Praise for the Rosato & DiNunzio Series

"Scottoline is an A-lister all the way, and her Rosato series is always an A-plus."
—*Booklist* (starred review)

"Scottoline's third entry in her Rosato & DiNunzio series does not disappoint. Fans will be on the edge of their seats eager to discover what happens next."
—*Library Journal* (starred review) on *Corrupted*

"There is nothing as riveting as a skilled writer creating tense courtroom scenes and Scottoline does that in *Corrupted*."
—*The Huffington Post*

"Scottoline excels at turning societal issues of the day into suspenseful plot points, a proclivity she takes to a whole new level in *Corrupted,* out-Grishaming Grisham. After twenty-plus books, she has written her best ever, as tightly fashioned as it is nail-bitingly suspenseful. A masterpiece of pitch-perfect storytelling balanced against emotional angst."
—*Providence Journal*

"Pop culture's current crop of female lawyers owes a great deal to the attorneys at Rosato & Associates . . . The deliciously dramatic and slightly over-the-top *Betrayed* reaffirms that after more than twenty novels, the Edgar Award–winning Scottoline is still able to create surprising, suspenseful plots with likable, daring heroines at the center."
—*The Washington Post*

"*Betrayed* is populated with the kind of smart, funny women you love to watch working crime scenes."
—*All You*

"Scottoline writes terrific legal fiction with warm, smart characters and lots of humor and heart. Her legion of fans will be happy with this one, and it should find her new readers as well."
—*Booklist* on *Betrayed*

CORRUPTED

Also by Lisa Scottoline

Rosato & DiNunzio Novels
Betrayed
Accused

Rosato & Associates Novels
Think Twice
Lady Killer
Killer Smile
Dead Ringer
Courting Trouble
The Vendetta Defense
Moment of Truth
Mistaken Identity
Rough Justice
Legal Tender
Everywhere That Mary Went

Other Novels
Most Wanted
Every Fifteen Minutes
Keep Quiet
Don't Go
Come Home
Save Me
Look Again
Daddy's Girl
Dirty Blonde
Devil's Corner
Running from the Law
Final Appeal

Nonfiction (with Francesca Serritella)
I've Got Sand in All the Wrong Places
Does This Beach Make Me Look Fat?
Have a Nice Guilt Trip
Meet Me at Emotional Baggage Claim
Best Friends, Occasional Enemies
My Nest Isn't Empty, It Just Has More Closet Space
Why My Third Husband Will Be a Dog

CORRUPTED

A Rosato & DiNunzio Novel

Lisa Scottoline

ST. MARTIN'S GRIFFIN ✱ NEW YORK

CORRUPTED. Copyright © 2015 by Smart Blonde, LLC. All rights reserved. Printed in the United States of America. For information, address St. Martin's Press, 175 Fifth Avenue, New York, N.Y. 10010.

www.stmartins.com

The Library of Congress has cataloged the hardcover edition as follows:

Scottoline, Lisa.
    Corrupted / by Lisa Scottoline. — First edition.
        p.   cm.
    "A Rosato & DiNunzio Novel."
    ISBN 978-1-250-02793-1 (hardcover)
    ISBN 978-1-250-02794-8 (e-book)
 1. Women lawyers—Fiction.   2. Murder—Investigation—Fiction.   I. Title.
    PS3569.C725C67   2016
    813'.54—dc23

                                                    2015025569

ISBN 978-1-250-10461-8 (trade paperback)

Our books may be purchased in bulk for promotional, educational, or business use. Please contact your local bookseller or the Macmillan Corporate and Premium Sales Department at 1-800-221-7945, extension 5442, or by e-mail at MacmillanSpecial Markets@macmillan.com.

First St. Martin's Griffin Edition: August 2016

10   9   8   7   6

To Laura Leonard and the entire Leonard family,
with gratitude for their inspiration, friendship, and love

We shall not cease from exploration
And the end of all our exploring
Will be to arrive where we started
And know the place for the first time.

—T. S. Eliot, *Little Gidding*

CHAPTER ONE

Bennie Rosato hadn't taken a murder case in years, but she'd have to take this one. She'd been working late when the call came in, from a time she didn't want to remember and a place she didn't want to revisit. Still, she'd said yes. She couldn't assign the case to an associate, either. Nobody paid her debts but her. And she wanted redemption.

She lowered her head, hoisted her bags higher on her shoulder, and powered her way to Philadelphia police headquarters, near the tangled ramps to I-95 and the Schuylkill Expressway. It was almost midnight in the dead of January, with the sky frozen black except for a full moon, round as a bullethole. There was no one else on the street except a homeless man, rattling a can of coins at the cars stopped at a red light.

Bennie beelined for the building, called the Roundhouse owing to its shape, which was two massive circular sections stuck together like an old-school barbell. The design was no longer innovative, nor was the building, and cracks lined its precast-concrete façade. Its three stories of smoked windows were set lengthwise, and fluorescent lighting from within showed that blinds were broken or missing in every pane. **PHILADELPHIA POLICE DEPARTMENT**, read dark metal letters on the wall next to a mailbox, an overflowing trash can, and a Port-a-John.

Bennie opened the smoked glass door and let herself into an

entrance with a wooden shield of the PPD next to a window of bulletproof glass. A young officer came to the window to meet her, wearing a blue shirt and a white UnderArmor turtleneck that revealed the telltale thickness of a Kevlar vest.

"Can I help you, miss?" he asked.

"Yes." Bennie liked him immediately, as she was in her forties and couldn't remember the last time anybody called her miss. "I have a client in Homicide. His name is Jason Lefkavick."

"Hold on a sec." The officer consulted an old computer for a moment. "Detective Gallagher will meet you upstairs at the Unit. Go to the door on your left. I'll need to see ID, inside."

"Sure, thanks." Bennie entered the massive round lobby, produced her ID, went through the metal detector, then took a grimy elevator to the fourth floor, where the ceiling lights flickered and the floor tile was gray with filth. She passed a bathroom with an open door and a leaking faucet. Running overhead were exposed wires and plumbing wrapped with duct tape.

HOMICIDE, read an old plaque ahead, and the hallway ended in a closed wooden door with a keypad and a dark window of reinforced glass. She knocked, facing her own reflection. Her hair was a tangle of long blond curls twisted into a topknot by a ponytail holder, and she tried to smooth it in place. She wore only light makeup, now worn off, so her wide-set blue eyes were unlined. She was fully six feet tall, which came in handy in a courtroom, if less so on a date. She hadn't seen anybody since she and Grady broke up. She'd have thought she was dead below the waist, but for the fact that her legs were so dry they itched all winter.

"You must be Bennie Rosato." The door was opened by a bald detective with brown eyes and a ruddy complexion. He had on a white shirt with a dark green sweater, khaki slacks, and loafers and looked about her age, but was shorter. He flashed a professional smile and extended a large hand. "I'm Mike Gallagher, good to meet you."

"You too, Detective." Bennie shook his hand, stepping inside a cramped waiting area with rubbery black benches and two large bulletin boards labeled WANTED FOR MURDER, with thirty-odd photographs of men, and one woman.

"Call me Mike. I've heard a lot about you. I know you were a buddy of Azzic's and he spoke well of you."

"Thanks." Bennie managed a smile but felt too antsy for small talk. "So do you think I can see my client?"

"Sure, no problem. Follow me." Detective Gallagher led her past the memorial wall, then into the squad room, which was mostly empty. The only remotely modern appliance was a medium-sized flat-screen television playing football highlights on mute; the walls were a scuffed light blue and the dropped ceiling a grimy white, with more bundled wiring. The gray tile floor was dirty, and crammed everywhere were mismatched file cabinets covered with taped notices about Courtroom Numbers, Phillies tickets, Computer Training for the Forensics Lab, and a bumper sticker that read, YOU BOOKIN'?

"The squad room's the same, I see." Bennie followed him past the cabinets.

"Still a dump, right? They're talking about moving us uptown, God knows when." Detective Gallagher stopped in front of the closed door to Interview Room A and slid aside a large barrel lock.

"Did you videotape your interview with him?"

"No, the machine's broken. You'll see it dangling in the corner."

"How about the audio?"

"We gave up on audio recordings. It sounded like everybody was underwater. The D.A. told us he couldn't use them. Take as long as you like, then come find me. My desk is the first one on the right." Detective Gallagher gestured to a connecting room behind him. "A word of warning. It's not pretty in there."

"The room? Why am I not surprised?"

"No, your client. And don't blame us, we didn't do it."

"What do you mean?" Bennie asked, concerned.

She opened the door, and got her answer.

CHAPTER TWO

The last time Bennie had seen Jason Lefkavick, he was only twelve years old, so it made sense that he looked different, but that wasn't the headline. His forehead looked pink and puffy, and over his left eyebrow, a swollen, reddish lump rose with a cut matted with drying blood. His left eyelid had shut to a slit, and the sclera of his eye was blood-red around a sliver of watery blue iris.

"Jason, yikes, what happened?" Bennie closed the door behind her and dumped her bags on the beat-up black table.

"It's okay."

"Did you see a doctor?"

"The nurse, she came in. It doesn't need stitches."

"You should see an eye doctor."

"She said it's fine. It's fine." Jason shrugged it off.

"Okay, well, good to see you, even in the circumstances." Bennie appraised him, and he was still short, about five-foot-six, but he'd lost weight and acquired a wiry build. His face had become long and lean, with prominent cheekbones, and his hair, which he'd shaved on the sides, had darkened from its previous sandy brown. Sinewy biceps popped through the armholes of his white paper jumpsuit, and tattoos of Chinese calligraphy, praying hands in blue, a sacred heart, and a blurry barcode blanketed both forearms.

"I didn't know if you'd remember me."

"Of course I would." Bennie took off her coat, but static electricity made it cling at the hem, so she unpeeled it from her khaki suit. She set it on the table, which held an open can of Coke and a greasy pile of chicken bones on waxed paper. There was a two-way mirror in the far wall, above two holes that were fist level. You didn't need to be a detective to figure out how they got there.

"Thanks for comin'."

"You're welcome. How have you been?" Bennie gave him a hug, though she didn't generally hug her clients. Jason hugged her back briefly, and she caught a whiff of chicken, beer, and cigarettes.

"Almost twenty-five."

"Really?" Bennie said, though she knew that already. She still thought about him.

"You got to be a big deal, huh? Famous lawyer, all that." Jason smiled, keeping his lips closed, and Bennie remembered that he was self-conscious about his crooked incisors.

"No, not at all."

"Not gonna lie, I didn't think you'd come."

"Of course I'd come. I would never not." Bennie sat down in the hard plastic chair opposite him, realizing that his demeanor had changed, too. He sat back with a belligerent uptilt to his chin, and his manner was more disaffected than it used to be, like a street thug's. If she hadn't known him, she might have been afraid to be alone with him. He wasn't handcuffed.

"Jason, listen." Bennie felt pressure in her chest, which she'd been carrying for over a decade. "I know it was a long time ago, but I owe you an explanation—"

"No, you don't owe me anything." Jason cut her off with a hand chop.

"But I'm so sorry for—"

"I don't want to go there. What's done is done." Jason pursed his thin lips. "Really."

Bennie let it go, for now. "How's your dad?"

"He died. His heart got him, when I was twenty."

"I'm so sorry."

"Can we move on?"

"Okay, let's get started." Bennie bent down and pulled a legal pad from her bag, facing him. They were oddly close because the interview room was so small, its only contents the black table and two chairs, though Jason's was bolted to the floor.

"Look, Bennie, I'm not gonna lie, I can't pay you right away."

"Don't worry. It's on the house." Bennie wouldn't have dreamed of asking him for a retainer. She stopped short of saying *I owe you*.

"You don't gotta do that." Jason ran a hand over his head. "I'm no charity case, yo."

"Don't worry about it, yo."

Jason didn't smile. "But you gotta know, I'm not takin' any deals, I didn't kill anybody. They say I did it, they gotta prove it. I didn't do it. I'm not guilty."

"Good." Bennie wasn't going to ask him if he did it anyway, no experienced criminal lawyer would. *Still*, she'd never been comfortable with the don't-ask-don't-tell of the defense bar, which was only one of the reasons she'd gotten out.

"I'm innocent, straight up. I was framed."

"Okay, I believe you, and I need to get the facts." Bennie rummaged through her messenger bag and found a pen.

"It was Richie. Richie Grusini. Remember him?"

"What?" Bennie froze. "What are you saying? Richie did it? He committed the murder?"

"No, Richie's dead. He got killed."

"Richie was the *victim*?"

"Yeah, he's dead. I'm not cryin', believe me."

"You didn't tell me it was Richie, when you called me." Bennie tried to wrap her mind around it. She had thought Richie was a part of Jason's past—and hers.

"I know, I worried you wouldn't come."

"I would have, anyway." Bennie let the awkward moment pass. "Did the cops tell you they're going to charge you?"

"No, but that detective thinks I did it. Gallagher. He tried to get me to make a statement, but I told him I wanted to call you. I wouldn't sign the papers."

Bennie knew he meant the papers required by Miranda to determine a waiver of counsel, ironic given Jason's history. "Let's get some background, so I'm up to speed. Jason, tell me where you live."

"403 East Gansett Street. In Fishtown."

"Okay." Bennie should've known from the chicken wings. The homicide detectives thought the way to a confession was through a defendant's stomach. If he was from South Philly, they got cheese-steaks from Pat's or Geno's, and if he was from Olney, they got crab fries from Chicky & Pete's. The chicken wings would have come from Byrne's at Kensington and Lehigh.

"I live in a house with a roommate. It's a chick. Gail Malloy."

Bennie made a note. "How long have you lived there?"

"Moved there six months ago, from home."

"Is she your girlfriend?"

"No, I don't have a girlfriend."

"How about a job?"

"I wait tables at Juarez, you know, the chain. It's in East Fish-town."

"Good. Got any friends?"

"Just Gail, my roommate. She works at Juarez, too. She manages it. She's cool."

"What's her cell number?"

"I wanted to call her but they only let me make one call." Jason rattled off a number, and Bennie wrote it down.

"Have you been in any legal trouble, as an adult?"

"Only misdemeanors. I didn't serve any time."

"Any weapons involved?'

"No.

Bennie made a note. "So tell me what happened tonight."

"Okay." Jason sniffed. "Anyway, after work, I wanted to eat, so I go into this bar, Eddie's, on Pimlico Street. I sit down and who do I see but Richie Grusini, sittin' at the bar. You know the story with me and Richie."

"So what happened?"

"I had a few beers and I guess it just got to me, watching him laugh with his buddy, having a good time. He was flashin' all this cash, and this girl was coming over to them and she was hangin' all over him." Jason shook his head, looking down. "Anyways, I thought to myself, where's the justice? Here he is, he got everythin', and he never paid for what he done to me, he *got away* with it, so I decided to do somethin' about it, not just suck it up."

Bennie didn't like the way this was going.

"So I get up and say to him, hey, 'member me? Right away he shoves me, and we're in a fight and they throw us out."

"Is that how you got the bump on your forehead?"

"No, that came later."

"What time did this take place?"

"About 11:00? The game was still on."

"How many people at the bar?"

"I dunno, about nine?"

Bennie made a note. "Including the bartender?"

"No."

Bennie wrote *ten witnesses*, which was ten too many. "How many beers had you had?"

"Three."

"Were you drunk?"

"No. So the bartender threw us out, and Richie's buddy left, and I was going to let it go, like we went opposite directions, I took a lef' to the bus but Richie and his buddy went to the right, and the bartender, he watched us split up. I waited at the bus stop, and I saw where Richie went, and the bartender went inside. But the bus didn't come, and I got madder and madder and I was like, why not, so I turned back and I went after Richie, like, down the street. He turned into an alley, and I figured he was gonna take a leak, and I went after him."

"Why?"

"I wanted to have it out with him, I admit it." Jason's pale skin flushed. "I wanted to tell him how he ruined my life. I went up to him in the alley and he was standin' at the middle, facin' the wall about to unzip his pants, and then all of a sudden, he hits me, really hard, right above my eye." Jason gestured at his injury. "I fell back and my head hit the ground, and I *def* passed out. Then

I don't know what happened, how long I was out. But when I woke up, Richie was lyin' there in the alley and blood was everywhere, like, coming from his throat, and there was this big, like, cut. That's prolly how I got the blood on me. He was all still, like, he wasn't moving." Jason's good eye widened slightly. "I couldn't believe it, and I got up and in my hand was a hunting knife. I don't know where it came from, it wasn't mine I swear, but Richie was dead, then there were sirens and people were yelling and the police came and arrested me."

Bennie couldn't tell if he was lying, but this wasn't the time to find out. "So you're saying somebody killed Richie and put the knife into your hand?"

"Yes, they framed me. Richie was a mean bastard, he musta had tons of enemies. Anybody coulda killed him."

"But how would they know you and Richie were there? Did they follow you into the alley?"

"Prolly, yes. They set me up!"

Bennie hid her doubt. "Did you notice anyone following you into the alley?"

"No, but anybody coulda seen us. It's an alley but the front part is wide enough to park in. There was a white pickup there."

"Whose was it? Was it Richie's?"

"I don't know, all I know is, I didn't kill him."

"Was anybody else in the alley?"

"No, not that I saw."

"Did anybody pass by and see you and Richie fight?"

"No one was around, I don't know."

"Were any stores open, near the alley?"

"No, I don't think so."

"Was there any noise during your fight? Did Richie yell at you or shout?"

"No, why?"

"I'm wondering if we can find a witness, somebody who heard something. Like somebody from one of the surrounding buildings, in an apartment or something."

"I didn't see anybody, I don't know who the hell killed him, but that guy took out the *trash*. You know the story, you remember." Jason shook his head in disgust. "I'm not sorry he's dead, I'm *glad* he's dead."

Bennie let it go, switching gears. "Jason, did the police give you your Miranda warnings when they arrested you?"

"Yes."

"You didn't say anything to them after that, did you?"

"Yes, I did." Jason frowned. "I was so freaked, I started talkin', like I couldn't shut up."

"What did you say?" Bennie held her breath.

"I said I didn't do it, I don't know how it happened, but I wasn't sad about it. I told 'em, '*Good!*' I told 'em, 'About damn time he paid for what he did to me,' and I got a lil' justice for once in my effing life!"

Bennie cringed inwardly. "Did you tell Detective Gallagher that, too?"

"Yeah, I did. He gave me Miranda warnings, and we went over the sheets." Jason gestured at the papers. "I know, it was stupid to say anything to the cops. I know better, *anybody* knows better. I do the dumbest things, you don't even know." Jason's shoulders slumped, as if he were deflating.

"When did you call me?"

"After he wanted me to sign the form, I figured I need a lawyer."

"Did you tell the police you'd been drinking?"

"Yeah, the cops asked in the alley, but I told them I wasn't drunk. I *wasn't*. I'm not. The detective asked me that, too."

"Okay." Bennie didn't expect Jason to understand the legal significance of the alcohol. It could have nullified his statements, but his admission that he wasn't drunk would cut against him. Bennie wasn't hearing any basis for a motion to suppress. "When they brought you here, did they take your blood? DNA? Skin?"

"Yes. They also took pictures of the blood that was on me. They cleaned me up, after."

"Was there blood on your clothes?"

"Yes, but I swear, I *didn't* do it."

"Then how do you think blood got on you?" Bennie hid her puzzlement.

"I don't know, whatever, I *didn't* kill him. Somebody else put that knife in my hand, and I'm *not* goin' to go down for it, no matter what."

"Okay, that'll do for now." Bennie set her pad on the table. "This is very serious. I have to tell you, they have enough to charge you with first-degree murder."

"So let 'em charge me, but I'm not pleading guilty to a murder I didn't do."

"Jason, the sentence for first-degree murder is life in prison, without possibility of parole. It's mandatory."

"I know that."

"I'm sure I can get you a deal for ten, at most. If you plead guilty to third-degree murder—"

"You have to get me off. I didn't do it. End of discussion."

"I'll be right back." Bennie rose. "I have to see Detective Gallagher."

"No deals, Bennie." Jason scowled. "You know why."

CHAPTER THREE

Bennie found Detective Gallagher on an ancient computer in an office so cramped that his desk shared space with a coatrack, and sleeves brushed against his case files. "Hi, got a minute?"

"Sure." Detective Gallagher swiveled around, rolled a black chair from a nearby desk, and motioned her into it. "Please, feel free."

"Thanks." Bennie sat down in the chair, which wobbled slightly. She knew she had a losing cause, but that didn't mean she wouldn't put up a fight. "I don't think you have enough to charge him. The case is totally circumstantial."

"Doesn't mean it's not a case." Detective Gallagher retook his seat, his mouth a grim line. "Plus your client made a number of *res gestae* statements to the uniformed officer on the scene, as well as myself, during his interview."

Bennie frowned. By *res gestae* statements, the detective meant what Jason had said about being happy Richie was dead. "They weren't admissions, and he also said he didn't do it."

"True, but the jury won't be interested in the legal technicalities. Your client had bad blood with the victim. He handed us motive and he was found in the alley with the weapon."

"The knife wasn't his. It was planted on him. Someone framed him for this."

"Yeah, right." Detective Gallagher snorted.

"Are you even investigating that? Richie Grusini had enemies. You need to look into his character and his history. That kid was bad to the bone."

"Educate me."

"Well, he—" Bennie stopped herself. She knew they had enough to charge Jason, so there was no point to showing her hand. "Forget it, let me ask you, was Grusini found with his wallet?"

"Yes. Money and all."

"Phone?"

"Yes."

"Did you learn anything from it?"

Detective Gallagher frowned. "The A.D.A. will let you know, when they have to."

"How about a weapon? Did he have one on him?"

"*Your* boy had the knife."

"But Grusini. Any weapon?"

"No." Detective Gallagher spread his hands, palms up. "Bennie, be real. The way I see this case, these two had history, and it's a bar fight turned into a murder. Your client's a punk, not a cold-blooded killer. Problem is, a man is dead. According to your client, that's not the worst thing in the world. But the victim's family doesn't agree."

"Have you notified them?" Bennie ignored the pang in her chest.

"Yes. We have enough to charge your client with general murder. You don't need me to tell you, that's fifteen to twenty years."

Bennie knew, too well. It would be the prime of Jason's life, and after what he had gone through, could put him over the edge.

"On the other hand, if you let him talk to me, we can reduce it to third-degree murder, voluntary manslaughter. He'll do ten years, maybe less." Detective Gallagher cocked his head, and the institutional lights shone on his bald scalp. "Let's make a deal. I can get the D.A. to go for it."

"Jason didn't do it, Detective. He's innocent. He doesn't want a deal."

"He should. He's jammed up."

"He won't deal."

"You really gonna make them try this?" Detective Gallagher frowned, and Bennie knew why. Almost everybody made a deal in Philly, and the truth was, plea bargains were often in the defendant's best interests.

"I'll give it a shot, but he's going to say no." Bennie rose, resigned. A guilty plea would have been a no-brainer with any client but Jason Lefkavick.

She knew why, but she wasn't saying.

At dawn, Bennie found herself sitting in her coat in Arraignment Court, waiting for Jason to be arraigned. He'd declined the plea deal, and she understood. It had taken all night for him to be scheduled for arraignment, and though she hadn't gotten any sleep, she felt oddly energized. She'd never thought she'd get a second chance to come through for Jason, and it fueled her. She didn't love his story, but she couldn't bring herself to believe that the little boy she'd known had become a murderer, even after all he'd been through.

Arraignments were held uptown in the Criminal Justice Center, which was Philly's modern courthouse, its corporate cleanliness a relief after the atmospheric filth of the Roundhouse. The courtroom was a windowless gray box, and the gallery was empty except for her. All arraignments were via closed-circuit television, so an arraignment courtroom was unique; a bulletproof wall divided the gallery from the bar of court, and Bail Commissioner Lawrence Holloway spoke directly to a camera, as did the public defender and assistant district attorney, their voices piped to the gallery on the sound system. A large closed-circuit monitor sat between them on a cart, broadcasting prisoners held in precincts around the city.

Bennie watched as the defendants popped onto the TV, one after the other, like the worst nightmare reality show of all time. Each was onscreen for only a matter of minutes, and some cried, cursed, or even spat at the camera. They would nevertheless be formally charged with murder, rape, arson, or the like, then granted or denied bail. Murder wasn't generally a bailable offense in Philadelphia, but Bennie was going to give Jason everything she had this time, conceding nothing.

She heard some noise in the hallway and turned around. There were glass windows in the doors, and through them, she could see what was causing the commotion. About to walk into the courtroom was something Bennie had never expected to see again.

Her past.

And he looked even better, the second time around.

PART ONE

Thirteen Years Earlier, December 16, 2002

What transpired would make us pause for careful inquiry if a mature man were involved. And when, as here, a mere child, an easy victim of the law, is before us, special care in scrutinizing the record must be used.

—Justice William O. Douglas, *Haley v. Ohio,* 332 U.S. 596

CHAPTER FOUR

Bennie Rosato could win a murder case and run a law firm, but she couldn't buy presents to save her life. She couldn't find anything good for fifteen bucks and she hated what she'd bought. She hated wrapping gifts, too, and it didn't help that she'd forgotten to buy wrapping paper, so she was using a sheet of yellow legal paper, trying desperately to form it around a sphere, which was probably the hardest shape to wrap. She wished she could gift-wrap fifteen bucks but gathered that wouldn't be in the holiday spirit.

She could hear her associates yapping away outside her closed door, ready to begin the Secret Santa. She had three young associates, Mary DiNunzio, Judy Carrier, and Anne Murphy; all female, but Bennie hadn't intended it that way. She hired only the best and the brightest, and they happened to come with ovaries. She wasn't a girly girl herself, and truth be told, she was the closest thing they had to a male lawyer. She'd read somewhere that there had been a study measuring the testosterone of all types of lawyers, and the results were that male and female trial lawyers had higher levels than everybody else. Bennie was pretty sure hers qualified her as incapable of wrapping gifts, as well as applying liquid eyeliner.

Also included in the Secret Santa was their young receptionist, Marshall Trow, and their investigator, Lou Jacobs, a retired cop. Lou was Bennie's good friend and right hand, and his age and experience gave him the authority to keep the associates in line, like the Office Daddy to her Office Second Wife. The associates adored him, going to him with their complaints and drama, which were mostly about Bennie herself. It always struck her as vaguely ironic that Lou was considered less threatening than she, though he carried concealed.

"Rowf!" Bear barked, facing the door and waving his feathery tail, getting excited at the sound of the happy chatter on the other side of the door. He was a chubby golden retriever, a breed always ready for a party. He knew something nonbillable was happening because nobody was working, ringing phones went unanswered, and faxes were being ignored. Plus the air smelled like cake. The only thing goldens liked better than cake were balls, which was how Bennie got the idea for her gift. She figured that if Bear would like it, so would Mary.

"Boss, you almost ready?" Mary called from the other side of the door.

"One more second." Bennie formed the legal paper with her cupped hands, then tore a long strip of Scotch tape off the roll. She wrapped the tape around the gift a few times, like a spaceship orbiting the earth. "Okay, come on in."

"Yay!" the associates called out in unison, like an estrogen chorus.

Bear barked again, as the door was opened and a noisy Mary, Judy, and Anne piled into Bennie's office, followed by Lou, grinning broadly.

"Merry Christmas!" Mary held a sheet cake that read Happy Holidays in red-and-green lettering.

"Happy Hanukkah!" Lou called out. "Even though it ended on the seventh. Let's not get technical. What'd you get me, Bennie?"

Bennie set her anxiety aside, petting Bear's head. "You're not my Secret Santa. Tough break."

"So no Maker's Mark?"

"Bingo." Bennie noticed Mary eyeing her cluttered desk, obviously wondering where to set the cake down without getting in trouble. Mary DiNunzio was proverbially short and sweet, a South-Philly Italian-American with a tendency toward codependency. Mary was a better lawyer than she knew, but generally loath to step out of line, as exemplified by her conventional blue suit and nude pantyhose, which Bennie regarded as cruel and unusual punishment.

"Here's cake!" Mary set down the cake with a brave smile. "Would you like a piece? It's vanilla."

"Let's do the presents first!" Anne Murphy called out, which surprised no one because she was the firm's Material Girl. Lovely and model-thin, with green eyes and glossy red hair, Anne stepped forward, clapping her manicured hands. Today she had on a sleek black knit dress with black suede boots, an outfit that made her look like a licorice stick, but Bennie didn't care what the associates wore, only that they won.

"Yes, presents!" Judy Carrier started jumping up and down, which was her default mood, and if every office had a free spirit, Judy was theirs. A tall blonde from northern California, she painted for a hobby, and Bennie sensed it wasn't coincidental that the associate had a brilliantly creative legal mind. Unfortunately, every day was Casual Friday for Judy, who today had on a long, multicolored Oilily sweater over her jeans, with cobalt blue clogs that matched her latest crazy hair color, courtesy of Manic Panic dye. Bennie thought it was a good look if you liked M&Ms, but she kept her own counsel.

"Rowf!" Bear jumped up and down along with Judy, and Bennie waved them both into better manners, having better luck with the dog.

"Carrier, don't get him riled up," Bennie said, trying to keep the annoyance from her tone, as it was a national holiday. She looked around, and the receptionist was missing. "Where's Marshall? We can't exchange gifts without her."

Mary waved her off. "She said to go ahead and get started. She wanted to check the answering machine to make sure none of the calls was important."

"Good." Bennie approved. Secret Santa wasn't worth a malpractice action.

"Oh, by the way," Mary said, tentative. "I wanted to ask you about next week, with the holiday. Are we closing the whole week?"

"No, why would we?" Bennie couldn't get any work out of anybody as soon as Thanksgiving passed. The associates started taking long lunches, and she'd even caught Murphy shopping online while she defended a deposition.

Carrier jumped in, coming to her best friend's rescue. "Boss, Christmas is Wednesday of next week, and Christmas Eve is Tuesday, so what's the point of opening on Monday, and then afterwards—"

"Do we have to discuss this now?" Bennie wished they discussed their cases with the same enthusiasm as their vacation schedule.

"I might go skiing with some friends and I have to get a plane ticket. It's cheaper if you buy it earlier."

Murphy nodded. "Last year you said we might close the office on Christmas week or between Christmas and New Year's. Remember?"

"No," Bennie answered, though she could see the problem with plane fares.

"You said you would see how busy we all were, and it seems like none of us is that busy. You know how it is around the holidays. The courts slow down, everything slows down. None of our cases is that active."

Bennie frowned. "Neither are mine, but that doesn't mean I'm closing the office. The courts may slow down, but they don't close, and I'll be here."

"So what should we do? Are we allowed to take off, then?"

"Here's what I think." Bennie decided just to speak to them like equals, since one day they would be. "You're all professionals. Put on your big-girl panties and stop asking for permission. Your practice is *your* business. You should take time off when you feel that you can take time off. Answer to your clients and yourself, not to me."

"O-kay," Judy said slowly, and the other two associates looked vaguely astonished.

Lou started chuckling softly. "You meant that in a nice way, right, Bennie?"

"Of course. I respect their judgment. They should use it. End of discussion." Bennie wished she were better in the maternal department, but she didn't get a lot of practice, unless you counted golden retrievers. She looked around, ignoring the awkward moment. "So who wants to give out the first present? DiNunzio, why don't you go first?"

"Okay." Mary accepted a perfectly gift-wrapped box from Judy and handed it over the desk to Bennie. Her brown eyes shone. "I'm your Secret Santa, Bennie! Merry Christmas!"

"Ha!" Bennie laughed, surprised. It was pure chance that she had picked Mary, and she hoped that Mary's gift didn't outclass hers. She accepted the gift and tried to relax. "This is fun!"

Lou snorted. "Bennie, you're not fooling anybody. You'd rather be working."

Judy laughed. "Right, if it's really fun, you don't have to say it's fun."

Anne giggled. "I mean, who says that?"

Mary mock-frowned. "Give her a break, she's trying."

"Fun is overrated." Bennie tore off gift wrap covered with Grinches, which she assumed was coincidental. Under the paper was a square white box, and she opened the top and pulled out a white mug that read, I CAN SMELL FEAR.

"You're not mad, are you?" Mary asked.

Bennie burst into laughter. "No, of course not! I love it, thanks!"

Lou chuckled. "You should buy a case."

"Funny." Bennie set the mug down on her desk, picked up her own gift, and handed it across the desk to Mary. "DiNunzio, you should get the next present, since I was your Secret Santa."

"Great!" Mary accepted the gift with an expectant smile, turning it this way and that. "What could this be? It's so soft!"

"Nice paper, Bennie." Lou snorted again. "What, did you run out of tinfoil?"

Bennie shot him a look. "Please, I'm a busy, self-important woman. Plus can *you* smell fear? I can."

"How cute!" Mary extricated the gift from the legal paper, then held it up. It was a pink squishy ball with a worried face painted on one side.

"What the hell is that?" Lou asked, chuckling, just as Bear jumped up and tried to get the ball from Mary's hand.

Judy frowned, puzzled. "Is it a dog toy?"

"Of course," Anne answered, her tone helpful. "Bennie got it so Mary can play with the dog, obviously."

Bennie's heart sank. "No, it's not a dog toy. It's a stress ball."

"Rowf!" Bear jumped up, snatched the ball from Mary, and bounded out of the office with his prize. The three associates started laughing.

Lou smiled. "It's the thought that counts."

Suddenly Marshall appeared at the threshold, a concerned look in her blue eyes. Her light brown hair was pulled back into its low ponytail, and she had on a denim smock with a white turtleneck underneath. "Bennie, I hate to interrupt, there's a call from a new client. He left two messages on the answering machine and just called back."

"Who is it?" Bennie asked, and the associates and Lou quieted down.

"His name is Matthew Lefkavick. He says it's an emergency."

"Okay." Bennie headed for the office door. She wasn't that busy and she could use a new case. "You guys have fun, I'll take it in the conference room."

"But you'll miss the *fun*," Lou called after her, and Bennie responded by flipping him the bird. She hurried into their nicer conference room, which was large and rectangular, dominated by a long table of polished walnut and allegedly ergonomic black mesh chairs. Bennie grabbed the phone on the credenza. "Bennie Rosato."

"Hi, I'm Matthew Lefkavick. I'm calling about my son, Jason."

Bennie thought the man sounded upset, though if he had been crying, it was over now. "I understand, what seems to be the problem?"

"They took him to jail, just like that. He got in a fight and they took him to jail."

"Did he have a weapon?" Bennie rolled one of the chairs over, sat down, and eyed the view from the panel of floor-to-ceiling windows, facing west, showing off the Center City skyline. The cold sun gleamed off the metallic top of the Mellon Center, the whimsical Mickey Mouse ears of Commerce Center, and the spiky ziggurats of Liberty Place.

"No, nothing like that."

"What was he charged with? Assault?"

"No, they didn't charge him. They just took him, they *took* him away. They picked him up right out of school!"

"School?" Bennie asked, surprised. "How old is he?"

"Twelve. He's only in middle school. He got into a fight and they took him right to court and put them in jail. They can't do that, can they?"

Bennie thought it sounded crazy, but it wasn't her field. "Sir, I don't represent juveniles. Where are you located? Are you in Philadelphia?"

"No, up northern PA. Mountain Top."

Bennie had never heard of it. It sounded like a fake name. "Where is that?"

"Near the Poconos. It's not that far, a two-hour drive, tops. Please, you have to help me."

"Sir, there are major differences between the juvenile system and the adult criminal justice system. The procedures are different, the court rules are different."

"How? What's the difference? One's just the junior version of the other, isn't it?"

"No, not at all." Bennie knew it was a common misconception, as if juvenile justice were the kiddie table of the law. "The juvenile justice system isn't adversarial at all. The proceeding isn't a trial, which results in a conviction of a crime. It's an adjudication hearing, and when a child is adjudicated delinquent, the idea isn't to convict and punish them, but to rehabilitate them, because they're still young enough. That's why adjudication hearings, unlike criminal trials, aren't public."

"I know, they're secret!"

"No, just private, to protect the juvenile's identity. Their names in the case captions are in initials only, and the records are kept sealed."

"Jason doesn't need rehabilitating. He's a *great* kid."

Bennie couldn't ignore the pain in his voice. "I'm sure, but the judge made a determination, and they don't even put a kid in out-of-home placement unless they've already considered the less restrictive alternatives. It's called restorative justice."

"What's the difference if you call it a sentence or placement, and they put him in jail!"

Bennie didn't have a quick reply. "I do think you need help, but I'm not an expert. Unlike a lot of states, our juvenile justice system is decentralized, and a lot of power is given to the juvenile court judges in the counties."

"You *sound* like an expert."

"All lawyers sound like experts when they're not. You need a local lawyer. He'll know the ins and outs, and the judges tend to favor county lawyers. They'll consider me an outsider—"

"But that's what's good about you. It's like a club up here, and they all know each other, and I'm on the outside looking in!"

Bennie knew the feeling. She'd felt like an outsider her whole life. "Did you try the public defender?"

"Yes, and they won't help me. I read about you in the newspaper, it said you take on the cases for the little guy. Well, *I'm* the little guy."

Bennie knew which article he was talking about. She had cringed when the reporter had written that phrase.

"You have to help me. I got nowhere else to go. He's my boy, my only boy. He's all I got. His mother died, and she had a way with him. The two of them, they were thick as thieves. Ever since she's gone, it's like, he's lost."

Bennie felt the words resonate in her chest. Her mother had died only recently, and she still missed her, every day.

"Please, I'm begging you. Just come up and talk to me, I can pay you, I'll pay you. I need my son home. He's been in jail one night already. He never even slept away."

Bennie couldn't believe it. A twelve-year-old boy who'd just lost his mother, sitting in a cell.

"Can I just have an hour of your time?"

"Rowf!" Bear barked, bounding into the conference room, the stress ball in his mouth.

CHAPTER FIVE

Bennie set off at six o'clock, and darkness fell as she drove north on Route 476 in congested rush-hour traffic, traveling past Quakertown and Allentown, where the elevation began to change, higher and more up and down as she got closer to the Pocono Mountains. Snow blanketed the sides of the highway, since the outskirts had gotten more snowfall than the city in the last storm. The big-box stores and warehouses morphed into RV dealerships and manufacturing businesses, then into miles and miles of woods, their tree trunks exposed and limbs bare and black, like etchings in an inky drawing.

She switched onto Route 80, then traveled on back roads through the small-town landscape of aging two-story clapboard houses only steps from the road, their porches decorated with Christmas lights, plastic icicles, and inflatable Santa heads. Zoning seemed fairly chaotic, mixing residential and commercial; the homes were interspersed with Family Dollar Stores, Turkey Hill convenience marts, fire halls, churches, a John Deere dealership, and Masonic lodges, their signs advertising Spaghetti Suppers and Bingo Nights.

Her ears began to pop as the elevation grew even higher, and she passed a colliery, a reminder of the region's once-booming coal industry. She navigated onto Route 81 and found South Mountain Boulevard heading into Mountain Top, where civilization seemed to reappear in the form of a Weis Market, gas stations, and McDonald's, as well as independent businesses, selling cigars, cigarettes, and lottery tickets. She took Church Road and Nuangola Road, finally turning off the commercial district into a rural residential area that contained Heslop Road, where Matthew Lefkavick lived.

Bennie turned onto the street, and a pristine blanket of snow lay everywhere. There were no streetlights, and she flicked on her high beams, catching a fox off guard, his blood-red eyes glimmering before he dashed off into the woods lining the street. There were only a few houses along the road on multiacre lots, and the neighborhood looked solidly middle-class, with well-maintained Cape Cods and ranches set back from the road, behind front yards with snow-covered swing sets and homemade nativity scenes, aglow with multicolored lights.

She looked for the house number on the black mailboxes and stopped when she got to the Lefkavicks', cutting the engine. She wrapped her coat closer around her, grabbed her purse and messenger bag, and got out of the car, breathing in a lungful of freezing air. Snow shimmered in the moonlight, its hard crust making a twinkling layer around the Lefkavicks' house, which was of golden-yellow clapboard, a bright spot in the darkness some three stories tall. Its porch roof was lined with multicolored lights, which lit her way down a brick path to the front door.

She hurried toward the house, noticing a large bay window to the right of the door, filled with shelves of knickknacks, and as she climbed onto the wooden porch, there was a wooden bench with a matching porch swing. She was about to knock when she heard barking coming from inside, and at the same moment, the door was opened wide, by a heavyset bald man in a flannel work shirt and jeans.

"Bennie, come in, it's cold out there!" Matthew shook her hand, tugging her inside the house, with a smile that looked relieved. A small black-and-white mutt barked excitedly, jumping around his workboots.

"Thank you, Matthew."

"I can't thank you enough for coming. They say snow's on the way, but not until later." Matthew opened the door. "Go on out, Patch, run your willies out."

"What about traffic and cars, with the dog?" Bennie watched the little dog run into the snow.

"Around here?" Matthew closed the door, extending a hand. "Here, let me take your coat."

"Thanks." Bennie shed her coat, glancing around. The house was small, but neat, with a living room to the left, furnished with blue quilted couches, matching chairs, and a blue hooked rug. To the right was a large kitchen/dining area, with a round wooden table set with three blue-checked place mats. In the center was an arrangement of blue silk flowers.

"Ever been up here before?" Matthew took her coat to a wall closet with a louvered door, hanging it up neatly.

"No. I never leave my office."

Matthew chuckled. "Rice Township is on the north side of the county. On the east is Wapwallopen Creek, with Nuangola Borough on the west."

"What's with these names?"

"They're Indian, Delaware mostly, though the Iroquois settled this part of the state, too. Back behind the house is all woods, state game lands, pretty but a pain in the butt this time o' year." Mathew motioned out the back window.

"How so?"

"The hunters start around four thirty in the morning, which gets the deer runnin' and the dog barkin'. They gut the deer and leave the innards, so the dog's out all day, eatin' God-knows-what and draggin' home bones. I love to hunt, and Jason could field-dress a deer by the time he was ten, but he didn't like to hunt. Used to turn his stomach."

"I hear that."

"We got quite a lot of history in Rice Township, they call it the Ice Lakes Region. My father worked in the icehouses." Matthew gestured at a wall over the TV, which showed framed black-and-white photographs of men walking behind a draft horse and plow, in the snow. "That's my dad harvesting ice. That went by the wayside when modern times came along."

"Where do you work?"

"I'm a fabricator at Parnell Ironworks in Mountain Top, it's been here a long time, too, makes garage doors, hurricane doors, insulated doors, fire doors, and whatnot. I've done real well with them, gotten promoted up to supervisor. I'm a member of Mountain Top Legion Post 781, and of course, our parish is St. Mary's. Jason's an altar boy." Matthew paused, faltering. "God knows why I'm tellin' you this, I guess so you know we're a good family."

"I can see that." Bennie smiled, touched.

"Our family name, the Lefkavicks', it *means* something to me, it means something in this *town*. Nobody's ever went to jail from the Lefkavick family, nor my wife's side, the Brushevskis." Matthew met her eye, determined again. "That's why I can't abide what they did, lockin' my son up like a common criminal. My mother and father, they'd be turnin' over in their graves with the shame of it, and my wife, this would kill her." Matthew ran a wrinkled hand over his bald head, frowning deeply. "Anyway, can I get you a cup of coffee? I just made some."

"Thanks, that would be great."

"Good, make yourself comfortable." Matthew pulled out a chair at the table, and Bennie set her purse and messenger bag on the floor, then sat down, facing the bay window that she had seen from the outside. On the windowsill rested a homemade case that had displayed things made of Legos: houses, cars, a tiny railroad station, an oversized shoe, a truck, a grandfather clock, and an entire forest with Lego butterflies.

Bennie was astounded. "Who made all these? Did Jason?"

"Yes, he's been playing with Legos since he was a little boy." Matthew came over to the table with a thick mug of black coffee. "Want cream or sugar?"

"Neither, thanks." Bennie accepted the mug and took a sip of the coffee, which tasted hot and delicious.

"Jason started buildin' when he was little, his mother got him the first set. She found some at a garage sale, and he took to it like crazy." Matthew crossed to the display case and plucked a blue brick truck from the shelves, setting the rubber wheels spinning. "He made this when he was only four. Keeps a catalog in his room and every card has a picture of what he made, when he made it, and how many hours it took." Matthew set the truck back on the shelf. "My wife always said he'd be an engineer someday."

"He sounds like quite a kid."

"He is." Matthew pulled up a chair opposite her, and in the light from the overhead fixture, Bennie could see unevenness on the skin over his cheeks, a residual pitting from childhood acne scars. His forehead showed a pinkish indentation where his hairline used to be, and his eyes were a rich, warm brown behind his steel-rimmed glasses, each lens with a visible bifocal window at the bottom.

"Tell me what happened yesterday, as far as you know."

"Okay." Matthew reached for his coffee and took a quick sip. "I was at work, and I got a call that Jason and Richie got into it at school."

"Seventh grade. A twelve-year-old." Bennie still couldn't wrap her mind around it. She tugged a legal pad from her bag.

"Yes, at Crestwood Middle School in Mountain Top."

"Who's Richie?"

"Richie Grusini." Matthew shook his head. "Kid's a bully, a loudmouth, a *hood*, he gives Jason a hard time, always has, since elementary school."

"Are they in the same grade?"

"Yes, but my wife used to take care o' all this. She knew everything, I'm playin' catch-up. I've been hearin' about Richie Grusini since I don't know when. They all tease Jason, he's pudgy like us. My wife used to make homemade pierogies, they were great." Matthew paused, grief furrowing his forehead. "Once I said to my wife, I'm going over to the Grusinis', give 'em a piece of my mind.

She said it would make it worse for Jason. Jason said the same thing. Richie told Jason, 'snitches get stitches.'" Matthew swallowed hard. "So I didn't say nothin', I wanted my boy to fight his own battles, I sure do regret it now."

Bennie could imagine the bind as a parent, which seemed no-win.

"Jason just finally snapped, he just *snapped*. He pushed Richie, then Richie pushed back." Matthew rubbed his face. "So then the lunchroom monitor calls the principal, and the police arrest Jason and Richie."

Bennie couldn't believe what she was hearing. "Was anybody seriously hurt?"

"Jason was the one who took a punch and he didn't look that bad to me. I told him when I saw him, you're fine. Richie didn't have a mark on him." Matthew shook his head. "The way I was raised, that's jus' boys bein' boys, the worst you should get is detention, maybe suspension, that's it."

"Right, I agree."

"But not with the 'zero tolerance,' that's the new thing. They started it at the schools, all over the district. That's the policy, after that shooting in Columbine, when those kids shot up that high school, in '99."

"In Colorado, you mean?" Bennie didn't see the relevance.

Matthew nodded. "Like I said, my wife was the one who was always in the school. She told me they don't tolerate any trouble anymore, they take the troublemakers out of school, and they go right to juvie." Matthew hesitated. "I told her, 'good'! I liked the idea. Too many troublemakers, they ruin it for the good kids like Jason. *They're* the juvenile delinquents, not Jason."

"So then what happened?"

"They took him to the courthouse and I met them there. It's right in town, you can't miss it."

Bennie had a terrible sense of direction, especially where there was no graffiti to guide her. "What time did you get called?"

"About 3:15."

"So he was arrested around 12:15 and you don't get called until three hours later?"

"Yes, when I got there, they had him handcuffed!" Matthew's eyes widened in disbelief. "He was tryin' not to cry, and the cop said we hadda see the judge right then, so we did."

"Was he alone or with Richie?"

"Alone. I took him aside so we could talk. He felt bad I had to leave work, the poor kid."

"Is there a reason you didn't call a lawyer?"

"The cop said we don't need a lawyer, he said nobody gets a lawyer for juvie court."

Bennie knew that had to be wrong. "What was the cop's name, do you remember?"

"Remember? I know him. Wright Township police only have a handful o' cops. It was Johnny Manco, he goes to our church. So then he took us to the courthouse door. We went to a table and they gave us this sheet and the lady said if we signed it, and pled guilty, it would go easier for Jason."

"Let me see that." Bennie accepted the paper when Matthew slid it toward her and the top line read, **WAIVER OF RIGHT TO COUNSEL**. Underneath that it read:

A. I understand the rights listed above. Check one: yes, no.

B. I wish to proceed with the intake interview without a lawyer. Check one: yes, no.

I will have my own lawyer. Check one: yes, no.

I cannot afford a lawyer and desire a public defender to represent me. Check one: yes, no.

Bennie noted that on Part A, the "yes" box had been checked in pen, and on Part B, the first sentence had been checked yes, **I wish to proceed with the intake interview without a lawyer.** "What's an intake interview?"

"I don't know. There was a lady at the back of the room, she's a probation officer, I think, just sitting at a table in the back of the courtroom. You tell her what happened, and they just shuffle you into the courtroom."

"Why did you sign this?"

"She said the same thing the cop did, 'don't make a big deal of it, that it'll go a lot easier for him if he doesn't have a lawyer.'" Matthew paused, stricken. "I let him down. I never thought this could happen."

Bennie's heart went out to him. "Don't blame yourself. It's not your fault."

"I should've known better."

"If you knew better, you wouldn't need a lawyer. And I'd be out of business."

Matthew managed a smile, and Bennie returned her attention to the form, which had a signature line at the bottom, after: **Acknowledgment: I acknowledge the above-named juvenile is my child, and I hereby waive his right to counsel.** After that was Matthew's signature.

"Did the judge ask you or Jason any questions about having a lawyer?"

"No."

"Also, you signed this waiver form, but I don't believe that you can waive Jason's rights to counsel."

"I figured it's like a permission slip."

"Legally, it's not the same thing. He has constitutional rights." Bennie decided it was time for the short course in juvenile justice. "There's a landmark case, *In Re Gault*, decided by the Supreme Court in the sixties, and it guarantees the same constitutional rights to juveniles that adults have. Any waiver of a constitutional right has to be knowing and intelligent. His wasn't." Bennie set the sheet of paper aside. "Okay, you said you went to the public defender. What happened?"

"They told me I make too much money." Matthew snorted. "First time I ever heard *that*."

"But it's not your income level that's relevant, it's Jason's, and he's indigent." Bennie didn't get it. "Tell me what the judge said, during the adjudication."

"There was no 'judication,' the whole thing didn't take but three minutes! The judge yelled at him, you're going right to jail, then the officers came over and they put him in shackles!"

"Around his ankles?" Bennie asked, shocked.

"Yes, so he couldn't even walk, and they took him to River Street."

"What's River Street?"

"It's juvie. He's going to be there *ninety days.*"

"Three months?" Bennie couldn't imagine how such a long sentence was justified.

"It's awful. We were going to pick out a tree this weekend. The first Christmas without his mother, he'll be behind *bars.*" Matthew shook his head, plainly heartsick.

"And what about school, homework, tests? Isn't this almost the end of the semester?"

"He'll miss all that time in school. They say they'll teach him in juvie, but Jason likes school, gets good grades, A's and B's. It's all he has, that and this house, his toys. Me, now that his mother is gone. He's a *kid,* for Christ's sake!"

"What about his friends?"

"Not many, he's kind of a loner."

Bennie set the pad aside. "Here's the problem, legally. Appeals from the adjudication by the juvenile court are to the Superior Court, but appeals are too slow. It can take six months to a year to get a case heard on appeal, and Jason's sentence will have expired by that time."

"So what do we do?"

"We have to think of something else. I'll have to get creative." Bennie felt her blood flowing faster.

"So, you'll take this case? I'll pay you what it takes, I have money. My wife and me, we saved for Jason's college fund. I'll take the money from there." Matthew knitted his fingers together. "I read about you, you'll get him out. You're smart, you're a Philadelphia lawyer. There's nobody else I can turn to, I went in town, there's no juvenile lawyer or whatever you call it. Please, get him out for his mother's sake."

"Okay, I'll do it. But if it looks like I'm out of my depth, I'll let you know and I'll help you find an expert."

"Thank God." Matthew got out of his chair, and before Bennie could stop him, he hustled around the table, opening his arms. "Thank you so much!"

"You're welcome." Bennie rose, hugged him back, then released him. "So, let's get started."

CHAPTER SIX

Bennie drove Matthew down East North Street through Wilkes-Barre, where streetlights illuminated brick homes and businesses decorated with Christmas lights, but there was no foot traffic. They passed the low-slung brick dormitories for King's College, a local Catholic university, but there were no students on the street. Bennie was beginning to realize that the density levels were so much lower than she was used to, and the weather was a factor as well. Snow was beginning to fall, and flurries swirled in the cones of light cast by the streetlights.

"Cold out," Bennie said, just to make conversation. Matthew had grown quiet as they approached the detention center.

"Storm's coming. You might have to stay over at the Hilton. It's the only place around."

"Okay." Bennie had seen it, coming in. She didn't think she'd have a problem getting a room.

"The wind's whippin' off the river. It's icy."

"What river?"

"The Susquehanna. That's what the North Street Bridge is over."

Bennie spotted the elevated bridge, which was four lanes heading into the darkness with the mountains behind. Ahead lay a big intersection with a modern building to the right, and to the left, a massive limestone edifice with stately columns in front, graceful arches at the entrance, and a silvery dome, illuminated at night.

"That's the courthouse," Matthew said, evidently reading her mind. "Turn right at the light."

Bennie saw the River Street sign in the snow, then turned. There were modern office buildings on her left, but on the right were small, run-down clapboard houses. She drove higher uphill, and at the very peak stood a long, boxy building, encased in shadow.

"That's it." Matthew's tone was quiet.

"There's no sign."

"They don't need one. Everybody knows what it is."

Bennie turned onto the driveway, which wound around the side building, going straight up to the peak of the hill, with a wall of black rock on the right and a guardrail on the left. She spotted a grimy old redbrick building, which looked to have three or four stories, with bars over the windows. It was shaped like a rectangle with a wing at either end, and she drove around to the left wing, since that was where the driveway led. There was a small parking lot near the entrance, and Bennie pulled in, cutting the ignition.

"I appreciate you doing this." Matthew pressed his glasses up on his nose. In his lap sat a white plastic bag he was bringing Jason, which contained socks, long underwear, and Legos. "We wouldn't be here if you hadn't read the riot act to that lady."

"It's my job." Bennie had insisted on seeing Jason outside of visiting hours, arguing that as his counsel, she couldn't be denied. She grabbed her purse and messenger bag, then turned to Matthew. "I hope you don't mind my meeting with him alone."

"No, I'll say hi, then I'll say I have to go to the bathroom. Give you two some time." Matthew opened the car door, clutching the white plastic bag.

"Let's go." Bennie got out of the car, catching a frigid gust of wind in the face as she closed the door behind her. She looked down to the river, which snaked thick and black at the foot of the hill, and she saw a large dark building, its roof ringed with concertina wire, along the riverbank. It had an older portion in back, of lighter tan brick, and its roof looked like an ancient medieval castle with turrets at the corners. Story-high cyclone fencing and barbed wire surrounded the entire compound.

"That's the adult prison," Matthew said, his breath wreathing his head in the cold.

Bennie shuddered, then turned around. LUZERNE COUNTY DETENTION CENTER, read a white sign beside a rusted double door with peeling green paint, set under a green metal awning. A single light flickered above the door, and down the left side of the building was a tiny yard with cyclone fencing topped with concertina wire. Brutal wind and icy snow swirled off the river, making the setting grimly Gothic. The sky was completely black and starless.

Matthew shoved his hands in his pockets, shaking his head. "I can't believe my boy is here, I just can't believe it."

"I know." Bennie couldn't believe any kids were in such a horrible place. Matthew gestured her ahead, and they climbed the few concrete steps to the doorway, where they pressed an aged buzzer. There were no security cameras, and in the next few moments, an older guard in a blue uniform came to the door, unlocked it, and opened it narrowly, blinking against the snow.

"Hello, I'm Bennie Rosato, counsel for Jason Lefkavick, and this is his father, Matthew Lefkavick. We called ahead."

"Oh, you're the one." The guard looked from Bennie to Matthew, then opened the door. The doors emptied into a grimy vestibule with a worn linoleum floor and walls of peeling gray paint, and after they produced IDs, they were led down an equally run-down corridor to a small visiting room that contained a few battered wooden tables with mismatched chairs. The guard left them to retrieve Jason.

Bennie sat down, setting her things on the table, while Matthew remained standing, gazing expectantly at the door on the other side of the room. He was in motion as soon as the door was opened and Jason was led into the room by the guard. Bennie was struck immediately by how little Jason was, not even five feet tall. His chubby, prepubescent frame filled out the blue jumpsuit, and his brush haircut showed a child's indifference to appearance. The instant Jason saw his father, he took off running into his arms.

"No running!" shouted the guard, from a station by the door, but neither father nor son paid him any mind, embracing in the middle of the quiet, empty room. Bennie watched the scene, praying she could get this kid out of this dump. She watched as Matthew gave Jason the bag of toys, looped a heavy arm around his shoulder, then walked him over to Bennie.

"Bennie, this is Jason and he's happy to talk to you. You guys have a nice chat while I go to the bathroom. Understood, son?"

"Okay." Jason nodded, looking down as his father left.

"Hi, Jason." Bennie couldn't remember the last time she'd talked to a seventh grader, if ever. "I'm sorry you're here, pal."

Jason didn't meet her eye. "Me, too. It sucks."

"So, I'm a lawyer in Philadelphia and your father called me to see if I could help you."

"Can you get me out of here?" Jason's blue eyes widened with hope.

"I hope so," Bennie answered, watching her words. It was always tricky business to manage the client's expectations, and she never felt that more acutely than she did now.

"Do you think I will be out this week?" Jason's short forehead buckled. "I really want to be home by Christmas. I want to finish the castle."

"The what?"

"The castle. King Leo's castle."

"King Lear?"

"No, Leo." Jason reached into the bag and pulled out a handful of tiny black Lego bricks and some small figurines, which he emptied on the table, then lined up. "I can work on part of the castle here, but have to be home to finish. I try to cut the hours it takes, each time."

"Oh I see." Bennie smiled, impressed by his industry. "I saw the ones you built in the dining room. They're incredible."

"Thank you." Jason smiled back, then pursed his lips again, covering his teeth. "I can do so much better now. I can build faster, too, like, if you build a lot of Legos, you figure out how it works. It's logical. And you have to use your imagination, and it takes patience. I have a lot of patience, that's what my mom always says. Said."

"Patience is a good thing." Bennie took her pad from her messenger bag and set it in front of her. "Why don't you tell me what happened, with Richie?"

Jason's face changed immediately, as if a protective mask had just descended over his young features. "I don't even know, it was just weird."

"How so?" Bennie left her ballpoint pen on her pad, so he would feel encouraged to talk.

"I mean, they tease me, Richie always teases me, because well, you know." Jason flushed, pursing his lips. "I'm kind of husky, and also because of my teeth, like, I have these teeth in front they say I'm like a vampire."

"You don't look like a vampire."

"There's this movie called *Dracula 2000* and they say *I'm Dracula 2000* and they thought that was funny. They said they saw it but they're liars because they can't see it, it's rated R."

Bennie's heart went out to him. "That must be tough, getting teased like that."

"I mean, a lot of kids get teased, so, like, I try not to let it bother me." Jason looked down at the figurine in his hands. "That's what my mom used to say, like, pretend you're like a duck and it just rolls off your back."

"And what happened, at lunch? What made it different?"

"They were just calling me names, like they always do. 'Fat Boy.' 'Tank.' 'Blubber Boy.' 'Albino Gorilla,' every day they got a new name. 'Bootylicious,' was last week, on account of the song." Jason seemed to deflate, his soft shoulders slumping.

"Did Richie hit you or something?"

"No."

"You can tell me. I won't even tell your dad, if you don't want me to."

"You know, Richie starts calling me Bootylicious and then everybody joins in, that's what it's like." Jason shrugged.

"Isn't there a monitor in the cafeteria? Or somebody who can stop it?"

"Yes, but she doesn't see." Jason started fiddling with the figurine again. "The cool thing about Legos is that you can *do* things with them, like you can make them shoot the catapult, and they joust, and there's even a dragon minifig."

"What's a minifig?"

"This is a minifig." Jason brightened, holding up the figurine. "This is King Leo, it's a new theme they have, Knights' Kingdom. It's, like, a big war, and King Leo is a good king and they're lion knights."

"Cool," Bennie said, willing to take the conversational detour only because Jason brightened again.

"The way it works is the knights have to protect the castle against Cedric the Bull. And they have to fight for Queen Leonora and Princess Storm, even though Princess Storm is a warrior and she fights, but not as much as King Leo or Richard the Strong." Jason picked up a small plastic figure with a blue helmet. "This minifig is Richard the Strong. He helps King Leo defend the castle and he's really a good guy. Cedric the Bull is the *worst,* and they have a story, that's what I like about it, too."

"What's the story?"

"Well, Cedric is, like, the son of a king, but he got cheated out of his land because there were, like, thirteen sons, and he is really, like, *angry* about it, and that's why he wants the land that belongs to King Leo."

Bennie thought it sounded like King Lear, but maybe that was reading too much into plastic toys.

"And Cedric has a guy who helps him named Weasel, who knows all about traps, and Gilbert the Bad."

"I'm guessing Gilbert the Bad is bad."

"Duh, right?" Jason rolled his eyes. "But Gilbert the Bad is really smart, and Boris, too, those are the bad guys. Like a lot of people think Legos are just for little kids, but they're really not. The coolest is Richard the Strong." Jason wiggled the figure. "He figures things out, protects the Queen and the Princess. He, like, *helps*. He's just, like a good guy but he's not the main guy, he's like strong. He like, stands up for justice."

"Maybe he'll be a lawyer someday."

"Ha!" Jason giggled, an adorably carefree sound, incongruous in the grim surroundings. "He's already better than a lawyer."

"Nothing's better than a lawyer."

"What? No way, he's, like, *awesome*! Like if anybody does or says anything bad about Queen Leonora or Princess Storm, he'll fight them!" Suddenly Jason's happiness evaporated.

"What, Jason? What's going on?"

"I guess that's, kind of, what was different, in the cafeteria." Jason's eyes filmed, but he kept his gaze on the toy. "I was walking by with my tray, and Richie started saying bad things about . . . my *mom*."

"Like what?" Bennie felt a pang. Her mother had been depressed, and as a child, Bennie remembered kids teasing her, the tall girl with the crazy mother.

"Richie said my mom was as big as a *house*, and that she was fat, then he told this joke, 'how fat is your momma,' 'when she sits around the house, she sits *around* the house.'"

"That's not funny." Bennie was beginning to think that the problem with her practicing juvenile law wasn't the expertise, but the emotionality.

"Then he said, that's why my mom . . . *died*, that she got a heart attack because she was a big, fat *pig*."

"Oh no." Bennie couldn't imagine the cruelty of the words to the grieving boy. "What happened after Richie said that? Did you hit him?"

"No, I started, like, crying." Jason kept his head down, his lower lip trembling. "I was trying not to, but I couldn't help it and then they started laughing harder, so then I dropped my tray and

I shoved Richie, and he shoved me back." Jason wiped his eyes with the palm of his hand. "Next thing I knew, I was on the ground and he was on top of me, and they called the police."

"Did you tell the cops?"

"No."

"The judge?"

"No, I was too scared. The courtroom was so big it looked like a castle!" Jason's glistening eyes went wide again, this time with fear. "And the judge was sitting on this big tall desk, way up high like a *king*, and he started yelling right away. He came to our assembly last year, he goes to all the schools and he tells them, if you make trouble or break the rules, I'm going to put you in juvie."

Bennie wasn't completely surprised to hear that the judge had spoken at school, because the judiciary in Pennsylvania were elected instead of being chosen by merit selection. One of the unfortunate results of the antiquated system was that judges frequently spoke at schools, Rotary Clubs, and even farm shows, pandering like common politicians, instead of guardians of the law.

"Yeah, and then they just put me in handcuffs and they even put them around my *legs*."

Bennie still couldn't wrap her mind around putting shackles on a seventh grader. In the Philadelphia criminal system, shackles weren't even used for accused murderers anymore.

"I felt like I was going into a *dungeon*."

Bennie didn't interrupt him, but from the looks of the detention center, a dungeon would've been an upgrade.

"I couldn't even walk, and I felt so bad. They got me out and I didn't even get to say good-bye to my dad. He musta been embarrassed in front of his boss. All the people from his work, they came to my mom's funeral . . ." Jason's voice trailed off and he bit his lip. "I feel like I'm a bad kid, now."

"No, you're a good kid—"

"But I'm in *jail*. They *lock* us in our rooms, and the other kids in here, they're *bad* kids. And they're *big*, they're all bigger than me. I'm the youngest. Even Richie is older than me."

"Richie is here, too?" Bennie questioned the wisdom of sending a bully to the same detention center as his victim. With adult offenders, she could have asked for a separation order, requesting a court to assign them to two different prisons.

"Yes, he's on my hall."

"Is he giving you a hard time?"

"Yes." Jason shook his head, still facing down.

Bennie felt her blood boil. "Stay away from him. Try to avoid him, as best you can."

"I'm going to be here, like, forever. I'm gonna miss *Christmas*." Jason bit his lower lip hard, but it trembled nevertheless.

"I'm going to try my hardest to see what I can do about that. I'll be here tomorrow to talk to you and tell you what's going on."

"Okay. Thanks."

"Good, you hang in here." Bennie collected her pen and legal pad, and slid them back into her messenger bag. "You're not too old a kid for me to hug, are you?"

"I guess not," Jason answered, with a shaky smile. He got to his feet, and Bennie went over and gave him a hug, though she couldn't remember the last time she'd hugged a child. She couldn't deny a surprisingly maternal twinge she felt, especially when she realized that Jason was clinging to her, longer than necessary.

"You're gonna be okay, buddy," Bennie said softly.

Praying she was right.

CHAPTER SEVEN

Bennie drove along, the case weighing on her mind and heart. She hated seeing Jason in juvie and when she'd dropped Matthew off, she tried to reassure him without raising his hopes—or her own. Meanwhile, the snow was falling too hard for her windshield wipers to keep up. The radio was full of storm predictions, but she had one last thing to do. She stopped the car and cut the ignition in front of the house.

GRUSINI, read reflective letters stuck on the black mailbox. Matthew had given her the address, which was in Slocum Township, adjoining Rice Township to the west, but even more rural. Bennie grabbed her purse, got out of the car, and hurried through the snow to a narrow house of white clapboard. The porch ceiling sagged, and the glass housing of the fixture beside the door was missing, exposing its bare bulb and illuminated peeling paint of the façade. Saran Wrap had been duct-taped over the front window, but lights were on inside, coming through sheer curtains.

Bennie climbed onto the porch and pressed the doorbell, but didn't hear it ring, so it must have been broken. She opened the screen door and knocked hard, and after a moment or two, the front door was answered by a woman with short, dark brown hair and a weary smile.

"Yes?" she said loudly, to be heard over the background noise of children. She had a pretty, if lined face, with lively dark eyes, a strong, hawkish nose, and a broad mouth, and she was wiping her hands on a white sack dish towel. Her petite frame seemed lost in an oversized blue Nittany Lions sweatshirt, with jeans.

"Doreen Grusini? I'm Bennie Rosato, and I'm wondering if I could come in and talk—"

"No, I'm busy." Doreen cut her off with a hand chop, holding the dish towel. "I'm fine with my religion and I gotta bake cookies for my son's school. Thanks for stopping by."

"Doreen, I'm a lawyer, and I'm here about what happened with your son Richie and Jason Lefkavick." Bennie fished in her wallet for her business card and handed it over. "I represent Jason, but the way I see it, the boys are in the same boat. Neither of them belongs in juvenile detention for a school fight."

"Hmph." Doreen arched an eyebrow, squinting to read the card in the light from the porch fixture, then looked up scowling. "You've got some nerve! Jason started it, you know. He shoved Richie for no reason."

"I'm not here to argue with you, I'm hoping we can help the kids."

"I don't need your help. My son wouldn't be in jail but for *your* client!"

"I'll just take fifteen minutes of your time—"

"I don't have fifteen minutes and I don't know what the point is."

"It's just to talk about the boys, and see if we can figure out a way to—"

"Oh, I get it, you're looking for me to *hire* you, but I have news. There's no way in the world *that's* happening." Doreen started to close the door.

"No, not at all, please." Bennie stopped the door from closing. "The boys aren't against each other anymore, they're both against the prosecutor. *Please*, I'll take five minutes. Five minutes."

"What kinda name is Bennie?" Doreen frowned.

"Short for Benedetta."

"You're Italian?"

"Through and through." Bennie could pander if it would help Jason.

"My ex was Italian, and I hate him."

Arg. "This is about your son, not your ex."

"Well, all right then." Doreen pocketed the card and opened the door. "Come in, you're letting in cold air."

"Thank you, so much." Bennie stepped inside the small house, looking around as Doreen closed the door behind them.

The children weren't in sight, but their noise reverberated through the walls. The living room was to the left and the kitchen to the right, the same layout as the Lefkavicks', but the two interiors couldn't have been more different; while the Lefkavick home was neat and orderly, albeit empty-feeling, the Grusinis' was vaguely chaotic, cluttered with children's toys, clothes, and games. The living room was stuffed with worn plaid furniture, but DVDs and video games lay open all over the brown rug next to joystick controllers, and ice-hockey sticks sat against the wall, with a pile of ice skates, black gloves, and helmets.

"Mommeeeee!" a child yelled, from upstairs. "He's hitting me! He's hitting me!"

"Don't make me come up there!" Doreen yelled toward the stairwell, and Bennie followed her into a toasty kitchen with sunny yellow walls. It was shaped like a cozy U, which ended in a rectangular wooden table on which a small TV played *Third Watch*. Shiny cookie sheets sat next to a large mixing bowl on the table, and the aroma of baking sugar cookies made her mouth water.

"Smells great," Bennie said, to show she came in peace.

"I suppose you want a cup of coffee?"

"No, I'm fine, thanks. I just had some."

Doreen cocked her head. "You're from Philly."

"Does it show?"

"Like you're wearing a sign. South Philly?"

"No, west."

"Does that make a difference?"

"Believe it or not, all the difference in the world."

Doreen smiled, seeming to warm up. "Okay, well, sit down. Oh, wait!" Her smile disappeared as she picked a blue backpack off the chair, then dropped it on the tile floor. "I tell them not to leave their crap on the chairs, but do they listen? Here, sit."

Bennie sat down.

"You're going to have to talk while I bake the cookies, because if I stop, I'll never get the twins bathed and in bed."

"That's fine. Can I help?"

"No, thanks." Doreen was already stabbing the cookie dough with a teaspoon and dropping it onto the cookie sheet. "I'm no Martha Stewart. They're holiday cookies because I say they're holiday cookies. They're not red, they're not green. They're not shaped like reindeer, Santa, or any of that happy horseshit, but they taste good."

"That's all that matters."

"Right. Kids don't know the difference. If it's sugar, they eat it."

Bennie hadn't expected to like Doreen, but she was beginning to. "You got your hands full."

"That's one way to put it. I hate the holidays. You know why? Whatever you have going on, there's just *more* of it at the holidays. You have to buy *more* food. You have to do *more* errands. You have to buy *more* presents. If you bake, you have to bake *more*. If the kids are busy in school, they're *more* busy. Every single thing is *more*." Doreen paused as more yelling came from upstairs, then she resumed making the cookies. "I worry when they're quiet. If they're loud, they're alive."

"So I guess Richie has siblings?"

"Two brothers, six-year-old twins." Doreen dropped another ball of batter onto the sheet, making a neat row, and Bennie was getting the sense that Richie wasn't uppermost on Doreen's mind.

"So about Richie. Were you there, at the courthouse?"

"Yes, it was *ridiculous*."

"I heard they put them in shackles."

"Right, *ridiculous*," Doreen said again.

"I just came from River Street. It's horrible to think of them being there. They're too young for an out-of-home placement, in any event. Were you considering getting a lawyer? I'm going to file a petition on Jason's behalf, and if you do the same thing, that makes our position much stronger."

"How? Jason's a nerd. They butt heads all the time. They're not friends."

"It doesn't matter, at this point. They're both in the same situation vis-à-vis the Commonwealth." Bennie caught herself speaking legalese. "They have a common enemy now. The system."

"Hold on, let me see if the first batch is done." Doreen stuck the spoon in the batter, crossed into the kitchen, and grabbed a quilted pot holder in one hand while she opened the oven door with the other. She squatted, eyeing the cookies, and the light from the oven illuminated her strong, if pretty, profile. She closed the oven door, stood up, and tossed the pot holder back on the counter. "This is what I hate about making cookies. You take them out too soon, they're gummy, but if you leave them in another minute, they burn." Doreen came back to the table and picked up the spoon. "So you were saying . . ."

"I was curious what you're going to do about Richie. I think his and Jason's civil rights were infringed, their constitutional rights. Did Richie have a lawyer? They have a right to counsel."

"No, they told us we didn't need one." Doreen dropped another cookie on the sheet.

"They were wrong."

"How would I know? I'm a hockey mom, not a lawyer."

"Did you sign a waiver form?"

"Yes, it's around here somewhere." Doreen dropped another cookie, finishing another row.

"So, about Richie, what sentence did he get?"

"Sixty days."

"Jason got ninety."

"Told you, he started it."

Bennie let it go. "Did the judge know that? Did you get a chance to present Richie's side of the story?"

"Are you kidding? No way. We were in and out of the court-room in five minutes. The judge gave Richie a lecture, then sentenced him to River Street." Doreen frowned as she scooped out some cookie dough. "I don't even know how the judge knew about the fight, I guess from the probation lady. We told her that Jason started the fight. He pushed Richie and he should've known better. My son's not going to take that crap and he's twice Jason's size."

Bennie couldn't let it stand uncorrected. "You know, it's true that Jason pushed Richie first, but Richie was teasing him, saying his mother was fat and that's why she died."

Doreen looked up sharply. "Is that true?" she asked, her lips set in a firm line.

"Yes."

"How do you know?" Doreen forgot about the cookies for a moment, resting the spoon on the edge of the bowl.

"Jason told me. He owned up to pushing Richie, but that's tough for a kid to deal with, the death of a mother. He started crying and just lashed out."

"Christ!" Doreen spat out, disgusted. "I'm sorry about that. That's horrible, that's really horrible. Richie didn't tell me. Tell Jason's father, I'm very sorry about that."

"Thank you, and I will tell him that. He's grieving, too, they both are. You can imagine."

"Of course I can." Doreen picked up the spoon and scooped out the cookie dough, practically throwing it at the cookie sheet, like paintball. "You know, Jason's mom, Lorraine, was a sweet-heart, always at the school, helping out. I never do that crap, I don't have the time, but she was the one, making the phone calls, running the canned-goods collections, doing the bake sale, what-ever it was, she did it."

Bennie had no idea how many extra things mothers did these days. Or maybe they did them in the old days, too, but her own mother had opted out, because of her illness.

"Poor woman, so what, she was fat, but you gotta die of some-thing. I just quit smoking, I got the patch, but it'll kill me in the end, if my kids don't." Doreen kept throwing cookie dough at the sheet. "I swear, I don't know what to do with Richie, I just don't. He's angry, we never know what mood he's gonna be in when he comes home. Last week I had to break up a fight with one of the twins. I swear, I thought Richie was going to choke him."

Bennie tried not to act as shocked as she felt.

"They say 'boys will be boys,' but this is way beyond that, and the thing I worry about, besides when he beats up on his brothers, is when they start acting like him. If they grow up thinking they should be like him, then they'll start bullying everybody, even *me*."

"That sounds tough." Bennie felt for her. "I'm not a mother, I don't know what I would do in that situation."

"You know what?" Doreen looked up from the cookies, her dark eyes flashing. "You wouldn't do anything, because there's nothing you *can* do. When Richie was little, I could punish him, I could make him take a time-out. I could take stuff away from him. Or I could beat his butt with the belt. But now, he's *way* bigger than I am. He pushes me *back*. He doesn't listen to a frigging thing I say!" Doreen threw up her hands, still holding the spoon. "He's mad because his father left, so am I! Welcome to the club, kid! You think I wanted to be on my own with *three* kids? Or what else, he's a bad seed, he gets it from his father, that's possible, too! What am I, Dr. Phil? I don't know what to do with him! And to be honest, sometimes I can't stand him."

Bennie fell silent, and for a moment the only sound was the children upstairs, but Doreen seemed not to notice, gesturing at the front door with the spoon.

"And when I hear him out there, his footsteps on the porch, I tense up. The twins do, too." Doreen's dark eyes blazed as she gazed down at Bennie. "It's the truth, the absolute *truth*. I'm on eggshells. I thought of sending him to military school, but now he gets arrested, he's a juvenile delinquent!"

Bennie could see how much Doreen loved her son, but at the same time how deeply she was troubled by him.

"Here's the silver lining, maybe they can turn him around at

River Street, scare him straight. Maybe he'll listen to *them* because he sure as hell won't listen to *me*!"

"MOMMMEEEE, OWWWW!" yelled one of the kids upstairs, his cry unmistakably urgent.

"Oh no!" Doreen dropped the spoon, turned away, and hustled for the stairwell. "Sorry, you'd better go!"

CHAPTER EIGHT

Bennie headed back to Wilkes-Barre toward the hotel, more determined than ever to get justice for Jason, since he'd been so
clearly victimized by Richie, a boy troubled enough to victimize
even his own family. She followed the street around a curve and
spotted a lighted sign for Larry's Beef 'n Brew, a long rectangular
building of pine paneling plastered with white plastic banners advertising Miller Lite, Yuengling Beer, and the NASCAR Sprint
Cup Series Schedule. Bennie realized she hadn't eaten dinner and
doubted the hotel would have room service this late, so she
pulled in.

She cut the engine, grabbed her purse, and got out of the car,
hustling into the building through the snow. She yanked open the
door, and the men at the bar turned to see who'd come in, every
expression telegraphing: YOU'RE NOT FROM HERE, AND
WE SUSPECT YOU HAVE OVARIES.

Bennie smiled back politely, deciding where to sit. The place
was a medium-sized room, dimly lit by recessed lighting in a
dropped-tile ceiling. Beer bottle caps the size of hubcaps shared
the paneled walls with mounted deer antlers, photographs of the
Rat Pack, and sketches of Frank Sinatra that looked hand-drawn.
The kitchen was at the back, there were a few tables on the right
and a U-shaped bar with a TV on the left, where an older bartender served a handful of male patrons hunched over bottles of

Rolling Rock. One man wore a baseball cap with an embroidered revolver above the words **I DON'T CALL 911**. Bennie decided not to sit at the bar, as she had no problem calling 911.

She opted for one of the tables alongside a lineup of lighted cases with refrigerated beer and another TV, playing the Weather Channel on mute. She pulled up a chair, slid out of her coat, and sat down at one of the square pine tables. The menu was a trifold plastic affair, and she lost herself in the down-home fare of kielbasa, Texas Tommy, and Italian sausage, even though she was a vegetarian.

"How can I help you?" said the bartender, setting down a tumbler of water, and Bennie looked up. He smiled, a short man with gray hair, a white shirt, and worn jeans.

"I'd like a grilled cheese, please."

"Kitchen's about to close, but I'll see what I can do. Be right back." The bartender left, and Bennie rummaged in her purse for her cell phone, which she flipped open. Heads turned at the bar, and she pressed in the phone number, realizing that she was the person everybody hated, the certified big deal who talked on the cell phone in public. Still, she had a client to update. The phone rang once, and Matthew picked up.

"Bennie, how did it go?"

"I talked it over with Doreen, and she apologizes for Richie's behavior. But I'm not sure we can count on her help going forward, and I'm going to stay over, do some legal research, and see what I can do tomorrow."

"Do you think you'll be able to get him out?"

"I won't know anything until I do the research, so I'll let you know tomorrow. Fair enough?" Bennie looked over as the front door opened, letting in a blast of cold air and a very tall, darkhaired man in a brown Carhartt coat and jeans, who nodded to the men at the bar.

Matthew was saying, "That would be wonderful. Thank you so much."

"You're welcome, good night." Bennie pressed END, noticing that the man in the Carhartt coat was eyeing her with a vaguely cocky smile. He was handsome, but she couldn't remember the last time she'd been picked up in a bar with antlers.

"Do you mind if I join you?" the man asked, crossing the room toward her table. "I'm Declan Mitchell—"

"Um, I'd rather not—"

"—Doreen Grusini's brother. You must be Bennie Rosato."

"Oh, sure, sit down." Bennie blinked, taken aback.

"I just missed you at my sister's." Declan eased his large frame into the seat, oversized for the table. He had to be six-foot-five and maybe 230 pounds. "I was on the way home when I saw your car."

"How did you know it was mine?"

"The residential parking sticker for Philly."

"Observant."

"Occupational hazard. I'm a state trooper."

Bennie thought it explained his size and demeanor, which was generally authoritative. It didn't, however, explain his hotness. Not that she was interested. She went for the brainy, bespectacled type who tried harder, not the drop-dead-babe type with the world on a string. She glanced reflexively at his hand, which lacked a wedding band.

"I wanted to talk with you about my nephew Richie."

"Sure." Bennie noticed that over Declan's shoulder, the bartender was coming over, carrying a glass of water.

"Sergeant Mitchell," the bartender said, with a grin. "You want the usual? Meatball sandwich?"

"Please, if Sara's still around to fix it for me."

"For you, she's around. For you, she'll kill the cow with her bare hands." The bartender turned away and lumbered off toward the kitchen, and Declan faced Bennie with a sheepish smile.

"Sorry about that."

"No worries." Bennie didn't say, *Must be tough being the hot single cop in a small town.*

"So you sue law enforcement for a living." Declan's tone was matter-of-fact, without rancor.

"Among other things, but how do you know that?"

"You left your business card with my sister. I looked up your website. You won a three-million-dollar case against the Philly police." Declan's eyes flared a rich, disapproving brown, roundish and wide-set. "Last year, you even won a case against *us*."

"I'm weeding out your bad apples. You can thank me anytime."

"Don't hold your breath." Declan snorted. He had a strong, straight nose and a largish mouth, with full lips. In fact, he had the lips Bennie always wished she had, which were wasted on a man.

"Anybody who breaks the law has to account, even if they wear a badge."

"So that's how it is, Philly? *You* uphold the law?"

"Yes, I serve and protect. I just don't have to write it all over my car, like some people we know." Bennie kept it light, wondering if she could get him on her side, for Jason's sake. "Did you talk to your sister about us joining forces? Because I really think we can help both kids if we work together."

"Now you're making sense. Strength in numbers." Declan's expression darkened, a frown crossing his face. "Doreen told me what Richie said to Jason about his mother. Sorry."

"Thanks. The two boys have an ongoing problem, as you may know."

"No, I didn't know. I've been out of touch with Richie. We used to get along better than we do."

"Richie bullies Jason because he's overweight. It's not fair and it has to stop."

"Richie's had a rough go since his dad took off."

"That's no excuse. Jason's mother died, and he doesn't bully anybody. No kid deserves to be tormented at school. Richie needs limits and counseling."

"I agree." Declan met Bennie's eye, his dark gaze direct. "I had him in counseling. He stopped going. He pushes back against authority, including me."

"Your sister seems to think juvie will scare him straight."

"It won't. It's incarceration. Nobody comes out of prison better than they went in."

Bennie heard the tinge of pain in his tone, as well as the conviction in his words, which rang true. So maybe he was smarter
than she thought.

"That's why I caught up with you." Declan raked his thick hair
with his hand, shifting forward in his chair. "We should team up.
If we can get one kid out of River Street, we can get the other
one out, right? Their interests aren't in conflict."

"Exactly what I was thinking." Bennie shifted forward, too,
heartened. "Their legal arguments are identical. They both signed
the same form, which is constitutionally defective."

"If I'd been there, I wouldn't have let her sign that form. By
the time I got to the courthouse, it was over." Declan's frown
deepened. "Richie got the lighter sentence because Doreen told
the judge I'm with the PSP. She leads with that when Richie gets
in trouble."

"I see." Bennie remembered that PSP stood for Pennsylvania
State Police. She wondered if Declan's connection to law enforcement could help Jason, too.

"Anyway, I don't want Richie in River Street another minute."

"I know, it's disgusting."

"The problem isn't the building. River Street is a catchall. They
don't segregate the firestarters, kids with substance abuse problems, even sexual offenders." Declan shook his head. "Last week,
I arrested a seventeen-year-old for assault with a deadly weapon. A
bat. He was sent to River Street. They're there for ag assault, bur-
glary, arson, heroin, and meth. They're much older than Richie.
They're men."

Bennie shuddered to think of Jason in jail, playing with his
Lego set. "Is there a lot of crime out here? I didn't think there
would be."

"We have fewer murders than Philly. That's only a matter of
density. I'm not going to let my nephew learn to be a criminal
from professionals. I want Richie out."

"And I want Jason out. There has to be a way." Bennie spoke
from the heart, since she didn't have to manage his expectations.
"There's no provision for rehearings, but I have to go back to

Common Pleas Court, for starters. Also my alternative argument would be for at-home placement and only the lower court can order that."

"So you file something?"

"Exactly, and right away."

"What do you file?" Declan frowned, puzzled.

"It doesn't matter what it's called. Whether I call it a petition or a motion, it's just a way to talk to the court."

"Form over substance."

"Exactly." Bennie liked that he understood. "I'm going to get something in front of a judge tomorrow, if it kills me."

"Would you represent Richie, too?"

Bennie hesitated. "I shouldn't."

"Why not, if their interests aren't in conflict?"

It was a good question. "They could be, down the line."

"And you'd throw Richie under the bus?"

"If I had to, yes. I'm not about to apologize for it. Jason wouldn't be in jail but for Richie's bullying."

"Whoa. Relax." Declan bristled.

"I am relaxed." Bennie hated it when people told her to relax.

"You're tough."

"You have no idea."

"Play nice." Declan recoiled. "We're on the same team."

"Okay. Fine." Bennie tried to dial it back. She rowed a single scull. Life was an individual sport. "Look, the best thing for both kids is if you get Richie a lawyer, somebody local, who specializes in juvenile law. Then we can cooperate and share information like co-counsel."

"I got the name of a lawyer in Hershey who does juvenile work. I'll call him and see if he'll take the case."

"Good. Hire him. I'll email him whatever papers I draft. He can copy them and file them right away, too. I was about to go to the Hilton and do some research. I have my laptop."

"The Hilton in Wilkes-Barre? It's closed for renovation."

"For real?" Bennie asked, dismayed. "Is there another one nearby? I don't want to drive home this late."

"You can't drive to Philly in this weather. You don't have four-wheel drive. We already closed part of I-80."

"What about another inn, or a bed-and-breakfast?"

"The nearest one is too far." Declan frowned. "I live five minutes from here, over the hill. Stay at my place. I have plenty of room."

"No, thanks." Bennie thought it was too random. She hardly knew him. She wasn't even sure she liked him, Mr. Always Gets What He Wants.

"You have no choice. You can't drive in this."

"There has to be an inn closer." Bennie reached for her phone to check.

"Not as close as my house. There's accidents everywhere. It's going to snow until three in the morning." Declan turned and signaled to the bartender, who was already on his way to the kitchen.

"But I have work to do."

"Work in my home office. Use my computer and printer. I'm not taking no for an answer." Declan pushed out his chair, just as the bartender came from the kitchen, carrying a brown bag.

"Declan, here we go. Grilled cheese and a meatball sandwich. I'll put it on your tab."

"Thanks." Declan took the bag. "Good night, Lee. Say hi to Susan for me."

"Good night." The bartender nodded. "Hi to Melissa, too."

"Will do." Declan returned with the bag, and Bennie assumed Melissa was his girlfriend.

Poor thing.

CHAPTER NINE

Bennie wolfed down her grilled cheese as she followed Declan's black Chevy pickup, his tires churning through fresh snow. She couldn't see much through the driving storm, and there were no other cars on the road. She would have been crazy to drive much farther, trying to find an inn. The only lights were their high-beams, as the two cars traveled together onto a winding road that narrowed from two lanes to one.

Bennie wiped her greasy fingers on a napkin, and they turned left onto Declan's driveway, which led to a farm in the middle of a snowy, wooded pasture. She craned her neck to see a small barn in front of a modern A-frame house, its distinctive roof visible only because of the moonlight. Declan parked next to a snow-covered pickup and horse trailer, and Bennie pulled in next to him, cut the ignition, and got out of the car. Her foot sunk into about five inches of newfallen snow.

"Bennie?" Declan stood by the pickup with his front door open, illuminated by the interior light. "I have a chore to do. Come with or go inside?"

Go inside. "Come with," Bennie answered, to be polite. She grabbed her purse and messenger bag, closed her car door, and chirped it locked.

"Why'd you lock your car?" Declan took off, chuckling.

"Bears could break in." Bennie followed him, walking in his footsteps, which were too far apart, even for her.

"Bears hibernate, Philly."

"I knew that." Bennie picked her way after him, and Declan switched on a light, illuminating a wood barn with a snowy overhang that covered two stalls, with a horse in each, a white one and a black one. Their heads popped up, their tufted ears swiveled forward, and their big eyes blinked comically. They had on thick green blankets that buckled under their chests.

"Meet Ember. He's a draft cross." Declan rolled the stall door aside and patted the dark horse on its neck. Steam came from its shell-pink nostrils, clouding the air. "Do you ride?"

"No, I drive." Bennie had never seen horses, up close. "They're so big."

"They're retired police horses." Declan patted the horse again. "He's friendly to everybody but lawyers. Don't feed him your fingers."

"Funny." Bennie patted Ember's neck, which felt strong. His color was a glossy black, with fur so thick it buried her knuckles.

"He was my partner." Declan gestured at Bennie's purse and messenger bag. "Give me your things. I'll put them in the tack room."

"What do you mean, your partner?" Bennie handed him her bags, and Declan opened a door at the end of the barn, turned on a light inside, and took her stuff into a small room with saddles mounted on wall racks and other horsey paraphernalia.

"I'm a field rider with the mounted unit. Ember served with me. I rescued him from the kill pen at New Holland." Declan came back holding a bucket containing duct tape, a white jar, and packaged rolls of black bandages, then set it down on the concrete floor in front of the stalls.

"Do you have a squad car, too?" Bennie had never met a mounted policeman. Meanwhile, of course Declan rode a horse. He'd have all the local girls swooning, plus he'd generate a lot of bad *mounted* puns.

"Yes, I have a patrol car. The PSP has twenty-five horses stabled at the Academy in Hershey. We maintain a mounted unit at the BES." Declan went back into the tack room, and there was the sound of water running.

"What's the BES?"

"Bureau of Emergency Services. Since 9/11, we get called for security. We do search and rescue, crowd control, ceremonial duties. When we get the call, we go down to Hershey, pack up the horses, and deploy as needed."

"How long have you been doing this?"

"Since I graduated from Penn State. I'm stationed at Troop N, Hazleton Station. There are mounted officers in every troop of the PSP. Each troop has three or four field riders who can be detailed as needed." Declan came back holding a large rubber tub of water, which looked cloudy. Steam rose from its surface, and he set it down on the concrete.

"What's that?"

"Water with Epsom salts. I pulled the mare's shoes for the winter. I'm worried she has an abscess. This will only take a few minutes." Declan unlatched the other stall door and rolled it aside, leaving it wide open for the white horse.

"Yikes, won't she run out?"

"Of course not." Declan got a halter from a hook, looped it over the horse's furry ears, and led her onto the concrete, where she stood. He picked up her front leg, bent it at the knobby knee, and took off a gray boot made of duct tape, then placed her hoof in the tub of Epsom salts.

"She's *stands* in the water, like that?"

"Most horses will." Declan patted the horse's neck. "Police horses are drilled to stand for extended periods."

Suddenly a gust of snow flew under the overhang, and Bennie turned, scanning the scene behind her. A snowy pasture surrounded them, glowing a bluish-white in the moonlight. Snowflakes swirled in the air, and moonbeams flowed through the bare branches of the trees, etching inky shadows across the white pasture. "It's gorgeous here," Bennie said, meaning it.

"Thanks. I feel lucky. Blessed. When I come home, I forget everything. It's a life that suits me. A place that suits me." Declan knelt beside the horse, bathing its foot with a cupped palm. "I was thinking about what you said. That you uphold the law."

"I was only joking."

"I know. But it made me think. I don't uphold or protect the law. I protect the people." Declan shook his head, still at his task. "I feel it more strongly since 9/11 and the war in Afghanistan. The world has become a dangerous place. The people I care about need protecting, more than ever before. Look there. See the house behind the treeline?" Declan pointed behind her with a wet hand, and Bennie turned to see a lighted farmhouse with a barn in the distance.

"Yes?"

"The Walshes live there, Helen and Jacob. They're ninety now. They were friends of my parents. Had three girls. Jacob keeps bees, and Helen makes everything out of honey. They think it's good for your skin. All I can tell you is, they don't look a day over eighty-seven."

Bennie smiled.

"When I think of what I do and why, I think of them and the other families here. I didn't realize it until tonight, talking with you. I have a purpose here. I'm set in my ways. It's not always good, in relationships. There's no compromise in me."

Bennie wondered if he was talking about Melissa but didn't ask. "I understand that. I never go out and I don't even miss it."

"You're not seeing anyone?" Declan took the horse's hoof out of the water, grabbed a small towel, then dried it off.

"As if it's your business?"

"I take it that's a no," Declan said, with a faint smile. He set the towel down, picked up the white jar, uncapped it, and dug out some gray paste and smeared it under the horse's hoof. "Why?"

"I work too much, a typical trial lawyer, you know."

"No, I don't. Tell me."

"Tell you what?"

"Tell me about yourself. What do you do with your free time?" Declan tossed her a roll of duct tape. "Tear off a bunch of ten-inch strips of tape. Put them on the stall door in a line."

"I don't have any free time." Bennie unrolled duct tape with freezing fingers and ripped it with her teeth, but she wished she were at the Hilton, working. She didn't like talking about herself.

"Hobbies?"

"None." Bennie stuck the first strip on the door, God knew why. Because Declan liked ordering her around.

"I thought you were cooler than this, Philly. You're not living up to your website."

"Nobody does." Bennie stuck the strip on the door, then unrolled another, eyeing Declan as he wrapped the horse's foot in cotton.

"It said you were an Olympic rower."

"Almost. I missed qualifying." Bennie tore off the strip with difficulty.

"What got you into rowing?" Declan covered the horse's hoof in cotton, then reached for the black cloth tape, which he began to wind around the cotton.

"I'm tall and I suck at basketball." Bennie tore off another strip, wondering why she found rowing, or it found her. She liked the physicality of the sport, the testing of her own limits. How far could she go, and how fast. How strong she could be, how powerful.

"So no room for dating?"

"Are we almost done here? I have work to do." Bennie stuck another strip of duct tape on the door.

"I offered you the chance to go inside. You said no." Declan kept winding the black tape around the cotton, then pressed it together so that it adhered to itself.

"I was being polite."

"So stay polite. I'm almost ready for the duct tape. Hurry."

"You like to give orders, don't you?" Bennie ripped off another strip of tape.

"And you like to duck questions." Declan looked up, arching an eyebrow.

"I'm in court all the time. I'm too busy to date anyone." Bennie stuck the strip to the door with the others. "When you're on trial, you're busy all day and all night, too. You have to prepare witnesses, draft evidentiary motions, think about direct exam and cross. You don't have control of a trial schedule. You go according to the court's schedule."

"I get that. Enough tape, thanks." Declan rose, went to the door, and took two strips, weaving them together.

"Plus, the trial's only for one client, and you have other active cases. I have a great staff and I like to pay them well. My business model is different, more equal. I like it that way, but payroll keeps me up at night." Bennie heard herself explaining her business, which she'd never articulated before, even to herself. "I love my life, like you, but it takes a lot of doing. I thought it would be easier when I was younger."

"I get that, too." Declan wove the duct tape together, his fingers working nimbly, and Bennie had no idea how, but he was making a lattice of duct tape.

"Every day is wall-to-wall. There's no time for a relationship, to give anything to a relationship. I pour everything into my business and trying to grow it. My firm has to get to cruising altitude, and I'm not there yet. If I didn't have a dog that I could bring to work, I wouldn't even have a dog."

"Cats are easier. I have Catmandu." Declan went back to the horse with the duct-tape lattice, picked up her leg, and pressed the lattice onto the black tape.

"Are you done yet?"

"Almost." Declan folded the duct tape around the hoof, making a MacGyver-like shoe.

"It's cold."

"Finished." Declan rose and led the horse back to her stall. "Say good night to Melissa."

"Melissa is the *horse*?"

"Yes." Declan rolled the door closed. "How do you know about Melissa?"

Bennie's mouth went oddly dry. "I heard the bartender mention her."

"Who'd you think she was?" Declan asked, with a knowing smile.

CHAPTER TEN

The next morning, Bennie was in the car bright and early, and the countryside was even more beautiful, with new snow lying on the rooftops and icy sleeves covering the bare limbs of the trees. She followed the winding road, with the pale sun rising in a frigid blue sky, thinking unaccountably of Declan. He was gone by the time she got up, and she'd showered, changed back into the same clothes, and ate cereal from his well-stocked kitchen cabinet. His refrigerator had everything, and judging from a stash of Hershey's products, he was a chocoholic. His house had been what she'd expected; a three-bedroom, inexpensively but neatly furnished, with a family room containing a locked gun rack, a big-screen TV with Madden video games, and a bookshelf full of biographies and detective fiction. The *Wilkes-Barre Times Leader* arrived on his doorstep this morning, which did not surprise her, along with the *New York Times,* which did.

Bennie was heading to the courthouse to file the petition she'd written last night. She'd been up all night researching and writing, but she felt confident of success. She was right on the case law, *Commonwealth v. Monica*, and even the statutory law, Section 6337 of the Juvenile Act. Her trump card was an on-point precedent she'd found—*In re A.M.*, in which the state's appellate court had held that an admission by a juvenile was a critical stage at which the juvenile had a right to counsel. The case had been decided in January 2001, reversing an adjudication by Judge Zero Tolerance, the *same* judge that Jason had. It was almost too much too hope for, a home run.

Bennie steered onto the main road, traveling behind a tractor-trailer whose chunky tires sprayed road salt and dirt. She reached for her phone, pressing Matthew's number. The phone rang a few times, and Matthew picked up. "Matthew, good morning," she said. "I'm heading toward the courthouse to file a petition to get a rehearing in Jason's case."

"That was quick! Do you think we'll win?"

"All I know is that we should, but I don't know if we will." Bennie switched on her windshield wipers, trying to clear the road salt from the truck.

"Can Jason get home by Christmas?"

"We have a chance. I asked the judge to schedule the Commonwealth's responsive pleading in three days, instead of the standard ten. If the response comes in this week, then the judge might schedule a hearing on Monday of next week, which could get Jason home on Christmas morning."

"That would be great!"

"But no promises."

"When will we find out?"

"I don't know."

"Please keep me posted."

"I'll update you at the end of the day."

"Good. I'm at work now. I better hang up. God bless you."

"Bye for now, Matthew." Bennie hung up, touched. She cared about all of her clients, but there was something about representing a kid that got to her like nothing else had, ever before. She turned right onto the highway, merging behind the tractor-trailer.

About an hour later, Bennie was turning left onto Pennsylvania Avenue and passing the stately limestone courthouse, situated in the center of a parklike parcel covered with snow. Parking was around the back, and she steered into the long lot, past cars and white police cruisers lined against a wall. She found a spot,

grabbed her stuff, and got out of the car, then hurried to the closest entrance, in the basement of the building. She went through
a newish metal detector and retrieved her stuff. Security had
heightened since 9/11 and the war, and Bennie hated that the
courthouses wouldn't be easily accessible to the public, a notion
enshrined in the Constitution itself.

She went down a hallway, passing administrative offices, and a
sign that read DOG, HUNTING, FISHING, SPORTSMEN'S FIREARMS,
BINGO AND SMALL GAMES-OF-CHANCE LICENSING, something
she'd never seen in Philadelphia's City Hall. She got into an elevator and traveled upstairs, then was let off into the most beautiful
courthouse she'd ever seen. The floor of the foyer was covered with
a darkish tan marble, and the space was dominated by a double-
banked stairwell of gray-and-white marble. The atrium was three
stories high, ringed with rose-gray marble balconies, but the pièce
de résistance was a domed mosaic ceiling and at its very apex, an
orb of stained glass.

Court employees with laminated ID lanyards crisscrossed the
lobby, and groups of lawyers talked together, carrying old-school
briefcases. Bennie found the clerk's office, which had a modern
glass door retrofitted into a carved arch of white marble, and went
inside to an antique mahogany counter, incongruous with com-
puters, fax machines, and the gray cubicles of the staff. She slid
her petition from her messenger bag as a clerk walked over with
a pleasant smile. She was an older woman with short, feathery
gray hair, and she had on a sweater sporting a sequined Christmas tree.

"Good morning, how may I help you?" she asked, slipping on
a pair of reading glasses with a sea-glass lorgnette.

"Hi, I have some papers I'd like to file with the juvenile court
judge." Bennie passed them to the clerk, who pointed to the
capitalized title of the papers, EMERGENCY PETITION FOR READ-
JUDICATION IN THE MATTER OF J. L., A JUVENILE.

"What's an 'Emergency Petition for Readjudication'? I've never
heard that term."

Because I made it up, Bennie thought but didn't say. "I represent a juvenile who was adjudicated delinquent last Friday. I believe his right to counsel was violated and I'm seeking a rehearing of the adjudication of delinquency."

"But there is no local court rule that provides for rehearing of adjudications. I don't even think there's a rule in the Pennsylvania Rules of Civil Procedure that allows such a thing." The clerk's hooded eyes fluttered behind her reading glasses.

"There may not be, but at the same time, there is no court rule that prohibits the filing of petitions not sanctioned by court rule, if you follow." Bennie knew it sounded circuitous, but she was right on the law.

"Which law firm are you with? I'm sorry, we haven't met."

"I work with my own law firm in Philadelphia."

"That explains it." The clerk slid the papers back. "You may do it that way in Philadelphia, but that's not how we do it here."

"It shouldn't make a difference, it's a Common Pleas Court. You can enter it in the docket like any other petition or motion."

"The Clerk's Office has to reject filings that don't comply with local rules."

"But this filing doesn't run afoul of any local rules. I can file any motion with the Juvenile Court, and if that's improper, it would be up to the judge to deny it."

"But the judge is busy this week. He's presiding over the double murder trial in 302. It's a big deal, all over the news."

"He does criminal cases, as well?" Bennie was surprised that a Juvenile Court judge heard other matters, yet another difference between the courts in the city and out here.

"Yes, two days a week he hears juvenile cases, and the other three days he hears civil or criminal cases."

"Is there only one Juvenile Court judge?"

"Yes." The clerk kept fluttering her eyes, and Bennie realized she just wanted to follow the correct procedure, which was impossible, because there was no procedure.

"Look, I get that this is an unusual petition. But let me tell you, I clerked for a state appellate judge, and in my experience, judges don't like it when other people make decisions for them. If I were you, I'd accept the papers for filing and let him deal with it. It's the safer course, don't you think?"

The clerk smiled, relieved. "Now *that's* the truth. I'll make sure these get filed and entered in the docket."

CHAPTER ELEVEN

Bennie followed the curved hallway of the courthouse, her boots clacking on the marble floor. She kept going until she came to another curved arch with a retrofitted door that read, **OFFICE OF THE DISTRICT ATTORNEY**. She entered, walked to another antique counter, and spotted a young man in a gray suit and tie, with the telltale short haircut of a prosecutor.

"Excuse me, can I speak with you?" Bennie asked the prosecutor, who nodded and strolled over. He looked about thirty years old, his alert brown eyes vaguely caffeinated and his fresh morning shave aromatic.

"Sure, what is it?"

"I represent a juvenile who was sent to River Street. I just filed some papers that I need to serve on you—"

"I'll accept service." The prosecutor held out his hand.

"Thanks. Did you handle the matter? I haven't gotten the transcript yet." Bennie dug in her messenger bag, extracted the service copy of the papers, and handed it to the prosecutor.

"No, it wasn't me. There's only one guy who does Juvenile Court and he's not in right now."

"Do you know when he'll be back?"

"No idea."

"These are emergency papers. I'm going to try to get a readjudication if not today, then tomorrow. Can you alert him to that fact, so we're good to go when the judge gives the word?"

"Will do. I'll leave a note on his desk." The prosecutor checked his watch.

"Let me ask you one last question." Bennie flipped to the last page of her petition, which was the waiver form that Matthew had given her. "You see this form?"

"Yes, what about it?" The prosecutor glanced at the form quickly.

"This is a form they're using in Juvenile Court, which purports to be a waiver of the right to counsel. You can see the signature line for the parents, who are permitted to sign on the juvenile's behalf—"

"I have a trial I have to get ready for, so could you get to the point?"

"I think it's constitutionally defective and—"

"What's your question?"

Bennie didn't mind getting a hard time. On the contrary, she liked a good fight. "My question is, did your office develop this waiver form?"

"I don't know."

"Do you think the judge developed it?"

"No idea."

"Is the District Attorney around?"

"You want to see my boss?" The prosecutor smiled slightly. "He's trying the double homicide."

"How about the First Assistant?"

"Everybody's there but me. I'm Cinderella and I have to get ready for the ball. Thanks." The prosecutor slid the papers off the counter and edged away with them.

"Please have your colleague call me. My cell phone number and email are on the papers," Bennie called after the prosecutor, as he made his way through the warren of cubicles and disappeared. She left the office, crossed the lobby, and consulted a court directory festooned with red-and-green tinsel, which told her where else she had to go. Lawyering wasn't always fireworks, but she wanted to get to the bottom of that waiver form.

Bennie found a wide marble stairwell and headed upstairs to the judge's chambers. She reached the fourth floor, got a copy of her papers ready, and opened the heavy wooden door onto chambers, which had a waiting area with blue cloth chairs and a coffee table with Pennsylvania Bar Association journals. A secretary sat at a small wooden desk, which held a computer monitor, neatly stacked files, and a green mini Christmas tree, its multicolored lights aglow.

"Good morning." Bennie introduced herself, stepping forward with her papers, and the secretary looked up, a middle-aged woman whose dark hair was pulled into a low ponytail. She wore oversized glasses with blue acetate frames that matched her eye color almost exactly. She had on a blue jumper, white blouse, and a red sweater.

"Yes, how can I help you?"

"I'd like the judge to have a courtesy copy of papers that I just filed, seeking an emergency hearing this week."

"Oh. My." The secretary accepted the papers, her thin lips pursed. "The judge is very busy. I doubt he'll be able to schedule a hearing this week."

"I'm hoping he can schedule something after court is out of session today or before it convenes tomorrow morning."

"I'm not sure that will be possible. I wouldn't get your hopes up."

"I won't, thanks. Does he take a break at midmorning, during trial?"

"Yes, usually," the secretary answered, reluctantly.

"I assume he hasn't taken that yet, since it's on the early side." Bennie glanced at the wall clock, a bronzed-eagle affair that read 9:30. Most trials took a break at 10:30, when the judge had to pee, the staff had to smoke, and the lawyers had to double-bill somebody.

"He hasn't taken a break yet."

"Good. So maybe you could show him the petition then?"

"Thank you. Good day now." The secretary averted her eyes, seeming to dismiss Bennie, who wasn't leaving just yet.

"I know that the judge uses a waiver-of-counsel form in his courtroom. Do you know if he generates the form himself?"

The secretary hesitated. "Perhaps you should take that up with the judge. Good-bye now."

"Okay, thank you." Bennie let it go, having become *persona non grata* in thirty seconds, which was a personal best. She left chambers, hurried down the hall and down the stairwell four flights, then left the courthouse by the side entrance. The air was bitterly cold, and she found herself running down the slate walkway to the sidewalk, then scurrying across the street toward the courthouse annex, a modern building of tan brick and smoked glass windows. The edifice lacked the vintage grace of the courthouse, but she was hoping for a friendlier reception at the public defender's office.

Bennie made a beeline for the entrance, climbed a set of concrete steps, and let herself past an open door. It led to an office space that was modern, with gray rugs, inexpensive fluorescent lighting, and a white counter. A handful of gray cubicles filled the room, and only one of the desks was occupied, by a woman on a computer, who flicked long brown hair from her shoulders, got up, and came over, wearing a coarse-knit Mexican sweater and jeans.

"Hello, how can I help you?" the woman asked.

"I'm wondering if I could talk to whoever does the juvenile work here."

"He's not here now. I can take a message for you."

"Let me ask you a quick question." Bennie got out a spare copy of her papers and turned to the waiver in the back. "This is a waiver used in Juvenile Court, which I think is constitutionally defective. Do you have any idea where this form came from?"

"No."

"Have you ever seen it before?"

"No."

"Is it more likely it came from the D.A., the judge, or somebody else?"

The woman shook her head. "I can't say. Fact is, we don't get a lot of juvenile cases."

"That brings me to my other question. My client's father was told he didn't qualify for a public defender because he made too much money. The client whose income you should've been looking at isn't the father's, but the son's. The son is a student and he would've easily qualified for a defender."

The woman bristled, flicking back her hair again. "I wasn't the one who said that and I don't know why it was said."

"Thanks. I'd love a call back, from whoever knows." Bennie pulled a business card from her wallet, left the building, and headed back to the courthouse. She had boxes to check and enemies to make.

Nobody becomes a lawyer to be liked.

CHAPTER TWELVE

"Good morning, may I help you?" asked an older court stenographer, who appeared at the Transcription Services counter. She had a narrow face framed with close-cropped silvery-gray hair and she wore a prim blue suit and earrings shaped like Christmas trees.

"Yes, I'd like to order a transcript." Bennie fished her bar card from her wallet, pulled out another copy of her petition, and set both on the counter.

"I've never seen an 'Emergency Petition for Readjudication' before." The court stenographer skimmed the petition, then looked up. "What's the emergency?"

"A twelve-year-old was wrongly sent to River Street and I'd like to get him out as soon as possible."

"Twelve years old?" The court stenographer lifted a graying eyebrow. "That's quite young to be misbehaving."

"He wasn't, it was just a minor fight at school."

"I see." The court stenographer pursed her lips. "The judge doesn't tolerate any sort of misbehavior in school. Somebody has to keep the schools safe."

"My client was being bullied by another boy. That's how the fight started, it wasn't his fault." Bennie had spent enough time in courthouses to know that everybody talked about the cases, and a good word could travel.

"But it takes two to tango, and you can't be too careful these days. My sister lives in Windber, near Shanksville. You know, where Flight 93 crashed."

"Is that near here?"

"Only three hours west. The poor souls on that airplane, my heart breaks for them, and I hate to think what would've happened if they crashed into a neighborhood. These terrorists, they're inhuman."

"I agree with you, but my client isn't a terrorist. He's a child."

"Hmph. If you're in the right, you should prevail."

Bennie let it go. If only that were true. "How long will it take to get the transcript?"

"Fifteen minutes. It will be easy to transcribe because the juvenile judge doesn't waste any words."

"So I hear." Bennie realized that the court stenographer could have some behind-the-scenes information. "Have you worked in the judge's courtroom as a stenographer, when he hears juvenile cases?"

"Yes, he's very intelligent, and he's tough but he's fair."

"That's good." Bennie kept her tone casual. "When you've been in his courtroom, have you noticed how often the juveniles are represented?"

"Rarely, if ever. Now, come back in a few minutes, I'll have the transcript ready."

"Terrific, thanks." Bennie took off for the stairwell, reached the third floor, and approached the crowd in front of Courtroom 302, the double murder trial. Reporters with notepads and spectators in heavy coats packed the balcony, mingling with local police in black insulated jackets and thick gun belts. She wedged her way toward one of the cops, who stood in front of a set of long metal tables by a metal detector.

"Officer, I'd like to go in and observe the judge. I have a case before him and I want to see how he operates."

"I get it, like recon." The cop smiled in a knowing way. "Wish

I could admit you, but I can't. We got a full house. Nobody's getting in unless somebody comes out."

"What about standing room?"

"We don't allow it." The cop leaned toward her, lowering his voice. "But I can tell you something about how he operates. Is it a criminal matter or civil?"

"It involves a juvenile."

"Oh." The cop shook his head. "He's tough on kids. He's known for it. You know what his nickname is?"

"Judge Zero Tolerance?"

"No. Napoleon."

"Thanks," Bennie said, getting the picture. She made her way back toward the stairwell, descending two floors to the first floor, where she headed back to the Transcription Services office. She walked back inside just as the court stenographer emerged from the hallway, carrying a few papers.

"Perfect timing," the court stenographer said, with a smile.

"Finished already? How much will that be?"

"Five dollars."

"Great." Bennie slid a five from her purse and handed it over.

"Hold on while I get you a receipt." The court stenographer stepped away from the counter.

"Thanks." Bennie opened the transcript, which was only four pages long, counting the title page and the certification by the court reporter. It read, *in toto*:

> JUVENILE OFFICER: Mr. Lefkavick, please step forward.
> (Whereupon, the party was sworn in.)
> THE COURT: You've been charged with fighting in school, how do you wish to plead?
> THE JUVENILE: Guilty.
> THE COURT: Based upon his admission, I'll adjudicate him delinquent. What makes you think you have the right to do this kind of crap?

THE JUVENILE: I don't, sir. I never—
THE COURT: How long have you been at Crestwood?
THE JUVENILE: Uh, since, I'm in—
THE COURT: You heard me speak at assembly?
THE JUVENILE: Uh, yes.
THE COURT: Told you what type of conduct I expected from children in that school, relative to the juvenile justice system?
THE JUVENILE: Uh. Yes.
THE COURT: Is fighting acceptable in school?
THE JUVENILE: No, but—
THE COURT: No buts. What did I say would happen if you acted in an unacceptable way in school?
THE JUVENILE: Um, I don't remember.
THE COURT: You don't remember? You don't remember me saying that if you did anything unacceptable in school that I would send you away? You don't remember me saying I won't tolerate violence in school? You don't remember those words?
THE JUVENILE: No, sir.
THE COURT: Were you sleeping?
THE JUVENILE: No, no.
THE COURT: You can't remember that?
THE JUVENILE: No, sorry.
THE COURT: I'll remind you of what I said, I walked into that school and I spoke to your student body and I wasn't just doing it to scare you, to blow smoke, to make you think that I would do that when I wouldn't. I'm a man of my word. You're gone. Send him up to River Street. Let him stay there ninety days. Let's see if that's time enough to remember the difference between right and wrong, acceptable and unacceptable in school. Thank you.
FATHER OF JUVENILE: No, wait, please, that's not fair. That's not what the lady said. Judge, please, you don't understand, he's a good boy.
THE COURT: Thank you.
(Whereupon, the proceedings were concluded.)

Bennie closed the transcript. She had expected the hearing would be inadequate, but seeing *how* inadequate turned her stomach.

"Here we go," said the court stenographer, returning to the counter with the receipt. "My, are you okay, dear?"

"No," Bennie answered, taking the receipt. "But thanks."

CHAPTER THIRTEEN

Sunlight struggled through the dirty windows, and Bennie watched as Jason made his way across the empty visiting room, his feet scuffing the gritty tile floor, his head downcast. Her heart went out to him, and she was still angry after what she'd read in the transcript, seeing how unjust his hearing had been.

"Hey buddy," Bennie said, as Jason reached the table, and up close, she noticed that his eyes were bloodshot and there were dark circles underneath them.

"Hi." Jason sat down heavily in the hard chair opposite her, slumping backwards.

"How're you doing?" Bennie heard shouting in another room, and the air smelled dirty and felt cold, though the ancient radiators knocked constantly.

"Okay."

"How did you sleep?"

"Okay."

"You should feel free to talk with me, even if you just want to complain."

"I'm no whiner." Jason swallowed hard, his little Adam's apple going up and down.

"It's not whining."

"Whining and complaining are the same thing."

"Not when the complaining is to a lawyer," Bennie said, gently.

"In fact, every lawsuit is started with a piece of paper that gets filed with a court. You know what that paper is called?"

"No, what?"

"A Complaint."

"Really?" Jason's eyes narrowed with adult skepticism.

"Truly. If you don't tell me your complaint, I can't do my job. Now, let's start over. Did you sleep okay?"

"No." Jason hesitated. "I was, like, afraid. It's dark, and there's weird noises, and these boys, they talk all night. They yell and I heard somebody crying."

"That's sad. I would cry if I were in here, too." Bennie wondered if Jason had cried. "Did you have any classes today? They're supposed to hold classes for you."

"They said they'll do that later. I don't know how." Jason bit his lip. "My teachers don't come here, do they?"

"No, they have different teachers." Bennie wasn't sure how it worked, in fact.

"My grades, they're going to go down. I'm already so far behind. We had to read a book over the weekend. *The Giver.* I didn't bring it and I only got done eleven pages."

"I'm sure you'll catch up," Bennie said, though she was worried. She wondered if this was what being a parent was like, giving comfort you didn't feel and reassuring someone when you were worried as hell.

"I told my dad and he's going to bring more books tonight. I can read in my room, I keep away from everybody, and Richie and the boy next door to me, he's *seventeen.* They call him Wrinkles." Jason lowered his voice. "I think he did something bad to a little girl. You know what I mean?"

Bennie's mouth went dry. "Stay away from him."

"Oh, I will," Jason shot back.

"What about Richie? How is he?" Bennie realized she was worried about Richie's being on the same hall as a sex offender. She never would've felt that way before, her loyalties newly confused.

"I stay away from Richie, too. I stay away from *everybody.*"

Jason's eyes went rounder, his fear plain. "I just try to stay out of everybody's way, like school, only worse."

"Are they bullying you already?"

"They call me names. The guard calls me Fats Domino."

"I could do something about that, you know." Bennie felt anger tighten her chest.

"No don't." Jason's expression changed, his eyebrows flying upward in anxiety. "Let it roll off your back. Like a duck, remember I told you?"

"I won't say anything, but you have to make me a promise. If you are in any kind of physical danger, I want you to go to the guard and tell him. If anybody shoves you, or pushes you, or tries to touch you"—Bennie was choosing her words carefully—"then I want you to go to the guard and I want you to tell him you want your lawyer. I will come, any time of day or night. You understand?"

"Okay. I promise. So when am I going to get out? After you win in court, like in *Law & Order*?"

"Not exactly, and you—"

"So will I get out after the jury says so?"

"There's no jury, just the judge. I just filed some papers, trying to get the judge to take another look at your case."

"What did he say?"

"He didn't say yet. It takes longer than—"

"So tomorrow?"

"No, at best, by the end of the week. The judge could deny my motion, which means he could just say no. We could lose. So try not to get your hopes up."

"Why would you not win, if you're right?"

"Good question." Bennie wasn't sure she could explain it. "Because the judge has the power and he can be wrong. He already has been, hasn't he?"

"Do you have to ask the *same* judge? Oh no." Jason sighed, his soft shoulders sagging. "The judge isn't going to change his mind. He's mean. Why can't you go ask another judge?"

"That's not how it works. I'm going to do everything I possibly can, Jason." Bennie reached across the table and patted his hand, which felt warm. "Just hang in there, can you?"

"The guard took Richard the Strong and my other bricks. They said I couldn't have them. They weren't approved."

"Who did that?"

"Just leave it alone. They put them in a box and they said my dad can have them next time he comes." Jason rallied. "He said he'll come tonight with my pictures."

"Pictures of what?" Bennie thought she'd burst into tears if Jason said his mother.

"Of Patch. I know, that sounds dumb, but, well, she always sleeps on my bed."

"It doesn't sound dumb. My dog sleeps on my bed, too."

"Cool." Jason's face lit up, for the first time. "Patch likes to run around at night. My dad always lets her, but my mother never did. She was too worried she'd get hit by a car." He frowned. "I'm worried she might, too."

Bennie remembered she had thought the same thing. "I'll ask your dad to keep her in at night. Would you like that?"

"Yes." Jason's eyes filmed. "She should stay in until I get home."

"Yes, at least until then," Bennie repeated, her throat constricting.

CHAPTER FOURTEEN

Bennie charged up the courthouse stairwell, her determination renewed by her visit with Jason. She reached the judge's chambers and opened the door on the secretary. "Hello, I'm—"

"Yes, I remember." The secretary was standing by the coatrack, putting on her parka.

"I'm checking to see if the judge was able to take a look at my petition."

"Yes, and he issued the order during the morning recess."

"Great!" Bennie said, surprised. "May I see the order? Did he give the Commonwealth three or ten days?"

"I'll give you a copy of the order. I sent it to the clerk for filing, but it may not have been docketed yet." The secretary crossed to her desk, opened a manila folder on top, slid out a paper, and handed it over.

"Thank you." Bennie skimmed the single paragraph, which read: **The Commonwealth shall file a responsive pleading in no more than three (3) business days.** She almost cheered. "This is wonderful! Thanks so much!"

"Now, excuse me, I'm on my way to lunch, and we keep chambers locked." The secretary walked to the door and held it open, but Bennie wasn't leaving just yet.

"According to this, he didn't schedule a hearing."

"I'm sure he will make that decision after both parties have filed their pleadings."

"Do you think it's possible to get the hearing by Christmas?"

"That isn't for me to say."

"Court isn't closed next week, is it?"

"No, it's closed only Wednesday, Christmas Day."

"By the way, is the judge in now?"

"No." The secretary gestured to the door again. "Please?"

"Okay, thanks." Bennie left chambers, went downstairs, headed for the exit doors, and hit the cold. She squared her shoulders, tilting into the wind as she headed to the parking lot. She reached the car, turned on the ignition, and pressed Matthew's number into her phone. The call rang once, then was picked up. "Matthew, good news. The judge ordered the Commonwealth to respond to our petition in three days."

"That's good?" Matthew sounded disappointed.

"Yes, remember, I told you, on the way in?"

"Yes, but Jason will have been in a whole week by then. He already feels like he's been there forever."

"I know, he told me. It's the best we could have hoped for, at this point." Bennie realized the only thing worse than being a child who was incarcerated was being the father of a child who was incarcerated.

"Well, thank you. What happens next?"

"If the Commonwealth files its response on Friday, I'm hoping that the judge clears his desk by the holidays—"

"So Jason would be home by Christmas!"

Bennie reminded herself to check him. "I'm trying, but that's not a guarantee."

"That's what lawyers always say, isn't it?"

"No, I'm not just saying it. There's too many variables that we can't control. By the way, I did go visit Jason, and he says, please don't forget to bring his book and pictures. Also I think he'd feel better if you kept the dog in at night."

"Okay, I'd better be going." Matthew sounded newly official, as if someone was in earshot. "Thank you, bye."

Bennie hung up and left the lot, driving through town while she returned calls from her clients. She had just hung up with one when the phone rang, and she picked up. "This is Bennie Rosato."

"It's Declan, checking in. Did you file the papers?"

"Yes, and the judge gave the Commonwealth only three days to respond."

"That's good!"

Bennie warmed. It was nice not to disappoint someone. "Did you get a lawyer for Richie?"

"I hired the guy I told you about."

"Great. If you send me his contact information, I'll send him a copy of what I filed. He should file one, too, ASAP." Bennie drove out of town, past the snow-covered trees. "Jason told me there's a sex offender on his hallway. Also, Richie's spending too much time with the wrong kids."

"That doesn't surprise me. I was planning on going over after work."

Bennie tried to visualize a state trooper walking into a juvenile detention center. "In your uniform, in those hats, with the chinstrap?"

"No, I change at work. We have lockers. We don't wear uniforms off duty. And those hats are called campaign hats. The chinstrap is tradition. Show some respect." Declan chuckled. "Were you okay at the house this morning?"

"Yes, thanks."

"Where are you now?"

"Heading home."

"Hey, I'm off this weekend. I'd like to drive to Philly and put our heads together. You free?"

"Sure. When?" Bennie thought it could help, but wasn't exactly a necessity.

"Saturday's best for me. I can be there for dinner. We can grab a bite."

"Okay," Bennie answered, wondering. Saturday night was date night, but this wasn't a date.

"Eight o'clock. I'll buy dinner if you don't bill me for the time."

"Deal." So it wasn't a date.

"Sorry, I'm getting a radio call. Can I catch you later?"

"Sure."

"Drive safe. Stay off the phone. Bye."

"Bye." Bennie hung up, hitting the gas. Fifteen minutes later, she got a text, which she read when traffic came to a standstill. It was from Declan and said simply:

It's not a date.

CHAPTER FIFTEEN

It took Bennie until after the close of business to get back to the office, and she stepped off the elevator to find Mary, Judy, and Anne hanging around the reception desk with the firm's private investigator, Lou. Marshall must've left for the day, and the associates looked like they were ready to go, too, dressed in their heavy coats and carrying their purses. They all turned to face her as she entered the room, but stopped their happy chatter. Only Bear came bounding toward her, wagging his tail.

"Hi, everybody." Bennie leaned over to pet the dog, scratching him behind his ears. "Is something the matter?"

"Nothing," DiNunzio answered quickly.

"Nothing at all," Judy added.

"We're happy to see you, boss," Anne said, smiling her dazzling smile.

"You don't *look* happy to see me." Bennie managed a smile.

Mary waved her off. "Of course we're happy to see you."

Judy added, "Yes, welcome back."

Anne chimed in, "How was your trip?"

Bennie turned to Lou. "Something's going on. What is it?"

"This." Lou stepped aside to reveal a pile of luggage stacked behind the reception desk. "They're knocking off next week and they're afraid you're going to yell at them."

Mary said, "That's not true."

Judy added, "Not true at all."

"Not in the least," Anne chimed in, still smiling, because she used to be a catalog model.

Bennie faced the associates. "What's not true, that you're not going anywhere or that you're not afraid I'm going to yell at you?"

Mary cleared her throat. "The thing is, after we talked about whether the office was going to be open next week, you said we should make our own decisions. So we did."

Judy added, "All of our cases are quiet, which never happens at the same time, so we thought we would plan a trip together. We found some good fares and we're going to Miami together."

Anne chimed in, "Our flight leaves tonight, and we'll be back the Friday after Christmas. We're only taking off a total of six workdays, even if you include Christmas Eve."

Lou turned to Bennie. "Please don't fire them. No one else will work for you. Except me."

"Lou, what about you? Are you taking off next week, too?" Bennie hid her emotions, trying to get up to speed.

"Hell, no. My people always get stuck holding the bag while you Gentiles gallivant around." Lou snorted. "You'll make it up to me on the high holy days. Or fishing season."

Everybody laughed, including Bennie, but she realized that the associates were waiting for her to respond. She had to admit, her historic reaction would have been disapproval, but she felt different inside. All the way home, she'd sung along with the radio even though she didn't know any songs. Suddenly it seemed okay if the associates took off. She could handle any new client who came in or the matter would have to wait until after the holidays.

Bennie shrugged. "I think it sounds like a great idea. Go, and have a great time. In fact, don't come back until Monday, and we can talk then about New Year's."

"Thanks!" said the associates, hugging each other, then Lou, and in the next moment, enveloping Bennie in a group hug fragrant with fading perfume and fresh estrogen. Bear jumped around, because goldens were never left out of a good time.

Mary picked up her plain nylon suitcase. "We should get going, then. We have to be at the airport two hours early to go through security."

Judy grabbed her stuffed backpack. "Miami, here we come!"

Anne struggled with two heavy designer bags. "I hope I didn't forget anything."

Bennie smiled. "Looks like you remembered *absolutely* everything."

Lou laughed. "One bag's for makeup, the other's shoes."

"Ha!" Anne headed to the elevator with the other associates, all of them saying, "Good-bye!" "Merry Christmas!" "Happy Hanukkah!"

"Bye!" Bennie called to them.

"Ladies, be safe!" Lou watched them go.

"We will, bye!" Mary called back as the elevator doors opened, and they bustled inside, then the doors closed.

"Aw," Bennie said, oddly touched after they had gone. Maybe she did have some maternal instinct, after all. She patted Bear's head.

Lou looked over. "What will we do when they leave for college?"

"Replace them, cheap."

"So how did it go in the boondocks?" Lou turned to her, with a smile draped by cheeks slackened with age. He was in his sixties, but still a handsome man, with flinty, knowing blue eyes, a strong nose, prominent cheekbones, and a ready laugh.

"A mixed bag." Bennie hoisted her stuff to her shoulder and headed for her office, with Bear in tow. "Walk with me."

"So you took the juvenile case?" Lou fell into step beside her, shoving his hands into the pockets of his khakis, which he had on with a navy sportcoat and white oxford shirt. "I knew you would. You're a sucker for an underdog."

"It turns out there's no underdog like a kid."

"How's it going?" Lou looked over as they walked down the corridor past the empty associates' offices. The sky outside the windows was just beginning to darken, and the city lights brightening, the neon spikes of Liberty Place glowing red and green for the holidays.

"So far, so good. I got a short response time on a petition."

"Hmm." Lou's eyes narrowed. "But you look like you won something."

"I won three days. It's a sad case." Bennie reached her office and shed her purse and messenger bag on the nubby Berber rug.

"But you don't seem sad." Lou followed her inside and eased into one of the soft patterned chairs opposite the desk.

"It's tough." Bennie didn't know whether to tell him about Declan, especially since there was nothing to tell. She crossed her desk and sat down, as Bear trotted to his dog bed and curled into a doughnut.

"But you're smiling funny. Last time I saw you smile like that, was well"—Lou paused—"oh my God, you got laid!"

"*What?* No!" Bennie burst into nervous laughter.

"Don't tell me, I know you. You only smile like that if you get paid or if you get laid. And if you didn't get paid—"

"No!"

"But something in that category." Lou wagged his arthritic finger at her, his hooded eyes narrowing. "What the hell is going on?"

"Nothing."

"You're the worst liar in the Bar Association. Tell me. I'll keep your secrets, you know that."

"Go, I have to work." Bennie waved at the door, but Lou didn't budge.

"I knew it when you let the associates go! Since when would you let them take off together? Even *I* thought it was crazy."

"You told me to let them go!"

"Because you wanted to, and the Bennie Rosato *I* know would never *want* to!" Lou's gaze locked on to her like an old pointer. "Who is he? You met someone. I can tell."

"Relax." Bennie shot him a look. "The only person I met is the uncle of the kid who started the fight with my client. His nephew's a total bully, who's given my client a hard time, almost his whole life. The kids are enemies and now they're in the same jail. Seventh graders."

"That's young to be locked up." Lou raised a sparse gray eyebrow.

"I know, and for *nothing*. For a school fight. It's all this zero-tolerance stuff, after Columbine and 9/11. Everybody's paranoid."

"Everybody's paranoid, with good reason." Lou fell silent a moment, and Bennie remembered he'd been close to two NYPD cops who were killed in the attack on the World Trade Center.

"I'm sorry, Lou. I didn't mean to bring it up."

"It's okay." Lou pursed his lips. "Anyway, back to the kids. So maybe the bully will grow out of it or get help. Either way, you can't hold that against the uncle, unless he's in denial."

"He's tried to help. He and his sister are at a loss about what to do with the nephew. So the boys are like codefendants and he's like a co-counsel."

"So who's this guy? Is he another lawyer?"

"No, a cop. But he's just a friend."

"A *cop*? Excellent!" Lou's lined face lit up, in delight. "Where?"

"A state trooper, a sergeant."

"A *statie*?" Lou's mouth dropped open. "Oh excuse *me*. No beat cop for my girl! You went on a date?"

"No." Bennie wasn't about to elaborate.

"Then, what?"

"We *met*, is all."

"Are you *meeting* again?"

"Saturday night, but it's not a date."

"This is incredible!"

"It's not." Bennie rolled her eyes.

"Astounding!"

"Enough." Bennie waved him off.

"It's been *so* long."

"Lou, slow down. I barely like him. He's bossy."

"So are you."

"Well, I'm a boss."

"So is he! A sergeant! My opinion, this is a good thing. A very good thing."

"Don't get crazy." Bennie chuckled. "You don't even know him."

"I know how he makes you feel. I can *see* that, and I want that for you."

"He doesn't make me feel anything," Bennie shot back, pretty sure it was true.

"Oh please!" Lou raised his hands, palms up. "Bennie, for once in your life, do something nice for yourself!"

"Lou, it's a man, not a manicure."

"You're entitled to enjoy yourself, it's as simple as that."

"We're friends, that's it. Colleagues. I'm not attracted to him and I'm sure he's not attracted to me." Bennie's mouth went oddly dry. "We're not teenagers anymore."

"What difference does that make? I'm older than you and I'm dating somebody new. Senior citizens get married every day."

"We have different lives. We live in different places. We're both set in our ways."

"You're not as set in your ways as you think. You just let the girls go on a road trip together." Lou's tone softened, and he cocked his head. "So what, the two of you, you're different? The difference has to make a difference, you know what I mean? It's good for you to date outside your comfort zone."

"We're *not* dating."

"You always pick the same type, kiddo. Ivy League eggheads, lawyers and judges. Enough already. Life is short. Live a little. Follow your heart, not your head. Have a fling. Enjoy." Lou shrugged happily. "If it turns into more than that, then you worry."

Bennie scoffed. "That's like seeing a burning building and running in."

Lou nodded happily. "In other words, like falling in love."

CHAPTER SIXTEEN

Bennie got home, opening the door while Bear scooted in ahead of her, his toenails clicking on the hardwood floor. She set her purse and messenger bag on the floor, slid out of her coat and hung it up on the coatrack, then flipped on the light switch, illuminating the small entrance hall and the scattered pile of the day's mail on the floor. She picked it up, went through it quickly, and set it on a cherrywood console table to be dealt with later. She didn't want to deal with mail just yet, having spent the last few hours trying to get work done at the office, between checking her BlackBerry for texts from Declan.

She looked around the house with new eyes, wondering if there was room for a man in her home, or her life. She loved the house, in the Fairmount section of the city, which she had bought as a shell and renovated with costly respect for its history, preserving its white plaster scrollwork and elegant crown molding. The first-floor layout was three large single rooms on a chain, the living room, dining room, kitchen, a floor plan typical of Philadelphia's colonial homes. Everything she saw was just the way she wanted it, wasn't it?

She walked through the living room, with its twelve-foot-tall windows that faced the street, and she had furnished it in an un-apologetically feminine vibe; comfortable sectionals in an oatmeal color with bright red-and-pink patterned pillows, lamps with ginger-jar bases in creamy melon hues, and oil paintings that showed flowers in vases. At least the TV was unisex. She crossed into the dining room, flicking on another light switch and noticing that everything in the room were objects she loved and had collected over the years, but all of them were about her.

She ran a critical eye over her beloved Thomas Eakins lithographs of rowers on the Schuylkill River, and the real oar mounted at the top of the wall, with the red-and-blue-painted blade of the University of Pennsylvania, her alma mater. Did she really date only Ivy League eggheads? What would Declan think about her having an oar on a wall? Why did she care what he thought anyway? It was *her* house. She went into the kitchen and turned on the light to see Bear trotting toward her with his metal bowl in his mouth, which was one of the cutest tricks she'd ever seen.

"Good boy, it's time for dinner," she said, reaching down to pet him and taking the bowl.

"Arf!" Bear danced excitedly as she went to the cabinet, dug a scoop of kibble, and dumped it into his bowl. She closed the cabinet and set the bowl down beside the refrigerator, continuing her home inventory. The kitchen was gender-neutral, but Declan's kitchen put hers to shame. He must've been a good cook because he had a knife block. All she had were knives and lawyerly sharp edges.

"So what?" Bennie asked no one in particular. Her countertops were clean and uncluttered, of a white Corian, and the cabinets were of a bright, warm pine, which coordinated nicely with a round cherrywood table off to the side. Her appliances were top-of-the-line, a Sub-Zero refrigerator and a Viking range, but the GE microwave got the most use, which proved that cooking was not a skill you could buy.

"Sue me, I'm not a chef," Bennie said aloud, but Bear was buried in his kibble. She went to the refrigerator and opened it wide, even though she knew nothing would be there except a few cans of Diet Coke, a wrinkled head of aging romaine lettuce, and a bag of shredded cheddar, because she was too lazy to chop. She bought everything presliced and even prewashed, having more valuable things to do than prepare her own food—unlike a certain state trooper, who squandered his time making sure that Pennsylvania's men, women, and children were safe from lethal harm.

Bennie grabbed a can of Diet Coke and the bag of shredded cheese, went over to the kitchen table, popped the tab of the soda and took a fresh, bubbly slug. She opened the Ziploc bag, dug inside with her fingers, and managed to extract a handful of cheese, which she shoved into her mouth. *Ring!* went her BlackBerry, at just the wrong moment. She reached in her pocket for the phone and checked the screen, which read DECLAN CALLING.

"Hi." Bennie swallowed, narrowly avoiding asphyxiation. "How are you?"

"I just left my sister's. She doesn't like the lawyer I hired. She thinks he's not good enough."

"What do you think?"

"I think he's fine. He practices juvenile law in Hershey. He was willing to drop everything."

"I already emailed him my petition and the judge's order, so he could copy them if he wanted to."

"I know, thanks. I told my sister that, too. She wanted me to fire him, so I did. Richie is her son, not mine. I want her to have a lawyer she's comfortable with."

"Understood. I bet I could rustle somebody up in the Philadelphia area, but I still think you'd be better off with somebody local, even Hershey."

"She wants to interview a few of them, then pick one."

"That's a tall order. There's not that many of them, and the real problem is time. If she wants to get Richie out by Christmas, you need to get a lawyer tomorrow. He has to file papers right away."

"I know." Declan sounded tense. "I'm going back to the drawing board."

"You know, there's a place in Philadelphia called the Juvenile Law Center. They might have some referrals in the area."

"I'll call them. Doreen can be a pain in the ass. You have any siblings?"

"No, it's just me." Bennie didn't have to tell him the whole story about her estranged sister Alice, at least not yet.

"And your parents? Are they still alive?"

"No, it's just me and Bear." Bennie wanted to shift the conversation. "If I get my hearing and win, whoever you hire has precedent, right there. The judge won't have any choice but to grant Richie's petition. So it's for the best that I go first."

"Good point." Declan rallied. "Anyway I'm home now. Melissa says hi."

"Does she?" Bennie smiled. "Did you ride tonight?"

"I'm on Ember now."

"As we speak? You're talking on the cell phone, on a horse?"

"It's a helluva lot safer than driving a car."

"Thanks, Dad. How's Melissa's hoof?"

"Better."

"Good." Bennie flashed on a bird's-eye view of the same moment in two separate places. Declan was outside on his horse, under the moonlight in a pasture of frozen snow, and she was inside, in a row house in the middle of a city, brick and mortar and people and cars, the moon obliterated by the reflection of electric lights. The settings couldn't have been more different.

The difference has to make a difference.

"You didn't answer my text," Declan said, after a moment.

"It didn't require an answer, did it?" Bennie asked, surprised. She hadn't known what to reply to the text, so she hadn't.

"No. Not really. Hey, I'd better go."

"Sure." Bennie thought she heard a softening in his voice, but it could have been her imagination.

"Drive safe."

"Take care," Bennie said, but the line was already dead.

CHAPTER SEVENTEEN

Morning sunlight streamed through Bennie's office window, and she'd just sat down at her desk when Marshall had materialized with some faxed pages. Bennie accepted the fax, surprised to see that it was the Commonwealth's brief in response to her petition. "They replied early? That's weird. They had until Friday."

"That *is* weird. Lawyers do everything at the last minute. Ask any legal secretary." Marshall's eyes shone an amused blue, her shiny hair was in its trademark braid, and her denim jumper paired with a white turtleneck and white tights.

"From the looks of it, it took five minutes to draft." Bennie flipped through the Commonwealth's response. "There's no substance to this brief. They don't address any of my arguments or deal with any of my precedent, which was directly on point. It's boilerplate." Bennie shook her head, and Marshall came around the side of the desk and handed her another fax.

"This fax came in after it. It looks like a judge's order."

"An *order*?" Bennie read the paper, which was an order in Jason's case, only a paragraph long. Her gaze zoomed to the bottom of the page, where it stated, **Petition for Emergency Relief is hereby DENIED.**

"Did you lose?"

"Yes," Bennie answered, stunned. "I don't get it. I had Supreme Court precedent on my side, U.S. *and* Pennsylvania. I even found the case on point from the same judge. He was reversed last year for the same mistake." Bennie rose, reflexively. She thought best on her feet, like most trial lawyers. She had an old boyfriend who used to joke that she was born standing up.

"The judge sounds stubborn."

"They call him Napoleon." Bennie simmered, eyeing the faxes.

"So, not the first judge on a power trip."

"I can't believe this." Bennie flipped through the sheets again. "Are you sure this is everything that came off the machine?"

"Except for the cover sheets, yes."

"There's no opinion with the judge's order?"

"I'll go check. Be right back." Marshall left the office.

Damn. Bennie read the order and reply brief again, her heart sinking. She had known it was a possibility that she could lose, but she deserved at least a rehearing. Plus, the fact that she had such good case authority merited at least a written opinion, wherein the judge explained his rationale for denying the petition. She looked up from the papers to see Marshall coming back, empty-handed.

"Bennie, that's all there was. I double-checked to make sure nothing got jammed."

"This order leaves a kid sitting in jail. A twelve-year-old boy." Bennie threw the faxes down in disgust.

"Are you going to appeal?"

"It's either that or burn the courthouse down."

"Peace is better than war."

"Litigation *is* war, only more expensive." Bennie gritted her teeth.

"Don't get riled up."

"Too late." Bennie felt her adrenaline flowing. "I became a lawyer to take down bullies like this. It feels *good* to get this angry."

"Don't get mad, get even."

"Why do I have to choose?" Bennie set the faxes side by side on her desk; the Commonwealth's response on the left and the judge's order on the right. "You know what else makes me mad? Look at the timing of these papers. First, we have a reply brief, filed a day early. That's a tipoff. Second—" Bennie checked the tiny numbers at the top of the faxed brief, which showed the time as 9:01 A.M. She compared it with the time the order had been faxed, which was 9:15. "—there's only fifteen minutes between the time of the reply brief and the judge's order. This must be a coordinated effort between the judge and the prosecutor."

"Really? How did that happen?" Marshall cocked her head.

"I think they're all buddy-buddy at that courthouse, and the judge and the assistant district attorney touched base on the timing, maybe because Christmas is around the corner. Their offices are in the *same* courthouse. They could have run into each other in the lobby, even the men's room." Bennie started counting off the days in her mind. "Assume the judge is already on a big murder trial and he doesn't want this case hanging over his head. So he tells the assistant district attorney to file his brief early. Or the A.D.A. takes it on himself to file early because he knows what the judge will do. There's only one judge and one A.D.A. who handle juvenile cases. They work together all the time, the two of them. They know each other."

"Then it does sound possible."

"It's more than possible, it's *likely*." Bennie threw up her hands. "I bet the judge waited for the A.D.A. to file his brief, because it would be improper for him to deny without their filing *anything*, then he denied my petition."

"Will they get caught?"

"No, the record doesn't reflect what time papers are filed. The docket shows only that they were filed the same day. But that they're fifteen minutes apart? It doesn't show that."

"Is what they did against the law?" Marshall frowned.

"No, but it's improper." Bennie knew the Code of Judicial Conduct because it was similar to the Code of Professional Responsibility for lawyers. "The Judicial Code says that judges should avoid the appearance of impropriety. The test is whether the conduct 'reflects adversely,' among other things, on the judge's impartiality."

"That would cover this, wouldn't it?"

"Yes, but I can't do anything about it. If I file a misconduct petition, I'd only make this judge madder at my client, and I'm sure he would argue that they discussed the timing, not the merits. This probably happens all the time in a small courthouse."

"Couldn't it happen here, though, too?" Marshall lifted an eyebrow. "Be real. Things get pretty chummy in Common Pleas in Philly."

"God knows that the Common Pleas Court of Philadelphia is no paragon of judicial virtue, but it's far less likely to happen here, if only because of its size." Bennie was thinking aloud. "Our Common Pleas Court has eighty-something judges, about twenty of whom handle juvenile cases, and there's probably a group of assistant district attorneys who handle juvenile cases. The offices aren't in the same building, and it's not the same thing, at all. It's clubby out in the counties, and I'm not in the club."

"Sounds like you have your work cut out for you, then."

"I sure do." Bennie raked a hand through her hair. "It's hard to know what to do first. I have to tell the client, who will be disappointed, and I have to hit the road, too. This isn't the day I planned." *Or the night,* she thought.

"Like my husband says, 'Do like the pilots.' 'Aviate, navigate, and communicate.' "

"Right." Bennie smiled. "So how does that apply to this?"

"Keep the craft in the air, figure out where you're going, and tell everybody what you did later."

"Gotcha."

"Good luck. See you later." Marshall left for the reception desk, and Bennie sat down and pulled her laptop closer to her, rallying. She would do some quick research, then cut and paste her petition to draft the appeal papers, so that wouldn't take too long. Pennsylvania procedure required her to begin the appeals process by first filing a Notice of Appeal in the Common Pleas Court, so she'd have to go back to Wilkes-Barre and file the notice, then drive to the Superior Court in Harrisburg to file the actual appeal, which she would also style as an appeal for emergency relief. By the end of the day, she'd feel more like a chauffeur than a lawyer, but the only person having a crappier day would be Jason Lefkavick.

An hour later, Bennie was back in her car, with the dog. She hadn't been able to get a dog-sitter, and nobody loved a road trip more than a golden retriever. Bear sat in the passenger seat, his brown marble eyes glued to the road, exercising better judgment than his mistress, who was already on the phone.

"Matthew?" Bennie knew the only way to deliver bad news was directly. "Unfortunately, the judge denied our petition for a re-adjudication."

"Oh no. Jeez, I thought you said we were going to win!" Matthew groaned, and Bennie heard anguish, not blame.

"If you remember, I said there's no guarantee. We should have won, by all accounts. We had the law and the facts on our side."

"So what went wrong?"

"He turned us down anyway. It happens. I can't explain it any other way, except that he has the power." Bennie filled Matthew in on her theory about the timing.

"You got that right. I'm sure that's what happened. It's, like, a conspiracy."

"In any event, I'm already in the car, and I'm filing an emergency appeal today, with the Superior Court."

"Do you think we'll win?"

"No guarantees, again, but I do." Bennie steered ahead, in light traffic. "The Superior Court is an excellent court, and we have a good argument on appeal because we fall within a certain exception."

"What exception?" Matthew asked, with a new note of distrust.

"Generally, an appellate court will deny an emergency appeal. They usually think that litigants can wait the six months to a year that it takes to get an appeal heard. Do you follow me?"

"Yes."

"But there's an exception for cases that would always moot themselves, like ours. By that I mean, juvenile sentences are usually less than six months. It takes more than six months for an appeals court to make a decision. The expiration of the sentence moots the appeal, every time. Understood?"

"Okay."

"Appeals judges will look favorably on an emergency appeal in a case like ours because if the normal timing were followed, Jason's appeal would never be heard. I want ours to be the case they take, the case they make an exception for."

"I would testify if you need me to."

"You don't have to. There's no testimony taken in appellate court. The judge will make his decision on the papers unless they grant me an oral argument. Then I'll make the oral argument to them, but you can come." Bennie reminded herself to manage his expectations. "But just so you're aware, here's the problem with our appeal. We still have the general rule about emergencies going against us. So I can't say *for sure* that we're going to win. They get emergency appeals filed from time to time, even in adult criminal cases. Nobody in jail thinks they should be in there any longer than they have to, follow me?"

"Yes, but it's a kid!"

"I'm hoping that it will appeal to their compassion. But courts are always aware that they're setting precedent when they act, and they might not want to make a new precedent and thus invite appeals in juvenile cases—"

"Whose side are you on?" Matthew shot back.

"Yours, but we have to be realistic. We just have to hope for the best."

"That's what they said after my wife had her first heart attack." Matthew sighed. "I'll start praying. Thanks for the call, I better get back to work. Thanks for keeping me posted."

"Sure, good-bye." Bennie hung up, switching lanes to pass a grimy tractor-trailer, then realized she should call Declan to update him and see how he was progressing with Richie. She slowed her speed, calling him.

"Please tell me you're not driving," Declan said, as soon as he picked up.

"You don't give up, do you?"

"Neither do you."

"Am I catching you at a bad time?"

"Little bit. Go ahead."

"I'll make it fast." Bennie wondered if Declan had somebody in custody or was even in danger. She felt a twinge of concern, but dismissed the thought. "I lost my petition and I'm filing an appeal. I'm on the way to Wilkes-Barre and Harrisburg. Anything new on hiring a lawyer for Richie?"

"I'll fill you in later."

"Declan, we're shifting into a higher gear. If you don't have a lawyer yet, you should get one with appellate experience."

"So you're coming this way?"

"Yes." Bennie detected a change in his voice, and it wasn't her imagination, but she stayed in work mode. "I'm staying in Harrisburg tonight and maybe the next day. The Superior Court can grant me oral argument at any time, and I have to be ready when they call. There won't be time to drive from Philly."

"So you're free tonight?"

"Well, yes." Bennie blinked. Bear looked over. They both thought, *Huh?*

"I have a better idea."

"What?" Bennie asked, knowing that whatever it was, she wasn't dressed for it. She had on her crummy jeans with an old blue sweater, and she'd packed a bag full of court clothes. Not that any of that mattered. It was a reflexive thought.

"Ever hear of Jim Thorpe?"

"No, who's he?"

Declan chuckled softly. "I'll text you, Philly."

CHAPTER EIGHTEEN

Bennie traveled until about five o'clock, and the wintry sky was graying by the time she reached Jim Thorpe, a town nestled in a valley between snowy mountains. She steered onto its main street, lined with cute boutiques, quaint restaurants, and antique stores, most of them two stories of red brick, with tall shuttered windows. Holiday lights twinkled in the trees, and couples, families, and tourists strolled along the sidewalks.

Bennie perked up at the picturesque scene, a welcome sight after a tiresome day of highway driving interrupted by courthouses and gas-station bathrooms. She drove uphill until she found the address that Declan had texted her, which was an inn. She had no idea what he was up to, but she presumed she'd find out, soon enough. She felt confused but vaguely excited, even though she hated to admit as much.

She steered into the parking lot, pulled into a space, and cut the ignition, checking her reflection in the rearview mirror. She looked predictably tired, her hair a mess, and a mustard stain from a road pretzel encrusted her sweater. Bear started barking, and she turned to see Declan coming toward the car. She opened the car door, whereupon the golden lurched out and jumped on him, tail awag.

"Sorry, this is Bear." Bennie grabbed her purse and the dog's leash, then closed and locked the car.

"He's cute. Good to see you." Declan looked tense, his forehead buckled. His broad shoulders were hunched, and he seemed buried in his green parka. If he'd been in a good mood on the phone, it had vanished.

"So what's up?" Bennie asked, concerned.

"It's a long story. I just pulled up, myself." Declan gestured to the back of the lot, where his pickup was parked. "You want to take a walk through town? Stretch your legs before dinner?"

"Okay. So, dinner? Is that your better idea?" Bennie fell into step with him, and they left the lot, joining the others on the sidewalk, with the dog tugging ahead.

"Partly. The inn has a nice restaurant. I made a reservation at eight. I also got you a room. The inn is a helluva lot nicer than anything in Harrisburg. Jim Thorpe's close enough to get to Harrisburg fast."

"Wow, okay." Bennie liked the idea, but it was a surprise. "I'll cancel the hotel in Harrisburg."

"Do. You're helping my family. I wanted you to know, I appreciate it."

"Well, thanks." Bennie felt uncertain. "You're not paying."

"I already did. Whatever progress you make will help Richie, too. I insist."

"I can't accept it."

"You have to." Declan paused. "Please."

"Okay, you're welcome."

"I got a room, too."

"Really." Bennie tried not to react.

"It's not what you're thinking." Declan managed a smile, his dark eyes shifting sideways to her. "I thought it would be a nice break. I come here all the time. I ski nearby."

"Oh." Bennie noticed a woman checking Declan out as they walked by. Glass storefronts cast lighted oblongs on their path, as they passed a funky store with handmade silver jewelry. Bracelets and earrings gleamed in the last light of the day, and a silver bracelet caught her eye, in passing. It was what she should've bought Mary, instead of the dog toy. "That's pretty."

"I'm not a big shopper."

"Me, neither."

"Anyway, I need time to deal with Richie." Declan's lips went tight, and he looked ahead as they walked along. "I got a referral of another lawyer from the Juvenile Law Center. They gave me the name of somebody in Kingston. He practices family law and he's branching out into juvenile law."

"What happened?"

"He didn't have time to meet with Doreen, but he agreed to give her a call today and they spoke." Declan appeared to be watching Bear, who trotted happily along, his tail pumping. The street climbed gently upward, revealing a darkening sky over the top of the mountain, with the stars waiting to shine.

"And?"

"She doesn't want to hire him."

"Why not?"

"She thinks he doesn't have enough experience in juvenile law."

"He couldn't have less experience than I do."

"It's her call." Declan's mouth formed an unhappy dash, and Bennie wondered if Doreen wanted to keep Richie in jail for Christmas, because by insisting on an unavailable lawyer, she was virtually guaranteeing that result. But that a mother would want her son imprisoned was too awful to contemplate, much less say.

"So now what?"

"I had one other referral. I called him and he's going to meet with Doreen tomorrow morning."

"So maybe that will pan out."

"We can only hope."

"Right." Bennie noticed an unusual building at the top of the hill, which looked like a medieval castle, surrounded by a tall stone wall made from gray and black fieldstones. A single tower pierced the darkening sky. "What's that building?"

"The Carbon County jail."

"Right in town?" Bennie asked, taken aback.

"It's closed now. It's a museum. See that?" Declan pointed to a rampart in front of the building. "The Molly Maguires were hanged there."

"The what?"

"This was a coal-mining region. Hard coal. Anthracite. It was dirty work, and a lot of the miners were Irish. The Molly Maguires were a group of miners, Irish immigrants. They were fighting the company for better working conditions. Four of them were accused of murdering company officials. They were convicted and hanged in public, right on that rampart."

"A *public* execution." Bennie recoiled.

"Yes. But it was controversial. The murders were investigated by private police hired by the mining company. Pinkertons. The prosecutor had ties to the mining company, too."

Bennie looked over. "So it was a way for the company to get rid of labor agitators."

"That's what some people say."

"Law doesn't always lead to justice, does it?" Bennie eyed the grim rampart.

"If you ask me, law leads to order. Not necessarily justice."

"Why do you say that?" Bennie had never thought of it that way before.

"I arrest people every day. But somebody else decides if they get charged and prosecuted. That's the only part of my job that I don't like. I don't have any say in what comes after. Any idiot can see the relationship between the number of arrests and the quality of life."

"For the people who don't get arrested."

"Right, for them." Declan nodded again. "It's like Judge Zero Tolerance. If you lock up the bad kids, you'll never have another Columbine. Nobody has to worry. The parents are happy. The teachers are happy. You'll have complete order."

"But you won't have justice."

"Right."

"Well, that's why God made appeals courts, and the Pennsylvania Superior Court is an excellent court."

"So you're optimistic?"

"Cautiously."

"Good." Declan stopped, turning to face her, his eyes newly troubled. "I went to see Richie after work. Something was off, I could tell as soon as he came into the room. He would barely talk to me. He was keeping me at a distance."

"Why?"

"The word's out that I'm a cop, after I visited him yesterday. A couple of thugs were giving him a hard time. They assumed I'm his father. He tried to set them right, but it doesn't matter. A cop uncle is as bad as a cop father, inside."

"Oh no." Bennie felt terrible.

"I should've seen this coming." Declan frowned. "It happened to a buddy of mine. His brother got locked up in Graterford, down your way. It's tough inside for anybody with family in law enforcement."

"Do they think Richie's a snitch or something?"

"No." Declan shook his head. "It's not that rational. Anybody related to cops bears the brunt of the hate against cops."

"Even if you had seen it coming, what would you do about it?" Bennie realized that Richie would be bullied the way he had been bullying Jason. Still, she wouldn't have wished it on him, especially since she could see how much pain it caused Declan.

"There's nothing to do. The cat's already out of the bag. It's a no-win situation." Declan squared his shoulders. "That's why I want him out of there, ASAP. It's driving me crazy. I don't know why it's not driving Doreen crazy, too."

Bennie hesitated. "I'm sure it is. She's his mother."

"If Richie were my son, I'd take any damn lawyer. I'd do anything, so he knew I was fighting for him. Like you are, for Jason."

Bennie didn't reply, and Declan continued, speaking from the heart.

"Doreen hasn't even gone to visit him yet. She says she's busy with the twins, and I know she is. But he matters, too." Declan shook his head, plunging his hands into his pockets. "His father checked out on him. Now she is, too. I almost said it to her on the phone. I wanted to ask her, 'what the hell are you thinking?' "

"What would she do if you said that?" Bennie could see the emotion etching fine lines into Declan's handsome face. Maybe he didn't always get everything he wanted. Maybe nobody did.

"Probably throw a fit. She doesn't like it when I play big brother. She thinks I judge her."

"Maybe if you say it in a way that's not judgmental?"

"I don't know how to be judgmental in a nonjudgmental way." Declan met her eye with an ironic smile, his crow's-feet wrinkling.

"Me neither." Bennie's heart went out to him, and she found herself feeling closer to him, in a real way. "I feel the same way about Jason. Both of these kids are in a terrible bind. In fact, the one thing I don't like about *my* job is that I can't always help the people I need to. I can't always win. I can't always get justice, and it never felt worse to me than it does in this case, with that little boy in that hellhole."

"But he's not even your family." Declan blinked. "You're his lawyer, not his mother."

"He feels like family to me. It's not abstract or intellectual, and you can't parse or analyze it. It's an emotion."

"I get that." Declan nodded sadly. "I swear to God, until Richie got locked up, I didn't even know how much I loved him. He's not an easy kid to love. But he's blood. *My* blood. I taught him to ride and fish. I was there when he was a *baby*. Now he's sitting in jail with gangbangers who hate him because I'm a cop. He could be in danger because of *me*."

Bennie saw the anguish in Declan's eyes and she could feel his need for comfort, almost palpably. She wanted to hug him, but stopped herself. She didn't know where the impulse came from, and she didn't want it to be misinterpreted. Instead, she flashed him a professional smile.

"Let's get you a drink," she said.

CHAPTER NINETEEN

Bennie let herself into her room, and Bear trotted ahead, trailing his leash while she closed the door behind her. Two lamps with cut-crystal bases flanked a lovely bed cloaked in dotted-Swiss bedcovers, with a filmy matching canopy. An antique bureau sat opposite windows covered with pink-and-red toile curtains, coordinating with rose walls. The total effect was overwhelmingly lovely, until Bear bounced onto the bed and started digging at the bedclothes with his front paws, making himself a doggie nest.

"Bear, no!" Bennie put her belongings on the floor, took off her coat, and headed for the bathroom to get ready for dinner. She went to the sink, washed her face, then dried off. She eyed her reflection, looking different to herself, somehow. Something was happening, but she couldn't put her finger on it. She didn't feel like herself. She was off the reservation. She was about to have dinner-that-might-be-a-date with an interesting, intelligent, and sexy man. Anything could happen, anything was possible, and nobody had to know. She was *free.*

She turned out the light, left the bathroom, and patted Bear good-bye. She grabbed her room key and slid it in her back pocket, leaving her purse behind. She reached the lobby buzzing with guests and hotel staff in Santa hats. She walked to the restaurant in the back where she spotted Declan already sitting at a table for two, wearing a work shirt and dark corduroy sport jacket, his perfect features illuminated by a flickering candle. Bennie felt a palpitation in her chest, but prayed she was just having a heart attack.

"Hi." Declan stood up and came around the table.

"Hi, I got it." Bennie reached for her chair, pulling it out before he could. "How's your room? Miss your gun rack?"

"Fine." Declan rolled his eyes, sitting down. "Like the place?"

"Yes." Bennie glanced around. The restaurant was large, quaint, and classy, with dark wainscoting, plaster walls, and real brass sconces that lit forty-odd tables covered with old-school white tablecloths. A holiday crowd filled the seats, mostly couples, with enough ties and jackets that made the place seem high-end, but not stuffy. Wine and beer flowed easily, and the air smelled like chicken with rosemary.

"I was thinking about getting our rooms through the weekend. What do you think?"

"Are you serious?" Bennie asked him, surprised. "Why?"

"I thought it would be good to have a home base. For the case."

"But it's only Wednesday night. I have to work."

"What work do you have the week before Christmas?"

"Jason's case, for one thing."

"Right, and that's here. Why drive back to the city, when you have all this?" Declan gestured out the window to the street, with its shops open and festive lights aglow. "I'm taking the week off. They owe me so many vacation days, I stopped counting."

"I'm self-employed, so there's no vacation days. My boss is a real bitch."

"If you can't stay, I get it." Declan shrugged. "I'm staying. I need time to deal with Doreen and Richie. It's a crisis, and I can't give it short shrift."

"Hmm." Bennie mulled it over. Her first instinct was negative, inside her comfort level, but maybe Lou was right. It was time to leave her comfort level behind. "The truth is, none of my cases is active, except for Jason's case. I have the laptop, so I can work if I need to. The dog is with me, so there's no reason to go back to the city. The firm will be okay with my receptionist holding the fort."

"See how you feel tomorrow. Let's have some wine. We're here. We don't have to drive anywhere." Declan picked up her glass and filled it partway. "Merry Christmas, and may the next one be better."

"I'll drink to that." Bennie accepted the glass from him, then took a sip and set the glass down. "Declan, let's talk a minute."

"About what?"

"About, this." Bennie felt impatient with her own inability to express herself, even her own discomfort. "The rooms, your staying, my staying, this dinner. This."

"What about it?" Declan cocked his head, his tone gentle, not a challenge.

"I thought we were friends, colleagues, co-counsel. Are we starting something here? Are we trying to have some kind of relationship? And how are we going to do that?" Bennie couldn't even stop to let him answer. "As you said, you don't like to compromise. I don't either. Where's the middle ground? York? Harrisburg? We're not twenty years old. It's complicated. We can't pretend that everything's easy."

"I hear you." Declan sipped wine. "We're adults. We have jobs and responsibilities."

"Right. Mortgages, bills, overhead, business expenses, depreciation—"

"—shift schedules—"

"—court schedules—"

"Don't forget staff."

"Staff, yes." Bennie threw up her hands. "What are we doing here, really? What do you want? What are you looking for? The only thing that makes sense is a fling. Is that what you want, a fling?"

"No," Declan answered quietly, setting his glass down. "I don't want a fling. If I wanted a fling, I would've gotten one room."

"So what do you want?"

"Something real. Something serious. Something that lasts."

Bennie's mouth went dry. It was just the answer she wanted, and the one she most dreaded.

"How about you, Bennie? What do *you* want?"

"I want the same thing," Bennie forced herself to say aloud, though it wasn't easy to be so vulnerable. "I'm not looking for a fling or one-night stand. Something like that, it's not worth the trouble or the time."

"Agree," Declan said, simply.

"But what about the compromising? Neither of us wants to compromise."

"Bennie, I don't have the answers. I'm feeling my way along, too. I didn't know I wanted any of this, not until I met you." Declan's dark eyes searched her face. "If you really want to know what I want, it's a chance with you. That's all. I never met a woman like you. It threw me off in the beginning, but I'd like to give us a try."

"You don't even know me."

"What I know so far, I really like. I like how honest you are. I like that you're smart. I like that you're sexy. I even like that you ask a thousand questions. I like how much you care about Jason. And your passion, about something other than yourself." Declan leaned over, looking directly into her eyes in the candlelight. "I didn't expect this to be easy. *You're* not easy. But I think there can be something between us. We're more alike than we're different. If anybody can figure this out, we can."

Bennie blinked. It was not only a great answer, it was the perfect answer. Declan had just delivered the best oral argument ever, and he didn't even know he was in court.

"Bennie, I've seen you take a chance when something matters to you, like on Jason's case. So why not take a chance on us?" Declan reached over the table and took her hand, holding it lightly. "Agree?"

CHAPTER TWENTY

The morning sun rose in a frigid sky, and Bennie flew down the highway. Last night she'd slept like a baby, after three glasses of wine and a delicious eggplant parm. Declan had walked her to the door of her room, but there was a family with kids in the hall and he didn't try to kiss her, which showed good judgment. Maybe. This morning they'd eaten breakfast in the inn's restaurant, then he'd gone for a run, volunteering to take Bear, which delighted her, if not the chubby retriever, who'd looked back at Bennie in panic as Declan tugged him away. By the time they'd rounded the corner, Bear's tail was wagging. So was Declan's.

Bennie reached Wilkes-Barre in an hour and turned right onto River Street, heading uphill for the detention center, her mood darkening. She turned into the driveway and pulled into the parking lot, unusually packed with white Ford vans bearing the state's official seal. She took the last available space, got out of the car, then hustled to the entrance, where two workmen in knit caps and blue jumpsuits were leaving with boxes.

"Good morning, gentlemen," Bennie said to them. "What's going on?"

"Moving equipment to the new place," the tall one answered, carrying some boxes out to the van.

"What new place?"

"They're replacing this dump, didn't you hear? It'll be open

January or February. It's new construction, up in Pittston. Your kid in there?"

"Yes," Bennie answered, without elaborating.

"Well, the new place is a damn sight better."

"Thanks." Bennie hoped Jason would be free by then, anyway. She entered the building, showed ID to the security guard, and went to the visiting room, where she sat down. Jason was led in by an older, African-American security guard she hadn't seen before, who flashed her a kind smile as the boy scuffed his way toward her, his head down and his demeanor even more depressed than she'd seen him last time.

"Hey, buddy." Bennie rose and gave him a hug, which he barely returned. "How you doing?"

"Okay." Jason slumped into the chair, plopping his head on his fist.

"You don't seem okay." Bennie went around the table and returned to her seat, eyeing him. His skin looked pale, and there were still dark circles under his eyes. His fleshy lips were chapped, and his mouth downturned at the corners, his sadness undisguised.

"My dad said the judge didn't change his mind. I'm never getting out of here." Jason kept his head on his fist, listless. "And now Richie and the big boys call me Fat Joe, after some rapper, then Richie got in a fight with them and the guards came."

"Oh no." Bennie would have to tell Declan, later.

"Guess what, my dad left Patch in at night. He's not letting her out anymore." Jason looked up, with a smile that felt to Bennie like a reward.

"That's a relief, huh?"

"He says he's going to walk her. I'll believe that when I see it." Jason chuckled, shifted his position, and Bennie noticed an odd flash of white skin above his left ear, where he'd been leaning on his fist.

"Jason, what happened to your head?"

"Nothing." Jason quickly covered the patch with his hand, and Bennie realized he'd been hiding it earlier.

"I saw, it looks white. Did somebody hurt you?"

"No."

"Then what's going on? Did somebody *hit* you?"

"No." Jason shook his head, his hand still firmly planted.

"Did you bang it on something?"

"No."

"Jason, please tell me what happened."

"Nobody did it to me." Jason lowered his voice.

"Did you do it to yourself?" Bennie asked, confused.

"No, it just came out."

"What came out?"

"My *hair*." Jason looked up, stricken. His face flushed pink. "My hair, it's, like, *falling out*. I found some in the shower and on my pillow this morning, and on my shirt when I took it off, around the neck. I'm afraid I'm going to be bald, like, I'm going to be totally *bald* like a *baby*."

"Oh no," Bennie said, alarmed. Her thoughts raced with possibilities. There were childhood cancers, an immune disorder, or it could even be psychological. "Do you feel sick?"

"No."

"Are you throwing up or anything?"

"No."

"Do you have a fever?" Bennie put her hand on Jason's forehead like a TV mom, but it didn't feel hot. "When did this start?"

"I don't know, it's just like, all of a sudden, like, my hair is falling out, and look, it's, like, happening to my eyebrows, too."

Bennie leaned over, noticing that his eyebrows seemed oddly sparse.

"Can you tell, like, right off? If the other kids see, or the big boys . . ." Jason didn't finish the sentence, and Bennie placed a steadying hand on his soft shoulder.

"Jason, you can't see it easily, but we need to have a doctor look at you. What did your dad say?"

"I didn't tell him, and he was sitting on my other side, so he couldn't see."

"Why didn't you tell him, buddy?"

"He was upset because we lost and like, I knew I would only make him worry more." Jason's eyes filmed, and his lower lip trembled. "Richard the Strong wouldn't say anything."

Bennie squeezed his shoulder. "I don't think Richard the Strong had to put up with what you're having to put up with."

"Yes, he did, he had battles."

"Well, he wears a helmet."

"You remembered." Jason managed a smile, and Bennie felt her heart lift.

"For all we know, he's bald under that helmet. So don't worry too much about trying to be like Richard the Strong."

"You said to."

"I know, but I was wrong." Bennie sighed inwardly. She had no idea how mothers did their jobs. It was impossibly hard, like taking the bar exam—every day for the rest of your life. "Jason, it's good to be brave, but you're going through a lot now, and it's okay to say that it's hard. Really hard, and really scary."

"It is," Jason whispered. His eyes glistened with unshed tears.

"I know, sweetie." Bennie felt wetness come to her own eyes, but blinked them clear. She'd sensed Jason needed her to be strong, which was another Mother Thing. "Anyway, what I was saying was we need to get a doctor, to check you out—"

"No, please don't, they'll know, they'll make fun of me." Jason wiped his eyes with his free hand. "Soon they'll *see*, if it doesn't stop, they'll see. I won't have any hair!"

"We'll deal with that when it happens, if it happens." Bennie hesitated. "It's possible that part of the reason this is happening is because you're stressed, which is normal. We can get you some help for that, too, somebody to talk to."

"Like *Frasier*, you mean a shrink. You think I'm crazy."

"No, not at all. Not crazy, but stressed. Worried. Anybody would be nervous and anxious in this situation. I would be."

"So why don't *you* see a shrink?"

"I have in my life, and I would again, if I needed to." Bennie had grown up with a single mother, who suffered from depression, and she'd been her mother's caretaker, from childhood. She'd done her time in therapy, which was why she was so incredibly well adjusted, if you didn't count her personal life.

"They have a shrink that comes here, I heard people saying, making fun of the boy who had to see him." Jason's eyes flashed with new panic. "Really, I *mean* it, they'll tease me, they'll call me crazy, I don't want anything like that to happen, I want them to leave me alone until I go home. When am I going home? Just tell me."

"I'm working on it, Jason." Suddenly Bennie had an idea. "Sit here. I have to go a minute."

"Why?"

"You'll see. Stay here. I'll be right back." Bennie jumped up, signaling to the guard. "Sir, I'll be right back. Please let him wait here for me."

The guard nodded back to her, and Bennie grabbed her purse, hustled from the room, waved her way past the security desk, and went outside. She caught up with the workman, loading a box on the van.

"Hi, remember me?" Bennie asked him, as he turned around.

"Sure, the mom."

"Can I ask you a favor? Will you sell me your hat for twenty bucks?" Bennie gestured at his black knit cap.

"What, why?"

"My son's head is really cold in there, and I don't want him to have to wait 'til I can buy him a new one."

"No problem." The workman slid the hat off his head. "Take it for free."

"Aw, I'm happy to pay for it." Bennie reached for her purse.

"Put your money away, 'tis the season," the workman replied, with a smile. "Merry Christmas to you and your boy."

"Thank you very much. That's very kind of you." Bennie gave him a grateful wave as she ran back up the steps, hurried inside, went back through the metal detector again, and was let into the visiting room.

Jason looked up, still resting on his fist to hide his bald spot. "Where did you go?" he asked, as she reached him.

"Here." Bennie passed him the hat. "Put this on. It's cold enough in here that everybody will think that's why you have it on."

"Where did you get it?" Jason brightened, picking up the hat and pulling it on. "Do I look okay?"

"Great!" Bennie threw her arms around him, and Jason got up and gave her a big hug back.

"Thanks!"

"You're welcome." Bennie patted him on the back, then let him go. "Now go back to your room and try not to worry, honey."

"Okay, Mommy." Jason's hand flew to his mouth. "Oops, sorry I called you that, it's 'cause my mom always called me honey."

"It's okay. Bye for now." Bennie smiled, concealing the strength of the emotion welling up inside her. She wasn't sure what to call the feeling, which touched a part of her heart so deep that she didn't even know it existed. She'd often wondered when she'd be a mother, but she'd never thought of herself as mommy. Just the sound of the word got to her. *Mommy.*

"Bye." Jason turned away, then scuffed out of the room, his head down in his new cap.

Bennie watched him go, her throat thickening. Her tears brimmed only after the door had closed, and the little boy was gone.

CHAPTER TWENTY-ONE

Bennie left the waiting room and went to the security desk in the entrance hall, where a young guard in a blue uniform sat behind the desk. "Officer Dulaney," she said, reading his nameplate. "I wonder if you can help me."

"Call me Stan. What do you need?" The young man looked up with a smile, his gelled hair shiny in the overhead light.

"I'm concerned that my client is having a health issue. What can I do to get him medical treatment? Do you have an infirmary on the premises?"

"We have a nurse who comes in, and a doctor, if necessary."

"Great. What about a psychiatrist?"

"We have one who comes in, Dr. Vita. You're a private attorney, correct?" Stan frowned slightly.

"Yes. Why?"

"We don't get many of those. There has to be a written request from the parent for the doctor or psychiatrist. You can't make the request."

"Okay, but I'd like to get it scheduled as soon as possible."

"We can get him into the nurse later today. Dr. Vita has a waiting list. I bet it'll take a month or two." Stan leaned over. "He's expensive. I heard it's a couple hundred bucks for an evaluation."

"Good to know, thanks. Good-bye now."

"Good-bye. Merry Christmas!"

"To you, too," Bennie called back, troubled. She left, hurried to her car, climbed inside, and started the ignition, then reached in her purse for her phone and plugged in the number for Matthew, who picked up after one ring. "Matthew, I just saw Jason. Can you meet me for lunch today? It's important."

"Yes, come by work at noon. Parnell Ironworks. I'll meet you at the employee entrance."

"Done. See you then. Bye." Bennie backed out of the space, turned around, and traveled down the driveway, then turned right when the traffic allowed, onto River Street. The dashboard clock read 10:15, and she pressed in the number for the Superior Court in Harrisburg.

"Prothonotary's Office. How may I help you?"

"Hello, this is Bennie Rosato, and I filed an Application for Emergency Relief and A Request for an Expedited Briefing Schedule with the on-call judge yesterday. Do you know if any of those have been ruled upon yet?" Bennie rattled off the caption as she entered traffic, driving with care.

"Please hold while I check."

"Thank you." Bennie felt her heartbeat pound, emotionally involved in a case in a way that was new to her.

"Ms. Rosato? We just received an order in this matter, granting your petition for expedited briefing."

"That's wonderful!" Bennie's spirits lifted, though she reminded herself that she'd gotten this tantalizingly close before. "How long does the Commonwealth have to file its response?"

"Until five o'clock tomorrow, Friday. We were about to fax a copy of the order to your office, but it just came in. It hasn't even been docketed yet."

"Did he rule on my Application for Oral Argument?"

"No, just on the briefing."

"Which judge was assigned to the case?"

"Judge Wallace Kittredge. He's new."

Damn. Bennie couldn't research him without a track record of his opinions. She didn't know whether he was Republican or Democrat, but even that wasn't a reliable predictor of the way he'd rule, and she cursed again the fact that Pennsylvania elected judges, instead of appointing them.

"Feel free to call later about oral argument."

"Thank you very much."

"You're welcome, Ms. Rosato. Happy holidays!"

Bennie hung up, then made her way toward Mountain Top, checking her email and messages on her phone when it was safe. She made a quick phone call to the office, which was picked up by Lou.

"Bennie, you just waking up?"

"No." Bennie flushed unaccountably. "Why are you answering the phone instead of Marshall?"

"She stepped away. So, did the earth move? Did you remember how to ride a bicycle? They say you never forget."

"I'm not that kind of girl."

"That kind of girl has a lot more fun than you."

"I'm doing just fine."

"But you're giving this guy a shot, aren't you?"

"I'm thinking about it."

"Mazel tov!"

"Shh, it's supposed to be a secret." Bennie braked behind a tractor-trailer, its big tires and mud flaps streaked with salt. She had never seen more salt than in northeastern Pennsylvania.

"Relax. There's no one around. Where are you? Aren't you coming in?"

"No, I'm staying in Jim Thorpe for the rest of the week."

"With Mr. Right? Excuse me, *Sergeant* Right?"

"In two rooms."

Lou snorted. "Gimme a break. What happens in Jim Thorpe, stays in Jim Thorpe."

"Keep it classy, would you?" Bennie couldn't help but smile. "How are things?"

"We're getting along fine without you."

"All right, I'm hanging up. Call me if you need me."

"Will do. Have *fun*."

"Bye." Bennie hung up, and the traffic eased, so she traveled to Mountain Top in about half an hour, wending her way through the town, then into the outskirts, which turned into wide-open spaces, broken up by light industry. She spotted the Parnell Iron-works sign in front of the offices, next to a windowless building of white corrugated metal. She followed the driveway and passed a sign that read **Employee Entrance**, where she parked. In time, she spotted Matthew emerge from the door, in a white paper jumpsuit covered with blue spray paint.

Bennie flagged him down, and he jogged toward the car, jumping inside just as she opened the door, letting in cold air. "Matthew, good to see you."

"Hi, thanks." Matthew folded into the seat and closed the door behind him. A chemical scent wreathed the paper jumpsuit, and there was a fine spray of faint bluish paint on his cheeks, but it stopped where his goggles and mask must have been. "Sorry I couldn't talk. It's one of those days."

"Can I take you to lunch? Do you have time to grab a bite?"

"No, I only take half an hour. We have a cafeteria but it's employees only. Can we just talk here, in the car?"

"Sure, I went to see Jason this morning—"

"Thanks." Matthew smiled, surprised. "I didn't know you were coming up."

"I'm staying, to make it easier." Bennie wasn't about to tell him about Declan, but it felt uncomfortably like a material omission. "I filed the appeal yesterday, and we got good news this morning, in that the appellate judge ruled in our favor on expedited briefing."

"So that tells you something, right?" Matthew brightened. "It's like he wants to hear about the case."

"Yes, but remember last time? We got exactly this far and then we lost." Bennie met his eye. "But I think we have a problem with Jason. His hair is falling out. I saw his scalp above his ear, and his eyebrows are thinning."

"What? I just saw him and he was fine." Matthew frowned. "Except he told me that Richie's ganging up on him, with the older kids."

"I'll see what I can do about that, if anything." Bennie felt conflicted, but pressed it away. "About his hair, he hid it from you, and I'm worried. He's going to see a nurse today, but I need a letter from you to get him seen by a doctor and a psychologist."

"A *psychologist*? Why?"

"I've heard that stress can make your hair fall out, haven't you?" Bennie kept her tone gentle. "I think it's called alopecia. He's worried that he's going to go completely bald, which does happen."

"I never heard of that."

"The psychiatrist at River Street can't see him for a couple of months, so I think we need to get him seen privately."

"Who's gonna pay for *that?* You know, they're charging me for Jason's court costs and for staying at River Street. Is that nerve or what? They're gonna take it out of my pay every week. The gal in Human Resources just told me, fifty bucks a week until I pay 517 bucks. Plus your fee, it adds up, no offense."

"I'll do everything I can for you on my bill, and you're probably insured for treatment for him. I really think he needs—"

"Pssh!" Matthew waved her off. "You're making too big a deal about this. You don't have kids, do you?"

Mommy. "No, but—"

"They have ups and downs. If you get him out of there, the whole dang thing will blow over. For free."

"I drafted a letter from you to the director of the prison, would you sign it?"

"He doesn't need a psychiatrist." Matthew raised his voice, slightly.

"I think he does."

"Well. I decide, I'm the client," Matthew said, flatly.

"Technically, Jason is my client."

"Then have *him* pay your bill." Matthew pursed his lips. "You do the lawyering and leave Jason to me. You just get him home, where he belongs."

"I'm doing everything I can." Bennie masked her frustration, and just then, her phone started ringing. She glanced at the screen, which showed Declan's cell phone number.

"Answer that if you want to."

"No, it can wait." Bennie pressed the button to voicemail, but the call made her nervous.

"I should get back to work anyway. The muckety-mucks are in today, and we got a big order from Canada. Sorry if I got loud, there. I try to be a gentleman, at all times."

"It's okay. I'm sorry I got pushy."

"I'd better go. See you." Matthew opened the car door, letting in a blast of cold air, then shut it behind him.

Bennie watched him head for the employees' entrance, then she picked up the phone.

CHAPTER TWENTY-TWO

"Hi, Declan, sorry I missed your call." Bennie kept the engine running for heat, looking through the windshield without really seeing anything. All she could think about was Jason, and there was nothing to see except snow, the corrugated building, and the cold pewter sky.

"Doreen and I met with the lawyer. I struck out again. She doesn't want to hire him."

"Why?" Bennie held her tongue, but it was becoming impossible to believe that Doreen really wanted Richie out of River Street.

"She didn't like him. She said he talked down to her."

"Did he?"

"No. Not to my mind. She and I had words. I told her she needed to hire somebody fast. She told me to back off. It wasn't pleasant."

"I bet. The Superior Court granted expedited briefing, so I hope I'm making some precedent for you."

"Congratulations." Declan's tone warmed. "It seems like you're making excellent progress. I'll try again. I'll find somebody else. Cast the net wider. I can't give up on Richie. I'm sitting outside River Street now, about to go in."

"I was just there, and it's going badly." Bennie didn't hesitate.

"Declan, Richie has to leave Jason alone. I mean, for real. Will you tell him that?"

"Sure. I'll lay down the law. Did something happen?" Declan sounded concerned.

"Keep this confidential, but Jason's hair is falling out, and I think it's from stress. I want to get him treated and I remember you said that you had a psychologist for Richie. Do you still have the name?"

"Yes, it's a husband-and-wife team in Wilkes-Barre. They treat children and adolescents. Richie saw the husband. I'll text you their name and information."

"Thanks. Also, I have bad news about Richie. Jason told me he got into a fight with some of the older kids."

"Oh no, was he hurt?" Declan asked, alarmed.

"I don't think so." Bennie could hear the beeping of his car door, which meant he was leaving his car, then heard the door slam.

"Okay, I'm going in. I want to check on Richie. By the way, I picked out a new place for dinner. They can take us at eight."

Us, again. Bennie liked the way it sounded. "Perfect."

An hour later, Bennie found her way into an upscale development in Mountain Top where Scott and Gloria McNamara maintained a joint office in the back of their modern contemporary home. Gloria was a petite woman, but she came off as wiry in a black fleece top, which she had on with jeans and loafers. Her blue eyes were sharply intelligent, her nose was fine, and her smile pretty. She wore her lemony-blonde hair in a layered brush cut and gestured Bennie into a leafy-patterned chair.

"Please, have a seat."

"Thank you for seeing me on such short notice." Bennie took the seat, looking quickly around. Psychiatric textbooks and journals filled white bookshelves, and framed botanical prints, a natural sisal rug, and a pickled-white coffee table gave it a cheery garden vibe. Indirect light flowed through windows on the back of the room, which overlooked woods.

Gloria took the matching chair opposite Bennie, crossing her legs. "So, what's going on with your client?"

"I represent a seventh grader at Crestwood Middle School who was sent to River Street for fighting in school, but the truth is, he gets bullied. Actually, by a former patient of your husband, a boy in his grade named Richie Grusini."

Gloria kept her pleasant smile in place. "My husband and I are respectful of our patients' confidentiality, so I don't know or discuss his patients."

"Understood. Jason's hair and eyebrows are falling out. I've heard of alopecia and I'm wondering if that's what it is."

Gloria made a note. "He should be seen by a medical doctor. Blood tests should be performed and his thyroid needs to be checked, before we pathologize it. Moreover, the differential isn't necessarily alopecia areata. His hair could be falling out for many reasons. It could be a side effect, a reaction to a drug."

"He's not on any medication. It looked like a round white circle."

"That does sound like alopecia areata, an autoimmune disorder caused by stress, but I wouldn't make a diagnosis without examining him." Gloria paused. "I've had a few patients with alopecia areata, and the hair falls out in patches, until baldness. The loss of eyebrows is disfiguring, and it can't be hidden with the wig, a cap, or sunglasses." Gloria frowned. "Jason will become more of a target. I've seen it happen."

Bennie cringed. "What's the treatment?"

"If it is alopecia areata, I would send him to a dermatologist who specializes in hair loss. They perform steroid injections in the scalp." Gloria rested her pen on her pad. "Sadly, there are life-long psychological repercussions to childhood incarceration."

"How so?" Bennie shuddered.

"As a child grows up, there are certain developmental windows, or, things that need to happen at certain times. Children need to socialize to develop peer relationships. They need to replace

parental relationships, and they need to develop a sense of identity and self-esteem." Gloria shook her head. "Juvenile detention
interferes with every one of these developmental stages, causing
untold harm."

"Really." Bennie felt the words like a weight in the pit of her
stomach. "Have you worked with kids in River Street?"

"No, but I trained in Pittsburgh and I worked with children
in juvenile detention there. Children who get bullied, you can
almost smell it on them. The victims get identified quickly, and
unchecked, bullying becomes a *Lord of the Flies* situation. When
I see children in that situation, my diagnosis is usually post-
traumatic stress disorder."

"PTSD, like from war?" Bennie asked, horrified.

"The analogy isn't unwarranted." Gloria pursed her lips. "It's
traumatic to be in a situation in which you feel endangered, victimized, or there's volatility. A child or adolescent will typically
experience a loss of control, a distrust of surroundings and others. Eventually that gets projected onto the world as a whole."

"What are the symptoms of PTSD in kids?"

"Nightmares, difficulty sleeping, difficulty concentrating, mood
swings, loss of self-esteem. A child or adolescent will shut down,
internalize his feelings, self-harm, or self-medicate. Or he can turn
that anger out, striking out and becoming aggressive."

"Jason is the former type of kid. He's not aggressive." Bennie
didn't add that the latter sounded like Richie.

"Don't be so sure. You told me on the phone, he pushed his
bully, didn't he? He could develop PTSD in River Street, and his
aggression will be triggered by certain things. His temper could
flare up at certain times. He could develop intermittent explosive
disorder."

Bennie fast-forwarded to a grown-up Jason, praying he didn't
develop those issues.

"I have seen striking out occur more often in children who
come from abusive homes. Kids who are aggressive have often
been aggressed upon or witnessed it in the home, like a husband
who abuses a wife."

Bennie found herself wondering if Doreen had been abused by her husband, before he left. "How do you treat PTSD in children? Let's say, if Jason develops it?"

"Talk therapy." Gloria cocked her head. "The more they tell their story, the more they attach their negative emotions to the story, and they realize the emotions belong to the story, not to them. You have to create a safe environment in which to do that."

"How do you create a safe environment, within a juvenile prison?"

"The safety is created in the therapeutic environment. It's not easy, but it's possible. I've done it, I know." Gloria's aspect brightened. "It's gratifying."

"So you think you could help Jason?"

"Yes. It would be $100 an hour, and the evaluation would take two hours. I might have to make a return visit, so that's $300 all told."

Bennie had to come clean with her. "His father isn't completely on board with therapy yet."

Gloria frowned. "I would need parental consent."

"I assumed that, and I'll work on it. That is, if I can't get Jason out of there."

Gloria nodded, gravely. "The sooner he's out, the better off he is. The longer he's incarcerated, who knows?"

CHAPTER TWENTY-THREE

Bennie checked her phone as she walked from Gloria's house to the car. The screen showed a message from the office, so she called back on the fly. "Hi, Marshall, what's up?"

"We got a fax from the Superior Court on your juvenile case."

"It's probably the reply brief by the Commonwealth. Can you fax it to the hotel?"

"I already did that. What I got is an order from Judge Kittredge. He granted your application for oral argument. Congrats!"

"That's great!" Bennie climbed in the car, putting two and two together. The Commonwealth had filed its reply brief, and Judge Kittredge had granted oral argument. That could only mean that the judge felt there was merit to her case, and the Commonwealth hadn't put his qualms to rest. Bennie started the ignition, jazzed. She was finally on the road to freeing Jason.

"Argument is scheduled for ten o'clock, tomorrow morning in Harrisburg."

"I hope he goes our way. I can't have that kid in prison another minute." Bennie steered out of the development, with its Sample Open flags flapping in the wind.

"If it's in Harrisburg, it probably makes sense for you to stay over again. I feel bad that you're stuck up there another night. You must be so sick of the boonies."

"No, it's growing on me." Bennie felt funny not telling Marshall the real reason she was staying over.

"Good. You got no calls. The world is shutting down for the holidays. I'll let you know if anything else comes in."

"Thanks. Tell Lou I said hi." Bennie wended her way through the streets of Mountain Top's nicer neighborhood.

"I will. Good-bye, and good luck tomorrow."

"Thanks, good-bye." Bennie hung up, her mood soaring. She pressed Matthew's number into her cell phone, modulating her tone to keep the excitement from her voice. She didn't want to get his hopes up again, only to have them dashed. The phone rang twice, and Matthew picked up.

"Matthew, I wanted to let you know that our petition for oral argument was granted by the judge. Oral argument is scheduled for tomorrow morning at ten in Harrisburg."

"Good! That's good, right?"

"Yes. It's good, but not a home run—"

"What's oral argument?" Matthew asked, excited. "What does that mean? Why do they call it that?"

"Oral argument is something held in open court, to clarify the written arguments that came before. It means that the judge wants to ask me a few questions before he makes his decision. It doesn't necessarily mean that he's going to go our way. I'm letting you know now, in case you want to be there. We can drive together." Bennie always made it a point to invite clients because it helped them understand what was going on. She also thought it influenced the judge by personifying the parties, though an appellate court was less likely to be influenced than a jury.

"Do I have to go? I can't get off, not this week."

"That's fine. I'll call you as soon as it's over to let you know how it went. Now, I just met with a child psychologist and she's concerned about Jason's hair falling out. She agreed to go and evaluate him at the prison and—"

"I said, I'll think about it. I have to get back to work. Thanks. I'll be praying for you, tomorrow morning."

"Thanks, Matthew. Good-bye." Bennie hung up and hit the gas, turning onto the main road. She would have to work late tonight and didn't have time for the dinner with Declan. She expected he would understand. If she won for Jason, it would help Richie, too. And the proverb went, the law was a jealous mister.

A frigid night had fallen, and Bennie sat working at her laptop at a card table in her bedroom, which had been temporarily transformed into an office. The inn's manager had rustled her up a printer, a surge protector, and an extension cord, so she was fully electrified, and copies of the cases she needed lay around her, having been Xeroxed by a bellman, because there was no business center. There was no room service, either, but she'd bribed somebody in the kitchen to keep her supplied with fresh coffee, in a metallic carafe that scented the room with caffeine. Declan had been a great sport about her canceling dinner, yet another test he passed, which he didn't know he was taking.

Bennie typed THE LOWER COURT'S WAIVER FORM IS UNCONSTITUTIONAL in oversized font, so she could read it from the lectern tomorrow. She knew what she wanted to say, but she had to shorten it, since oral arguments in the Superior Court were timed. She usually prepared by pretending her oral argument was a TV commercial, distilling its essence, then memorizing it, so that it sounded natural.

"One plain pizza, coming up!" Declan entered the room with Bear, who bounded in ahead, jumping on the bed.

"Thanks." Bennie kept working, preoccupied.

"Keep working. I get it." Declan set the pizza box and a large brown bag on the dresser."

"Thanks." Bennie glanced at him, as she typed. His gorgeous face was flushed from the cold and his thick hair in slight disarray from the wind, which made him look even more handsome. Whoever said looks didn't matter never dated anybody superhot. Still, she returned her attention to her argument.

"I'm going back to my room to find my sister a new lawyer. I have two more referrals. By the way, Richie swore he'd back off of Jason."

"Thanks," Bennie said, grateful, but she kept working. "Was he hurt in the fight?"

"He got a split lip. We can talk about it another time. Good luck tonight. We have to leave at six in the morning."

"You're coming with me, tomorrow?" Bennie had been so pre-occupied she hadn't even thought to ask him.

"Of course. I'll wear a sweater with a B on the front. Not for you. For Bear." Declan patted the dog on the head. "By the way, I fed him. Dry food, Purina. It was what they had at the grocery."

"Thank you, I completely forgot." Bennie kept writing.

"I'll keep him tonight. You won't have time to walk him." Declan picked up Bear's leash, and the dog jumped off the bed, behind him. "Good night."

"Good night," Bennie said, finding a new gear.

CHAPTER TWENTY-FOUR

Bennie sat at counsel table, waiting for Judge Kittredge. She felt both nervous and calm, a paradox familiar to any trial attorney. The paneled courtroom was lined with oil portraits of distinguished Pennsylvania jurists and filled with pews worn by time and use. The dais was of carved mahogany, and the lights were low, owing to ancient overhead fixtures with frosted glass. The air smelled musty because an appellate courtroom wasn't used on a daily basis, and most of the appeals in Pennsylvania were decided without oral argument.

Bennie glanced at the Commonwealth attorney, John Natal, whose name had been on their reply brief. He looked young, short, and preppy, with tortoiseshell glasses and a generic-prosecutor haircut. His reply brief to her application had been a rehash of his arguments below, in the same way that hers had, so it was anybody's guess what would happen today.

Bennie glanced at the wall clock, it was 10:05, which meant the judge was late, one of the prerogatives of the bench. The court stenographer had set up her stand, and the bailiff was busying himself at a desk beside the dais. The gallery was empty except for Declan, in a pew toward the back. His presence had already been noticed by the judge's attractive female law clerk, who sat at the side of the courtroom with a legal pad on her lap, stealing glances at him.

"All rise!" said the courtroom deputy, coming through the

pocket door, and everybody stood up as Judge Kittredge swept into the room in a heavy black robe. He was tall, thin, and in his forties, with a blonde mustache and a thatch of blonde hair, gray on the sideburns.

"Good morning, counsel, please sit down." Judge Kittredge shot her and Natal a quick smile as he ascended the dais.

"Good morning, Your Honor," Bennie replied, in serendipitous unison with the Commonwealth attorney, then they both sat down.

"Counsel for appellant?" Judge Kittredge sat down and motioned her to the lectern. "Let us have your argument."

"Thank you, Your Honor." Bennie rose, walked to the lectern, and set down her papers. Instantaneously, the green bulb on the lectern lit up, an electrical system operated by the courtroom deputy. "May it please the court, my name is Bennie Rosato, and I'd like to reserve two minutes for rebuttal."

"Granted."

"Thank you, Your Honor. I represent the appellant, a twelve-year-old boy who is presently incarcerated in the juvenile correctional facility in Wilkes-Barre, for pushing another student—"

"Counsel, your position is that your client's constitutional right to counsel was violated by the lower court, is that correct?"

"Yes, Your Honor." Bennie felt a surge of adrenaline, ready to jump right into the fray. "It's well established that juveniles have the constitutional right to counsel, and that waivers of constitutional rights have to be knowing, voluntary, and intelligent to be valid. My client was induced to enter a guilty plea and waived his right to counsel by signing a so-called waiver form that did not pass constitutional muster, nor was there any colloquy on the record to ensure that his waiver was knowing, voluntary, and intelligent."

"You rely as authority for your position on the case of *In re A.M.*, in which a panel of my colleagues reversed the trial court for failing to guarantee that the waiver was knowing and intelligently made in a juvenile proceeding. Correct?"

"Yes, Your Honor."

"However, I note that in *In re A.M.*, there was no written waiver of the right to counsel, as there was in appellant's."

"That's true, Your Honor." Bennie had made that point in her brief. "*In re A.M.* was decided only last year, and my sense is that the lower court judge developed the waiver in response to the panel's decision—"

"That may be true, but as you point out, that fact is not of record."

"True, but in any event, my argument remains the same. It's a distinction without a difference. The lower court judge may have attempted to correct itself by developing a waiver form, but that still doesn't pass constitutional muster. The waiver form used in the case at bar is like a simple release, a waiver of liability you'd expect to see at an amusement park. It simply is not enough to guarantee that a constitutional right was knowingly, voluntarily, and intelligently waived."

Judge Kittredge didn't interrupt, so Bennie kept talking, picking up her argument where she left off, which was the standard protocol at oral argument.

"Your Honor, in addition, the form requires that the minor sign, but he is under the age of contract in Pennsylvania, and it also requires the parent of the minor sign, but a parent cannot waive a constitutional right for a minor. In fact, in the case at bar, my client and his father did not know that they had the right to counsel or that one would be appointed free if they could not afford one, because they were told exactly the opposite. They asked and were told by the Public Defender's Office that they could not qualify for a public defender because of the father's income—"

"But none of that is on the record, counsel."

"Correct, Your Honor, which is precisely the problem. The record is inadequate because the proceeding below was inadequate. The transcript of the hearing is barely three pages. My client's father attempted to speak at the adjudication hearing and was cut off. My client, a *middle schooler*, was understandably intimidated, and in any event, we're not at the draconian point where we hold minor children accountable for not knowing their constitutional rights."

Judge Kittredge cocked his head. "So your position is that an on-the-record colloquy should've been conducted, the same as in an adult criminal trial, before what was essentially a guilty plea was accepted."

"Exactly, Your Honor."

"My research reveals that that is not yet the law in Pennsylvania with regard to juveniles. That specific, narrow question has yet to be decided by our state Supreme Court. It has not yet been reached, correct?"

Bennie's mouth went dry. "That is correct, Your Honor, though the Pennsylvania Supreme Court has made clear that juveniles have the same right to counsel that adults do. Therefore, any such ruling by you would be completely consistent with the current law of the Commonwealth, as enunciated by our Supreme Court. In addition to his right to counsel, my client was not informed of his right to be presumed innocent, his right to confront and cross-examine witnesses, or any of the other rights that are guaranteed by the Constitution before incarceration."

Judge Kittredge raised a hand, cutting Bennie off. "Your point is well taken, counsel. I share many of your concerns with the waiver form used below. Your legal analysis in this matter is sound. Certainly, I've heard of you by reputation, and you have not disappointed today."

"Thank you, Your Honor," Bennie said, surprised at the praise, though she had the feeling from the judge's tone of voice that a "but" was coming—and it would be the reason he'd ordered oral argument.

"But the issue in this matter, at this juncture, is that it comes to me as a single appellate judge, sitting as a matter of emergency relief." Judge Kittredge leaned over the dais, his tone sincere and unguarded. "If, in fact, counsel, you're asking me to rule that the waiver was constitutionally defective because an on-the-record colloquy was not held for this juvenile, then I would be making law in the Commonwealth of Pennsylvania *on my own*. It may well be the logical extension of the law, and it may well be consistent with what the Supreme Court and the Superior Court panel in *In re A.M.* intended. But they did not say as much, nor did they reach this specific and narrow question, and therefore, it is an extension of the law."

Bennie felt her heart sinking, but she didn't dare interrupt Judge Kittredge, who continued.

"So we find ourselves at a procedural impasse. I may decide this question on my own, or I may refer this matter to a panel of my colleagues for decision, so that we may address it in the normal course. Or, it may raise a question of such legal importance that it is addressed by the entire court, sitting *en banc*."

Bennie knew the last option would be a disaster, in terms of time. The Superior Court held its *en banc* sessions only a few times a year because they required the empaneling of the entire court.

"But that doesn't help your client, does it, counsel?" Judge Kittredge asked, reading her mind.

"No, it doesn't," Bennie answered, seizing her opportunity, even though the yellow light on the podium came on. "My client's sentence will have expired by then, and he stands in the shoes of every other juvenile, because juvenile sentences tend to be shorter term. If we wait for that occasion, then a profound constitutional defect will be permitted to stand, remaining essentially unreviewable and rendering a plain injustice for the juveniles of the Commonwealth."

"Thank you, counsel. I have your argument." Judge Kittredge turned to Natal, who was already on his feet. "Counsel, please come forward."

"Thank you, Your Honor." Bennie returned to counsel table, perching on the edge of her seat. She had made the best argument she could, but she wanted to see what the judge asked the Commonwealth, because that could be even more telling as to which way his decision would go.

Natal straightened up at the lectern, and the green light went on. "May it please the court, my name is John Natal, and I represent the Commonwealth—"

"Counsel," Judge Kittredge interrupted. "Let's get directly to this waiver form. Is Ms. Rosato correct that it fails to pass muster under the Constitution?"

"No. She is incorrect, Your Honor." Natal shuffled quickly through a set of papers, stopping at the waiver. "It states clearly at the top, 'Waiver of Right to Counsel,' and it reads that, 'I am aware I have the right to counsel in the juvenile matter before the Court. I have consulted and been advised by a responsible adult who is aware of the fifth and sixth amendments right guaranteed to me—' "

"Counsel, I can read it. My question is, is it valid under the Constitution of the United States and of the Commonwealth of Pennsylvania?"

"We believe it is, Your Honor. By its very terms, it both informs appellant and his father that they have the right to counsel and that they are waiving it by signing the form. It is in plain English, not legalese, and is self-explanatory." Natal set the form aside. "We believe that this Court should not be placed in a position, as appellant's counsel would have you do, in which it is not only extending the law of criminal procedure with respect to juveniles, but reaching its hand down into the court below and micromanaging its courtroom administration." Natal shuffled to the photocopied case on top of his stack. "It is well established in the Commonwealth that lower courts are accorded wide latitude in juvenile matters to conduct and administer their courtrooms as they see fit, under the case of—"

"Of course, that is subject to the Constitution. Is it not, counsel?"

"Yes, Your Honor, but in this matter, the lower court did follow and conform its procedure according to prevailing law. There is no current legal requirement for an on-the-record colloquy for juveniles who wish to enter a guilty plea to an adjudication, and the waiver form was signed not only by appellant's father, but by the juvenile himself. If appellant or his father had an objection or a question about it, they could've asked it in open court."

"What about Ms. Rosato's argument, that they felt intimidated or were otherwise silenced?"

"Your Honor, these are not matters of record, as you have correctly pointed out. For that reason, they may not be considered at the appellate level."

Judge Kittredge frowned. "The transcript *was* terribly brief, counsel."

"And that, Your Honor, is precisely the reason the waiver form is utilized. It streamlines the administration of justice in juvenile court, and that is all the more reason why juvenile courts should *not* be micromanaged at this upper level." Natal cleared his throat, and the yellow bulb lit up on the lectern. "If appellant's argument were to prevail, Your Honor, then even an on-the-record colloquy would not cure it, and it's difficult to see where it stops."

Judge Kittredge frowned again. "Please explain, counsel."

"With respect, Your Honor, an appellate court cannot speculate about what would have been said or what would have been done, in the absence of any indication on the record. If an appellate court follows that path, then it's a slippery slope indeed, extending not only to juvenile court matters, but to all manner of cases that come before Your Honor."

Judge Kittredge nodded, but didn't say anything, so Natal continued.

"Such a decision is of the utmost importance, not only in terms of procedure but in terms of substantive law, and it should not be decided by you as an individual judge, sitting alone." Natal looked down, and the yellow light on his podium blinked on. "Your Honor, the appellant has been adjudicated a juvenile delinquent for fighting in school. It is incumbent upon our juvenile courts to ensure that violence in our public schools is eradicated. Recent news stories of school shootings warn all of us of these dangers. This matter goes directly to the health, safety, and welfare of children in public schools, as well as of teachers and staff. For all of the foregoing reasons, the Commonwealth asks that you deny Appellant's Application for Emergency Relief."

"Thank you, counsel, I have your argument." Judge Kittredge turned to Bennie. "Counsel for appellant, rebuttal?"

"Thank you, Your Honor." Bennie strode quickly to the podium, and the green light blinked on. She reminded herself that the purpose of rebuttal was to refute only what the Commonwealth had said, and she knew exactly what she wanted to say.

"Your Honor, you have heard the Commonwealth say that you would be micromanaging if you granted appellant's application in this case, and you've heard him further suggest that forms such as this obviously facially invalid waiver are necessary, perhaps to prevent the occurrence of another tragic shooting."

Judge Kittredge's face grew somber, and Bennie worried that the Commonwealth's point had hit home, so she had to address it, right now.

"We are all mindful of that tragedy, as we are of the perilous times in which we live. Not only Columbine, but September 11, and the war in Afghanistan. We know that we will be facing legal issues in the days to come, which will require courts to strike a balance between our collective security and our individual rights. Going forward, it's important to focus on the facts and not to let our understandable concern for public safety render meaningless the procedural protections that safeguard our individual freedoms and those of our children."

Judge Kittredge nodded, so Bennie continued.

"This is not an application for relief that has anything to do with Columbine High School. This is about a twelve-year-old boy, an A student in Crestwood Middle School, who has never been in any kind of trouble. He gets bullied, and he finally pushed back when another student called his late mother a nasty name." Bennie knew the facts were outside the scope of the record, but she went for it anyway. "This is the sort of thing that occurs in every cafeteria and playground in the country. This is not a matter that belongs in any court at all, much less an appellate court, and we must exercise caution not to make it so, for that is the slippery slope I fear the most. Law must always protect justice, not injustice, though it is capable of either. Your Honor, I ask that you grant Appellant's Application for Emergency Relief. Thank you."

"Thank you, counsel." Judge Kittredge banged the gavel, his expression impassive. "Court is dismissed."

CHAPTER TWENTY-FIVE

"So how do you think it went?" Bennie asked Declan, as they pushed through the double doors of the courtroom, their parkas open.

"I think it went great." Declan looked over, his dark eyes shining and his face alive with animation. He reached out his large hand. "Give me your bag."

"Thanks." Bennie handed him her heavy messenger bag, knowing he'd insist anyway, and they walked down the corridor of rose marble. They were alone, and the ancient frosted fixtures shed barely any light.

"You were awesome. You did a great job." Declan grinned, hoisting the bag easily to his shoulder. "You even made me *like* lawyers. Really, I mean it. I get why you had to work so late, last night. When I saw the green light go on, I thought, damn. The green light makes it real. 'Ready, set, go!'"

"I'm fine with the green light; it's the red light I hate." Bennie smiled, and Declan smiled back.

"Because it's over then?"

"Yes, I have to shut up."

Declan chuckled. "You gave me hope for Richie. For the both of them. I think we won."

"How about we go with cautious optimism?" Bennie couldn't help but temper his enthusiasm, a practitioner's reflex.

"Hell, no. How could we *not* win? You were so convincing."

"Declan, you heard the judge." Bennie's heels clacked on the hard marble floor as they walked toward the glass exit doors. "He's with us on the substance, but not the procedure. He doesn't want to rule alone. Best-case scenario, we win, but not yet. Is that a win or not? Justice delayed is justice denied, isn't it?"

"I see what you mean." Declan's smile faded. "You know, I'm going to explore becoming Richie's legal guardian."

"What, really?" Bennie stopped in her tracks, and so did Declan. They stood in the sunlight coming through the exit doors. "When did you decide to do this?"

"It's been growing on me, from watching you." Declan frowned. "I didn't get a chance to tell you. Doreen is refusing to meet with the new lawyers I found."

"How is that even an option? Richie needs a lawyer." Bennie didn't hide her anger.

"I know. I think she's sabotaging me. Honestly, I don't think she wants Richie out."

"I wondered about that," Bennie said gently.

"You dropped everything for Jason. That's what Richie needs, too." Declan clenched his jaw. "If I were a lawyer, I'd do it on my own, like you did today."

"But guardianship?" Bennie wondered if Declan knew what he was getting into. "You can't be declared Richie's guardian unless you show that Doreen is unfit. That's a high standard. She didn't seem unfit to me, and it would be an ugly court battle."

"I don't think it will go as far as court. I already have Richie's okay. I'm hoping she'll go along."

"Do you think she will? I mean, how close are you two, anyway?"

"Not very. We used to be closer. Our whole family was close. But then my parents passed, a year apart. She took it hard." Declan's frown deepened. "She met her ex, and I couldn't stand him. I knew he was a loser from day one. I told her so, before they got married. That didn't help. You would think we got closer after they broke up. We didn't. It only made it worse I turned out to be right."

"So, do you really think she'll agree?"

"Yes. She wants somebody to solve this problem for her. She's like that. Richie thinks she'll agree, too. He wants to get out of River Street. He said he'd rather live with me. I could get him the help he needs, whenever he gets out." Declan managed a smile. "Even if he gets out later than we all want."

Bennie realized she hadn't called Matthew yet. "Oh, I almost forgot, Jason's father is waiting to hear how the argument went. Can you give me a minute?"

"Sure." Declan gestured outside. "I'll go get the truck and pick you up."

"Okay, thanks." Bennie slid her phone from her purse and pressed in Matthew's number, as Declan left the courthouse.

Matthew answered immediately. "Did we win?" he asked, anxious.

"The judge hasn't ruled yet. It's a difficult legal question, and even though we're right, the judge might be reluctant to decide it on his own—"

"Isn't that his job, to decide things on his own?" Matthew sounded confused. "Look, just tell me straight, is Jason getting out or not?"

"I don't know if or when he's getting out, yet, because I don't know when the judge will rule. I hope it will be before Christmas, but he doesn't have to do that if he doesn't want to."

"I hardly slept last night. It's Friday already. Do they decide on the weekend?"

"It's only one judge, and no, he doesn't. I'm sorry, Matthew. I want him out as much as you do."

"Don't they know the meaning of the word emergency?" Matthew sighed.

"I know it's hard, believe me, but this is as fast as courts move. In fact, I've never seen a court move as fast."

"It's like they don't care."

"They do, I think that's why we're making the progress we are."

Bennie could hear the hopelessness in his tone. "Did you visit Jason last night? Did you see his bald patch?"

"Yes, he showed it to me. He had the hat on."

"So what do you think?"

"I'll see if it gets better on its own. The nurse made an appointment for him to see the doctor, but they couldn't schedule it until after New Year's."

Bennie sighed inwardly. "Matthew, it's not going to get better, and his hair is going to fall out. The boys will tease him, even worse—"

"Uh-oh, Bennie, I gotta get back to work, my boss is on the floor. Would you do me a favor and visit him this weekend? I'll go Saturday, but I can't go Sunday. They offered me overtime, and if I work a double, I can get ahead of Jason's expenses."

"Don't worry, I'll go Sunday."

"Thanks. He was asking for you. He likes you."

"I like him, too. He's a great kid." Bennie's throat caught. "I'll let you know as soon as I hear anything from the judge."

"Thank you. Bye now."

"Good-bye." Bennie hung up, shaking her head. She slipped her phone back in her purse and saw Declan's truck pulling up near the courthouse entrance, so she went outside.

"How'd it go?" Declan asked, coming around the front of the truck to open the door for her.

"Thanks. He's disappointed, and I get that." Bennie climbed inside the truck and closed the door behind her. She set her purse on the seat, then noticed a gift on the console, wrapped with shiny red paper. An attached note card read, *For Bennie, Merry Christmas to my favorite lawyer. From, Declan.*

Declan opened the driver's side door, got into the truck, and closed it behind him with a grin. "Merry Christmas!"

"What's this?" Bennie asked, delighted. She picked up the gift.

"Santa came early, I guess."

"Aw," Bennie said, touched. "You didn't have to."

"I wanted to." Declan smiled warmly.

"But I don't have anything for you."

"That's okay. Open it."

"What a lovely thing to do." Bennie tore off the paper and lifted up the lid of a white cardboard box. Inside on a layer of cotton gleamed the silver bracelet she had seen in the store in Jim Thorpe. "Thank you!"

"You're welcome."

"When did you do this?" Bennie asked, happily surprised.

"When I went running. Bear picked it out. Put it on."

"It's so pretty." Bennie picked up the silvery circle, which caught the lights as she slid it onto her wrist.

"Let me see." Declan reached for her hand, brought it to his mouth, and kissed the side. "Beautiful."

"Declan—" Bennie said, then felt a rush of happiness that rendered her speechless, maybe for the first time ever.

"Yes?" Declan said, smiling, and in the next moment, he leaned over and kissed her softly, and she kissed him back, feeling her heart give way.

"Yes," Bennie answered, pulling away with a smile.

"Wow." Declan smiled. "I've been wanting to do that for a long time."

"Now you're talking dirty."

"No, I'm not." Declan smiled wider. "When I talk dirty, you'll know it."

"Ha!" Bennie felt an unaccountable thrill.

"So how about I take you to lunch? I made a reservation at the place we canceled last night."

"Too bad, you'll have to cancel again."

"Why? You have to work?"

"No, but we have better things to do." Bennie reached over and turned the key in the ignition. "Let's go home."

"On it." Declan laughed, putting the truck in gear.

They got back to the hotel, and Bennie hurried up the steps to the second floor with Declan at her heels. She had the room key ready when they reached her door, so she stuck it in the lock and twisted, then they both leaned on the door, so that when it opened, they practically fell inside the room, laughing.

"Arf!" Bear pawed them for attention, but they both ignored him, kissing while they wiggled out of their coats and fell back on the canopy bed, which was covered with photocopied cases. The dog barked a few more times, the papers crackled under their bodies, and the air smelled like stale pizza, but Bennie didn't care, kicking off her pumps and hoping they didn't land on Bear, who quieted, getting the picture.

Bennie lay back on the soft bed as they kissed, letting the world ebb away from her. She felt the softness of Declan's lips, the delicious weight of his body on hers, and the pleasure coursing through her system, relaxing her totally, making her feel a way she hadn't in ages. Her mind cleared and her thoughts vanished, even as Declan helped her out of her blazer, managing not to get it stuck on her new bracelet.

"Well done," Bennie murmured.

"You ain't seen nothing yet." Declan slid his hands under her blouse, so expertly that it made her shudder with arousal, and Bennie shivered under the warmth of his fingers as they ran over the top of her bra, which was when she gave herself over completely, surrendering to the happiness, the joy, and the sheer toe-curling pleasure that great sex could be, between two adults who cared deeply about each other.

There was more laughter than she expected, more sighs, and an unladylike cry that came from somewhere in Bennie's throat, loud enough that Declan had to cover her mouth to keep the inn manager from the door, leaving them both laughing. They made love until darkness had fallen and they were out of condoms, and they talked until the dog needed walking, then they realized they were starving, so there was yet another pizza, this time eaten together in bed, watching the end of some dumb college football game, cut short by more talking, more kissing, and ultimately, more lovemaking.

Bennie didn't care if they never left the room, and neither did Declan, so they didn't, agreeing that although Jim Thorpe was adorable, they'd seen everything there was to see, so they spent all day Saturday in bed, as well as Saturday night to Sunday just after dawn. They both fell back asleep, with nobody bothering to set an alarm, and Bennie woke up with her head on Declan's chest and his arm draped heavily over her, holding her close. She let wakefulness creep over her, in no hurry to move or change anything, just letting Sunday morning come on.

Sunlight warmed the bedroom, glowing in rays through the mullioned window. The only sound was the snoring of the dog at the foot of the bed, and the only movement the soft rising and falling of Declan's chest as he slept. Bennie closed her eyes again, trying to hold on to the peace of the moment and the happiness of being here, with him. That she was falling in love with him was a foregone conclusion, though she hadn't admitted it to him last night, nor even to herself until this very moment. She sensed that he was falling in love with her in return, though he hadn't said so either. She felt oddly sure of his feelings, and the only mystery was how she had gotten this far in her life without ever being this happy.

She thought back to her conversation in the office with Lou, and her early worries about how she and Declan would make the differences between them work, but she no longer felt the same fear. She sensed that they both cared too much about each other to let things get in the way, and she knew that she would make room for him in her life, and he would do the same for her. She simply felt too good to let the feeling go.

And he was a man worth compromising for.

CHAPTER TWENTY-SIX

Bennie shifted forward in the front seat of the truck, and Declan steered onto the driveway to the juvenile detention center. They had showered, eaten, and walked the dog, reentering the outside world happy, if sleepy. She turned to him, shifting into work mode in anticipation of seeing Jason.

"Okay, so Declan, do you want to go in first or shall I?"

"Whatever you want." Declan drove up the hill, eyeing the parking lot ahead, which held more cars than usual. "Sunday must be visiting day."

"I'll go in first and get situated with Jason. We'll sit on the right, and you sit on the left."

"The boys will see each other."

"Right, but they won't relate the two of us, and that's all I'm worried about."

"Okay." Declan reached the top of the hill, parked, cut the ignition, and kissed her briefly.

"Let's go see the kids." Bennie got her purse, climbed out of the truck, and closed the heavy door behind her. The sun felt warm and the wind blew gently off the river, a nice break in the weather. Declan put his arm around her, and they walked toward the entrance together. Another couple walked past them, looking back.

Suddenly, a shouted "hey!" cut the quiet Sunday afternoon, and they looked over to see Doreen leaving the detention center, holding the hands of her twin boys. "What the *hell* is going on here, Declan?" she shouted, startling the other couple, who hustled away.

"Doreen, relax." Declan let go of Bennie, and she stopped in her tracks, momentarily unsure. Doreen must've changed her mind about visiting Richie and she'd brought the twins, who looked adorable, if confused, in matching blue coats.

"Uncle Declan!" called one of the boys, breaking into a happy grin. They both started to run toward Declan, but Doreen yanked them back, advancing.

"Declan, who the *hell* do you think you are, trying to take my son?" Doreen's dark eyes flared with outrage. "Are you *screwing* Jason's lawyer? Is *that* who this is coming from? *Her?*"

"No, wait." Bennie's mouth went dry, and Declan stepped in front of her, protectively.

"Doreen, calm down in front of the kids—"

"Where do you get off, trying to take my son! Richie told me what you were cooking up! *I'm* his parent, not you!" Doreen threw up her hands without letting go of the twins, tugging them around. The boys started to cry, their identical little faces contorted with anxiety.

"Doreen, please." Declan raised his hands in appeal. "Get a grip—"

"Go to hell!" Doreen glared past Declan, to Bennie. "You're not taking my son from me! You're not going to screw your way into *my* family!"

"Doreen, that's *enough*," Declan snapped, stern. "We can talk about this calmly. Let's go somewhere and—"

"I'll fight you every step of the way, Declan!" Doreen ignored the wailing twins. "You think you're here to visit Richie? I took you off the visitors' list, you're not going to see him anymore! *I* get to say who sees him, not you!"

"Doreen, we can work this out—"

"Let him *rot* in there! Let him think about what he does! How he makes life horrible for me and his brothers! *You* can go straight to hell!" Doreen spat at Bennie while the twins cried, their little chests heaving. "He's not your son, Declan! He's *mine*!"

Declan guided Bennie toward the entrance. "Go inside. Hurry. I'll take care of this. Go!"

Bennie hurried away, shaken. She felt bad about Doreen, but worse about the boys, distraught over the confrontation between their mother and uncle.

"Oh, sure, typical freaking lawyer!" Doreen called after her. "Run away like the sneak you are!"

Bennie hurried into the detention center and put her purse on the conveyor belt to go into the metal detector, and Stan the security guard looked up from his newspaper. She could hear Doreen still yelling, but couldn't make out the words. "Sorry about that noise outside."

"It's not your fault." Stan gestured her through the detector.

"It's just kind of, upsetting." Bennie realized that Stan didn't connect her to the scene in the parking lot.

"It isn't the first time. This ain't Disneyland. I bet nobody fights in the parking lot of the Magic Kingdom. That mom, she's a pistol. She gave her son a *real* hard time during the visit. Calvin, you know, the black guard, he had to tell her to mind her tongue."

"Really?" Bennie asked, dismayed.

"Hey, my mom would've killed me, if I ended up in juvie." Stan shook his head. "Anyway, I heard your client got to the nurse, so that's good."

"Yes, thanks." Bennie picked up her purse from the conveyor belt, realizing the yelling in the parking lot had finally stopped.

"Go on, and I'll have him sent in."

"Thanks." Bennie went to the visiting room and sat down. The room was fuller than usual, maybe because it was the weekend, and families clustered around the tables, talking, hugging, and wiping away tears. She looked away, and in the next few minutes, the door on the other side of the room opened, admitting Jason, with Calvin at his side.

They were both smiling, and Bennie found herself on her feet, happy to see Jason, whose grin broadened when he spotted her, scuffing forward more quickly than usual. He still wore his black knit cap, and his eyebrows seemed sparser, but she kept that to herself. "Hey, buddy, give me a hug," Bennie said, but the boy was already wrapping his arms around her waist.

"Hi, Bennie!" Jason smiled up at her, his blue eyes bright. "My dad said I'm going home! He said you went to a better court, like the boss of the judge!"

"Well, not exactly," Bennie answered, caught up short. Suddenly she heard shouting from the direction of the entrance hall and heads turned toward the commotion. The door was flung open by Doreen, her dark eyes glittering as she scanned the tables.

"Where are you, you bitch?" she hollered. "You can't hide from me!"

"Stop, Mrs. Grusini!" Calvin hustled from the far side of the room, as shocked parents and children got up from their seats.

Bennie rose, horrified, putting Jason behind her. "Doreen, please, you need to calm down—"

"Stay away from my *freaking family*!" Doreen rushed toward Bennie, her fingers outstretched, but Calvin intercepted her, grabbing her by the arm and trying to pull her back toward the door. Parents rose at the tables, mothers protecting their children and fathers hustling to help Calvin.

"Go back to Philly, you *whore*!" Doreen struggled in his grasp, her face tinged with fury. "We were fine until *you* came here!"

"Doreen, please!" Bennie hustled Jason toward the back of the room.

"That's Richie's mom!" Jason gasped. "Why's she yelling at you, Bennie?"

"You *whore*!" Doreen kept shouting, pushing back against Calvin. "You're *screwing* my brother! You're trying to take my son away from me! You're a freaking *whore*!"

The door banged open, and Declan flew in and grabbed Doreen, tipping the balance in the men's favor, dragging her screaming and kicking toward the door. They got her from the room just as Stan came through the door, blood dripping from a gash near his gelled hairline.

"Attention, people!" Stan called to the crowd, gesturing. "We're going to lock this down! Visiting day is over! We need to lock this down!"

The crowd reacted, talking at once. "No, why?" "Come on, it takes me an hour to drive here!" "I wanna see my kid, I waited all week for this!"

"Sorry, it's procedure," Stan called back. "Say good-bye to your kids and have them line up at the door! Police are on the way!"

"Bennie, what's going on? What's happening?" Jason hugged Bennie around the waist, and she rubbed his back, holding him close.

"I'll explain later, honey." Bennie hadn't wanted Jason to know anything, much less to find out this way. "Don't worry about it. It's not your problem."

"Why lock it down?" a father yelled back, at Stan. "They got her out! It's over! Don't make it a federal case!"

"Sorry, sir." Stan pointed at the exit door. "Please leave. We have a security risk on the premises, we go into lockdown."

"That's bullshit!" one mother called out, though most of the parents and the crowd were giving their children final hugs and bidding them teary good-byes.

"Bennie?" Jason hugged her, and she hugged him back.

"You'd better go, honey. I'll come back tomorrow."

"But when am I going home? I just want to go home." Jason's eyes brimmed with tears, and Bennie's heart broke.

Stan came over, meeting her eye with concern. "Sheesh! Ms. Rosato, are you guys okay?"

"We're fine, but how are you? What happened to your head?"

"I hit it on the machine. She came at me when I wouldn't let her back inside." Stan shook his head in disgust. "That woman is straight-up crazy. If she has a beef with you, I'd stay out of her way."

Jason looked from Stan to Bennie. "That's Richie's *mom*. Is she really crazy?"

"Anyway, it's all over now." Stan placed a hand on Jason's

shoulder, with a reassuring smile. "Pal, you gotta go back to your room. Go get in line with the others, will you?"

"Okay." Jason shuffled off, joining the others, the last one in the line, his head down and his black cap as round as a period at the end of a very sad sentence.

Bennie stood with the parents, watching their children file out, then the door closed and the kids were gone. Mothers and fathers turned away, glancing over at her, their expressions resentful.

"I'm so . . . sorry," Bennie stammered.

"*Slut,*" someone hissed.

CHAPTER TWENTY-SEVEN

Bennie passed the afternoon sitting at a table in a nearby bar, watching the sun vanish from the sky through a dirty window outlined with Christmas lights. Her view was a lineup of dark vacant row homes, backgrounded by the adult prison, its concertina wire glittering like tinsel. Stuck into the patch of snow by the road was a white-painted sign, **BAIL BONDS—CALL ME FIRST TO PUT U BACK ON THE STREET.**

The bar was empty, and behind her, the bartender hummed tunelessly to himself. The air smelled like stale cigarette smoke, and the floor felt gritty. Dusty holiday lights festooned the paneled walls, and the TV over the bar played a football game on mute. Bennie could watch even though it was behind her, because of its flickering reflection in the window. The Eagles were losing.

Bennie checked her phone, but there was still no call or text from Declan, who had gone with Doreen to the police station. That was about two hours ago, and Bennie killed the time by answering email and calling Matthew. Her call had gone to voicemail, so she'd left a message. She remembered that he was working a double shift, but she wanted to tell him before he heard it from Jason. She'd have to come clean to Matthew about Declan, too, and she hoped he'd understand, in context.

A blast of cold air brought her from her reverie, and she looked over to see Declan entering the bar. He walked over heavily, his posture somewhat stooped, which struck her as unlike him.

"I'm sorry it took so long." Declan kissed her on the cheek, and Bennie could feel the tension clinging to him like frost.

"Sit down and have something to eat."

"I'm not hungry." Declan took off his coat, looking past her to the bartender. "Hey, pal, can I get Yuengling on tap?"

"No problem," the bartender called back.

Declan sat down heavily opposite Bennie, laying his hand on the table, palm up. "Take my hand, if you're still speaking to me."

"Of course I am." Bennie took his hand and squeezed it gently.

"I am so sorry." Declan met her eye, pained. "I'm so sorry I involved you with this. Forgive me, please."

"It's not your fault," Bennie said, touched. "I'm sorry it happened, too. Did the police charge her?"

"No." Declan looked up as the bartender came over with the beer and set it down. "Thanks, pal." He nodded at Bennie. "You need anything more?"

"No, I'm fine."

"Gotcha," the bartender said, leaving the table.

Declan picked up his beer. "As I was saying, they didn't charge her. The guard decided not to press charges. He said it was an accident. She hit him and he fell backwards." Declan sipped his beer, frowning. "It took her a long time to calm down. She was a raving lunatic. I've never seen my sister act like that. The kids were beside themselves. It was a nightmare."

"What do you mean? Who did she rave at?"

"Me. But then it was all over the lot." Declan raked his hands through his hair. "She screamed at the desk officer. The female uniform who helped settle down the kids. Then the captain came over. She heard him say something about putting her on a psych hold." Declan's eyes flared. "Oh my God. She called him every name in the book." Declan put his beer down with a heavy *clunk*, and his mouth formed a downturned line. "I talked them out of the psych hold because she begged me to. It was the only way I could get back in her good graces. But I really think . . . something's wrong with her."

"There must be," Bennie said quietly, having come to the same conclusion.

"I don't know what it is." Declan rubbed his forehead. "I mean, she's always had a temper. She was always like my mom, hot-blooded. But my mom never did anything like that. I mean, did you see the way she pulled the kids around? That's how she got back inside the detention center without me."

"How?" Bennie had been wondering.

"I convinced her to let me take them to the car. I didn't want them to hear what she was saying." Declan stopped talking, clenching his jaw, and Bennie squeezed his hand again.

"I'm sorry."

"She's sick. She's really sick." Declan kept working his chin, his voice hushed. "She couldn't control herself today. She couldn't control herself at the station."

"So now what do we do?"

"If you don't mind, I told her I'd go over there tonight. She's home, now." Declan sighed heavily, his chest expanding. "We should try to hash it out. We didn't get a chance to talk privately at the station."

"I don't mind. What do you want to hash out? Hiring a lawyer for Richie?"

"Yes, and I thought I would explain about us. Try to calm her down."

"Uh-oh."

"Only that she has to know this didn't come from you. It came from me. That I'm worried about the way she treats Richie."

"You know, the child psychiatrist I met with told me something interesting. It's common sense, but it might apply here. I don't know, you tell me."

"What?"

"What was Doreen's ex-husband like?"

"He was a carpenter, but he didn't like to work. He could never hold a job. He was a loser. A jerk. I wasn't surprised when he left because he was so immature."

"Did he have anger issues?"

"Yes." Declan mulled it over. "He had a tendency to yell. He was hot-tempered, like her. When they fought, they yelled a lot. Used to drive me crazy. It was nonstop drama, the two of them."

"Was he ever physically aggressive to Richie?"

"I don't think so." Declan frowned. "Why? You think he abused him?"

"It's possible, isn't it? The psychiatrist reminded me that kids who are physically aggressive have been aggressed upon. In other words, Richie is a bully because he probably gets bullied. Maybe his father abused him and Doreen."

"I can ask her about it."

"What about your becoming Richie's guardian?"

"I'll back down, if she'll agree to let him see a lawyer and a psychiatrist. And now, if she'll agree to see a psychiatrist, too." Declan lifted an eyebrow, straightening up. "I'll take you back to Jim Thorpe, go see her, and come back to the inn."

"That's a lot of driving for one night. You can stay at your house if you want. You don't have to come back."

"Please." Declan smiled, a little sadly. "I'm coming back to you tonight, if I have to crawl."

CHAPTER TWENTY-EIGHT

Bennie woke up on top of the bedcovers, realizing she'd fallen asleep in her clothes. Bear snored at the foot of the bed, and the lights in the bedroom were on. Declan's parka was thrown on a side chair, and she heard the faucet running in the bathroom. The bedside clock read 5:17, so he'd been gone almost all night. She shifted up in bed and took a sip of warm Diet Coke, in case he kissed her. She would still have crappy breath, but at least it would be carbonated.

Declan came out of the bathroom, still walking in a slightly stooped way, as if he shouldered a physical burden. His skin looked pale, making his five o'clock shadow more prominent, and his eyes met hers, anguished and bloodshot.

Bennie sat up. "It looks like it went badly."

Declan crossed to the bed and sat on the edge, placing his hand on her leg. "Sorry I woke you. I tried to be quiet."

"That's okay. What happened?"

"It started out okay. More like old times. We put the boys to bed together. We sat in the kitchen. We ate, we talked. I was able to reason with her. I told her I was worried about her and her emotional state. I told her I was on her side, I would help her. That we were family." Declan paused, pursing his lips. "We were able to come to terms on Richie. She told me she would put me back on the visitors' list. She'd let me get him evaluated. She even said she'd let me hire a lawyer."

"That's great."

"That's what I thought. She said I could hire any lawyer I wanted. Except you."

"Fair enough."

"She blames you—rather, she blames Jason—for Richie's being in River Street." Declan held up a restraining hand. "I know it's ridiculous. I know she's in denial. I'm on board with you. I think it's the other way around, that Richie is the one to blame for Jason's being in River Street."

Bennie felt her hackles rise, but kept that to herself.

"I told her I thought her ex abused Richie, and she said she doubted it. She never saw it, but she says he did have anger issues. I told her *she* had anger issues." Declan paused. "Then she got angrier."

"Which is to be expected." Bennie knew he saw the irony, so she didn't need to point it out.

"Yes." Declan nodded. "She's sensitive. She doesn't like to be criticized by her big brother. I knew it wasn't going to be a picnic. I didn't think she would react that badly, though. I've been underestimating the extent of her problem. In fact, I didn't think she had a problem. Now I do."

"She yelled?"

"Yes. I told her about us. She wasn't happy about that. Don't worry. We agreed to disagree." Declan patted Bennie's leg. "I don't need her permission to see you."

"Good." Bennie liked that he'd stood up for her and their relationship, even though they were just at the beginning.

"I was getting ready to leave, but I went upstairs. I told her I had to use the bathroom. That wasn't the real reason." Declan swallowed hard. "Let me back up a minute. On the way over to the house, I remembered something. It was what was bothering me about the way she was yanking Mikey around. I remembered why it bothered me. He broke his arm, playing ice hockey. He's only had the cast off a month ago. It had to hurt him, yanking him around that way. It was the same arm, his right. So I went upstairs to see him. To check him out."

Bennie was starting to get a bad feeling, but she didn't interrupt Declan.

"I turned on the light in the boys' bedroom. They didn't wake up." Declan's voice softened, pained. "I looked under his shirt. There were bruises on his chest. On his arm, too, there were bruises. But the boys, they're always getting banged up. The two of them, they're always coming up with bumps and bruises." Declan clenched his jaw. "She told me they fought with each other, typical boy stuff. Or from hockey. I get that, I played on the pond out back. I played in school, too. I was always getting banged up on the ice. I believed her."

Bennie cringed, though she said nothing.

"But the bruises on his arm were in a row. Like he'd been grabbed or pinched." Declan hesitated. "It's what they tell us to look for in child-abuse cases. There it was, on my own nephew."

"I'm so sorry," Bennie said, reaching for his hand.

"Wait, it gets worse." Declan cleared his throat, blinking. "So then I go look at Albert. Examine his chest, his legs. I see the same thing. Little red bruises, sometimes in a row, sometimes not. That's not what happens when you get hit with a stick or fall on the ice. They're not hockey injuries."

Bennie didn't say anything, sickened.

"Then all of a sudden, Albert wakes up. He's happy to see me. He hugs me." Declan's lower lip trembled, but he remained in control. "They're such great kids. Smart, happy, *good*. They listen to her. They don't deserve that treatment. No kid does."

"I agree," Bennie said, gently.

"All this time, I figured the twins were covered. They were the favorite, and Richie was on the outs. I worried about Richie." Declan sighed. "So I asked Albert, 'Did Mommy break Mikey's arm?' And he said, 'Yes.' I couldn't believe my ears. I said to him, 'Al, did she do it on purpose?' And he said, 'Yes.' "

"Oh no."

"And then—" Declan stopped talking and hung his head, unable to continue, and Bennie reached for him, holding him close. They embraced in the silent room, hugging each other, then Declan let her go. "I wanted to take the boys home, that minute. I wanted to call the cops. I wanted to call you. I wanted to go downstairs and *kill her.*"

Bennie shuddered. "What did you do?"

"I told Albert not to tell her what he told me. I told him to keep it a secret from his mother. If she knew what he said, she'd retaliate." Declan shook his head. "I wanted to confront her, but I didn't. She would just deny it. The boys would be in danger. So I didn't say anything. I said good-bye and I told her I'd see her for Christmas. Then I left and went to the lawyer's."

"He was in?"

"No, I called him. He met me at his office. He's a good guy. I've been there all night."

"Oh boy." Bennie's heart went out to him. "You could've called me. I would've been there in a second."

"I want you as far away from this as possible." Declan pursed his lips. "She already thinks you're behind it. I don't want to play into that. I don't want to make this about you. It isn't about you, or us." Declan touched her arm. "Can you understand? That's why I didn't call. I knew you'd come."

"You were right."

"I appreciate that you want to help, but this is about my family. It's about those boys and their safety. And Richie's, too." Declan shook his head. "I never thought he'd be safer in River Street than he is at home. God knows what she's been doing to him. She must be making him keep the secret about the twins. No wonder he hates her."

"So what are you going to do?" Bennie asked, horrified.

"I don't want to take her children away from her. I would never do that. The boys are hers and so's Richie, I know that. But I want them safe and I want her to get the help she needs."

"Right, totally."

"So the lawyer and I worked out an agreement, like a temporary custody agreement. One, she has to agree to a psychiatric evaluation on herself and the twins, and two, the twins have to have a physical exam. She has to give permission for that." Declan started to count off on his fingers. "Three, she has to agree to have psychiatric treatment for six months. During that time, I would take the twins. She could see them whenever she wanted to, at my house. Four, depending on what the psychiatrists say, she could take them home on visits. Supervised in the beginning, then unsupervised, until they transition back to living with her. Fifth, she also has to agree to let Richie get help from a psychiatrist and a lawyer."

"That sounds reasonable," Bennie said, proud of him.

"I thought of it myself."

"You'd be a hell of a lawyer."

"Thank you." Declan smiled briefly. "I'm trying to offer her something she'll go for. Something that's temporary."

"How would you do that, with work?"

"I'm going to take a two-month leave of absence to get the boys settled. After that, I think it will be fine. My shift ends at three. I live in the district. They're busy after school. They usually have practice. Albert wrestles with a club team. I can get them anywhere they need to go." Declan frowned. "The lawyer said we have to deal from a position of strength. So if she's not going to agree, I'll take her to court to become their temporary guardian. Then I'll have the power to accomplish all of this myself."

"I agree with the lawyer. It's the same thing as with Richie. You go to court only if you have to, and you prepare for that eventuality."

"Right. So we set everything up for tomorrow morning." Declan checked his watch. "Three hours from now. I came back to say good-bye."

"Oh, wow." Bennie tried to wrap her mind around it.

"I know it's a disappointment. Believe me, it isn't what I wanted for this week. Christmas is coming, and I wanted to spend it together. But it can't wait. I'm afraid for those kids. She could be getting worse. I can't let it wait, not another day."

"Oh, absolutely, I'm with you. I agree. You can't wait."

"I packed the truck. I don't know if I'm going to get back here this weekend. I don't know what's gonna happen in court."

"Of course, and you can't know. You won't know." Bennie touched his arm. "This is emergency litigation, like with Jason. You have to drop everything."

"I keep thinking back through the years. Times when she told me that they fell on the ice or got in a fight. I haven't been going over like I used to."

"You didn't know."

"I wish I had; I should've thought of it."

"You couldn't have." Bennie squeezed his arm. "It's unthinkable."

"I tell myself, the past is the past. Now I know and now I have to do something about it. You can't unknow what you know. Believe me, I wish I could."

"I understand."

"So I have to go. I paid our bill. I canceled my room, starting today. I paid for your room through Friday. You can stay through Christmas if you want." Declan hugged her briefly, but Bennie could tell that his mind was already elsewhere.

"You didn't have to do that."

"I wanted to. It's the least I can do."

"No, it's not. You didn't have to." Bennie reshuffled her schedule in her mind. "I probably should get back to Philly anyway."

"Do whatever you want." Declan rose, reaching for his coat. "I have to leave now, so I can get home and change if we have to go to court."

"You want me to come with you? I'm free and I can help." Bennie got up, getting ready for him to go.

"No, thanks. I'll call you as soon as I can. Next time you see me, I could be a father of two. Sorry, *three.*" Declan patted Bear, who lifted his head from his paws, sensing change in the air. "The boys still believe in Santa Claus. I didn't get all their presents yet. I don't even have a Christmas tree." Declan crossed to the door, and Bennie followed him, managing a smile.

"You can do it."

"Thanks." Declan kissed her softly, but absently. "Wish me luck."

"Good luck," Bennie said, watching him hurry down the hall.

CHAPTER TWENTY-NINE

Bennie woke up to the sound of Bear's barking and someone knocking on her door. She threw off the covers and got up, glancing at the clock. It was 9:15, and the morning sun poured through the windows. She hustled into the bathroom and grabbed a terrycloth bathrobe to cover her nakedness.

"Hush!" Bennie said to the dog, who quieted enough so she could hear someone talking through the door.

"Ms. Rosato, I have a message from the front desk. Sorry to disturb you."

"Coming." Bennie opened the door to see the young hotel clerk who had helped with the printer and computer setup. She held a manila envelope and offered it to Bennie.

"This fax came from your office. I wouldn't have disturbed you, but your receptionist said that it's important."

"Oh, thank you." Bennie came fully awake, hoping it was an order from the Superior Court in Jason's case.

"The receptionist said she left some messages this morning on your phone, but you didn't call back."

"Thank you." Bennie's heart began to pound. "I don't have a tip on me, but I'll take care of you at checkout."

"That won't be necessary, Ms. Rosato. Good-bye now." The woman turned away, and Bennie closed the door, crossed to the bed, and sat down next to Bear.

Her hands shook as she tore open the envelope, pulled out the fax, and read an order from Judge Kittredge, containing only a few lines: **Appellant's Petition for Emergency Relief SHALL BE REFERRED to a three-judge panel of the Superior Court, which SHALL BE EMPANELED on an expedited basis to hear oral argument and render a decision within thirty (30) days from the date of this order. Appellant's Petition is hereby stayed, pending decision of the three-judge panel. It is SO ORDERED. Kittredge, J.**

"Yes!" Bennie jumped to her feet. Judge Kittredge was implicitly agreeing there was substance to her argument, but he didn't want to make a decision on his own. So he ordered that her appeal be sent to a three-judge panel, which had the power to make a ruling on such an important point of constitutional law. She wouldn't be able to get Jason out by Christmas, but if she won, he would be out in a month. It was the absolute most she could have gotten.

Bennie picked up her phone from the night table, pressing the ON button. The screen stayed black, and she realized that she had forgotten to charge it last night, which was why Marshall hadn't been able to reach her. She plugged in the phone and checked her text messages, but there was nothing from Declan. She wondered how he was doing this morning, but she didn't want to call him and interrupt, even with the good news.

Her thoughts clicked away, analyzing the legal implications of Judge Kittredge's order. If the Superior Court panel went Jason's way, it would render unlawfully imprisoned any other juvenile who had been adjudicated delinquent using the waiver form, which included Richie. Declan wouldn't even have to bring a separate suit on Richie's behalf, and both kids would be automatically free. She had no idea what other juveniles would be affected, but there had to be others, and they would be freed as well—if she won.

She scrolled through her phone contacts, pressed Matthew's number, and the phone rang once, then twice, then it was answered. "Matthew, I have wonderful news. The Superior Court just referred Jason's case to a three-judge panel, to be decided in thirty days."

"Thirty days?" Matthew groaned. "Why do we have to wait thirty more days? That's *so* long."

"I know that's later than we hoped, but it's the best we could have done in the circumstances." Bennie understood his disappointment, since he was a father, and a layman. "The Superior Court *never* acts this quickly. They only rarely grant expedited appeals, much less schedule a special sitting, just for one case. The law has limits, Matthew."

"I guess it's better than nothing."

"Yes, it really is." Bennie didn't bother to toot her own horn. She had made remarkable strides in a case that she only got a few days ago. "I'm hoping that the good news will alleviate the stress Jason's been feeling, with his hair falling out—"

"Uh, well, Bennie, I did mean to talk to you about what happened at River Street yesterday."

"Oh, yes, of course." Bennie hadn't forgotten it, but it wasn't uppermost in her mind, since Judge Kittredge's order. "I can explain—"

"You don't need to. I heard about it from Jason. I called him last night to say good night." Matthew's voice grew tense, and Bennie knew she was in trouble.

"Matthew, I'm so sorry—"

"I was very shocked to hear what he told me. Is it true that you're dating Richie's uncle?"

"Yes, but—"

"You're fired."

"What?" Bennie absorbed it like a blow.

"You're fired. You're not my lawyer anymore or my son's." Matthew's words spilled out, in agitation. "You're sleeping with Richie's uncle. That's why you're up here. That's why you're staying in Jim Thorpe. You don't care about Jason at all."

"No, that's not true!" Bennie's mouth went dry.

"How could you do such a thing? Whose side are you on? My wife must be turning over in her *grave*. Here I am, I'm scrambling to pay you, working a double, and you're sleeping with the *enemy*."

"Jason's enemy isn't Richie, it's the Commonwealth—"

"That's the problem with you lawyers! You want to talk your way out of this. You can't. You let me down. You let Jason down. You don't care about us. You tricked us. You're a traitor."

"I care about you both," Bennie said, stricken. "I care about Jason. I love—"

"Jason told me what happened with that crazy mother, busting in to see you. She attacked you while you were there with *my* son! She beat up the guard! They had to call the cops and lock the place down! What if she hurt *Jason*?"

"I wouldn't have let that happen."

"Why did you get *involved* with these people? Mother and son, they're cut from the same *crazy cloth*! The uncle's prolly nuts, too."

"He's not, he's a state trooper—"

"Defend him, why don't you!" Matthew raised his voice, angry. "I don't have time to argue with you, I have to get back to work. I'll pay what I owe you, that's it. Don't you *dare* charge me for the time you spent in bed with the uncle, either."

"Matthew, please." Bennie felt desperate. "I'm *this* close to getting Jason out of prison. We're on the *one-yard* line. Let me argue the case this month. Let me get in front of that panel and finish the job. I won't charge you a penny. I can free him, I know it."

"No, I'm done with you. I'm going to find another lawyer. One who knows what loyalty is. Send me his file or whatever you call it. Stay away from Jason."

"Matthew, no, please. Let me just go visit him." Bennie felt her heart break at the thought of leaving Jason this way. "I don't want him to think I abandoned him. Let me say good-bye to him, not for my sake, but for his. He needs—"

"I have to get back to work. Leave him alone. Go back to Philly where you belong."

"Matthew?" Bennie said, but he had hung up. She remained motionless, holding the phone and sitting on the bed. Sunlight filled the empty room, which had fallen silent. She tried to collect her thoughts, but they tumbled over one another, impossible to parse. Her heart ached, and she found herself shaking her head, saying no in answer to a question that no one was asking.

Bennie knew Jason would be hurt, and he'd see it the way Matthew did, believing that Bennie didn't care about him. She didn't know what to say or what to do. She couldn't see Jason, and she couldn't call Declan. She had won in court, but it didn't matter. A wave of despair washed over her. She had no reason to be in Jim Thorpe any longer.

It was time to go home.

CHAPTER THIRTY

Bennie opened her front door and let herself in, exhausted, cranky, and depressed. She'd thought of nothing but Jason and Matthew the whole ride home, kicking herself. She dropped her stuff on the floor, slid out of her coat, and hung it up as Bear ran ahead, leaving pawprints on the mail, scattered on the floor. She left it lying there and walked to the kitchen. Bear trotted over, his bowl in his mouth, but she took no pleasure in his trick, scooped out some kibble, and dumped it into the bowl.

She went to the cabinet, slid out a glass, and filled it with water. It overflowed quickly, but she let the water run. She couldn't stop her thoughts from coming, or her regrets. She'd never been fired by a client, much less one she cared so much about, and as a result, she had jeopardized the well-being of an innocent child. She knew, down deep, that the loss she felt was more than professional. Losing Jason was something palpable, an emotion given flesh, and it was something like a mother's love.

She turned off the water and took a sip, then dumped it out, disgusted at herself. She'd always put her client's interests first, even above her own. The one time she'd let herself follow her heart instead of her head, she had lost. And so had Jason and Matthew. She tasted bitterness on her tongue, and she knew it was guilt. She bore responsibility for whatever happened to Jason from now on. She'd been so close to saving him; she had nobody but herself to blame for losing him. She looked down at the empty glass, and on impulse, threw it full force at the far wall, where it shattered, raining broken glass.

Bear startled at his bowl, and Bennie realized that she'd just done the stupidest thing ever. If the dog walked in the glass, he'd cut his paws. She cursed herself, got the dustpan and hand broom from underneath the sink, then began cleaning up the mess she'd made for herself. She was wondering if her life had just become too literal, when the phone rang in her pocket. She set the dustpan down, then reached for the phone to see that it was Declan.

"Hi," Bennie answered, cheered. "How's it going?"

"It's going, that's all I can say." Declan sounded tense. "I don't have long to talk. I wanted to give you the heads-up."

"Great, yes, go ahead."

"Doreen wouldn't agree to anything. She denies ever hurting the boys. She thinks she doesn't need a psychiatrist and neither do they. She took back everything she said about Richie. She won't let me hire him a lawyer or psychiatrist. So, it's on."

"Oh no."

"We filed our papers. Doreen's lawyering up. I have to testify tomorrow. The boys were taken out of the house to be examined by doctors. They also have to be seen by psychiatrists. It was tough. They freaked." Declan's tone sounded pained. "Christmas Eve is tomorrow night. They want to know if Santa's still going to come. The timing couldn't be worse."

"But it couldn't be helped, either."

"Right. I know. So tonight we're going to prepare my testimony. I've testified before, but never against my own sister. I hate that I have to call her an unfit mother in public."

"You're doing the right thing, Declan. You're all in. That's what's so great about you."

"By the way, my lawyer's heard of you. He says you're famous."

"Hardly. What's his name?"

"David Zilkha. We have to meet with our psychiatrist, too. We're putting on an expert." Declan paused. "Did you hear anything from the appeals court on Jason's case?"

"Oh right." Bennie had almost forgotten. "Good news. The judge sent the case to a panel of the Superior Court, to be decided in thirty days. It will be excellent precedent for Richie."

"That's great, congratulations!" Declan brightened. "I'm so proud of you. You must be so happy."

"Not exactly." Bennie hated to break it to him, when he had so much else on his mind. "I got fired. I'm not on the case anymore. Matthew found out about what happened at River Street, and he wasn't happy."

Declan groaned. "No, that's terrible. I'm so sorry."

"Don't worry about it. It wasn't your fault."

"Yes it *was*."

"No, let it go. I'm trying to. I'm hoping Matthew gets another lawyer right away, and practically all they have to do is show up. Jason will be free, and the decision will be controlling for Richie's case, as well. That's what really matters, that these kids get out."

"Babe, I'm so sorry."

"It's okay, really. The lawyer doesn't matter, justice is what matters, right?"

"Excuse me, hold on a sec." Declan paused at the sound of talking in the background.

"Declan, if you have to go, I understand."

"I do. Sorry. I don't know if I'll get to call you tonight."

"Don't worry about it. We'll talk when you can."

"Good night," Declan said, then hung up.

Bennie hung up the phone, slipped it back into her pocket, and resumed cleaning the broken glass. It reassured her to know that Declan had gotten the twins to safety, but it didn't help Jason and Matthew. Her guilt and sadness returned, and all she wanted to do was shed her bra and street clothes, put on her sweats, and read in bed until it was time to walk the dog and go to sleep.

So she did.

The next morning, Bennie woke up refreshed, trying to put Jason out of her mind as she showered, changed into a comfy sweater and jeans, made some coffee, then walked to work with the dog. The sun was high and the wind chilly, but not brutally cold, and her house in the Fairmount section was only a half an hour stroll from the office, down the breezy Benjamin Franklin Parkway that ran from the Art Museum to Philadelphia's City Hall. Red-and-green decorations and Hanukkah lights festooned the flagpoles along the parkway, and holiday traffic was unusually congested.

Bennie reached Center City, where last-minute shoppers carried bags bulging with gifts, and she remembered that she owed Declan a Christmas gift. She headed toward Walnut Street and lingered at store windows, forgetting that she hated to shop. She had only one gift to buy, and it was for a man she had fallen in love with, so maybe she liked shopping, after all. She ended up at the Burberry store, found her way to the men's department, and picked a gray cashmere scarf, then trotted to her office with her bag.

"Hi, Bennie!" Marshall looked over from her desk, having been talking to an older African-American woman in a blue wool coat. She was petite and attractive, and bifocals couldn't hide her bright brown eyes, slightly hooded. Her hair was short and tightly coiled, interspersed with fine gray strands.

"Good morning, all." Bennie walked over, and Marshall gestured to the woman.

"Bennie, this is Yvonne Walker. She wanted to speak with you about a new matter, but I didn't know you were coming in today."

"I changed plans, sorry about that. Hello, Yvonne." Bennie extended her hand, and they shook hands while Bear sniffed Yvonne happily, always glad to meet a new client.

"What a nice dog!" Yvonne smiled, patting Bear. "He must be well trained to be able to come to the office with you."

"He knows the owner. How can I help you?"

"I was just telling your receptionist that I lost my job, last month. They fired me."

"I'm sorry to hear that." Bennie couldn't help identifying with Yvonne, but didn't say so.

Marshall interjected, "This is quite a story, Bennie. Wait'll you hear."

Yvonne smiled, warming to her topic. "I was a claims adjuster at Graham Hill Trust. You know the insurance company?"

"Yes, I do." Bennie knew GHT as a Fortune 500 company based in New York, with offices in major cities around the country, including Philadelphia.

"I was terminated because of my age. So were my two best friends. We're in our sixties, the oldest people in the department, by far." Yvonne pursed her lips, which were lightly lipsticked. "The VP called it a reorganization, but all he did was reorganize us out. They replaced us with younger people, and our performance reviews have been wonderful. We're not about to take that lying down. We're the Stitchin' Bitches."

"What?" Bennie smiled.

"It's a quilting club. That's what we call ourselves. GHT insured many businesses in lower Manhattan and the home office got hit with a flood of claims after 9/11. Ever since then, they've been watching the bottom line. 'Nobody gets bonuses for paying claims,' that's what they say."

"Ugh, for 9/11? Have a heart. Haven't those people suffered enough?"

"Precisely." Yvonne arched a perfect eyebrow. "So we want to sue them and we have proof. You see, the three of us were on a conference call last month, when two of the bosses called. They told us we have to step up denials." Yvonne sniffed, indignant. "We finished the conference and we were about to hang up, but then we heard them talking about *us*. They thought we had hung up already, but we heard *everything* they said!"

"What'd they say?" Bennie asked, intrigued.

"The boss said to the VP, 'I cannot *wait* to get rid of those *old bags*. It's like having three grannies on the phone!'"

Bennie gasped.

"That's not all!" Yvonne's dark eyes flared. "The VP said, 'I think it's about time *we checked our bags*, don't you think? Let 'em go next week!' Then they started laughing!"

"My God." Bennie could imagine how hurtful that would have been, but it was also home-run evidence of discriminatory animus. "Did anybody hear this, besides the three of you?"

"Yes. Raymond did, a young adjuster. I told him to write it down. I thought it would come in handy if they fired us. Pretty good for an *old bag*, huh?"

"Ha!" Bennie laughed, feeling her juices start flowing again. She knew employment law like the back of her hand. She was back in Philadelphia in her own law firm, legally and physically on *terra firma*. She needed to move on from Jason and Matthew.

"So, will you represent us?"

"Happily," Bennie answered. "Let's get to work."

CHAPTER THIRTY-ONE

Bennie worked in the conference room, drafting a Complaint in Yvonne's age-discrimination case. She barely noticed that darkness had fallen and it was Christmas Eve, in a city twinkling with holiday lights. In fact, she didn't even realize she had missed dinner until Lou materialized in the doorway with an aromatic bag of takeout.

"Special delivery from Lou the Jew," he said, entering the conference room and setting the bag down in front of her. "Thai red curry. Vegetarian."

"How nice of you! How did you know I was here?" Bennie looked up from her laptop, and Bear stretched and walked over to Lou, wagging his tail.

"Marshall told me you came in and she knew you'd work through dinner." Lou eased into a chair, sinking into his best camel overcoat, which he had on with a tie and jacket.

"You're dressed up." Bennie pulled the bag of Thai food over, realizing she was hungry. Bear came around her side of the table, evidently coming to the same conclusion.

"Going out to dinner with one of my buddies and his wife. She likes fancy places, so I have to wear a noose." Lou tugged at his tie. "What are you doing here? I heard you won. I thought you'd be celebrating with Sergeant Right."

184 | Lisa Scottoline

"Nah. It might be a few weeks before I see him again, which sucks."

"What happened? I got a minute." Lou cocked his head in an encouraging way.

"He got held up on some family stuff, and I got fired, so nobody feels like celebrating." Bennie reached into the bag and took out the warm white container, small enough to be rice.

"Who would fire *you*? After you won?"

"Thanks, but let's not go into it." Bennie dug her hand in the bag and pulled out the bigger container, which had to be the red curry.

"So you're not working on the juvenile case?" Lou gestured at the laptop, Xeroxed cases, notes, and empty coffee cups littering the conference table.

"No." Bennie tried not to think about Jason. She had spent much of the day pressing him to the back of her mind, with varying degrees of success. "I took an age case that came in today. It's just what the doctor ordered. I get to sue a company that thinks it's okay to deny 9/11 claims *and* make middle-aged women feel like crap."

"God's work."

"Right." Bennie popped the top of the curry, releasing an aromatic blend of Thai spices, then reached in the bag for a plastic fork. "I have a great strategy for this case. It's reminding me of what a legal genius I am, thus restoring my sagging ego."

Lou smiled. "What's the strategy?"

"Our facts are so good that instead of doing the typical barebones complaint, I'm writing the most specific complaint in history, but I'm not going to file it." Bennie took the Styrofoam plate out of the bag, then forked out some rice, making a carbohydrate nest.

"What are you going to do with it?"

"I'm going to hand-deliver it to the bad guys on Monday morning. They'll be asleep at the switch, between Christmas and New Year's." Bennie dumped red curry onto the rice, making a deliciously fragrant mess. "I'm gonna threaten them with filing it, because the statements they made are so embarrassing that it's going to be the worst press ever. Then I'm calling my reporter friends and putting them on standby for a big story, on what is otherwise the slowest news week ever. Stop me when you're amazed."

"That was three sentences ago."

"Thank you." Bennie reached for the fork and scooped some red curry, which tasted awesomely tangy, into her mouth. "I hope I can get a nice juicy settlement in short order. I don't want my clients to have to wait for their money."

"What about Christmas?"

"What about it?" Bennie gulped down another mouthful of curry. "On Thursday, I have the other plaintiffs coming in to finalize their affidavits."

"You're going to war."

" 'Tis the season."

Lou chuckled. "That's my girl. Back in the saddle."

"More or less." Bennie thought of Declan and his horses.

"What about Sergeant Right?"

"Crazy about the guy. The guy is *great*." Bennie scooped more food into her mouth, happy to be talking about Declan with the one person in the world who knew about him. She wiggled her arm to show Lou her bracelet. "Look, he gave me this. Isn't it pretty?"

"Very pretty. I'm happy for you. You deserve to be happy. Everybody does, even lawyers." Lou rose and walked to the door. "Merry Christmas, honey."

"Have fun tonight."

"Will do." Lou left, and Bennie slipped Bear some rice, then got back to work. She kept at it until almost midnight, when she left the office. She grabbed a cab going home because it was too cold and too late to walk. She didn't really expect to hear from Declan, though she would've loved to, especially on Christmas Eve. She scrolled to the text function and typed in, **merry christmas eve!** She got home in no time, and went upstairs, changed into her favorite cottony nightshirt, and climbed into bed. She read a little, then turned out the light, trying not to think of Jason, frightened and alone in his cell at River Street, motherless on Christmas Eve.

For him, she prayed.

Bennie woke up to her phone ringing beside the bed. Groggy, she reached for it, and the lighted screen read Declan. She answered right away. "Babe?"

"Hey, sorry to wake you."

"Not at all." Bennie knew from his voice that something was terribly wrong. Her bedroom was still dark. The bedside clock glowed 4:48 A.M. "What's the matter?"

"Doreen had a car accident. She's in stable condition but she almost died. I'm at the hospital."

"My God." Bennie came instantly awake, sitting up.

"She hit a tree. She had major head trauma. She's been in intensive care all night. She's stable now."

"Was she alone in the car? Where are the kids?"

"The boys were with me. There's so much to tell, I don't know where to start. The headline is, we went to court and I testified. She threw a fit in court. I got temporary custody. The judge ordered the agreement that I wanted."

Bennie's thoughts raced ahead, though she felt disoriented in the darkness. Declan's anguished voice seemed disembodied, like she was in the middle of a bad dream.

"I got home, then I got a call. I called the neighbor to stay with the boys. I doubt it was really an accident. I think she tried to kill herself."

"No!" Bennie gasped.

"It's obvious, to me." Declan's voice grew hoarse. "She drove into a tree. She wasn't wearing a seatbelt. She always wears a seatbelt. I think she wanted to die."

"Why?" Bennie blurted out, but she could guess.

"I think she couldn't take losing the boys. Her secret is out. It was just too much for her. She had to face her illness and get in-patient help. Our expert said so. Now she'll get it, that's the only silver lining."

"But oh, I'm so sorry for her, and you, and the boys. Richie, too. Does he know?" Bennie tried to wrap her mind around what happened.

"Not yet. They say she'll recover her faculties but it's going to be a long process. It'll take three months for her to even get out of the hospital, then she'll be in rehab. It's horrible." Declan sighed. "I feel horrible."

"You had no choice."

"It's still no-win. I don't know how I didn't see it before. I shouldn't have stayed away. I would've known."

"Not necessarily, you wouldn't have."

"It's done now. What's done is done." Declan hesitated. "But Bennie?"

"Yes?"

"I don't know when I can see you again."

"I know. You told me."

"No, that was before. What happened tonight changes every-thing. Now I can't do the custody plan. There's not going to be any transition back to her for a year, if that."

"You don't know that yet." Bennie swallowed hard.

"Yes I do. I talked to her doctors. I talked to the shrink. This is bigger than I thought. It will take longer than I thought. It's an emergency. I don't want you to wait around—"

"I *want* to wait around," Bennie rushed to say, afraid of where he was going. "I don't mind waiting around. Besides, I have so many things to do, I'm doing them."

"Listen." Declan's voice softened. "I was happier with you than I have ever been in my life. You know that, right?"

Bennie began to get an ominous feeling. "Declan, wait—"

"No, please listen to me. It's not our time. It's just not. We have to end it. Our timing is wrong."

"You want to break up?" Bennie asked, stricken.

"Yes," Declan answered, his tone grave. "We have to. Face it. We're snakebit."

"Snakebit?" Bennie felt her tears come to her eyes. "What does that even mean—"

"It means that as much as I want to be with you, I can't. It won't work now. There's too much to deal with here. I can't take care of things here and have a relationship."

"Sure you can, we both can." Bennie tried to recover, to convince him. "When we get the time, we can get together, we can wait—"

"No, be realistic. I can't come to Philly because I can't leave the boys alone. You can't come here because I can't have you over. It's just too much for them." Declan emitted a sigh. "I haven't even told them Doreen is in the hospital. They'll freak. It's too much pressure on us. This isn't what you bargained for."

"I can change the bargain, I can be flexible. You're worth being flexible for."

"No, please. It's not fair to you. It's not fair to us. It's not fair to the twins." Declan's tone turned final. "You like that I'm 'all in.' Well, I'm 'all in' with these boys. If I don't give them a hundred percent now, they'll turn out like Richie. I can't let that happen. Not on my watch. I couldn't live with myself."

"Declan, we don't have to decide this now. It's too fresh. It just happened with Doreen. You haven't had time to process it."

"Yes, I have. I know how I feel. I know what I need to do, even if it's not what I want. These boys were brought into this world and they deserve more. Let me go, Bennie. Let us go. Try to understand."

"I *don't* understand!" Bennie blurted out, her throat catching.

"Aw, babe, don't cry."

"I'm not," Bennie said, tears brimming in her eyes. "You don't have to do this, not now. Just think it over."

"I thought about it. I'm doing the right thing for everybody."

"Not for me!" Bennie cried, raising her voice.

"It is. I know it is." Declan's resolve seemed to strengthen.

"These boys are my responsibility. This is my family. It's my house and I have to get it in order."

"But I can help—"

"I don't need help. If you want to help me, then let me do what I need to do. Let me go."

"I can't!"

"Yes you can. You can do anything. You're strong—"

"Declan, I'm not that strong, I'm begging you—"

"Don't, please. You know I'm right. I have to hang up. Take care of yourself."

"Declan, no, I love you!" Bennie cried out, desperate.

"Good-bye, sweetheart. Forgive me. I love you, too." Declan hung up, and the call went dead.

Bennie pressed REDIAL, frantic. She listened to her call ring, wiping her eyes. There had to be a way she could convince him. She had told him she loved him, and he loved her back. She couldn't let him go now. She couldn't let him go, ever. The call went to voicemail, but she hung up and pressed REDIAL again, a frantic urge she couldn't control and didn't try. Her whole life had been about arguing back, convincing, persuading when there was no hope of success, and she wasn't about to stop now. She couldn't take no for an answer, not to a question that mattered the most.

The phone rang and rang in her ear, then it went to voicemail again.

She hung up and pressed REDIAL, with tears in her eyes.

CHAPTER THIRTY-TWO

The next few days were a blur in which Bennie went through the motions but felt lost in her own world, disconnected from everyone around her. She woke up Christmas morning, forcing herself not to call Declan anymore or check the phone for texts or emails from him. She took off her bracelet and put it in the bottom drawer of her jewelry box, so she wouldn't have to look at it again. She put the cashmere scarf she'd bought him on the top shelf of the closet and spent the rest of Christmas finishing Yvonne's complaint. She went to the office the day after Christmas, met Yvonne and the other two plaintiffs, and hammered out detailed affidavits on her laptop. She spent the weekend finalizing the affidavits and by Monday morning had the complaints and the affidavits ready, then she had them hand-delivered to GHT and waited for the bomb to explode.

The associates came back from Miami, and Bennie listened to their funny vacation stories, trying to be a part of the action, but apart from it, inside. It struck her that none of them knew about Declan, Jason, or anything that had happened in her life, which had been turned upside down and then right-side up again, so that it looked exactly the way it always had, but was, in fact, utterly changed.

The rest of the month went much the same way, with the world getting back to business after the holidays, the clients calling with questions, the old cases becoming active again, and new cases coming in. Bennie got a hefty settlement for Yvonne and the others, and in any other frame of mind, she would've been deliriously happy. But she was muting her emotions, distancing herself from her own heart, so she felt only as if she had checked a box, completed a task on the Things-to-Do list entitled Getting Back to Normal.

Bennie noticed that in time she thought about Declan less and less, and she stopped checking her phone for texts. Lou would ask her about Sergeant Right, but she put him off and he stopped. She got an official notice from the Superior Court on Jason's case scheduling oral argument, which meant she was still Attorney of Record and Matthew hadn't hired another lawyer yet. She called him several times to ask what was going on, but he didn't answer or return her calls.

The time for oral argument came and went, then she got another notice from the Superior Court, dismissing Jason's appeal for lack of prosecution. She read it again and again, heartbroken. Matthew must never have hired another lawyer. It didn't make sense, but she couldn't figure out what happened. She'd tried to put the case out of her mind, but she didn't succeed. She couldn't forget Jason. She couldn't stand not knowing whether he was still in River Street, moved to the new facility, or back in middle school. She called River Street, but didn't get an answer, so she assumed it had been closed completely. She called the new facility, PA Childcare, but they wouldn't give her any information over the phone, one way or the other.

So one Sunday afternoon, Bennie found herself driving back up north, keeping her emotions at bay. She was determined not to feel a single feeling today, but only to gather information. She drove to PA Childcare in Pittston, though it wasn't easy to find, unsigned and surrounded by dark brown woods, covered with snow and ice. She pulled into the long, winding driveway, which led down into a new parking lot, then got out of the car.

The building was brand-new and modern, a sprawling low-profile edifice with a flat roof and an exterior of large brown bricks below, but tan bricks above. Behind it was a paved yard bordered by shiny new cyclone fencing and atop it, barbed concertina wire that glinted in the sun. She walked to the glass box of an entrance, set under a brick overhang, and entered a harshly bright anteroom with a tan tile floor and eggshell-white walls that smelled of fresh paint. There was a window with a smoked glass barricade, scored with a large hole in the center, and behind it she recognized Stan Dulaney, the young guard.

"Hey, old friend!" Bennie called out, and Stan turned, breaking into a smile and coming over to the window.

"Hi, how you been, counselor? What do you think of the new place?" Stan gestured around him in a proprietary way. "A damn sight better than River Street, eh?"

"It sure is. I'm sure it's better for you, and for the kids."

"I saw they took you off the visitors' list. What's up with that?" Stan frowned.

"I hope Jason got another lawyer." Bennie didn't elaborate. "Did he?"

"Not that I know of." Stan shrugged.

"I just came up to check on him. Is he still here?"

"Lefkavick? Sure. Where else would he be?"

Bennie's heart sank. "Can I see him?" she asked, hoping against hope.

"No, sorry." Stan shook his head, his lower lip puckering. "Wish I could. You know that."

"I know. Tell me, how is he? How's he doing?"

"He's okay, I guess." Stan glanced behind him, then leaned closer to the glass. "Totally bald now. Got no eyebrows. It's not a good look, to be honest, like a hard-boiled egg. He wears that cap you gave him, but it doesn't help."

Bennie sighed inwardly. "Do they tease him?"

"What do you think?"

"Did he ever see a doctor?"

"Not that I know of."

"How about a psychiatrist? Dr. Vita?"

"I don't know, sorry." Stan shrugged. "Don't worry. He's only got, like, two weeks left. All he has to do is keep his nose clean. If he doesn't reoffend, he's home free."

"Right." Bennie tried not to feel the tightness in her chest.

"We just got a kid back, he reoffended and he got a five-year sentence for aggravated assault. He's not getting out of the system until he's eighteen."

"Jason's not that kind of kid." Bennie hesitated. "How about Richie Grusini, who came in with Jason? Is he still here?"

"Yes, he went home but he's back. Got in another fight at school. Ninety-day sentence this time." Stan shook his head. "The uncle sees him all the time. He brings the twin boys every Sunday. Cute kids." Stan checked behind him, again. "We got new rules here, really strict. I don't think they'd like me giving you this information."

"Understood. Take care of yourself."

"You, too," Stan said, turning away from the window.

Bennie stood still a moment, alone in the entrance hall, unable to leave the building just yet. She tried to imagine Jason somewhere inside, behind the locked doors and the painted cinderblock walls, all by himself. She wished she could burst through the doors, knock down the walls, and claw her way to him, then grab him, drive off with him, and set him free. But she couldn't, and she didn't. She had to let him go.

She left the building and walked to her car, shoving her hands in her pockets, her head down. She hoped the tension in her chest would dissipate and she climbed into her car, started the ignition, and left the grounds, making her way over the snowy back roads. She drove on autopilot, without really focusing, her heart aching and her breathing shallow. She had driven these roads before, and it was almost as if her car were driving itself. Or at least, that was what she told herself when she turned onto the back road that led to Declan's.

Bennie reached his house and slowed to a stop on the street, leaving the engine running. She didn't know why she was here, but she couldn't *not* come. Snow lay everywhere in a pristine blanket, marked only by deer tracks, and nobody was outside.

Smoke curled from the chimney on his roof, but she couldn't tell if there were lights on inside. His truck was parked next to the barn, so he had to be home, and she felt an ache in her chest, the sensation undeniable.

She thought about going in to see him, and how easy it would be. All she had to do was turn off the engine, get out of the car, and knock on his door. The twins would probably be there, too, but she would find a way to explain her presence. If she went in, she would get to see Declan. She would get to hold him again. She could whisper in his ear, hear him laugh, talk to him. She imagined them stealing a kiss, maybe even sneaking upstairs to his bedroom.

It could happen. She could make it happen. But she knew she wouldn't. Because she couldn't be alone with Declan and hide the truth.

That she was pregnant with their child.

Bennie hit the gas. She loved him.

So she let him go.

PART TWO

Philadelphia, January 2015

I see it all perfectly; there are two possible situations—one can either do this or that. My honest opinion and my friendly advice is this: do it or do not do it—you will regret both.

—Søren Kierkegaard

CHAPTER THIRTY-THREE

Bennie faced the front of Arraignment Court, fighting for emotional control. Declan was entering the courtroom, somber as he supported a distraught Doreen, who had aged more than he had. Identical teenage boys with dark hair and long bangs were with them, their expression stricken, and they had to be the twins, Richie's brothers Mike and Albert. Behind the group was a pretty, petite blonde in her thirties. Bennie wondered if she was with Declan, his girlfriend, or even his wife.

The sight of them sent her into a mental tailspin, corkscrewing backwards through time. She flashed on an image of Declan's face, his confident smile. His arms, his body. The two of them, their heads together, talking in bed all night. She heard the sound of his deep, rich laugh. The terse rhythm of his sentences. She felt the brush of his razor stubble.

The entire courtroom seem to recede for a moment, and the gray-white walls, the modern black pews, the floor-to-ceiling bulletproof glass that separated the bar of court from the gallery, all of her surroundings fell away from her. Bail Commissioner Holloway, in his suit and tie, shuffled papers on his desk at the dais, and yet another defendant appeared on the closed-circuit-TV screen, but all of them went out of focus. The assistant district attorney stood up and said something, then the female public defender replied, their amplified discussion piped through the courtroom, but Bennie could barely hear their voices, lost in her own world.

We're snakebit.

Bennie hadn't seen Declan for thirteen years, and she was astounded that her feelings were that fresh, the wound still new, and the memory of him sharp enough to leave a bleeding edge. She never would have believed it if she hadn't experienced it, but there was a physical reaction. Her cheeks were on fire, her mouth went dry. It didn't feel like love: it felt like panic. She thought she'd sent those emotions packing, but evidently they'd been lying in wait, perfectly preserved in a part of her mind she never accessed, like a room nobody opened anymore.

Her heart was pounding, but she tried to get her act together. Bail Commissioner Holloway was speaking on the closed-circuit-TV screen; Bennie heard Declan and the others whispering among themselves, but Bennie couldn't understand the words. Declan had to have recognized her; she was the only other person in the gallery and she was six feet tall, with a messy blonde topknot.

Her mind raced. She had to have understood at some level that Declan could reappear tonight, but she hadn't let herself think about that. He would be totally unprepared to see her because he couldn't have known that Jason would call her. Or maybe he did know, maybe he was prepared, she had no way to tell. Either way, he had to be hating her now, for representing Jason in Richie's murder.

Bail Commissioner Holloway banged his gavel, then the monitor screen went to static gray before the next defendant would appear. The courtroom fell abruptly silent, and Bennie could hear Declan and the others settling into a pew in the middle of the courtroom, on the right, as far as possible from her. They were still whispering, though she didn't know why, then she realized they didn't want her to hear, because there was no one else in the room.

Bennie checked her watch, 7:45 A.M. She shifted position on the hard pew, trying to get her head in the game. The purpose of an arraignment was to formally charge the accused with a crime, as well as to set bail. Murder wasn't generally bailable in Philadelphia, so Bennie wasn't expecting to win, but Jason deserved her best try. She owed him nothing less and she couldn't blow a second chance to help him.

"Next up is *Commonwealth v. Lefkavick*." Bail Commissioner Holloway recited the docket number, then turned to the bailiff. "Please, let's have defendant, Jason Lefkavick."

Suddenly, the static on the monitor vanished and Jason's face popped into view on the screen. He looked subdued and tired, his eye swollen a darker pink. Bennie rose and left the pew, hearing Doreen talking loudly behind her.

"What the *hell*, Declan?" Doreen was saying. "Is that *her*? She's back? And what, he gets to be on *TV*? He doesn't have to face me? He doesn't have to look me in the eye for what he did to my son?"

Bennie tuned out Doreen, crossed to the transparent door at the bar of court, and was buzzed in. She went to the lectern as the public defender stepped aside, saying, "May it please the court, Bennie Rosato for defendant Jason Lefkavick."

"Good morning, counsel." Bail Commissioner Holloway shifted some papers on his desk, and the public defender sat down at counsel table, which held a system telephone. Bennie would have to use the phone if she wanted to speak with Jason, but the bail commissioner, assistant district attorney, public defender, and even Declan and his family would be able to hear. Bennie always thought the procedure violated the right to counsel, never more ironic than in this case.

"Thank you, counsel." Bail Commissioner Holloway looked into the camera facing him. "Mr. Lefkavick, I am the bail commissioner. Stay facing the camera and speak clearly, please."

"Okay." Jason squinted into the camera, his eyes narrow and his head tilted slightly back, which gave him a hostile demeanor. Watching him, Bennie wondered if he'd become his own worst enemy.

Bail Commissioner Holloway continued, "Mr. Lefkavick, you have been charged on the general charge of murder, do you understand?"

"Yes."

"Thank you." Bail Commissioner Holloway turned to the prosecutor's table. "Is the Commonwealth opposing bail in this matter?"

"Absolutely, Your Honor." The assistant district attorney went to his lectern. "This was a senseless and vicious murder of an innocent victim, whose throat was slashed and who bled to death. In addition, Your Honor, the defendant is most definitely a flight risk, and under no circumstances should the possibility of bail even be considered."

"Thank you, counsel." Bail Commissioner Holloway turned to Bennie. "Ah, Ms. Rosato. You've been sitting there a long time. I'm sure you have something to say about whether your client should receive bail."

"I do, Your Honor." Bennie adjusted the microphone, making it higher. "I am requesting bail for Mr. Lefkavick. Though it's true that he's able to travel, he has neither the intent nor means to do so. He lives in the city and has a job which he enjoys and he needs to work."

"Does he have roots in the city?"

"Not in the city, but in the area. He grew up in Mountain Top, Pennsylvania." Bennie knew it was one of the standard factors to consider, though she felt strange saying it in front of Declan, Doreen, and the boys.

"Does he have any family in the city?"

"No, Your Honor. His mother and father are deceased, but he has friends and coworkers in the city."

"How long has he lived here?"

"Six months, Your Honor."

"Does he rent or own?"

"He rents, Your Honor."

"Thank you, counsel." Bail Commissioner Holloway pursed his lips, then turned to the camera. "Mr. Lefkavick, I am denying bail in this matter. Please sign the paper in front of you. You will come back to court and appear at your preliminary hearing." Bail

Commissioner Holloway banged the gavel. "This concludes your arraignment."

"Okay, Your Honor," Jason said, before he vanished into static.

"Thank you, Your Honor." Bennie turned, went to the bullet-proof door, and when they buzzed her, pushed it open into the courtroom, where she had no choice but to face in Declan's direction. He was comforting Doreen, who was crying in his arms, her hoarse sobs echoing in the gallery. Bennie felt a wave of guilt, and Declan didn't meet her eye. Neither did the twins, but the blonde did, resentment etched on her pretty features.

Bennie went back to her pew, stalling to give them time to leave before her. She zipped up her coat slowly, noticing that Declan had managed to get Doreen on her feet and was guiding them all out of the pew and into the aisle. They went outside into the hall-way huddled together, and only then did Doreen begin to cry in earnest, her sobs heartbreakingly loud.

Bennie swallowed hard, trying not to feel the twisting in her gut. She waited until she couldn't hear crying anymore, then rose, left the courtroom, and climbed the stairs to the lobby, swimming upstream against the court clerks, bailiffs, administrative staff, security guards, and other courthouse employees arriving at the Criminal Justice Center. To them, it was another day in the justice business, but not to Bennie, Jason, Declan, or Doreen.

For her and for them, it was the beginning of a reckoning.

CHAPTER THIRTY-FOUR

By the time Bennie got back to the office, everyone was in the conference room for their weekly meeting. She ducked her head inside to see them milling around the brewing pot of coffee at the credenza, Mary yammering about her upcoming wedding with Marshall and Judy, and Anne being chatted up by John Foxman, their new male associate. Bennie was getting the impression that Foxman was attracted to Anne and Judy, a love triangle that Rosato & DiNunzio needed like a hole in the head. She'd learned the hard way that law and love didn't mix.

Lou looked over. "Bennie, aren't you coming in?"

"I can't. How busy are you?"

"For you, I have time. Why?" Lou set down his coffee, and everyone else turned in her direction.

"Hello and good-bye, all." Bennie flashed a quick smile. "I can't stay because I picked up a murder case last night. Lou, can you come with me?"

"Sure," Lou answered, already in motion. "Let me go get my coat. Meet you at the elevator."

"Great, thanks." Bennie let Lou pass her.

Mary smiled, cocking her head. "Bennie, why'd you take a murder case? Is it high-profile?"

Judy chimed in, "I didn't see anything online."

"We're court-appointed," Bennie lied, not about to fill them in.

Anne raised a manicured hand. "I can take a murder case. I'm not that busy."

"No, I got it." Bennie kept her face a mask. "If you're not that busy, please watch my desk for me. I'll be gone most of the day."

"Okay."

"Thanks, bye." Bennie left the conference room, met Lou at the elevator, and they climbed inside.

"So fill me in, boss."

"Remember that juvenile case I had a long time ago? Like thirteen years ago?"

"Honey, I don't remember yesterday." Lou chuckled.

"Remember that trooper that I dated? Sergeant Right?"

"Oh. *That* guy. Him, I remember." Lou's eyes flared.

"Exactly, and he's the uncle of the victim. My client in the murder case is the boy from the juvenile case."

"Oy." Lou exhaled loudly. "Give this case to Anne. You don't need the aggravation. It took you years to get over that guy."

"Not really." Bennie knew it was true, but it wasn't only about Declan. It was about the baby, whom she still thought about, when she permitted herself. The elevator reached the ground floor, where they stepped out and crossed the lobby together.

"I bet you're *still* not over him."

"I *am* over him," Bennie said, though she wasn't.

"Now I understand why you're so cockamamie today."

"I'm not cockamamie today," Bennie said, though she was.

"Meanwhile I can't wait to meet this jerk. Introduce me, I'll punch his lights out." Lou pushed the exit door and held it open for Bennie while she went out and looked for a cab. It was a cloudy day, gray and colorless, but that could've been her mood. People hurried past them on the sidewalk, looking at smartphones and carrying covered cups of overpriced coffee. The street was congested with the morning rush, and a few blocks up, behind a white boxy SEPTA bus, was a Yellow cab, which flashed its headlights at her.

"Why?"

"For breaking your heart."

"He didn't break my heart. It was the circumstances."

"Oh please." Lou shook his head. "The guy's a jerk. What was his name again?"

"Declan."

"Even a stupid name." Lou rolled his eyes. "I keep telling you, you need one of the tribe. All these guys I want to fix you up with, and you won't go."

"I'm not in the market right now." Bennie watched the cab get stuck in traffic.

"You haven't been in the market since *Declan*."

"Don't be silly. I've seen Grady since him." Bennie looked over to see Lou's shrewd blue eyes narrowing. He didn't look much older than he had then, except for deeper lines on his forehead, weathered from weekend fishing, and a tiny surgical scar on the tip of his strong nose.

"You wouldn't commit to Grady. The two of you, always off and on. The world doesn't stand still, Bennie. You have to shit or get off the pot. You were never all in with him, and he knew it."

All in. Bennie thought of Declan. "Okay, enough. Could we get back to the murder case, not my love life?"

"Evidently, the murder case *is* your love life." Lou wagged his arthritic finger at her. "He's the one that got away. Everybody has one, and he's yours. But here's the thing you gotta realize, Bennie. Sometimes the one that gets away, gets away for a reason."

"Thank you, Oprah."

"After they get away, you build them up. You didn't get enough time to hate each other."

"Are you serious?" Bennie saw the Yellow cab move a few feet, then stop again.

"Mark my words. I know, I'm divorced twice. How long were you and him together?"

"A weekend." Bennie knew it sounded like a short time, but it only took a weekend to turn a life upside down, because it had hers.

"Like I said. So don't build him up." Lou pursed his thin lips. "And anyway, why aren't you in the market? Don't you want to have kids?"

"If it's not going to happen, it's not going to happen." Bennie cringed inwardly. She would tell Lou a lot, but she wouldn't tell him everything. Not the things she didn't tell herself.

"Bennie, you're too young to close up shop."

"Lou, I'm a woman, not a store."

"Forget this guy. Get out of this case."

"No." Bennie wished the cab would get here already. "Declan and the case are two different things. Our client is Jason Lefka-vick. His father fired me, and it was because I was with Declan. I owe him one. I got a chance to redeem myself and I'm not going to blow it."

"Okay, so what's the facts?"

"Jason sees Richie Grusini, his childhood enemy, in a bar and they get into it. They get tossed, and Jason follows Richie into an alley, where he was taking a leak."

"Classy."

"They get into it again, in the alley. Jason ends up unconscious on the ground and when he wakes up, there's a knife in his hand. He says it's not his, and Richie is dead, his throat cut. He says he was framed. He says he didn't do it. I believe him."

"When were *you* born? Yesterday or the day before?"

"I don't think he did it. Richie was a bad actor. I'm sure he had enemies. We have to find them."

"Did his enemies know he'd get in a bar fight? Did they happen to have a knife on hand, so they could plant it on our unsuspecting client? Right off the bat, it's obvious his story's a lie."

"Try not to prejudge, Lou." Bennie watched as the cab headed toward them, switching lanes.

"Did they offer him a deal?"

"We said no. He doesn't want one."

"Why not?" Lou frowned.

"Because he didn't do it, and he believes I can prove him innocent. He trusts me. Still." Bennie's mouth went dry. "I'm going to take him to trial and get an acquittal."

"Whether he's innocent or not. Welcome to the NFL."

"No." Bennie felt relieved to see the cab almost to them. "He deserves the best defense I can give him and he's entitled to the presumption of innocence. You should give him that, too. We're his legal team, and believe me, we're all he's got."

"See, *this* is what I love about you!" Lou gestured grandly. "There's a legal presumption of innocence, and you pretend it's not a joke."

"Thank you, I think." Bennie permitted herself a smile, as the cab pulled up and Lou opened the door for her. She climbed inside, sliding over, and Lou got in behind her, closing the door. She leaned toward the driver. "Hi, we need to get to Eddie's Bar on Pimlico Street in Port Richmond. The cross street is Dunbar."

"No problem," the cabbie said, lurching into traffic.

Lou looked over, brightening. "Port Richmond? I love it up there. They say it's gentrifying, but I liked it better before. I hate yuppies."

"Nobody says 'yuppies' anymore."

"*I* do. I say everything nobody says anymore. I make it a point." Lou's eyes lit up. "We should get a pizza at Tacconelli's. You have to call ahead to reserve the dough, that's how good it is. Plus we could swing by Stock's on the way back, take a nice pound cake back to the office. You like vanilla or chocolate?"

"Either."

"Hmph." Lou reached in his pocket for his phone. "I'm calling about the dough."

Later, the cab slowed to a stop as it approached Eddie's, in the middle of the block, but Bennie spotted police cruisers parked at the entrance to Dunbar Street. "Lou, I think that's the scene, midblock on Dunbar."

Lou craned his neck. "Looks like they're breaking it down."

"Driver, you can stop here," Bennie said, and the cab pulled over, double-parking behind one of the cruisers.

"I'll go talk to the uniforms and work my blue magic." Lou hustled out of the cab, leaving the back door ajar. Blue magic was his cop network, which came in handy on their cases.

But Bennie had a feeling this case was going to take that, and much more.

CHAPTER THIRTY-FIVE

Bennie stood at the entrance to the alley, in horror. Blood stained the filthy concrete floor, glistening in the shade and blacker in color where the concrete sloped down. She realized that she had never met Richie, who was so hated by Jason and so loved by Declan, and it seemed awful that she would see his blood before she had seen him. Despair swept over her, as well as sorrow that it had come to this, regardless of who had killed him; Richie had been a victim as surely as Jason had, of his own mother. And his benighted, troubled, tragic life had ended here, too soon.

Bennie tuned out the activity behind her, the uniform cops who were talking to Lou, gathering the yellow plastic tape, or loading wooden sawhorses onto a municipal truck to be carted off, now that the crime scene had been released. She wondered if Declan had been here and seen the blood, and knowing him, she guessed he had. She couldn't imagine the grief that he'd felt at the sight. She didn't know whether he'd gotten custody of Richie, but that wouldn't have mattered. Declan loved Richie, and it would have killed him to lose the boy, especially this way.

Bennie found herself walking toward the blood, her step as reverent as a funeral procession. She caught a whiff of its distinctive metallic odor, mixing with the garbage smells, then stopped at the edge of the dark pool. The blood was so still that it reflected the light from the sky, like a dark red mirror. On impulse, she knelt, eyeing its surface, which had frozen, forming a thin red crust. She looked down and saw her own image looking back at her.

She realized with a start that Richie's blood was a part of her. He had been Declan's nephew, and she had been pregnant with Declan's child, so this very blood had been inside her body, and the very same DNA had flowed through the veins of her own child. She had lost the baby, miscarried when she was two-and-a-half months pregnant, and she would never forget that night, down to the most minute detail. She'd gone to the bathroom, and there was blood on the tile floor, drops like so many red starbursts. Then there was blood in the toilet, too, and other things, but that was too much of a memory to bear.

Bennie found herself reaching toward the dark mirror, unconsciously hoping to reconnect with something long gone.

"Bennie, what the hell are you doing?" Lou called out, hurrying up behind her. "Don't touch that! God knows what's in it. He could've had AIDS, Hep C, or anything."

Bennie came out of her reverie, rising, and Lou helped her to her feet, frowning with concern.

"Are you okay?"

"I'm just tired is all." Bennie composed herself, swallowing hard. "I didn't get any sleep last night."

"Hmph." Lou gestured at the blood, his lip curling in distaste. "They couldn't clean up the blood last night because the hose froze. They left to get some hot water."

"Okay. So. What did you learn? Anything?"

"Yes." Lou gestured to the left side of the alley, which was wide. "This is where the victim parked his truck. That's why he came into the alley, he parked here."

"Good to know."

"Also, I found out there's seven stores that have street cameras on Pimlico. There's also cameras on the traffic lights at either end of Dunbar. The detectives and the uniforms canvassed last night and they're getting the videos. I assume they're going to show our boy going into the alley after the victim."

"The cumulative effect won't be good at all, and you know the D.A. will try to use every one. I've never known a prosecutor to be subtle." Bennie got her head into the game. "But who knows? They could show someone else coming into the alley."

"That would be nice. Do you believe in Santa?"

Bennie let it go. "They could show somebody leaving it, too."

"Like I said."

"Or what actually happened during the fight. How Jason got knocked out. Who planted the knife on him." Bennie tried to visualize the fight, at the location of the bloodstain. "But forget that, I think the pallets would block the view from the street."

"And it would've been dark." Lou glanced around at the roofs of the buildings on either side of the alley, which were two stories high. "I don't see any security lights or motion detectors."

"Me neither." Bennie faced the back of the alley and saw that it didn't go through to the opposite street, but ended in a cinder-block wall, some five feet high. A recycling bin sat in front of the wall, and a trash can lay on its side. She gestured at the cinder-block wall. "Anybody could've gone over that wall. That's not very high. They could've used the trash cans to climb up. The ledge on top is flat, so it's easy to get over."

"How can you stand on the side of a trash can? It would roll like a log."

"Maybe somebody stood on it when it was on its side, then it fell over when they jumped back over the fence."

Lou arched a graying eyebrow. "So you think somebody could come in the other side?"

"Yes, that's possible. That's consistent with what Jason tells us."

"Why? How would they know? You think there was noise? Nothing's open in this street at night, and it's not residential." Lou pointed left, then right. "This left wall is a check-cashing agency, now out of business, and the right wall is the back of a medical supply company, which was closed at that hour."

"I don't know, I can't answer that yet." Bennie knew it was the question Lou had raised before, but she was trying to develop reasonable doubt. "I was hoping the alley was open on the back, which would be a slam dunk."

"Bennie, think about this for a minute. I don't think Jason is leveling with us."

"Lou, you said you were going to give him the presumption."

"I'm not saying that he's guilty. I'm saying that maybe it didn't happen the way he said." Lou cocked his head. "He tells you that he didn't know who the knife belonged to and that he woke up with it in his hand. But maybe what happened is that he followed the victim into the alley and the two got in a fight." Lou walked down the alley and stopped before the blood. "Pretend I'm Jason, and I want to finish what I started in the bar. I pick a fight with the victim while he's trying to take a leak. Who's the victim again?"

"Richie."

"All of a sudden, Richie pulls a knife on me. I have to defend myself. I get the knife from him and I kill him in self-defense. Isn't that more likely than somebody planting the knife, *framing* me?"

"It's possible, sure."

"Bennie, who's more likely to carry a knife, Jason or Richie?"

"Richie."

"So that fits my theory." Lou nodded.

"It's certainly possible, but it's not what Jason said."

"He wouldn't be the first client to lie to us."

"Why would he lie?"

"Because knuckleheads lie all the time, and he's a knucklehead!" Lou threw up his hands. "He tells you a story that makes him look like he doesn't know anything. He think that makes him look less guilty, when it doesn't. Why? Because he's a knucklehead!"

"I don't know, Lou." Bennie couldn't bring herself to agree.

"Okay. Try another scenario. The knife could've been Jason's. Is that possible?"

"Yes."

"Maybe Jason comes in the alley and he pulls the knife on

Richie. He doesn't want to kill him, he wants to scare him." Lou clapped his hands together. "But Richie calls his bluff and grabs the knife from him. They struggle, and our client kills the victim in self-defense. That could've happened too, couldn't it?"

"Yes, it could have," Bennie conceded.

"Who's bigger?"

"Richie."

"There.

"So if that was me, and I was the knucklehead, and it's my knife, I wouldn't *say* it was my knife. That would make me look really guilty. I mean, you walk in with a knife, you're the bad guy. So I say, 'I don't know where the knife came from.'" Lou smiled, newly animated. "Do you know the stories that knuckleheads tell? Do you know the *lies* they try to get away with? You know my favorite all-time knucklehead story?"

"I forget."

"We get a call that somebody stole a TV in Northern Liberties. So me and my partner, we're in the neighborhood and, lo and behold, we see a guy running down the street with a TV. We roll up and stop him. I say to him, 'Yo, where'd you get that TV?' He says, 'What TV?'" Lou burst into laughter. "'*What TV!*' Can you beat that? No! Bennie, don't you see? That's all our client is doing. He's just saying, '*What knife?*' 'I don't know nothin' about no knife!'"

"You might be right, but let's table it for now." Bennie looked back at the back wall. "I still wonder about that wall, if a person could climb it, and what's on the other side."

"Of course you do, because you're stubborn. I assume it's Yearling Street, but there's only one way to find out."

"Yes, I know." Bennie looked down at Richie's blood, which lay between them and the wall. "But I don't want us walking through this blood. It's disrespectful."

"And a health hazard." Lou cocked his head. "What about if we approach the wall from the other side? Let's go around the block, go down Yearling, and scale the wall from there." Lou slid his phone from his coat pocket. "But first let's take pictures of the

212 I Lisa Scottoline

way we found everything in the alley, before the uniforms get back with the hot water."

"Okay." Bennie pulled her phone from her purse, then took pictures of everything she saw, knowing she would study them for hours between now and the day of trial. Lou did the same thing, and they walked back and forth, in and out of the alley, taking pictures of everything. Bennie poked around in the litter that lay everywhere in the alley, just in case somebody had dropped something or something had fallen, but she found nothing noteworthy, while Lou measured the relevant distances, walking off the feet with his Wallabees.

"The alley is sixteen feet wide where he parked, and a truck is generally about eight feet wide, so there's not much room to move. The alley narrows to eight feet after the parking spot, and it's about five-hundred feet to the wall in back. I'm guesstimating."

"Good to know." Bennie made a note in her pad, and they looked at each other. Nobody had come to wash the blood away, and it lay freezing in the shade.

"Wait here a minute. I'll go see what happened to the uniforms." Lou walked away, dumping the pallets where they'd been, and Bennie took more pictures, wrote more notes, and poked around more trash until Lou came back with two men in long white aprons stained with blood and short rubber boots, also bloody.

Bennie gasped. "Is this a nightmare?"

"No, this is Nacho and Diego, and they don't speak English." Lou gestured at the two men. "They work at the Polish butcher shop and they're willing to help us for only twenty dollars apiece. See those doors down there, on the right?" He pointed, and Bennie noticed two black metal doors on the right wall toward the back of the alley. "The closer one is the back door of the butcher shop. They get their deliveries this way, which between you and me, can't comply with any code. Don't tell L & I. In any event, when it comes to cleaning up blood, they're the experts."

"But where are the cops?"

"Nowhere to be found, and their cars are gone."

"Isn't it their job to clean up a crime scene?"

"Technically, no. It's the job of the homeowner or the property owner, but nobody's claiming ownership of a bloody alley. Our new friends have a hose that runs hot water, so come out and let them do their stuff."

"Okay, thanks." Bennie left the alley and stood next to Lou, then one of the men turned on the hose and squirted the blood, while the other started sweeping reddish water toward a drain with a push broom. Steam rose from the blood the moment hot water hit it, and the metallic smell filled the air, making Bennie queasy.

"You okay, kid?" Lou put an arm around her. "Why don't you wait in the street until they're finished?"

"I'm okay," Bennie said, but she held on to Lou. She watched the powerful hose spray the blood toward the drain, turning up the trash and litter from the bottom of the alley, like the most grotesque sort of washing machine. A ballpoint pen, a cigarette lighter, a long tube sock, a slew of cigarette butts, handwritten papers, a hoagie wrapper, a baby pacifier, newspapers, and a condom flowed toward the drain, human detritus like shards of life among the death.

None of it made any sense to Bennie, all of this blood and loss, and after they had washed the blood away, she still couldn't get it from her mind, even as she checked the back wall, and the trash cans, searching for something she didn't completely understand.

CHAPTER THIRTY-SIX

Bennie rallied as they left the alley and turned onto Pimlico, backtracking along the route that Jason would have taken last night. Pimlico wasn't a major artery, but it had two-lane traffic and was lined with small businesses that had seen better days. They passed the medical supply store, its glass front covered with peeling ads, then the Polish butcher, marked by a red-and-white awning that read STAN'S FINEST HOMEMADE POLISH KIELBASY, above a handpainted list of items: Pasztet, Zwyczajna, Salceson Wloski, Krakowska Swieza, Mysliwska!

"No yuppies here," Lou said, with approval.

They approached Eddie's Bar, a small neighborhood tavern with one tiny window stuck into a grimy white stucco wall, and it had a neon sign that flickered Lech's Beer, next to which someone had graffitied Blech's Beer! Old cardboard placards rested on the windowsill: 6 Packs To Go. Credit Cards Not Accepted. Phillies World Series Champions 2008.

Lou eyed the bar, with a growing smile. "This looks like a great dive bar."

"Is that a thing?"

"Of course, like the Irish Pub. Don't you know that bar?"

"Have we met? I don't spend a lot of time barhopping."

"How about Doobies? You'd like that place. The owner won't

carry Coors because of the seal hunt in Canada. I bet he's a vegetarian, too."

"Good, I'll say hi at the next vegetarian convention."

They reached the entrance to Eddie's, and a concrete step to a plain wooden front door, with a handle encircled by grime. Lou pointed up at the transom. "Check it out."

Bennie looked up to see a white security camera mounted above the door, next to a light. "Duly noted."

"After you," Lou said, opening the door.

"Thanks." Bennie went inside, waiting a moment while her eyes adjusted to the darkness. The bar smelled vaguely like hot dogs, and it was a medium-sized room with a wooden bar on the right, which held two men hunched over beers, facing a TV showing ESPN on low volume. On the left side of the room, behind a red tile divider, was a dining area with wooden tables and a chalk-board menu that showed hamburgers and salads, as well as pier-ogies, sweet red cabbage, pickle soup, white borscht, and bigos.

Lou took a seat at the bar, and Bennie followed suit, figuring they'd play their approach by ear, the way they always did. She wanted to get any and all versions of what happened last night in the bar, find out what else anybody knew, and best-case scenario, find out what they told the police. Lou must've caught the eye of the bartender, who gave him a high sign that he'd be right over.

Lou turned to Bennie. "Let me do the talking," he said under his breath. "This guy's my age, but not as handsome. Also I think he's a retired cop."

"How do you know?"

"I can tell. A lot of my buddies started working in bars when they got off the job. There's beer and tipsy broads. What more do you need?" Lou chuckled at his own joke. "Also for security. Cops know how to spot a knucklehead right off the bat. If you have a cop tending bar, the knuckleheads find other bars to go to."

"Interesting," Bennie said, meaning it, as the bartender ambled over. She wouldn't have guessed he was a former cop, because he was short, wide, and had thick glasses that made his brown eyes look even smaller. He wore a blue polo shirt with his jeans and a waist apron.

"What can I get for you folks?" he asked, his gaze shifting from Lou to Bennie, though he barely smiled.

"I'm Lou Jacobs, and my associate is Bennie Rosato. We're here about a fight that happened last night, which led to a murder. Were you here?"

"No, the night guy was. I only work days." The bartender turned to Bennie, frowning. "You that lawyer?"

"Yes." Bennie knew it could go either way, if he'd been a cop.

"Way back when, I used to work in the 37th Precinct, and you sued some of the brass."

Lou interrupted, "Don't be giving my boss a hard time."

"I wasn't going to," the bartender said, with a crooked smile. "I never liked them anyway."

Lou laughed, and Bennie joined him. She knew they had broken the ice, and they would need a good rapport if they were going to learn anything.

The bartender gestured toward the back of the restaurant. "You wanna know how it went down, ask the waitress. Emily, the owner's daughter. She's in the back."

"I'll go, thanks. Be right back, Lou." Bennie rose, walked through the dining area, and found a hallway behind. There were restrooms on the left, and past them a young woman stood at an electronic cash register in a nook on the right. She had short brown hair and a soft, pretty face, the contours of her cheeks illuminated from below by the green-and-blue lights on the machine. She turned, as Bennie reached her. "My name is Bennie, and the bartender said I should talk to you. I represent Jason Lefkavick, who was here last night."

"Oh, sure." Emily brushed bangs from her forehead, showing pained greenish eyes. "He's such a nice guy! I don't believe he would do something like that."

"I don't think he did. Can you tell me how you know him?"

"He comes in all the time. He's a regular."

"Since when?"

"Since the summer, that's when I first met him."

"Okay." Bennie made a mental note. That was about six months ago, which was when Jason moved to Philadelphia.

"I remember because we hit it off that first day. He seemed real quiet but I noticed that he had the same tattoo as me." Emily pulled up the sleeve of her blue sweater and showed Chinese calligraphy on the inside of her forearm. "We thought it was so cool when we got it, now everybody has it."

"You said he's a regular, but how often does he come in? Once a week or more?"

"No, every night, for dinner."

"Really," Bennie said, surprised.

"I like him, and we used to talk. If I weren't married, I'd date him." Emily smiled, her lips shiny with lip gloss. "He looks tough, but you can see that he isn't, really. He used to talk about his mom. She died when he was little. He talked about his dad, too. Jason's just a nice, quiet guy."

"What happened last night?"

"Well, it was just really weird. Out of character."

"How so?"

"Every time he comes in, he has a routine. A lot of regulars are like that. They have their own set table, they order the same thing. He gets pierogies and the soup special, mostly."

"So he didn't sit at the bar?"

"No he never did. Here, I'll show you." Emily led Bennie to the dining room, and they stopped at the table on the right against the wall. Emily gestured. "This is where he sits. It's the worst table in the house because it's next to the bathrooms, and sometimes, well, you know, it's smelly."

"I get it." Bennie sat in Jason's seat, took out her pad, and set it on the table.

"And you can't see the TV from here, either. The crowd that comes in here, even if they're in the dining room, they want to see TV."

"Hmm." Bennie looked over, trying to see the view that Jason would have. The TV was angled away toward the bar patrons, so all he would've seen was the side. He could see the people sitting at the bar, but it wouldn't be that easy to see him from the bar, sitting in the back. The divider was four feet tall, so all that would show of him was the top of his head.

"I don't think he did it. They must have the wrong guy." Emily sat down, opposite Bennie. "First off, he doesn't even know Richie."

"Wait, do you know Richie?" Bennie made a note, but didn't show her hand.

"Richie Grusini? Sure. He comes in sometimes, sits at the bar. He comes after work."

"Do you know where he works?"

"Ackermann Construction in East Falls, I think. It says on his shirt."

Bennie made a note. "Was he big?"

"Yes, just under six feet, and he had a beer gut. I don't know him. My dad doesn't let me bartend. He likes me to work in the dining room."

"So how do you know Richie?"

"Everybody knows Richie." Emily rolled her eyes. "He's the kind of guy that if he's in a room, you know it. He's a loudmouth, especially when he drinks. He's a mean drunk, on top of it. He looks at your chest when he talks to you. He knows more about my bra than I do. I hate that."

"Me too." Bennie made a note, mentally filling in some of the blanks, and it wasn't squaring with Jason's story. "Tell me what else you know about Richie, other than where he works."

"Not much, really nothing."

"Does he come in alone or with someone?"

"A buddy from work, a tall guy."

"What's his name, this tall guy?"

"I don't know, but I know he's from work because they both wear the logo sweatshirts. My dad or Sammy, he's our night bartender, would know his name."

"If I give you my business card, do you think you can ask either of them to give me a call?"

"Yes, if it helps Jason."

"Great, thanks." Bennie went into her purse, extracted a business card from her wallet, and passed it across the table. "Was Richie with the tall guy, last night?"

"Yes."

"What does he look like, besides tall?"

"Tall and skinny, with brown floppy hair parted in the middle." Emily rolled her eyes again. "Like what dude wears their hair parted in the *middle*?"

"When Richie got thrown out, did the tall guy leave with him? I assume so."

"I wasn't paying attention to them. It was Jason I was worried about."

"Now, to get back to Richie, he's not married, is he?"

"God, I hope not. He doesn't wear a ring and sometimes he comes in with a girl, but never the same one."

"So no girlfriend?"

"I don't think so. There was a redhead, there used to be a blonde, and a brunette before her. He's going through all the fake hair colors."

"Do you know any of their names?"

"No, my dad or Sammy might. Whatever, they're all the same. Too much makeup, too-tight jeans, you know. He was just the kind of bad boy that those biddies like. Me, I hate that type."

"Me too."

Emily smiled. "We should hang out."

"Do you know if Richie lives with anybody, a roommate?"

"I don't know."

"Do you know if he has any family around here?" Bennie knew the answer, but she wanted to verify it, given that Emily already had so much misinformation.

"I don't think so. He's not from around here."

"How do you know that?"

"He doesn't have a Philly accent, like us."

"Poor guy."

Emily smiled.

"Okay." Bennie flipped a page of her pad. "So what happened last night between Richie and Jason?"

"It was the craziest thing, I didn't see it coming. I knew something was bothering Jason, so I asked him, and he told me that it was the anniversary of his father's death."

Bennie made a note, but didn't interrupt Emily.

"I felt bad for him, because I'm really close to my dad and that would suck if he died. Jason doesn't have either parent, he's, like, an orphan." Emily paused, blinking. "Anyway, he drank more than usual. Usually he has two beers, then he stops. This time he had three. He didn't get mean, he got quiet. He finished his dinner, and I cleared his place. He always gets black coffee after, so I turned to get his coffee. He always lets it cool. He doesn't like it hot."

Bennie kept taking notes, letting her talk.

"But when I came back with the coffee, he was already walking toward Richie at the bar. He tapped Richie on the shoulder and said to him, 'do you know what today is?' And Richie turned around and he looked surprised, then it was like one second later that Richie hauled off and shoved him backwards so hard he fell over."

Bennie imagined the scene, taking notes.

"I couldn't believe it! We don't get fights in here. This is a neighborhood place, and everybody knows it. Practically everybody at that bar is a regular."

"Right."

"So all of a sudden, everybody clears the barstools and people start standing up in the dining room, and Richie gets the better of Jason right away, climbs on top of him and gets him on the floor, and everybody has to pull Richie off. Sammy, he's huge, he used to be a bouncer. My dad would've been here last night, but he's in the hospital for his gallbladder. Anyway, Sammy got Richie off of Jason and threw them both out."

"Who left the bar first, Richie or Jason?"

"Sammy got Richie out first. I went over to Jason to see if he was okay, and he was. Sammy said he had to go, too, and Jason didn't put up a fight. Sammy escorted him out."

"Was he angry when he left?"

"No, just kind of stunned and sad."

"Did he say anything to you that suggested he was going to go after Richie?"

"No, not at all. It took awhile for everybody to settle back down, and I felt terrible for Jason." Emily shook her head. "He could've been sad about his dad's passing, you know? Or maybe he just got sick of hearing Richie mouth off from the bar. A lot of times when Richie gets loud, we get complaints from the people in the dining room." Emily hesitated. "God forgive me, I know it's a sin to speak ill, but I can't help it. My dad always says that bars are like people and every bar has an asshole. Richie's ours."

"Did you tell this to the police?"

"Sure. Did they arrest Jason already?"

"Yes, he's in custody now."

"Oh no. You know what really gets to me, about last night? Before Jason went over to Richie, he left me this, right beside his beer glass. I didn't even get his check yet." Emily reached into her jeans pocket, pulled out her wallet, opened it up and showed Bennie a hundred-dollar bill. "Can you believe that?"

"Wow."

"Right? How nice is that?" Emily folded the wallet back up and slipped it back in her pocket. "It's sweet, right? It's like he knew he was going to get in a fight with Richie and he wanted to make sure that I didn't get stiffed. I told my husband, and he said Jason must've wanted to say good-bye to me, like he had a crush. Either way, it's a sweet thing to do. Jason's a gentleman. He's not the guy who cuts somebody's throat."

"Right," Bennie said, though she was thinking it sounded like evidence of premeditation. "Did you tell the police about the hundred-dollar bill?"

"No, I forgot about it. They only asked me about the fight."

"Well, thanks." Bennie breathed a relieved sigh. She'd already learned enough to worry her.

But she still had a few more stops to make.

CHAPTER THIRTY-SEVEN

"So what did you find out?" Bennie asked Lou, while they climbed into a cab they'd caught in front of the bar.

"I learned that everybody hates Richie. The night bartender wanted to ban him from the bar, but the owner wouldn't let him."

"That's what I learned, too." Bennie climbed in the backseat and slid over, and Lou got in beside her, slamming the door. She leaned over to the cabbie, who was an older man. "Can you take us to 403 East Gansett Street?"

"On it." The cab took off.

"That address is in Fishtown. It's five minutes away. Who lives there?"

"It's Jason's house. I called his roommate Gail and left her a message, but she didn't call back."

"I also got the names of the other people at the bar, who will probably be witnesses for the Commonwealth. The night bartender had made a list and given it to the police, but they kept a copy." Lou slipped a hand inside his coat, pulled out a wrinkled piece of paper, and handed it over. "Here you go."

"Great, thanks." Bennie skimmed the list of names, none of which meant anything to her, then put the paper in her purse. "Jason ate dinner there almost every night, because Richie ate there. Evidently, Jason sat at a table in the back, which gave him a great view of Richie, but Richie wasn't able to see him because of the divider. Remember the divider?"

"Sure."

"So bottom line, it wasn't a chance meeting that night, and Jason has been going there for a long time, following Richie."

"Stalking him?"

"For lack of a better word, yes."

Lou frowned. "Did the waitress tell the detectives this?"

"No, she didn't realize that Jason knew Richie from before. But they'll put it together. I think they told the detectives enough to figure it out, and what they didn't tell the detectives, Jason did. He blabbed when they picked him up. He's told them he hated Richie."

"So he handed them motive."

"Yes." Bennie looked out the window, watching them pass older row homes with façades of aging gray brick or unfinished stucco. They were only two stories high, with four windows facing the street, and air conditioners rusted in the second-floor windows, where the bedrooms were. Black bars covered the first-floor windows and the front doors, some curlicued scrollwork that cost extra.

"Chin up, Bennie."

"This is not an easy case."

"An easy case would bore you."

"I wouldn't mind being bored right now." Bennie flashed on the blood in the alley, shuddering.

"You say that, but you don't mean it." Lou shifted forward in the seat as the cab slowed to a stop. "This is the 400 block of East Gansett Street, we're here."

They got out of the cab and walked to number 403, a gray brick house with black plastic awnings over three of the windows. Bennie said, "By the way, the roommate's name is Gail Malloy."

Lou looked over. "It's a girl, you be primary."

Bennie walked up the stoop and rang the bell, and in the next moment, the door was opened by a petite, wiry woman who looked to be in her early thirties. She was obviously upset, her forehead knit and her eyebrows sloping unhappily downward.

"Are you Bennie, Jason's lawyer, right? That's what you said on the phone."

"Yes I am, and this is my associate, Lou Jacobs."

"Please, come in." Gail stepped aside. She was slight, with sandy brown hair cut in short, cropped layers, and she had on a pressed white shirt, black slacks, and black shoes. "The police were just here, that's why I didn't return your call, I didn't want to do it when they were here. They told me that Jason was arrested for murder. They searched his room, they took his laptop. This is awful!"

Bennie hid her dismay. "Could we come in and talk about it?"

"Sure, sorry, come on in." Gail let them into a small living room that held a brown fabric sofa, wooden end tables with knobby legs, and a coffee table with a red tile top. Indirect daylight poured through the barred windows, and no lamps were on.

"Gail, who came here, was it detectives or uniformed police?"

"Two detectives and two uniformed cops. They think Jason killed Richie. I know he hated Richie, but I don't think he killed him. I told them that. That was okay, right?"

"Yes, you have to tell them the truth. What else did they ask you and what did you tell them?"

"They asked me a lot of questions about where he was last night, but I didn't know for sure. I only know that when I came home this morning, he hadn't come home last night. Please sit down." Gail gestured at the sofa, her hand flopping back to her side. "I was just about to leave for work. You want coffee or something?"

"No thanks. Do you have time to talk with us?"

"Sure, about half an hour."

"Great." Bennie sat down on the sofa with Lou, and Gail sank into a black vinyl recliner, catty-corner to them. Opposite the sofa was a table with an older-model TV and a tangled pile of video game controllers and joysticks.

"Where's Jason now?"

"He's in custody. He won't be released on bail."

"Oh no." Gail's short forehead knit with concern. "Can I go see him after work? Do you know where they have him?"

"Generally, he would get transferred from the Roundhouse to PICC, up on State Road near the Police Academy. I'll find out if he'll be there tonight and let you know." Bennie slid her legal pad and ballpoint pen from her purse. "So, you said Richie's name like you knew him. Did you?"

"No, I never met the guy. I only know his name because Jason talked about him all the time, he told me everything about him." Gail shook her head again. "I think he moved to this neighborhood because it's near Richie."

Bennie could hear Lou sigh. "Did he say where Richie lived?"

"No."

"Do you know how he found out where Richie lived?"

"Online? He's had a thing against him, he told me, ever since they were kids."

"Did he ever say to you that he wanted to kill Richie?"

"Yes, only once or twice, and only when he drank. I never thought he really would." Gail's dark eyes filmed. "I know he's not that kind of person, but he did have a temper. My partner Marie's a nurse at the VA Hospital, that's how we met. She always tried to get him to go to a shrink, but he wouldn't. She thinks he has PTSD. He lashes out, when you don't expect it."

"Really?" Bennie flashed suddenly on her meeting a long time ago, with the child psychiatrist in Mountain Top. She remembered they had discussed the possibility that Jason could develop PTSD, as a result of his childhood incarceration. She didn't know which way it cut; on the one hand, it might be a defense, but on the other, it made her wonder if Jason really had killed Richie. Bennie put it out of her mind for now. "Do you have any idea whether Jason had a hunting knife?"

"I never saw one. I doubt he has any kind of weapon."

"Did he ever mention any friends of Richie's? Richie was at the bar last night with a tall guy he worked with at Ackermann Construction."

"No."

Bennie shifted gears. "Let's back up a moment. Would you tell me about yourself?"

"I'm from Mayfair, all my life. I went to Prendy, then I did a year at community college, but I didn't like it. I enlisted in the Army in 2003. I did two tours in Afghanistan, in Operation Enduring Freedom."

"Thank you for your service."

"Yes, thank you," Lou added.

Gail nodded, with a brief smile. "Thanks, but I didn't see much action. I was a Fobbit, I never left the base. It was paradise compared to what some guys went through. But you know, I've known a lot of people who had to kill. Jason didn't have that killer instinct. He was just a softy."

"How long have you known Jason?"

"Half a year, when he moved here. He answered my ad on Craigslist. We liked him, Marie and I. I didn't really want a male roommate, but no one else was answering the ad and the night he came over for the interview, he did the most amazing thing."

"What?"

"You know, not everybody around here is superwelcoming to gay women." Gail leaned forward, resting her arms on her thighs. "My neighbor on the right, he hates me. The night Jason came over, my neighbor was giving me a hard time. Right away, Jason stood up to him. He said, 'It doesn't matter who she is, it matters who *you* are. So be a gentleman, at all times.' It backed the neighbor down, totally. That's who Jason is. He always has my back."

Bennie made a note, touched.

"So he moved in, and he lucked out on timing. I needed a new waiter at the restaurant, so I hired him. He did great. He's a hard worker." Gail shook her head. "He just couldn't get his head out of the past. I don't know if you know, he went to juvie when he was in middle school. It was really awful."

Bennie listened, pained. "I do know that, I was his lawyer. Did he ever finish high school or get a GED?"

"No, neither. He was in and out of juvie until he was eighteen.

He got off track and never got back on, to hear him tell it. I don't know if he told you, he doesn't like to talk about it."

Bennie could imagine it happening, after Jason's life derailed at River Street.

"His dad lost his job and became very depressed. Money was an issue. Jason got a job working after school, but he couldn't keep up with his schoolwork."

Bennie guessed it was why Matthew hadn't hired another lawyer. He didn't have the money, but she would have done it for free.

"He became truant, acted out, and ended back up in juvie with Richie. From what I hear, they both grew up in jail. Then when Jason's dad died, he told me he took it badly, and we could see it. He blames Richie for his dad's death. His dad died of heart disease, but Jason said it was a long time coming, like he had constant heart problems because of the stress. Lately, I could see that Jason was bumming, and he told me that the anniversary of his father's death was coming up."

Bennie sighed inwardly.

"His moods come and go. He gets depressed. He's quiet most of the time, but when something triggers it, he snaps out. Still, I don't think Jason did it. I just can't believe that he would kill anybody."

Bennie switched tacks, to see how much Gail knew. "What did Jason do in the evening, like for dinner? Did you guys ever eat together?"

"No, he ate at Eddie's. The cops said that's where he was last night. We both worked at the restaurant in the daytime, then I have dinner with my girlfriend at her house. I stay over there a lot, too. I was at her place last night."

Bennie realized that Gail must not have known that Jason was stalking Richie. She didn't want to taint her testimony, so she didn't tell her.

"Does Jason have a car?"

"Yes, but we take the bus to work."

"Why don't you take the car?"

"There's no parking."

"Did the cops search it?"

Gail blinked. "No, come to think of it. Jason keeps the keys in a basket in case I need to borrow it." She crossed the room to an old basket on a console table and plucked out some keys. "Presto."

"I'd like to check his car, if I may."

"Sure, if it helps the cause." Gail crossed back and handed over the keys, and Bennie put them in her purse.

"Where's the car now?"

"Parked on this street, somewhere. It's an old white Toyota."

"I'll find it." Bennie switched gears. "You say the cops took his laptop?"

"Yes, it was in his room and they searched his bedroom. I wouldn't let them search anywhere else because they didn't have a warrant for it. That's the law, right?"

"Yes." Bennie rose. "Do you think we could see his room?"

"Sure, there's a scrapbook of his father's you should see. Jason used to read it over and over. He was showing it to me just the other night, in my room, so the cops didn't get it. I didn't keep it from them intentionally, I just forgot to mention it."

"Let's see it," Bennie said, though she sensed she knew what it might contain.

CHAPTER THIRTY-EIGHT

Bennie and Lou entered Jason's room, which was small but pleasant because its single window faced south, allowing a shaft of sunlight to warm the room, which had no rug, only bare pine floors. The bedroom contained a queen-size bed with a shabby blue blanket, white bookshelves that held a few paperbacks and a cardboard box, and a wooden chest of drawers, hanging open from being searched. The laptop cord lay on the floor, still attached to a surge protector. The closet door stood ajar, and Jason's clothes had been pushed to the side, above his shoes and sneakers, mounded willy-nilly. There was nothing on the walls, which were white. There was no TV or radio.

Bennie walked over to the shelf. She scanned the paperbacks, then pulled out the cardboard box, which was open. The sight caught her by the throat. Inside was a colorful pile of Lego bricks, their plastic still as vivid, bright, and perfect as the day they were manufactured, and on top was a figurine she recognized immediately, suddenly remembering what Jason had said about the toy.

This minifig is Richard the Strong.

"Aw," Bennie said to herself, picking up the figurine. It couldn't have been more than two inches high, made of plastic, with a silvery crown, a blue vest, and black pants. It had a silvery sword, but it was broken. "Jason loved this toy."

"Hmph," Lou said, and they both turned to the door as Gail reappeared, holding a thick black plastic scrapbook.

"Here we go."

"Thank you." Bennie accepted the scrapbook.

Gail hesitated. "Can I ask you something? What happens now? When does he go to trial?"

"Three to six months."

"What about his rent and his other bills? I mean, what do I do?"

"You can send the bills to me, I'll take care of them."

"You mean you'll pay?" Gail's eyebrows lifted. "Sweet!"

"Send them to me at my office." Bennie felt Lou shift position beside her.

"Thanks. Okay, I gotta finish getting ready for work." Gail left the room, and Bennie set the scrapbook down on the bookshelf and thumbed through the first two pages, which contained old newspaper clippings.

"Bennie, why are you covering this kid's bills? And do we really have time for scrapbooks?"

"You want to know why he spent his life in juvie? Take a look at this."

"I know why he spent his life in juvie. He spent his life in juvie because he's messed-up."

"He didn't start out that way." Bennie went to the first page of the scrapbook.

"Tell me what it says, I don't have my reading glasses." Lou squinted.

"Okay." Bennie read the headline to Lou. "It says, 'Kids-for-Cash Scandal Rocks Luzerne County.' "

"So?"

"Well, the last time I saw Jason was in 2002. I was trying to get him out of a detention center on River Street in Wilkes-Barre, Luzerne County. It was run-down and disgusting. He was moved to a new place called PA Childcare in 2003. It was all nice and modern, I saw it once." Bennie would never forget that cold winter day, when she'd tried to see Jason at the new detention center, then had stopped in front of Declan's house. "It was still a prison, but everybody said it was going to be so wonderful."

"Okay." Lou folded his arms, listening.

"There's only one Juvenile Court in Luzerne County, and it was run by Judge Ciavarella. He was the one who adjudicated Jason as a juvenile delinquent and put him away. Judge Ciavarella put thousands of children away for minor things like fighting in the classroom, posting things about their teachers online, or acting out in general. The policy was called zero tolerance, and in fact, he was called Judge Zero Tolerance."

"I remember those days."

"Right, everybody thought it was because of Columbine. Nobody wanted violence in schools." Bennie felt resentment tighten her chest. "But what nobody knew was that Judge Zero Tolerance was part owner of the new for-profit prison and that he was in cahoots with Judge Conahan, another judge on the Common Pleas Court. The judges guaranteed the builder of the new juvenile detention center that it would be kept full."

"Oh, man." Lou cringed. "I think I remember hearing about this."

"It didn't get half of the attention it should have. They got reimbursed by the county for the kids they incarcerated, and they even made the parents pay the fees. They garnished the wages of the parents when they couldn't pay. It made the local papers when it came to light, and some national media." Bennie flipped through the scrapbook pages, reviewing the headlines she knew so well. It had broken her heart when the news of the corruption scheme came to light. She knew instantly that Jason had been one of those children. "It began to unravel in 2007, when a high-school girl and her mother made a fuss. Just like Jason, she had signed a waiver form. Her mother called the Juvenile Law Center and they looked into her case."

"The Juvenile Law Center in Philly?"

"Yes. They petitioned the Supreme Court, and to make a long story short, they subpoenaed all the juvenile court cases under Judge Ciavarella and found out that Luzerne County was sending a markedly disproportionate number of kids to the new juvenile center, and also that a disproportionate number of them had waived their right to counsel. Unlawfully." Bennie still blamed herself. The legal argument she had raised before the Superior Court had been exactly right, and if she had gone forward, she could have exposed the scheme much earlier.

"They won the suit?"

"And then some, as you can see." Bennie flipped through the next few pages, which held clipping after clipping, preserved under plastic. "They got the FBI and U.S. Attorney involved. The government brought federal criminal charges, alleging that Judge Ciavarella and Judge Conahan accepted nearly $2.6 million from PA Childcare and another facility that they built during the same time."

"That's *real* money." Lou's eyes flew open.

"Judge Conahan pled guilty to federal criminal charges and so did the other former co-owner, a lawyer named Robert Powell. The developer, Robert Mericle, also pled guilty."

"What about Judge Ciavarella?"

"He wouldn't plead. He went to trial, in 2011." Bennie flipped forward to the page that reported the trial results, JUSTICE FINALLY DONE. "He was found guilty of tax evasion and theft of honest services, which technically means he didn't report the income. He's doing federal time, as we speak. He was sentenced to seventeen years. Judge Conahan was sentenced to twelve years."

"What a shame." Lou shook his head.

"The scandal took place from 2003 to 2008, and they estimate it affected more than two thousand five hundred children and more than six thousand cases." Bennie skimmed the statistics from one of the articles, then looked up at Lou. "Can you imagine, the numbers of children who were affected? Children. Jason was a great kid taken out of his home, for no reason, and he was railroaded into a juvenile detention center to line the pockets of corrupt judges. It ruined his life. It ruined his family."

"Oh boy."

"I don't know if you saw in the paper, but they just settled a federal civil class action that was brought on behalf of the kids. The lawyers did it *pro bono,* but the most any kid got was a settlement of $5000. Does $5000 pay anybody back? Does $5000 begin to compensate for what happened to Jason? How much is a childhood worth?"

Lou's face turned grave, and Bennie flipped the page of the scrapbook, where it abruptly ended in a black page.

"None of the settlement is in the scrapbook, because Jason's father died. Can you imagine, that he kept this scrapbook? That he watched this horror unfold, knowing that it took his son from his home? No heart could withstand that." Bennie experienced a wave of regret. "I knew Jason's father, and he was a good man. A kind man. It was the anger and stress that killed him. The corruption, and the betrayal of his son. Who's to blame for his death? The crooked judges? Richie? Jason himself?"

Lou sighed, heavily. "It's not so black-and-white."

"Not at all. Causation never is, in any case. But in this one, it's a killer." Bennie closed the scrapbook, and its padded cover made a soft noise that punctuated her sentence. "I let Jason down, a long time ago. The justice system let him down, too. He was a sweet kid, and the system turned him into what he is today. He probably does have PTSD. Justice stole his childhood, and we have to set this right. We owe him one."

"Is that why you're gonna pay the kid's bills? That's above and beyond the call, Bennie."

"I want Jason to have a home, after trial. Because we're gonna win, if it's the last thing I do." Bennie put the scrapbook back, planning her next move. "Let's go."

Half an hour later, Bennie and Lou had found Jason's grimy, battered white Toyota, which was so old that it didn't have an automatic door lock. Bennie slid the key in the lock, twisted, and opened the driver's-side door, looking around. It smelled of stale cigarette smoke, and the seats were gray cloth. There was a well in the console, which held a few coins but nothing else.

"Looks pretty clean," Bennie said, looking in the skinny shelf on the door and finding only pens and a pack of matches.

Lou went around the passenger side and peered through the window. "Can you unlock me?"

"Sure, hold on." Bennie leaned in the driver's seat, reached over, and unlocked the other door.

"Thanks." Lou ducked his head inside the car and opened the glove compartment, which contained a few neatly folded maps, some CDs without the jackets, and a brown plastic bottle of Coppertone. "Nothing here."

"I don't really expect to find anything. I just want to be thorough. That's my thing, as you know."

"Yes, I do know. Your thoroughness drives me crazy. But then again, if I got into trouble, I'd want you on my side."

"Likewise, sir." Bennie got out of the car and went to the backseat. It was completely empty except for a folded-up newspaper and a box of Kleenex. There were gray rubbery pads on the floor, but they were remarkably clean, and she guessed Jason didn't use the car that much.

"Bennie, come here. I found something."

"What?" Bennie came back around to the front, peeking inside. Her heart sank at the sight. There, resting on Lou's open hand, was a Colt .45 revolver.

"It's loaded." Lou handled the gun with care, pressing open the barrel, which showed the flat bottom of a bullet in each of the exposed chambers. He unloaded the bullets, dropping them expertly into his cupped palm.

"Oh no." Bennie sighed. "I never would have thought he'd have a gun. Neither did Gail, remember?"

"Never say never." Lou pointed to some crude scratching on the shiny metal of the gun. "Look. Serial number filed off. Automatic felony. Illegal gun. So what do we do? Take it or leave it?"

"Take it. God forbid somebody breaks in. We'll keep it in the safe at work."

"Okay." Lou put the gun and the bullets into his pocket. "So, why do you think he had a gun?"

"Protection from Richie?"

"I'm not the jury, Bennie. I'm asking you." Lou got out of the car and closed the door.

"Same answer. Alternatively, I don't know." Bennie locked the door with the key. "Oddly, I think it's a good thing for us. It suggests the knife wasn't his."

"How?" Lou came around the back of the car to the sidewalk.

"Because if Jason was out to kill Richie, he would've kept the gun on him. After all, if he has a gun, why does he use a knife? You could say it was a lesser-included type of weapon."

"Pretty good, counselor." Lou smiled. "Now where do we go next?"

"Hold on, I gotta look up the address." Bennie slid her phone from her purse.

"I could eat something."

"So what else is new?" Bennie said, scrolling.

CHAPTER THIRTY-NINE

Bennie and Lou sat in the backseat of the cab, while it drove slowly down past the line of brick row houses. She'd looked up Richie's address on her phone and he lived in Kensington, the neighborhood adjacent to Port Richmond. She eyed his house as they approached: 736 Potter Street, a gray brick row house in good repair with a bowed-out bay window. There were white bars over the door, but not the window, and the roof looked new. She didn't know whether Richie rented or owned, but she made a mental note to have Lou run it down later. He was busy now, eating marble swirl pound cake.

"Bennie, you sure you don't want a piece?" Lou brushed a dark crumb from his chin. On his lap was the Stock's waxed-paper bag, and on top of that was the pound cake, which he'd sawed into thick slices with a plastic fork.

"I'm fine, thanks." Bennie returned her attention to the street, scanning the cars and trucks parked on both sides. She wondered if any belonged to Richie, his tall friend, or even Declan. It would make sense that they would be at Richie's house the day after the murder.

Lou leaned to the driver. "You want a piece of pound cake?"

The driver, an older African-American man, glanced in the rearview. "Sure, thanks."

"I'm Lou, what's your name?"

"Thomas."

"Here we go, Thomas." Lou handed cake through the plastic window, and Thomas received it with a backhand.

"Thanks."

Bennie shifted forward. "Thomas, we're about to drive by the house. Just drive like everything is normal."

"Will do." Thomas chuckled under his breath. "This is the most fun I've had in years."

Bennie kept her eyes on the house, trying to see inside the bay window, but she couldn't. It was sunny outside, but dark inside the house, though she could see an unusual amount of activity.

"See anything?" Lou asked, his mouth full.

"Yes, but not enough." Bennie shifted up in the seat. "Thomas, please go around the block one more time, then find a place to park on the opposite side of the street from the house. I want to see if anybody goes in and out."

"No problem," Thomas answered, his mouth full.

Lou looked over, swallowing. "You're staking out the house."

"Yes, I want to know who the tall guy is and what other friends Richie has." Bennie didn't mention Declan. The last thing she wanted was to see him, or him to see her.

"Wait, I have an idea." Lou wiped off his fingers, leaving grease from the rich cake on his thin napkin. "Thomas, go around the block one more time, drive past the house, but don't park. Bennie, you take your phone and make a video of all the license plates on cars on the right side of the street. I'll make a video of the license plates on the left side of the street. Then when whoever leaves the house, we can see which cars they go to, and I can run those license plates by some of my buddies."

Bennie smiled. "So you're not just in it for the carbs."

"It's brain fuel, honey." Lou grinned, and Thomas drove forward, took a left turn, then rounded the block and came up on the other side of Potter Street, where Bennie and Lou got out their phones and filmed the parked cars.

Thomas lapped the block again and returned to the top of Potter Street, where he slowed, looking for a parking space. "How about that space on the end? If I were going to pick somebody up on the street, this is where I'd wait."

"Great, do it."

Thomas pulled the cab into the spot.

"Thanks. Leave the meter running, and we'll just sit awhile."

Lou wiped off his hands on a napkin. "I knew I shoulda got coffee."

Bennie looked over. "Lou, it's a stakeout, not a restaurant."

Lou chuckled. "It's the same thing. I always gained weight on stakeout detail. It's the one thing they get right in cop movies."

Bennie returned her attention to the house. "They have to come out sooner or later, don't they?"

"Usually, later," Lou answered, setting the cake aside to get out of his coat, and Bennie did the same. Thomas listened to the radio, while Bennie and Lou kept checking the house, in between checking their emails. Only a few cars came down the street, which was one-way going north to south, but none of them stopped at Richie's. Half an hour turned into an hour, but the cab stayed warm because of the sun, which was bright enough to give Bennie a headache or maybe it was the tension, she didn't know which.

Suddenly, a black Chevy pickup turned onto the street, and she did a double take. The truck was covered with so much whitish salt that it had to have come from outside the city, and just one glimpse at the driver's seat told her it was Declan. "That's him!" Bennie folded over completely, hiding her face from view.

"*Him?* Whoa." Lou shifted up in the seat.

"Who?" Thomas asked, from the front. "The bad guy?"

"No," Bennie answered.

"Yes," Lou answered, at the exact same time.

Thomas chuckled. "You folks better get your story straight."

"There's no story," Bennie said, folded over.

"That's her old boyfriend," Lou added.

"Lou! Really?"

Lou waved her off. "Thomas can be trusted, not like the blabbermouths at the office."

Bennie stayed down. "What's Declan doing, Lou?"

"Parking. That's a big-ass truck he's driving. Compensate much?"

Thomas laughed. "Good one, Lou. City's no place to have a truck that big."

"He doesn't live in the city," Bennie said, then wondered why she was even bothering. "What's he doing now?"

"Walking to the house. He's carrying an Acme bag. Musta gone food shopping."

"Is he alone?"

"Yes. He's not bad-looking, for a jerk."

"He's not a jerk." Bennie's heart pounded at the thought that Declan was so close. She wanted to see him again, but then again she didn't.

Thomas clucked. "He's got nice shoes, you gotta give him that. *Very* nice shoes. That man knows how to *dress*."

"Bennie, you can sit up now." Lou touched her arm, and she popped up.

"That was close."

"Your face is flushed." Lou's gaze shifted sly to her.

"The blood rushed to my head because I was bent over."

"I'm sure that's it." Lou burst into laughter.

Thomas checked the rearview, his eyes narrowing. "That's love, Lou. She's got the look of love."

"That's enough, gentlemen." Bennie looked away, as the front door of the house opened, and three women came out, talking in a group.

"Look, we have activity." Lou shifted up in the seat, raising his phone.

Bennie did the same, zooming in closer and taking pictures. She could see that there was a redhead with two brunettes, though she couldn't make out their facial features from this distance. They dabbed at their faces with white Kleenex.

"Bennie, I wonder if the redhead's the one you told me about, the one that Jason saw with Richie at the bar."

"You have a good memory, Lou."

"Smarter than I look."

Bennie kept taking pictures, just in case. The women hugged each other, then separated, walking in three different directions. "You getting this, Lou? They must've driven separately."

"Yes, I'm on it. I switched to video to make it easier."

"I like the redhead," Thomas said, from the front seat. "I like her boots. I like when women wear those boots."

Bennie kept an eye on the redhead as she crossed the street to a white SUV, wrapping a black leather jacket around her, which she had on with black tights and black suede boots, the sexiest mourning outfit ever.

Thomas clucked again. "I like when people take personal pride in their appearance. Nobody does anymore, always runnin' around in those Uggs. My wife asked for 'em for Christmas, so I got 'em. They weren't cheap. Now she never takes 'em off. Every time she wears 'em, I say, 'Ugh.' She doesn't think it's funny."

Bennie watched through the camera phone as the redhead started the engine and after a moment, pulled out of the spot. She took a picture of the license plate. "I got the redhead," she said.

"I got the two others." Lou pointed, from behind his phone. "Check it. When it rains, it pours."

"What?" Bennie looked up to see two men leaving the house, one short and older, with gray hair, but the younger one was tall and thin, with floppy brown hair parted down the middle. Bennie raised her camera, in excitement. "I think that's our tall guy. That's Richie's friend."

"On it." Lou nodded, filming.

Bennie watched the two men get into a small brown VW, pull out of the space, and drive down the street. "I'm so tempted to follow them."

"No, I'll get the information we need."

"Good." Bennie felt jazzed. "Now we have one more stop. Thomas?"

Thomas started the ignition. "I hope you folks never leave."

CHAPTER FORTY

Bennie and Lou approached the prison by yet another cab, after grabbing a pizza at Tacconelli's to kill time until the authorities had transferred Jason to the Philadelphia Industrial Correctional Center, or PICC. PICC was located just north of Port Richmond, so it didn't make sense to go back to the office, and Lou was happy to eat again while Bennie returned phone calls and answered email.

"I'm so full." Lou groaned, rubbing his tummy. "I can't believe I ate the whole thing. Just like that commercial, remember?"

"No. You always ask me if I remember that commercial, and I tell you no."

"You remember."

"No I don't." Bennie chuckled, though it faded as they traveled farther up State Road, a four-lane boulevard that ran roughly parallel to I-95, leading to a massive concrete complex containing four prisons: PICC, Curran-Fromhold Correctional Facility, Riverside Correctional Facility, and the oldest, the House of Correction.

"I'm looking forward to meeting Jason."

"He's a good guy, underneath the tough exterior."

"Not to mention the loaded gun and the explosive temper." Lou looked over slyly as the cab traveled north, and they both caught sight of PICC, a modern, maximum-security prison that sprawled over several city blocks.

"Here we are." Bennie eyed the prison through the window, and the cab switched lanes, then slowed to a stop in front of the entrance.

"I got the fare." Lou reached for his wallet.

"Thanks." Bennie got out of the cab and faced PICC, its solid red brick façade unbroken except for three rows of narrow windows, set lengthwise; it was the standard design for prison windows, but it always reminded Bennie of razor cuts in a row. High cyclone fencing surrounded its perimeter, concertina wire topped its flat roof, and spiky steel towers stabbed the sky. They walked to the main door, of heavy gray metal, and entered a waiting area, half-full of inmates' families in the plastic bucket seats. A few toddlers made their way between the chairs, and one little girl patted the glass front of the vending machine, leaving smudgy fingerprints. The walls were off-white, the tile floor was grayish, and the overheated air smelled dusty.

"Can I help you?" asked the female guard from behind the front counter. She had on a black uniform with a badge and an electroplated lapel pin, and she stood in front of a vast panel of smoked glass that held one of the prison's satellite security centers. Silhouettes of uniformed guards moved back and forth behind the smoked glass, passing in front of a massive bank of monitor screens.

"I'm a lawyer, and this is my associate." Bennie pulled her bar card from her wallet and handed it over, and Lou did the same with his driver's license.

"Thank you, fill out the request slip, and sign the OV book." The guard noted their IDs, returned them, and pushed two yellow clip IDs across the counter, and as Bennie and Lou signed the OV book, for official visitor, filled out a request slip to summon Jason.

"Thanks." Bennie pushed the forms back and clipped the yellow badge to their clothes.

"You're welcome. What's in the briefcase?"

"Legal papers." Bennie used the generic term for anything that lawyers carried, which was the only material not considered contraband.

"Put your purse in the locker, over there." The guard gestured left, to a U-shaped area of lockers beside the door. "No cell phones, cameras, recording devices. It won't be long for them to bring him down."

"Thanks." Bennie and Lou went to the locker area, stowed their coats, her purse, and his phone inside, then lingered by the security counter. She found her attention drawn to the children in the waiting room, flashing on her reflection in Richie's blood in the alley, then on what Lou had said.

Don't you want kids? You're too young to close up shop.

"You're up, Ms. Rosato and Mr. Jacobs," called the guard.

They walked to the metal detector, and went through, with Bennie putting her messenger bag on the conveyor belt. The female guard gestured them forward, and Bennie retrieved her bag as a second guard unlocked another gray metal security door that admitted them to the prison proper. Bennie and Lou passed through the door, which locked behind them with a stereotypical *ca-thunk* that echoed off the harsh tile surfaces. They walked down the corridor, where they hit the battered elevator button and when the cab came, they rode it to the third floor. They stepped off, facing a smoked glass window, and on the other side sat a guard.

"Here for Jason Lefkavick." Bennie passed her request slip under the window and it was taken by a large hand.

"Room 32," said the guard's muffled voice, and the door to her left opened with another loud *ca-thunk*.

They walked through it to a corridor with a set of doors, each leading to a numbered cubicle. Inmates entered the cubicles from doors off a secured hallway on the other side, and all the doors locked when they closed. Each cubicle was about four-by-six and contained bucket seats facing each other, and a Formica counter separated inmate from lawyer. On the wall was a tan phone that summoned the guard in case of trouble.

Bennie reached the second door and opened it, going inside with Lou. "Hi," she said to Jason, who was sitting slumped on the other side of the counter, in a baggy orange jumpsuit. She flashed on seeing him so many years ago, when she was trying to get him out of River Street. He was a hurt little boy then, but he was an angry man now. He seemed edgier, in a more hostile mood from last night, his thin lips flat and his mouth tense.

"Hey." Jason extended a hand over the counter, but he averted his eyes.

"This is Lou Jacobs. He works at our firm as an investigator. He was with the Philly police for many years."

"Hi, Jason," Lou said, with a warm smile. "It's nice to meet you."

"So, Jason, how are you doing?" Bennie asked, but she knew the answer.

"Terrible." Jason shook his head. "You have to get me out of here. Can't I get bail? Can't we appeal?"

"No, there's no appeal right. I'm sorry, but you're here until trial."

"How long's that gonna be?"

"Six months, and I won't give them any extensions. I'll hold their feet to the fire."

"Shit!" Jason looked away, sucking in his cheeks.

"I know, and I'm sorry." Bennie wanted to get to the point. "Jason, about what happened last night. We've done some investigating, into the alley and the bar, and I talked to your roommate."

"You talked to Gail? Why did you do that?" Jason's lips parted in surprise.

"I told you I was going to. I need to learn as much as possible about the facts, so I'm not blindsided at trial."

"I could've told you anything."

"It wouldn't be the same." Bennie could see he was testy, so she chose her words carefully. "I want you to know you can tell me the truth about anything. I'm your lawyer, and everything you say is privileged. That's true of Lou as well."

"Okay, so? It sounds like you want to ask me something."

"I'd like to understand how Richie got killed."

"I told you that already." Jason frowned.

"I'm having a hard time imagining another person coming into that alley and framing you—"

"Well, they did, that's all I can tell you." Jason threw up his hands. "Like I said, I was unconscious, I was knocked out. When I woke up, Richie was dead."

"There's something I want you to understand. Self-defense is also a defense to murder."

"I know that!" Jason slammed the table with his fist, and Bennie didn't like his display of temper.

"Relax. What I'm trying to say is that if you went into the alley to confront Richie, and he pulled a knife on you and you had to protect yourself, you wouldn't be—"

"That isn't the way it happened. I told you the way it happened."

"Jason, I need you to tell me the truth."

"I didn't tell you the truth? I am telling you the truth!"

Lou rose slightly. "There's no call for that, son."

"I'm not your *son!*"

"Jason, please. We're both here trying to help you." Bennie noticed the guard look over, so she let it go for now. "I need to ask you about something else. I talked to Emily, the waitress at Eddie's. I'm thinking that you go in there because Richie goes there—"

"What's the difference?" Jason's eyes widened, with new outrage. "It's like you're checking up on me. You're my lawyer, not theirs. You're supposed to be helping me, not spying on me. I told you, I was framed. Have you investigated Richie like you're investigating me? Richie has enemies, trust me! Go find them!"

"Jason, be reasonable." Bennie bore down. "I have to understand what the prosecution's going to say, so I can construct a defense for you. The detectives know you go to Eddie's every night—"

"So, I like it there."

"So let me finish." Bennie held up a hand. "It looks like you were stalking Richie, and that's evidence of premeditation—"

"I wasn't *stalking* him! I'm not, like, a creeper or anything."

"Then what were you doing?"

"Eating dinner like everybody else! What's the matter with that? It's a free country, isn't it?"

"Jason." Bennie modulated her tone. "If you tell me the truth, I can figure out a way to deal with it."

"I did tell you the truth, I am telling you the truth!"

"I'm sorry, but that's not believable."

"Nobody knows anything! Nobody was in that alley but me and him."

"Whose knife was it, yours or Richie's?" Bennie bore down.

"The guy who framed me!" Jason's shout echoed, and the guard caught Bennie's eye, but she waved him off.

"Why do you have a gun in your car?"

"How do you know that?" Jason scowled. "What business is it of yours? Who said you could go in my car? How did you get in?"

"Okay, let's switch tacks. The police were at your house and they took your laptop."

"Dammit!"

"What will they see in it that's relevant to this case?"

"I don't know." Jason ran a hand over his head, ruffling up his hair, and Bennie could see his fingers shaking.

"Did you ever use it to look up anything about Richie? Like where he lives or—"

"I did!" Jason threw up his hands. "Why does it matter?"

"Okay, let's leave that aside for now. We'll talk many more times before trial. Let's catch our breath a moment." Bennie sat back in her chair, as if she could relax him by her own body language. "You seem more upset than before."

"You would be, too! You think it's a joke in here? These are some major-league gangbangers! It's stressing me *out*!"

"I totally understand that." Bennie kept thinking about the PTSD diagnosis, predicted so long ago by the child psychiatrist. "If you want, I can talk to somebody and you can see a professional, a psychologist—"

"I'm not crazy, I'm *pissed off*. You get it? I'm pissed off and I have good reason to be! I'm in jail for something I didn't do and I can't get out!"

"Listen, I know this is a hard time for you. I know this is the anniversary of—"

"How do you know that?"

"Jason, I'm investigating to help your defense. I'm on your side—"

"Like before? Like you were before?" Jason jumped to his feet, his fair skin flushing red. "You think I don't remember? You coming to River Street? You acting, like, all nice to me? Like you're my *mom* or something?"

"Jason, sit down, please." Bennie rose, a wrench in her chest.

"Calm down, Jason." Lou stood up, putting a hand in front of Bennie. Jason swatted it away, but the impact knocked Lou off-balance, and he bumped into his chair, which fell over, clattering.

"Who the hell are *you*, old man?" Jason exploded. "What the hell do you know! You used to be a cop, so you think you know everything! You don't know anything I've been through!"

"Jason, stop it!" Bennie spotted the guard hurrying toward Jason, who yelled louder.

"I lived *my life* in jail!" Jason yelled at the top of his lungs, his face bright red, his neck veins bulging. "Now I'm back in! Do you know what that's *like*? Do you have *any idea*? Get me outta here!"

"Sit down!" the guard bellowed. "Sit down! Sit down, right now!"

"Bennie, let's go!" Lou kicked the chair aside, took her arm, and hustled her through the cubicle door, just as it was unlocked by another guard on the outside.

"Come with me!" The guard grabbed Bennie's other arm.

"Go ahead, Bennie!" Jason kept raging. "I don't need you, I don't need *anybody*!"

It was already after the close of business by the time Bennie and Lou got back to the office, where they parted ways. He went home, and she went through her mail, checked a few things, and then left the office, grabbing her last cab of the day. She slumped in the backseat, as twilight came on and the air got colder. She felt her eyes close, a stress reaction to the events of the day, especially Jason's outburst. She hadn't seen that coming, and there in the darkness, alone in the backseat, she let herself face her doubts about whether he was innocent.

The thought made her heartsick, for Jason, for Richie, for everything that had happened. But there was no going back. She had to defend him, and she was going to win. She just didn't know how. The case was barely triable. Jason's story didn't travel. And she could never put him on the stand to testify. The cab drove slowly down her street, then it stopped, and Bennie paid the cab driver. She slid out of the seat, hoisted her bags to her shoulder, and closed the door behind her. She walked between the parked cars to her house, where she noticed that someone was sitting on her front step.

She didn't have to look twice.

Her heart knew him, on sight.

CHAPTER FORTY-ONE

"Hi," Bennie said, dry-mouthed.

"Hey." Declan rose slowly. The only light came from a fixture beside her neighbor's front door, and Bennie could see the outline of his gorgeous profile, the darkness of his eyes, and his crow's-feet that had only grown deeper. He looked handsome, tall, and strong, with his hands in his pockets the way he used to. Declan still did it for her, even after all these years, and she felt her heart lodge somewhere in her throat.

"I'm sorry about Richie." Bennie knew it was the automatic thing to say when someone died, but less so when someone was murdered, maybe by her own client.

"Thank you. Do you mind if I come in a minute? I want to talk to you."

"No, sure, right." Bennie looked down in her purse, rummaging around for her keys, using the time to compose herself. She didn't know what he wanted, and she didn't know what she wanted, either. She knew only one thing that they needed to talk about, but she didn't know when she could talk to him about that, especially not now.

"Do you still have Bear?"

"No, sadly, he passed." Bennie found her keys, walked past Declan to the stoop, went up the steps, and unlocked the door. She stepped awkwardly aside to admit him, finding herself suddenly too close to him in the entrance hall. She thought she caught a whiff of his aftershave, but it could've been her imagination. "Do you still have the horses?"

"No. They passed, too."

"Sorry." Bennie closed the door behind them, as Declan stepped out of the entrance hall and into the living room. Alone, she took a moment to center herself, then slipped off her coat and hung it on the hook. "Can I take your coat?"

"No. I'm not staying long."

"Okay." Bennie felt a *thud* in the middle of her chest. She didn't know what else she expected. She hadn't expected anything. But somehow, something inside her didn't want to hear *that*. She left the entrance hall and went to the living room, where she switched on the light.

"This is a nice house." Declan looked around. "Very you."

"Thank you." Bennie managed a smile, remembering so long ago, when she couldn't imagine fitting him into her house and her life, then she couldn't imagine her life and her house without him. In the end, she'd lived her life without him.

"I'm a lawyer now." Declan looked over, his hands still in the pockets of his parka, which was green. "I caught the bug when I saw you in Superior Court that day."

"Wow. So where do you practice?"

"Mountain Top. General practice. My own firm."

"That's great." Bennie could see he was keeping his distance. He barely met her eye, as if they'd never been intimate, and she understood. He had moved on, probably with the blonde.

"It was hard seeing you at the arraignment."

"Yes, I felt the same way," Bennie blurted out, a stab at intimacy that was doomed to fail.

"That's what I came to see you about."

"Do you want to sit down or anything?" Bennie gestured at the couch, but her arm fell at her side when Declan shook his head.

"No, thanks. Obviously this is difficult. Strange. Awkward."

"All of the above." Bennie couldn't resist the urge to make a joke, just to blow off the pressure, but somehow the lid stayed on the pot.

"You saw the boys at the arraignment. The twins. I got custody of them. I raised them." Declan looked away, his eyes scanning the living room, but not really alighting anywhere. "They go to Crestwood. Get good grades. Doreen cleaned up her act, too. It took awhile but she did it."

"That's good, too." Bennie sensed he was trying to build up to something, but she didn't know what.

"I tried to help with Richie, but it was too late." Declan hung his head a moment, and Bennie fought the urge to go over and hug him.

"I'm sorry, I truly am. It's so sad."

"Yes, it is." Declan looked up sharply, meeting her eye. "Jason killed him."

"Declan, we don't know that—"

"Please don't." Declan held up a palm, his lips pursed. "I picked out Richie's casket today. Doreen was too upset to go. So were the twins. We're going to bury him after they release the body. He was like a son to me, Bennie. He was my *son*."

Bennie swallowed hard, feeling his grief. Declan had just lost a son. She could never tell him that he had lost another child, first.

"I tried to turn him around. I couldn't." Declan shook his head, his voice suddenly hoarse, but his emotions in complete control. "I got him all the help I could. It was too late."

"You can't blame yourself."

"That's not who I blame. I blame Jason. Jason killed him."

"No, he didn't," Bennie said softly, but even she wasn't sure she believed it, after that display at the prison.

"Oh, right. Somebody framed him for the murder of his lifelong enemy." Declan scoffed, but it had a hollow sound. "You don't really believe that, do you?"

"I can't discuss this with you—"

"I know you. You're not buying his story for one minute. You can't be."

"Declan, Jason is my client. I can't discuss what I believe or don't believe. You're a lawyer now, you should understand that."

"You're right. I didn't come here to discuss Jason's ridiculous story. I came here to ask you not to represent him."

"What?" Bennie asked, aghast.

"Don't represent him."

"I am. I have to."

"No you don't."

"I owe him."

"No you don't. They fired you. You don't owe them anything."

"Matthew fired me because of *our* relationship." Bennie felt all the regret and guilt coming back to her. "If I hadn't been with you, Matthew wouldn't have let me go. I would've taken Jason's case to the Superior Court. I would've won. It would've made new law. They would've found out about Kids-for-Cash, years earlier. I would've put a stop to it. I would've prevented all that pain for Jason, Richie, *all* of those kids."

"You don't know that."

"Yes I do." Bennie let it go. It killed her. She would never forgive herself, ever. She could only hope to make it right for Jason, now.

"But your representing him, it's tearing me apart." Declan frowned, with a new urgency. "It's tearing my family apart. If you represent him, there's a chance he'll get off. I can't let that happen. I need to see Jason punished. Doreen needs to see Jason punished. So do the boys. It's *justice*."

"Declan—" Bennie said, but she wasn't sure how to finish the sentence. She wasn't about to argue about what justice was, in this case.

"You know he's guilty. He hated Richie."

"They hated each other. They were victims of the same judge, the same corruption."

"Kids-for-Cash didn't kill Richie in that alley. Jason did. Jason crossed the line. That's murder. We want justice for Richie. He deserves it."

"If I didn't represent him, somebody else would."

"Right. He'd get a public defender. He couldn't afford anybody else. They'd lose. The evidence is overwhelming."

"That could *still* happen. Don't overestimate me. My representation doesn't guarantee a win. I'm good, but I'm not that good." Bennie felt herself in the odd position of running herself down. All this time she had been worrying that she'd lose the case, now she worried she'd win.

"Don't be modest. You're the big gun. Everybody knows it, and I don't want to take a chance." Declan took a step toward her, his eyes searching hers. "If you ever cared about me, if you ever loved me, I'm asking you to quit."

"Declan, you know I loved you," Bennie said, her heart speaking out of turn.

"And I loved you, too. We loved each other, and that was real." Declan touched Bennie's arm, and she came alive inside at his touch, palpably reconnecting her to him, after so many years.

"So don't say that then, and don't ask me to quit."

"But I can't watch you get Jason off. I can't do it. It's not tenable. You're tearing me up. The whole family, it's just too hard."

"I don't understand." Bennie couldn't believe her ears, her emotions in tumult. "You're asking me to dump Jason, because it's hard for you? That's not right."

"He came between us once. Don't let him come between us again."

"What *us*?" Bennie blurted out. "There's no *us*. I haven't heard from you since then. You're with some blonde now."

"I'm not with any blonde." Declan shook his head.

"That blonde in court."

"She's Doreen's best friend." Declan refocused on Bennie, anguished. His hand squeezed her arm gently. "I haven't been with a woman who mattered since you. There's no one in your league."

Bennie felt her heart leap with hope, to hear the words. She felt the same way. She never thought Declan would come back into her life. She never thought she'd get pregnant and lose his baby. She didn't know how to tell him and she didn't know how not to, but this wasn't the time.

"Bennie, I know this is crazy. Seeing you again, I thought maybe we were getting a second chance. But not if you represent Jason. If you represent Jason, I can't. I can't do it. I can't justify it to myself."

"So if I give up Jason, I get you?" Bennie took a step backwards, shocked, and Declan's hand fell from her arm.

"That's not how to put it—"

"But that's the truth. That's what you're saying. That's not fair."

"It's not about fairness."

"Yes it is, you're giving me an impossible choice. If I give up my client, I get you." Bennie shook her head, stricken. "Either you want us to get back together or you don't. It's about us, not our job."

"It's not that simple. I can't bring myself to do it if you help Jason get away with murder. The murder of my *son*."

"But *I* can't put my personal life before my job. I did that last time, and look how it turned out." Bennie felt tears come to her eyes.

"Don't put Jason first. Put us first."

"It's not about Jason, it's about me. It's about my obligations and the way I feel."

"Come on, Bennie!" Declan threw up his hands. "Jason doesn't deserve you! He doesn't deserve *us*! He *killed* Richie!"

"I feel terrible that Richie was murdered—"

"No, you don't—"

"Yes, I do! Believe me, I do." Bennie had to convince him. "But I can't walk away from Jason again. I won't do that. Even if I get you in the bargain."

"You're sure?" Declan's eyes burned into her with a bitterness that had once been love.

"Yes," Bennie answered, miserably.

"Then, good-bye." Declan strode to the door.

PART THREE

Six months later, July 20, 2015

Cross-examination is the greatest legal engine ever invented for the discovery of truth.

—John Henry Wigmore

CHAPTER FORTY-TWO

"All rise for the Honorable Judge Martina Patterson!" called the court crier, standing aside at the pocket door.

Bennie rose at counsel table, on unusually weak knees. It was the first time she'd felt uncomfortable in a courtroom, and it was because of Declan. She hadn't seen him since he'd left her house that night, and he was sitting in the gallery to her left, on the Commonwealth's side. He lingered in her peripheral vision, looking handsomer than ever in a gray suit and dark tie. She'd stolen a glimpse at him when she first entered, but then she'd hardened her heart and thought of Jason, who would be brought up from the basement of the Criminal Justice Center any minute. She had a murder case to win.

She composed herself, waiting for the judge to enter. The jury had been empaneled but had yet to be brought in, because this would have been the time the judge heard pretrial evidentiary motions: i.e., commonly, the defense would be raising a number of objections to evidence the Commonwealth intended to introduce at trial, but that wasn't going to happen. Bennie wasn't about to move to exclude any of the Commonwealth's proffered testimony. She had a different trial strategy in mind.

She glanced around, getting her bearings. Courtroom 907 was large, since only murder trials were held in the '07 courtrooms, with walls of gray acoustical tiles and a rug in a coordinated gray-patterned synthetic. Light filled the courtroom, filtering through three windows with pinky-mauve sheers that were incongruously lovely for criminal homicide.

The judge's dais was sleek, cherrywood topped with a wide panel of gold electroplate, and it was flanked by a polyester American flag and the blue state flag, and behind the dais, an ersatz bronze seal of the Commonwealth of Pennsylvania. There was nothing on the judge's desk except a wooden gavel, but the court clerk's desk was covered with a ficus plant in a clay pot, a red Phillies mug containing highlighters, a yellow tube of Jergens hand cream, and a plastic photo cube of a little boy.

The gallery held five room-wide pews of indeterminate blackwood marred with scratches, and Bennie tried to ignore the fact that she was being watched from the Commonwealth side, where Doreen and the twin boys sat with Declan. Behind them sat a trio that Bennie knew from her investigation and the prosecution's witness list: Richie's floppy-haired friend, named Paul Stokowski, sat with Richie's girlfriend, an overly made-up blonde named Renée Zimmer, and her friend, whose name Bennie didn't know.

Bennie had been given the names of both past and current girlfriends by the night bartender at Eddie's, but neither woman had returned her or Lou's calls, which was to be expected. She had also tried to interview Paul Stokowski but he'd also declined, in profane terms that had offended even Lou, who was the sole occupant of the pews on the defense side of the gallery. Bennie had asked him to watch the jury and see how they were reacting to the testimony, but he'd been glaring at Declan from the moment they'd entered the courtroom.

A reporter and a few stringers sat in the pews behind her, talking among themselves with their smartphones and notepads in their laps. The press that covered the courthouse beat had diminished, but Bennie recognized the veteran Karen Engstrom, who had undoubtedly looked up the docket for the day, spotted Bennie's name, and wondered why she was on the case, since there was nothing about the murder that was out of the ordinary.

"Good morning, counsel." Judge Patterson appeared in the

pocket door and swept into the room, flashing a cool smile. She was a tall African-American woman in her forties, whose lovely brown eyes looked even bigger because her face tapered to a delicate chin, with prominent cheekbones. Her dark hair was smoothed back into a chignon, showing the chic gleam of gold earclips, and she held a case file in a manicured hand.

"Good morning, Your Honor," Bennie replied, getting her head into the game. Judge Patterson had ascended to the bench only last year, which made the judge one more unknown in a case too full of unknowns.

"Good morning, Your Honor," said Juan David Martinez, the first assistant district attorney. Martinez was about her age, the rumored next in line to be district attorney, and he looked the part of an urban politician—a conventionally attractive man of average height and blocky build, with clipped black hair and friendly brown eyes behind gold-rimmed eyeglasses. He smiled in a camera-ready way, which gave him an affable vibe, though Bennie had heard that he was a killer in the courtroom.

"Counsel, please sit down." Judge Patterson ascended the dais, then sat in her tall black leather chair. "Ms. Rosato? Would you like to present any motions *in limine*, at this time?"

"No, Your Honor." Bennie rose, but didn't walk to the black wood lectern between the counsel tables. "Thank you."

Judge Patterson frowned, puzzled. "Ms. Rosato, have you received the Commonwealth's Brady materials, stating that they intend to introduce evidence of prior bad acts by your client?"

"Yes, I have." Bennie had a plan. "Your Honor, the 'prior bad acts' refers to the fact that my client and Mr. Grusini have had a mutual enmity since childhood, which led to their being incarcerated in a juvenile detention center. Your Honor would've permitted that evidence as proof of bad motive on the part of my client, is that correct?"

"Perhaps, yes." Judge Patterson nodded. "Though the fact that your client's record was expunged in the wake of the Kids-for-Cash scandal gave me pause."

"Your Honor, I've decided not to challenge the admissibility

260 I Lisa Scottoline

of prior bad acts by my client." Bennie glanced over at Martinez, who was on his feet, arching an eyebrow in surprise. "However, Your Honor, it goes without saying that it cuts both ways. If the Commonwealth seeks to use evidence of my client's prior bad acts with respect to his juvenile record, then I trust that Your Honor would also regard as admissible evidence of Mr. Grusini's prior bad acts and juvenile record, which was also expunged. As a practical matter, the two are inextricably intertwined and one probably couldn't come in without the other."

Judge Patterson looked over at Martinez. "Mr. Martinez? What is the Commonwealth's position? What's good for the goose is good for the gander, is it not?"

"Fair enough, Your Honor," Martinez answered, then shrugged. "I admit, I expected a motion *in limine* from defense counsel this morning, but so be it." He looked over at Bennie, with a half smile. "You wanna put all the cards on the table, Ms. Rosato?"

"I'd call it telling the truth." Bennie turned to face Judge Patterson. "Your Honor, I have prepared a stipulation regarding prior bad acts, which is neutral as to both parties and contains only undisputed facts. I think the Commonwealth can agree with it, which will save the Court's time." Bennie picked up the draft stipulation from counsel table. "It states verbatim that, 'Both Mr. Grusini and Mr. Lefkavick were wrongly adjudicated delinquent on December 16, 2002, as a result of a childhood fight in the cafeteria in Crestwood Middle School, and as such were victims of the Kids-for-Cash scandal in Luzerne County. Both Mr. Grusini and Mr. Lefkavick were wrongly adjudicated juvenile offenders and wrongly served significant amounts of time in juvenile detention, as a result of that judicial corruption."

Martinez crossed to Bennie, peering at the sheet. "I can agree to that. So stipulated."

"Thank you." Bennie handed him the stipulation.

"Excellent." Judge Patterson nodded, pleased. "Isn't it nice when we get along? Ms. Rosato, for the record, I would have ruled against you."

"Thanks for telling me. I'll sleep better tonight." Bennie smiled, and Judge Patterson smiled back.

"Counsel, please be seated. Sheriff, would you retrieve the defendant?" The judge gestured to the uniformed sheriff, who was already in motion toward a locked door on the right wall, which led to the secured halls behind the courtroom.

Bennie sat down, picked up her pen, and drew a line down the top page of her legal pad, the time-honored technique of trial lawyers everywhere. The left side would be used to make notes about the testimony, and the right about what to cross-examine on. Her open laptop, case file, and a plastic gold-toned pitcher were the only other things on counsel table, kept clear as a secret reminder to herself to try the case that came in, not the one in the file.

Bennie heard a jingling sound and turned to see the sheriff leading a handcuffed Jason through the door, dressed in the white oxford shirt and khaki pants she'd picked out for him. His hair was neat and his tattoos hidden, as she had instructed. The reaction from the gallery was instantaneous, with Doreen gasping and Declan whispering to her.

Judge Patterson looked over. "Order, please," she said, though her tone was gentle. "We understand this trial is difficult for the victim's family. However, it's vital that your emotional reactions be restrained, particularly when the jury enters the courtroom."

Bennie rose to greet an ashen-faced Jason. "Hi, how are you?" she asked quietly, as the sheriff undid the handcuffs.

"I'm okay." Jason managed a shaky smile, covering his crooked teeth the way he used to, which reminded Bennie of the sweet boy he'd once been. His temper had been becalmed by medication, a superficial fix she hoped would get him through trial. She still couldn't bring herself to believe that he was a murderer, despite the fact that his story about being framed hadn't panned out. She and Lou had investigated, but they'd learned that Richie didn't have enemies at Ackermann and he made a decent living, so it's wasn't as if he owed anybody money. Richie had no drug issues, and though he dated, they couldn't find any jealous boyfriends or husbands, either. In short, they had no leads or evidence on who would've killed Richie and framed Jason.

"Here, sit down." Bennie pulled out his chair.

"What do I do during court, again?" Jason whispered to her, sitting down, and Bennie took a seat beside him.

"Try and relax. Listen to the witness, but don't make any expressions or funny faces. If you have a question or comment, write it on my pad."

"Okay." Jason nodded, tense. His eyes darted around the room, and Bennie could see him taking in the court reporter, an older woman sneaking a last look at her smartphone, and the court clerk, placing a slim blue booklet on the seats in the jury box, which the jurors would use to take notes.

Judge Patterson gestured to the court clerk. "Tania, thanks. Would you please fetch the jury for us?"

"Yes, Your Honor." The court clerk went to the side door.

Bennie noticed Paul Stokowski and Renée Zimmer slide out of their pew in the gallery and leave the courtroom, which told her that they were going to be called as Commonwealth witnesses. It was standard practice not to have a witness listen to the trial because it could taint their testimony and make them impeachable before the jury. For that reason, Judge Patterson entered a sequestration order, applicable to both the defense and the Commonwealth, requiring potential witnesses for both sides to remain outside the courtroom until they are called to testify. Martinez hadn't otherwise shown his hand about whom he was going to call, and his witness list was long, the traditional kitchen-sink approach. Bennie was worried about only one of the names on the list—Declan's.

She leaned nearer to Jason, to show the jury she was on his side, and watched the jurors file in, getting a first impression as they entered the jury box. There was a pasty-faced young man who looked like a Programmer Guy; a thirty-something black woman built lean as a runner, Marathon Mom; a tattooed redhead with oversized black glasses, Brooklyn Girl.

Bennie slid from the case file the chart they'd been given by the Court, containing the jurors' names, ages, occupations, and general location of their residence. The jury composition was seven males, five females, and two female alternates, so even-handed that she doubted it would be a factor. The race of the jurors reflected the city's diversity: five white, four black, two Hispanic, an Asian, and an older Indian grandmother, so that wouldn't be a factor, either. Bennie missed the days when the law-yers conducted voir dire, questioning the jury and getting to know them. The rules had changed, and now judges conducted voir dire to save time, asking only the most routine questions, while the lawyers watched and took notes, then *picked* the jury. Bennie always found the word *picked* to be ironic in that lawyers don't actually *select* juries but actually deselect them, through the use of challenges which eliminate potential jurors that one side or the other believe might be somehow biased, resulting in those that remain unchallenged to comprise the actual jury. It wasn't the same because Bennie always used voir dire to establish a rapport with the jury, to benefit her client. Those days were gone, and she would be watching the jurors during trial. Until then, their specific leanings, beliefs, and personalities were part of the vast sea of unknowns.

"Good morning, ladies and gentlemen." Judge Patterson smiled as the jurors settled into their numbered seats.

"Good morning, Judge," "Good morning, Your Honor," "Nice to meet you," they murmured as a group, picking up their blue booklets and smiling nervously back at the judge.

"Thank you for agreeing to serve. We are aware that it's an inconvenience, but service on jury duty is essential to the admin-istration of criminal justice in this city." Judge Patterson gestured at Martinez. "Jurors, seated at the table nearer to you is Juan David Martinez, who represents the Commonwealth in this case, and at the far table is counsel for defendant, Bennie Rosato. Next to her is the defendant in this matter, Jason Lefkavick."

Bennie nodded pleasantly, though Jason stiffened.

"Jurors, please feel free to make notes in your numbered book-lets, and only in your booklets. They will be collected at the end

of the day and may not be taken home. Additionally, you are asked
to refrain from watching or reading media about this case. You
are instructed not to discuss this case among yourselves at anytime
until all the evidence has been submitted, both sides have rested
their cases, and I have provided my instructions on the law. Only
at that time may you begin your deliberations. Now, we may
begin. Mr. Martinez?"

"Thank you, Your Honor." Martinez jumped up with a toothy
smile, buttoning his jacket as he walked over to the jury box.
"Ladies and gentlemen of the jury, thank you very much for your
service. We're here on a very grave matter, the gravest. The defendant, seated over there in the new white shirt, is charged with
the premeditated murder of a young man named Richie Grusini,
which took place on Monday night, January 12, of this year.
Richie, who was only twenty-six years old at the time of his
murder, leaves behind his mother and grieving family." Martinez
nodded in Doreen's direction, which was one of the cheapest
tricks in the book, because it wasn't permissible in an opening to
refer directly to a victim's family.

The jury looked over at Doreen and Declan, but Bennie kept
her face front, not to contribute to his stage directions. Martinez
was an experienced enough lawyer to have a bag of lawyerly tricks,
and she had a few of her own. Among them, she'd always refer to
Martinez as the prosecutor, because it was a word people mixed
up with persecutor, which sometimes wasn't far from the truth.
She put on her game face and listened as Martinez continued.

"I like to keep my opening short and let my witnesses do the
talking for me. The evidence of guilt in this case is simply overwhelming, in both hard evidence and supporting circumstantial
evidence. Suffice it to say that you will hear testimony that the
defendant and his victim, Richie Grusini, had a history of conflict since childhood, when they got into a childhood fight in a
middle-school cafeteria, in 2002. But to fast-forward to a year ago,
the evidence will show defendant moved to Philadelphia, rented
an apartment only a few blocks away from Richie, and began
stalking him."

Bennie was about to object to the stalking characterization, but let it go. She didn't want to appear as if she were hiding something.

"You will hear evidence that one Monday night this past January, Richie was seated at the bar in his favorite restaurant with his best friend, minding his own business, when the defendant interrupted the victim, Mr. Grusini, and picked a fight. An altercation ensued, and the two men were asked to leave the premises. Ladies and gentlemen, you will hear that what happened next is why all of us are here and that, what should have ended with the defendant simply walking away, ended with Richie lying dead in the alley outside the bar with his throat slashed."

Bennie watched the jury focus on Martinez, who held their rapt attention.

"The Commonwealth will prove that Richie left the bar and walked to an alley-like area around the corner, where his car was parked. But still, Richie wasn't safe from defendant. The evidence will show that defendant pursued Richie into the alley and that there, the defendant murdered him by stabbing him in the throat with a hunting knife, which was found, dripping Richie's blood, still in the defendant's hand."

Bennie watched as Marathon Mom's eyes flared in horror. Mouths dropped open in the front row, and Funny Guy exchanged appalled glances with the older Asian juror, sitting next to him.

"This is a classic case of premeditated and brutal murder. You will hear testimony that the defendant *himself* told officers at the scene that he was not sorry that Richie was dead, even as that poor young man lay bleeding to death."

Bennie kept her expression impassive as she caught Brooklyn Girl frowning behind her big black glasses.

"You have heard people use the term murder on television and movies, but in Pennsylvania, we use the term criminal homicide, and it is defined as the intentional, knowing, reckless or negligent causing of the death of another human being. Murder in the first degree, which is the charge here, is the most heinous crime known to man. It is defined as criminal homicide when the killing of another human being is intentional, and the evidence will show that that is exactly what happened to the victim in this case, at the hands of the defendant."

Martinez gestured at Jason, then continued.

"The Commonwealth will show you the actual murder weapon that was used, and we will produce additional forensic evidence, as well. Ladies and gentlemen, this is a horrific and indescribable tragedy, and you can be certain that by the time the evidence is closed and the Judge has charged you on the law, that same evidence and that same law will leave you with only one alternative, namely, to look this defendant squarely in the eye, just as he looked Richie in the eye when he cut his throat, and return the only verdict that the facts and the law will allow, namely, a verdict of murder in the first degree. Thank you." Martinez started back to his seat, and Bennie didn't wait because she wanted to dispel any mood he'd created by his opening.

"Good morning, ladies and gentlemen," she said, approaching the jury box, where she began to relax, feeling at home. She blocked Declan, Doreen, and the twins from her mind, kept Jason uppermost, and took a moment to make eye contact with the jurors, as calmly as possible. She never tried to wow a jury with an opening, but to plant the seed of a reasonable doubt about the Commonwealth's case.

"Thank you for agreeing to serve on this jury. You have a grave responsibility on your hands, the fate of my client, Jason Lefkavick." Bennie gestured briefly to him. "That's Jason sitting at counsel table, and as you can see, he's a young man. And yes, the prosecutor was right about one thing—Jason is wearing a new shirt, because I made him. We're all trying to look our best in court today, and that is not a crime. In fact I'm wearing a new shirt, for that very reason." Bennie kept her tone light, but not joking, and knew she'd made her point when she saw Brooklyn Girl smile. "So now that we've dispensed with wardrobe snark, let's get to what's important."

Bennie paused, just to make a break in their concentration.

"You have just heard the prosecutor tell you what he thinks the evidence will show in this matter, but I'm here to tell you something even more important—what the evidence will *not* show. This case is about a deadly argument that took place in an alley between two lifelong enemies, Mr. Grusini and my client, Jason, and there are no witnesses to what actually occurred." Bennie paused, for emphasis. "The prosecutor talked about videocameras, but there is no video that captured what happened in the alley. The prosecutor talked about best friends, but there is no best friend who saw what happened in the alley. I'm asking you to keep an open mind as the testimony goes in and to listen not only to what you are being told, but to what you are *not* being told."

Bennie felt heartened to see Brooklyn Girl nod in a knowing way, and she continued.

"The most important thing that you are *not* being told by the prosecutor is who really started the fight that led to Mr. Grusini's death. The prosecutor said that Mr. Grusini was minding his own business and that my client Jason was the aggressor, but in fact, the evidence will show that the opposite was true." Bennie spoke to them naturally, because it was the only way she knew how to speak to a jury, just like she spoke to everyone else. "The question in this case is not a complex one, and it comes down to, 'who started it?' The prosecutor claims that Jason started it, but I think the evidence will show that it was *Mr. Grusini* who started it. You will be the one to decide that question ultimately, and I have complete confidence that you will do so correctly. After all, 'who started it' isn't a complex legal question, but a matter of common sense. It's familiar to anybody who's ever raised a child—or for that matter, to anyone who's ever *been* a child."

Bennie had improvised this last part for Marathon Mom, who nodded in agreement, and the grandmotherly juror in the front row smiled.

"The evidence will show that my client, Jason, acted only in self-defense. Self-defense is a justification, which is the right of everyone in our Commonwealth, where, as you will learn, we have a stand-your-ground law that gives every Pennsylvanian the right to stand his ground and defend his own life, whether he is threatened in his home or anywhere in public, like in an alley. You are justified in using deadly force to defend yourself where there is a threat to imminent harm and there is no other means of escape from the situation. The evidence will show that is exactly what happened in this matter."

Bennie had no idea how she would make a self-defense case without putting Jason on the stand, but she wasn't about to promise the jury that they would see him testify. No trial lawyer would ever make a promise in an opening that they couldn't deliver. Her strategy was to establish self-defense through cross-examination of the Commonwealth witnesses, and her only consolation was that she had no other choice. Still, Bennie sensed that if she looked up Insanely Risky in the dictionary, there would be a picture of her, right now.

"You have heard the expression that there's two sides to every story. Well, that's true. So when the prosecutor has his witnesses up on the stand, he's telling you his side of the story. I get to tell our side of the story when I cross-examine. Real cross-examination isn't like on TV. It's not about being mean to the witnesses or making them cry. It's about eliciting facts from them that the prosecutor doesn't want you to know about, but that I do. I'm going to have questions for each witness, which will tell you our side of the story, so I'm going to ask you to listen carefully for when I do that."

Bennie paused.

"The most important point of law that you need to keep in mind, and one that Judge Patterson will instruct you on, is that even though we are claiming self-defense, we do not have to *prove* self-defense. Under the Constitution of this country, the burden never shifts to Jason or to me to prove *anything* in a criminal trial. That burden always remains with the prosecutor, and my client, Jason, is absolutely innocent unless and until the prosecutor proves him guilty beyond a reasonable doubt."

Bennie paused to let the concept sink in, and Programmer Guy seemed to understand immediately, raking a hand through scruffy hair. The other jurors seemed to be listening to her, returning solid eye contact or cocking their heads in a way that suggested she had planted the seed she wanted.

"We know that things are not always what they seem. Sometimes we need to look beyond the surface and question what we are being told. You're smart people and you will need to do that, starting now. Look for the holes in the prosecution's case, which I think falls far short of proving anything beyond reasonable doubt, much less the most heinous crime known to man. Thank you so much."

Bennie turned away from the jury, and Martinez popped up, trying to steal her thunder, the way she had stolen his.

"Thank you, counsel." Judge Patterson nodded. "Mr. Martinez, ready?"

Bennie got back to her seat, touching Jason's shoulder before she sat down next to him. He was frowning, and she realized why when she saw the note that he had written on her legal pad.

I CAN'T BELIEVE YOU DID THAT! I TOLD YOU IT WASN'T SELF-DEFENSE!!

Bennie tore off the page, and Martinez called his first witness.

CHAPTER FORTY-THREE

The Commonwealth's first witness was Officer Ryan Underwood, the arresting officer. Underwood was in his late thirties, with lively brown eyes behind wire-rimmed glasses, short brown hair, and sunburned cheeks that he'd gotten coaching his son's Little League game. He was absolutely professional, even likable, as Martinez took him through the preliminaries, his years on the Philadelphia police force, the number of crime scenes he'd been at, and how he'd been called to the crime scene that night.

Martinez entered into evidence an enlarged black-and-white photo of the alley on Dunbar Avenue, and Bennie didn't object because it was devoid of blood, a body, or anything else prejudicial. Martinez stood beside the easel, gesturing. "Now, Officer Underwood, when you arrived at the scene, where did you find the victim's body?"

"It was lying faceup, on a slight diagonal, right here." Officer Underwood pointed to the middle of the alley. "The victim's head pointed south toward the front of the alley and his feet toward the back of the alley. North."

"Officer Underwood, what, if anything, did you determine about the victim when you arrived at the scene?"

"He had no pulse or vital signs. His throat had been cut, and his clothes were extremely bloody. I attempted to administer CPR, but it was too late."

"What do you mean by too late?"

"That they were mortal injuries. The victim had already passed. He bled to death."

Bennie could have objected because the officer wasn't qualified to give cause of death, but this wasn't the time to quibble. Sniffling came from Doreen's direction, and two of the jurors glanced sympathetically at her, but Bennie kept her attention focused on the witness. Martinez returned to the witness box, standing close enough to the jury box to be chummy. It was another trick that Bennie used herself, and she wondered briefly if their tricks would cancel each other out.

"Officer Underwood, isn't the wide part of the alley, to the left, where you found Mr. Grusini's truck parked, is that correct?"

"Yes."

"And Mr. Grusini's truck was a 2009 Ford F-150, white in color, correct?"

"Yes."

Bennie knew he was leading the witness, but didn't bother to object because it was permissible to elicit preliminary information.

"Officer Underwood, the defendant in this case is Jason Lefkavick. Do you see him in this courtroom and can you identify him?"

"Yes, at that table." The witness pointed.

"And you have seen him before, is that correct?"

"Yes, I arrested him at the scene."

"Officer Underwood, how did the defendant appear to you when you first saw him at the scene?"

Bennie thought it was vague, but she let it go. She wasn't going to object unless it was absolutely necessary. She was putting all her money on cross.

Officer Underwood answered, "He was in a sitting position and he seemed kind of groggy."

"Your Honor, I would like to move into evidence Commonwealth Exhibit 2, a large hunting knife with a jagged edge."

Martinez crossed the courtroom to Bennie, making much of showing it to her. She didn't react and, mercifully, neither did Jason.

"No objection," Bennie said, her tone neutral.

"So admitted." Judge Patterson nodded, and the court clerk made the appropriate notes and labeling.

Martinez returned to his spot, holding up the knife like the Sword of Damocles. "Officer Underwood, have you ever seen this knife before today?"

"Yes."

"Please tell the jury where you first saw this knife."

"I took it out of the right hand of the defendant at the scene of the murder."

"Was its condition any different than it is today."

"Yes, it was covered with blood."

"Now, Officer Underwood, did you have occasion to speak with the defendant at that time?"

"Yes."

"What was your conversation?"

"I asked him if he was okay. He said yes. I advised him of his Miranda rights, then I informed him that the victim was deceased, and he said, 'Good, I'm *glad* he's dead.'"

Bennie kept a poker face as the jury reacted with a collective frown. It was home-run evidence of motive, fulfilling the "intentional" requirement for murder in the first degree. It was also a damning admission, which was why it didn't qualify as hearsay, but Bennie wouldn't have objected in any event. A few of the jurors checked Jason to see if he was reacting, but he merely blinked.

Martinez held up a hand. "To clarify, Officer Underwood, you're testifying that the defendant said he was *glad* that the victim was dead?"

"Yes."

"You're sure that's what he said?"

"Absolutely."

"Officer Underwood, did you ask him why he said that?"

"Yes."

"And what did the defendant say to you in response?"

"He answered, 'It's about damn time he paid for what he did to me and I got a lil' justice for once in my effing life!' " Officer Underwood paused. "Obviously, he used the f-word."

Bennie eyed the jurors, and the grandmother in the front row scowled.

"Officer Underwood, did you ask him what he meant by that?"

"No."

"Officer Underwood, how did he seem when he said that?"

"Very angry."

"Did you smell alcohol on his breath or on his person?"

"Yes, on his breath."

"Officer Underwood, did he seem so inebriated to you that he didn't know what he was saying?"

"No, not in my opinion."

"Did you give him a breathalyzer test?"

"No, it's not procedure in those circumstances."

"Thank you."

Martinez paused. "Officer Underwood, after that, did you transport defendant in custody to the Roundhouse?"

"Yes. My partner and I did."

"Did you have any further conversation with respect to the murder?"

"No."

"Thank you for your testimony, Officer Underwood." Martinez looked up at Judge Patterson. "I have no further questions at this time, Your Honor."

"Thank you, Mr. Martinez." Judge Patterson faced Bennie, who was already on her feet. "Ms. Rosato, cross-examination?"

CHAPTER FORTY-FOUR

"Yes, thank you, Your Honor, I do have cross-examination." Bennie crossed to the witness box and stood exactly where Martinez had, not to be outchummed. "Good morning, Officer Underwood. You testified on direct examination that you saw my client, Jason, in the alley, but you were not asked where he was located in relation to Mr. Grusini. Where was he located, in relation to Mr. Grusini?"

"He was here." Officer Underwood pointed to the exhibit, farther back in the alley.

"For the record, you're gesturing nearer the back wall of the alley, isn't that correct?"

"Yes."

"So that means that when you came to the alley, the first person you encountered was Mr. Grusini's body and behind him was my client Jason?"

"Yes."

"To the left was Mr. Grusini's pickup truck, isn't that correct?"

"Yes."

"Officer Underwood, how much space would you say was between Mr. Grusini's body and his pickup truck?"

"I would say, about two feet."

"Thank you." Bennie didn't ask the next question, *was there enough room to permit Jason to leave the alley by the front?* The issue with any cross-examination was twofold: what did the witness know and what was he willing to say? Bennie was experienced enough to know not to push it too far and risk losing everything; Officer Underwood would say that he didn't know, and he wasn't willing to give her the conclusion she needed.

"Now, Officer Underwood, did my client Jason give you the knife freely?"

"Yes."

"He didn't try to hide the knife, did he?"

"No, he did not."

"He didn't get up and try to run, did he?"

"No."

"Officer Underwood, to another point about which you weren't asked. Isn't it true that Jason told you the knife wasn't his?"

Martinez jumped to his shiny shoes. "Objection, Your Honor, calls for hearsay."

Bennie faced the judge. "Your Honor, it's not hearsay if it comes in only for the fact that it was said, not for the truth of the matter asserted. I didn't object during the prosecutor's direct examination of this witness for that reason, and what's good for the goose is good for the gander."

Judge Patterson nodded, with a tight smile that showed she had gotten Bennie's reference. "Objection overruled."

Bennie turned to the witness. "Officer Underwood, isn't it true that my client Jason told you that the knife was not his?"

"Yes."

"What exactly did he say to you?"

"He said, 'this isn't my knife.'"

Again, Bennie stopped short of asking the next question, which would have been, *whose knife was it*? The witness didn't have personal knowledge to answer the question and he wasn't willing to admit that it was Richie's. She let it go, trusting that the jury would follow her train of thought; if the knife didn't belong to Jason, then it had to belong to Richie, and the only logical inference was that Richie had pulled a knife on Jason. The facts spoke for themselves, laying the foundation of a self-defense claim, even if Jason wouldn't.

"Officer Underwood, did Jason say that the knife wasn't his, in response to a question?"

"No."

"So he volunteered that information?"

"Yes, that's why I didn't believe it."

Ouch. It was a punch, but Bennie wasn't about to fall down. "You didn't believe it because he volunteered it?"

"Yes."

"But Officer Underwood, you testified that Jason also said he was glad that Mr. Grusini was dead, correct?"

"Yes."

"And Jason volunteered that testimony, did he not?"

"Yes."

"But you believed *that* volunteered information, did you not?"

"Yes." Officer Underwood blinked.

"So Officer Underwood, contrary to what you just testified, some volunteered information you believe and some you don't."

"Well—"

"The fact that Jason volunteered the information has nothing to do with anything, does it?"

"Uh, no, not really."

"Officer Underwood, excuse me a moment." Bennie crossed to the counsel table, picked up her exhibit, and approached the bench. "Judge Patterson, may I show this photograph to the witness?"

"You may." Judge Patterson took a look at the picture and handed it back to Bennie, who took it over to the witness box.

"Officer Underwood, I'm showing you a mugshot, and I am asking you if it represents the way my client Jason looked when you first saw him."

Officer Underwood frowned at the photo. "It does, and it doesn't."

Bennie had expected as much, but stayed the course. She could've introduced the mugshot later, but she wanted to make her point as early as possible. "Officer Underwood, is it fair to say that it's a cleaned-up version of what Jason looked like when you first saw him?"

"The defendant? Yes."

"Thank you." Bennie addressed Judge Patterson as she walked to Martinez and showed him the picture. "Your Honor, I am showing it to the prosecutor and I move this mugshot into evidence as Defense Exhibit 10."

"Any objection, Mr. Martinez?" Judge Patterson asked.

"No," Martinez answered, his mouth tight.

"Thank you." Bennie walked back to counsel table, set the photo down, and grabbed its enlarged version, which she carried to the metal easel and placed on top of the picture of the alley. The jury reacted almost instantly, shifting in their seats, which was enough to satisfy her. Jason's mugshot showed flecks of dried blood on his forehead and blackening his eyebrow. His left eye was red, puffy, and swollen shut, and his enlarged goose egg looked as big as a baseball, which was the desired effect.

Bennie gestured at the exhibit. "Officer Underwood, as you can see, this is a larger view of the photo that is Defense Exhibit 10." She approached the witness box. "Officer Underwood, does the exhibit accurately represent the injury that you saw on Jason's face on the night in question?"

"Yes."

"That's the way it's similar, correct?"

"Yes."

"The way it's different is that his injury was much bloodier when you first saw him, correct?"

"Define 'much bloodier.'" Officer Underwood didn't look at the jury because cops were trained not to, which made them seem evasive even when they weren't. Until the PPD figured that out, Bennie would take advantage, every time.

"Officer Underwood, please tell the jury, in your own words, how much blood was on Jason's injury when you first saw him?"

"There was some blood."

"Yes, but how much blood?"

"It was dark, so it was hard to see."

"Was there a small, a medium, or a large amount of blood?" Bennie controlled her sarcasm to be respectful to the witness, especially with so many unknowns among the jurors. But so far, she was loving this testimony. The more they talked about the blood on Jason's injury, the less they were talking about the blood on Richie's neck.

"I would say there was a medium amount of blood."

"And where exactly was Jason bleeding from?"

"From the forehead."

"So above his eye is where this injury is, is that what you mean?"

"Yes."

"Could you show us on the photograph where the blood was on his eye?"

"Yes, right here." Officer Underwood pointed generally to Jason's eye, which was all Bennie needed. She wanted to give the jury permission to keep looking at the exhibit, which showed Jason's features grossly distorted by the injury; his eye and nose were swollen, and the white of his eye was completely red, which was disturbing.

"Officer Underwood, did you ask Jason how he got this injury?"

"No."

Bennie stopped short of asking the next question, which was, *didn't you assume that he had been punched by Mr. Grusini?* She didn't need to go there, and the jurors had the same powers of deduction as the witness; Jason had a goose egg on his forehead, so he got punched by the only other person in the alley, who was Richie.

"Officer Underwood, did you offer any medical assistance to my client?"

"No."

"You merely put him in handcuffs and arrested him?"

"Yes."

"Even though he looked like *this*?" Bennie gestured at the photo.

"Yes," Officer Underwood repeated, belatedly.

Bennie took the exhibit down because she knew jurors grew inured to gruesome exhibits over time, then she returned to the witness box. "Officer Underwood, you testified that Jason was groggy when you first saw him. What did you mean by that?"

"Dazed."

"Did you have any opinion about why that was so?"

"Objection!" Martinez jumped up. "The witness is not qualified to give a medical opinion. He's not a doctor."

Bennie faced Judge Patterson. "Your Honor, I'm simply asking the officer to explain what he meant. He formed an initial impression, groggy and dazed, and we all understand that he's not diagnosing an illness."

"I'll allow it." Judge Patterson lifted an arched eyebrow. "But don't go too far, Ms. Rosato."

"Thank you, Your Honor." Bennie turned back to the witness box. "Officer Underwood, what did you mean when you said my client was groggy?"

"He appeared to have been drinking and also he was regaining consciousness."

Bennie flared her eyes, for show. She would leave aside the inebriation because she had a plan for that later, but she could see the jury react to the revelation that Jason had been unconscious. "Officer Underwood, you had the initial impression that my client had just regained consciousness, didn't you?"

"Yes, but I'm not a doctor, so I'm not absolutely sure."

"Please answer my question. Did you or did you not have the impression that my client had just regained consciousness?"

"Yes, I did." Officer Underwood shifted in his seat. "It seemed like he was out and was just coming to, but I'm not a medical doctor."

Bennie didn't like that the cop was picking up on Martinez's cue and she knew the jury wouldn't like it either. "Officer Underwood, didn't you testify that you coach Little League for your—"

"Objection, relevance!" Martinez snapped, rising.

"Your Honor, if the prosecutor will permit me to finish, then I think the relevance will be clear."

Judge Patterson nodded. "I'll overrule the objection. But remember, not too far afield, Ms. Rosato."

"Thank you, Your Honor." Bennie returned to Officer Underwood. "Sir, I would gather that in your capacity as a Little League coach, sometimes you see children get hit in the head with the ball, or collide with each other on base, or even fight, is that correct?"

"Yes, it is."

"And do those children lose and regain consciousness, from time to time?"

"Yes."

"And isn't it also true that even the parents get into fights in the bleachers, from time to time?"

"Yes, unfortunately." Officer Underwood pursed his lips.

"Of course it is." Bennie glanced at Marathon Mom, who was listening with obvious interest. "So you have seen an adult regain consciousness, isn't that correct?"

"Yes."

"So Officer Underwood, when you say that Jason regained consciousness, we have every reason to credit your statement, isn't that correct?"

"Yes."

Bennie didn't ask the next question, which was *didn't you assume my client was knocked out by Mr. Grusini,* because again, she knew the cop didn't have personal knowledge of the answer and wasn't willing to give her the answer she wanted. She'd let the jury draw its own logical conclusion, again; Jason had a bloody bump on his forehead, so he had been punched there, which caused him to lose consciousness. Again, the facts spoke for themselves, even if Jason wouldn't.

Bennie glanced at the judge. "Your Honor, I have no further questions."

"Thank you, Ms. Rosato. Mr. Martinez?"

"Yes, Your Honor, I have redirect." Martinez crossed to the witness box and asked a few more questions, but Bennie didn't think he repaired the damage that she had done, so she didn't recross. Martinez would realize that he'd made a mistake by omitting bad facts, which allowed her to score. He wouldn't make the same mistake from now on. In fact, he was edgy and already on his feet.

"Your Honor, the Commonwealth is ready with its second witness."

CHAPTER FORTY-FIVE

Bennie picked up her pen, as Paul Stokowski was sworn in. She wasn't exactly sure of what he would say, since he had refused their interview requests, but he looked the way she'd expected him to look. His eyes were blue, round, and set close together; he had a long nose on a longish face, and his chin came to a point. He was tall and wore his sandy-brown hair parted down the middle, so that his bangs flopped up on both sides, a hairdo that gave him an incongruous beachy vibe in a city not known for its surf. He was fully six feet, with muscled biceps under a short-sleeve blue shirt, which he had on with khaki pants, a wardrobe choice that made him look like everybody's bro. The only note of the bad boy was a neck tattoo, but it was on his left side, which faced away from the jury.

Bennie guessed that Martinez had reshuffled his witness order, responding quickly to what had happened this morning. The conventional order of witnesses for the Commonwealth would've been arresting officer, medical examiner, detective, then fact witnesses like Stokowski and whoever else. But Martinez was evidently responding to her who-started-it argument, skipping law enforcement and going straight to Stokowski. It was good and bad news because it showed that Martinez was sure-footed enough to counter her argument, but it also meant that he probably hadn't had the time to prepare Stokowski, because witnesses weren't usually prepared until the night before they took the stand.

Martinez approached the witness box. "Mr. Stokowski, how long have you been friends with the victim?"

"Five years. We worked together at Ackermann Construction in East Falls. We've worked the same framing team all this time. We're both master carpenters. We do a lot of molding and sills, like that." Stokowski faced the jury when he spoke, and if he was nervous, it didn't show.

"Is this new construction or renovations?"

"Both. These days, mostly renovations. Lot of people like a new kitchen."

"Mr. Stokowski, would you say you and Mr. Grusini were best friends?"

"Absolutely." Stokowski smiled briefly, showing nice teeth. "He was my best man at my wedding."

"Please accept my condolences on your loss."

"Thank you." Stokowski's smile vanished, his face folding into lines of genuine grief.

Bennie slid her gaze to the jury, seeing that it'd hit home. They looked sympathetic for his loss and they liked him. Plus, sexism aside, most women could relate to getting a new kitchen, and most men to being a master carpenter.

"Mr. Stokowski, did you and Mr. Grusini often go to Eddie's bar?"

"Yes."

"How often would you say?"

"Once a week, either Friday night or in winter, to watch *Monday Night Football*. That's when I'm allowed out. We have two boys, so my wife needs a break. Sorry, honey." Stokowski smiled again, leaning over to catch the eye of someone in the gallery, presumably his wife.

The jurors smiled and looked back at the gallery.

Martinez paused. "Mr. Stokowski, have you ever heard Mr. Grusini talk about the defendant?"

"Yes."

"So you were aware that he had a prior relationship to the defendant?"

"Yes."

Bennie perked up, ready for a hearsay objection.

Martinez asked, "Mr. Stokowski, if you know, what was the nature of that relationship?"

Bennie rose, but didn't object because she didn't want to look bad to the jury, which was one of the reasons she'd drafted the stipulation about prior bad acts. "Your Honor, the prosecutor may want to save the Court's time at this point, by reading the stipulation for the record, or paraphrasing it, if he wishes."

Judge Patterson nodded. "Thank you, counsel. Mr. Martinez, that may be the best way to proceed, don't you agree?"

"Fine." Martinez turned to the witness. "Mr. Stokowski, did he mention to you that he and the defendant were both victims of the Kids-for-Cash scandal in Luzerne County?"

"Yes, he used to talk about that a lot."

"Mr. Stokowski, had you heard about the Kids-for-Cash scandal, prior to his telling you about it?"

"Yes."

"Would you explain the Kids-for-Cash scandal to the jury, generally?"

"Yes." Stokowski turned to the jury. "If you haven't heard about it, the Kids-for-Cash scandal was where a judge in Luzerne County sent kids to juvie halls for almost nothing, because the judges were crooked."

Some of the jurors nodded in a knowing way, and others frowned, hearing it for the first time. Bennie let it go. It was an informal way for the information to come in, but it was as good as any. She wanted the focus off the past and on the present, for Jason's benefit. If it came off that he'd been resentful since Kids-for-Cash, it would reinforce his motive to kill Richie.

"Mr. Stokowski, did Mr. Grusini mention to you that his initial incarceration, which began at only age twelve, was because he got into a fight in the middle-school cafeteria with the defendant, Jason Lefkavick?"

"Yes, he did."

"And as best you knew, Richie spent a lot of his childhood and young adulthood in juvenile incarceration, wrongly imprisoned because of this corrupt scheme, is that correct?"

"Yes."

Bennie let that go, too. It was sweeping under the rug any kind of wrongdoing that Richie was truly responsible for, but her eye was on the prize, which was an acquittal for Jason.

"Mr. Stokowski, what was Mr. Grusini's view of the defendant?"

"He didn't like him."

Bennie had been about to object, but was glad she hadn't. It was undoubtedly the truth, but a better answer for the Commonwealth would have been that Richie was indifferent to Jason. As it was, the answer helped the self-defense argument, but Stokowski had been out of the courtroom during openings and wouldn't know the defense theory of the case. And if Martinez hadn't reshuffled his witness list, he would have had more time to prepare Stokowski for all possibilities.

"Mr. Stokowski, was Mr. Grusini afraid of the defendant?"

"No way. Richie thought he was a joke."

Bennie thought it was an even better answer, for the defense. Jason shifted beside her, but didn't otherwise react to the testimony.

"Mr. Stokowski, what . . . do you mean by that?"

"When Richie talked about the defendant, he always called him 'Chunky,' like that chocolate candy. He was a fat kid. I guess he lost the weight now, but Richie wasn't afraid of him." Stokowski hesitated. "Maybe he should have been, the way things turned out. Richie wasn't the type to be afraid of anybody, he can handle himself."

Bennie wrote on the left side of her pad, *could handle himself.*

"Mr. Stokowski, let's fast-forward to the night in question. You and Mr. Grusini went to Eddie's and sat at the bar, is that correct?"

"Yes."

"Who sat on the left and who was on the right?"

"He was on the left and I was on the right."

"Mr. Stokowski, what time did you two arrive?"

"Around seven fifteen. We drove in separate cars, though."

"Mr. Stokowski, what did you do when you sat down?"

"You know, ate and drank, watched the pregame."

"How much did you personally eat and drink?"

"I had a cheeseburger and two beers. That's my limit when I drive." Stokowski spoke directly to the jury, who collectively nodded in approval.

"How about Mr. Grusini, how much did he drink?"

"He drank a little more, maybe a beer ahead of me, but he could hold his liquor."

Bennie wrote on her notepad, *could hold his liquor.*

"Mr. Stokowski, when you entered the bar, did you realize that the defendant was also in the bar, seated in the eating area?"

"No."

"Did Mr. Grusini realize that, if you know?"

"No, not to my knowledge."

"Did you or Mr. Grusini know that the defendant was even in Philadelphia, to your knowledge?"

Bennie could've objected, but let it go.

"No," Stokowski answered.

"Okay, so Mr. Stokowski, what happened on the night of the murder, at the bar, between the defendant and Mr. Grusini?"

"We were sitting at the bar, watching the game. I remember because the Eagles were ahead and that doesn't happen nearly enough." Stokowski managed a smile, and a few of the jurors nodded, commiserating. "Then all of a sudden, I looked over and there's this dude standing there between me and Richie, right behind us."

"Mr. Stokowski, do you see that person in the courtroom and will you identify him?"

"Yes, the defendant." Stokowski pointed.

"Okay, then what happened?"

"So I didn't know who the dude was, or the defendant, sorry, and all of a sudden he was tapping Richie on the shoulder and saying something."

"Mr. Stokowski, what did he say to Richie, if you know?"

"I do know, I heard it. He said, 'Remember me?' Then he said, 'Do you know what today is, you sick piece of shit?' " Stokowski looked from the jury to Martinez. "It's okay to curse, right? That's exactly what he said."

"Yes, with apologies for the profanity, we need to know exactly what he said."

"That's it."

Martinez nodded. "So then what happened, Mr. Stokowski?"

"So then Richie kind of pushed him."

"Now, before this took place, did Mr. Grusini do or say anything to the defendant?"

"No, like I say, our back was to the eating area. We didn't even know he was there."

Bennie didn't object because the question had been asked and answered, but she would if it went to one more question. She noticed a juror in the front row taking notes. Martinez was hammering home his Richie-was-minding-his-own-business point to show that Jason was the one who started it, in response to her opening. But the bar wasn't where it mattered. The alley was.

"Mr. Stokowski, before Mr. Grusini pushed the defendant, did he say anything to him?"

"Yes. He said, 'Get the eff out of my face, Chunk.' "

"Mr. Stokowski, in your opinion, was the defendant 'in his face'?" Martinez made air quotes.

"Most definitely. Richie pushed him away, and the defendant must've been drunk because he fell off-balance."

"Objection," Bennie said, because of the assumption about the drunkenness. She had bigger plans for that, later.

"Sustained," Judge Patterson ruled. "Jurors, you are to disregard the conclusion that the defendant was drunk."

"Thank you, Your Honor." Martinez returned his attention to

the witness stand. "Mr. Stokowski, when Mr. Grusini pushed the defendant, did he push him hard?"

"No, not really, but Richie was a bigger guy than him, so he fell over. When the defendant fell, he kind of kicked up at Richie, and Richie grabbed his leg, then all hell broke loose. The people at the bar jumped up, and the bartender stopped the fight, then he threw out Richie and the defendant."

Martinez paused. "Mr. Stokowski, how did the defendant react to being thrown out, from what you saw?"

"When the bartender picked up his arm, the defendant kind of pulled away in a very angry way, I guess that's what you would say."

"So he appeared very angry, to the best of your knowledge?"

Bennie let it go, knowing they were picking their words carefully.

"Yes, he was angry," Stokowski answered.

"Mr. Stokowski, what happened with Mr. Grusini, then?"

"The bartender asked him to go, too, and so we both left."

"Mr. Stokowski, what happened when you and the victim left the bar?"

"We said good-bye, we split up. I got a great parking space right in front, so I just got in my car and drove home." Stokowski ran his tongue over dry lips. "I feel bad about that now. I feel like I shoulda walked Richie to his car. He always parks, he always *parked*, in that alley on Dunbar Street. It was his secret spot, I think it went with the medical supply company. But I think about that a lot. What if I walked him to his car?"

"I understand," Martinez said gently.

Bennie could see that it had an effect on the jurors, but there was nothing she could do. She'd tried enough murder cases to know that she always felt lousy while the Commonwealth was putting on its case. The loss of life and the ripple effects of lethal violence were undeniably heartbreaking.

"Mr. Stokowski, when you left the bar, did you see the defendant at all?"

"No, just Richie."

"Mr. Stokowski, what was the victim doing when you saw him last?"

"He was walking down Pimlico Street toward Dunbar Street."

Martinez paused. "Mr. Stokowski, is that the last you ever saw of your best friend?"

"Yes."

"I have no further questions, Your Honor," Martinez said, but Bennie was already on her feet, crossing to the witness box.

"Mr. Stokowski, I have a few questions for you."

CHAPTER FORTY-SIX

"Mr. Stokowski, during this altercation in Eddie's bar, did you see Mr. Grusini land any punches to Jason's forehead?"

Paul Stokowski squared his shoulders, and his blue eyes regarded Bennie with a chill, expected in the circumstances. "No."

"What about elsewhere, did Mr. Grusini land any punches elsewhere?"

"No. It was more grappling, they were grappling."

"Conversely, Mr. Stokowski, did you see Jason land any punches on Mr. Grusini?"

"No, I don't think he threw a punch. He was more grappling back."

"Did anybody's clothes get torn, Mr. Stokowski?"

"No, not that I saw. The fight got broken up really fast, nipped in the bud."

"Mr. Stokowski, was there any further conversation between the two men?"

"No, just kind of grunting and cursing, but that's it."

"Any name-calling, Mr. Stokowski?"

"No."

Bennie thought back to what the waitress, Emily, had told her during their interview, about Richie's conduct when he drank. "Mr. Stokowski, to the best of your knowledge, did Mr. Grusini ever get into a bar fight, before the one in question?"

"Objection, relevance!" Martinez shot to his feet. "Your Honor, I don't see the relevance of the question."

Bennie faced Judge Patterson. "Your Honor, it has obvious relevance to the defense theory, which was explained in opening argument. I'd rather not describe it in full, since the witness did not hear the opening, but I'd be happy to approach the bench and explain."

Judge Patterson waved her off. "That won't be necessary. I'll allow it, but don't make me sorry I did."

"Thank you, Your Honor." Bennie faced the witness. "Mr. Stokowski, you testified that you have known Mr. Grusini for five years. Have you seen him get into a physical altercation in a bar before the one in question?"

"Yes," Stokowski answered, after a moment.

"How many in five years?"

"I don't know." Stokowski shrugged, uncomfortably.

"Between one and five, or between five and ten?"

Stokowski hesitated. "Between one and five."

"Thank you." Bennie didn't want to let it go, but it was too risky. She noticed the jury taking notes. "Now, Mr. Stokowski, you testified that Mr. Grusini 'could hold his own.' What did you mean by that?"

"I meant he could handle himself. He knew how to fight."

"And didn't you know that because of the fights you saw him get into?"

"Not really, I just knew it. I mean, he's a guy's guy. He worked construction. He was in decent shape, he could handle himself. It comes with the territory, you know?" Stokowski was saying too much, probably because he felt nervous during cross-examination, but it was helping Bennie's case, so she let him go.

"Mr. Stokowski, I would like to direct your attention for a moment to Defense Exhibit 10." Bennie crossed the room and picked up the enlarged mugshot of Jason, but she didn't turn it around yet. Instead, she kept the white side facing Stokowski while she spoke, leaning on the mounted exhibit. "I would like to show you a photograph taken of my client Jason at the time of his arrest and ask you a few questions."

Stokowski shifted around to face her, and Bennie walked over to the witness box and held up the exhibit, then turned it around, like a reveal. Stokowski recoiled, which was probably the most she could've asked for, and more than one juror noticed his reaction.

"Mr. Stokowski, Jason's face didn't look like this when he left the bar, did it?"

"No."

"There was no swelling around his forehead or his eye, was there?"

"No."

"Thank you. Excuse me a moment." Bennie walked the exhibit back and left it turned away as she spoke. "Mr. Stokowski, do you know if Mr. Grusini carried a weapon of any kind, such as a knife?"

"Objection." Martinez stood up. "That's outside the scope of direct examination."

"Your Honor, really?" Bennie crossed to Martinez's counsel table and picked up the bagged hunting knife. "This is Commonwealth Exhibit 2, the murder weapon. To whom it belongs has obvious relevance to this case, as well as my defense."

"Ms. Rosato, please narrow your question." Judge Patterson turned to Martinez. "Mr. Martinez, if you keep objecting at this pace, we're going to be here all week."

"Thank you, Your Honor." Martinez wilted into his seat.

"Mr. Stokowski." Bennie held up the knife in the bag, on her right side, which was away from the jury. "Did you ever see this knife before?"

"No."

"Do you know who it belongs to?"

"No."

"Do you know what type of knife this is?"

"No."

"Mr. Stokowski, are you a hunter?"

"Not anymore." Stokowski caught his wife's eye with a smile, but Bennie didn't want to break the mood with comic relief.

"So you never went hunting with Mr. Grusini, is that correct?"

"No, I never did."

"Do you know if Mr. Grusini went hunting?"

"Yes. He used to take off during deer season. A lot of the guys do."

Bennie put two and two together, on the fly. "The murder in question took place during deer season, did it not?"

"Yes."

"Do you know if Mr. Grusini carried a knife?"

"No, I don't."

"Mr. Stokowski, Mr. Grusini was your best friend and your best man, but you don't know if he carried a knife?"

"No, I don't."

Bennie wanted to ask him, *would it be out of character for Richie to carry a knife*, but again, she had to stop herself. Martinez would object, and Stokowski wouldn't give her the answer she wanted. "Do you know if Mr. Grusini carried a gun?"

"Objection, relevance!" Martinez rose, albeit sheepishly, but Bennie let it go.

"Your Honor, I withdraw the question. Mr. Stokowski, did you ever see Mr. Grusini pull a knife on anyone during the fights we discussed?"

Stokowski hesitated, and Bennie sensed she had struck gold, so she started digging.

"Mr. Stokowski? Yes or no? Did you ever see Mr. Grusini pull a knife on anybody during a fight?"

"Look, I never saw Richie pull *his* knife, I mean, I don't know if he had a knife." Stokowski pursed his lips. "I never saw him pull a knife off of himself, like from his pocket or anything. But once, I mean, I have to admit, he took a knife off the bar and he kind of held it out."

"He brandished a knife at someone?"

"I don't know what that means." Stokowski looked puzzled, but the jury didn't.

"It means to wave or point it at someone. Did you see Mr. Grusini brandish or wave a knife at someone during a fight?"

"Uh, yes," Stokowski answered, his reluctance plain.

"Mr. Stokowski, what kind of knife did he brandish?"

"It was just one of those little knives bartenders use, to cut up lemons and limes. It was on the white cutting board they always have. He reached over for it."

"So, a paring knife?"

"I guess so."

"In any event, not a butter knife?" Bennie noticed Marathon Mom taking notes in her booklet.

"No, not a butter knife."

"Mr. Stokowski, did Mr. Grusini aim the point of the knife at another person?"

"Yes, but he didn't stab him or anything. He just held it out."

"Who did he aim the knife at, on this occasion?"

"A drunk guy who came up to him, I forget."

Bennie let it go, because she was on a roll. "Was this fight in a bar, too?"

"Yes."

"At Eddie's?"

"No, Mayfair Bar & Grill."

Bennie made a mental note and she knew Lou would too, in the gallery. "How long ago did this occur?"

"Two years."

"Were the other fights we discussed in bars?"

"Uh, yes, I guess so."

Bennie didn't press it. She needed only the one. "So during this fight at the Mayfair Bar & Grill, after Mr. Grusini held out the knife, then what happened?"

"They threw us out."

"I see." Bennie glanced over at the jury, who had pricked up their ears. She had a hunch that Richie and Stokowski had been banned from the Mayfair Bar & Grill, but she couldn't take the chance, ask, and be wrong. Instead she asked, "Did you and Mr. Grusini ever return to the Mayfair Bar & Grill after that altercation?"

"No, we didn't."

Bennie let it go. The inference was there, and the jury wasn't stupid. "Mr. Stokowski, have you ever seen Mr. Grusini punch anyone so hard that they were knocked unconscious?"

Stokowski pursed his lips. "Only once, but yes."

"Where did that take place?"

"At an Eagles game, last year."

"Whom did Mr. Grusini knock unconscious?"

"I don't think he *meant* the guy to go unconscious or anything, but there was this jerk in the parking lot after the game, a Dallas fan, and he was annoying everybody, hooting and hollering, talking trash. They got into it, I don't really know how it started, but Richie ended it. The guy deserved it."

"I see." Bennie didn't react, because she had learned through experience that her reactions would cause the jury to mute their own reaction, when what she really wanted was the jury to react strongly. "Mr. Stokowski, did stadium security come, after that altercation?"

"No, we left." Stokowski's mood changed. He frowned, seeming to grow close-mouthed, and Bennie could tell that he felt that he'd said too much. She was guessing that Martinez felt the same way, but she couldn't take any credit. It had taken only a few simple questions to elicit Richie's true nature, and Stokowski was honest enough to tell the truth.

"Thank you, Mr. Stokowski." Bennie had almost forgotten something. "I have one last question. You testified that my client said to Mr. Grusini, 'Do you know what day this is?' Is that correct?"

"Yes."

"Did you ever find out what my client meant?"

"No."

"Thank you, Mr. Stokowski, I have no further questions."

Bennie turned and walked away, leaving the question hanging in the air. There was nothing wrong with leaving the jurors a mystery, after all.

"No redirect, Your Honor!" Martinez said, already on his feet. "The Commonwealth would like to call its third witness."

Judge Patterson, thinking about a midmorning break, asked Martinez for a proffer, and Martinez said that the next three witnesses were bar patrons who would corroborate Stokowski's version of the bar fight. Bennie had seen this coming, objected as their being cumulative, and offered to stipulate to the facts of the bar fight as established by Stokowski. Martinez agreed, and Bennie sat down, satisfied.

Martinez also put up an IT expert who had examined Jason's laptop and testified about the number of times that he Googled Richie, Ackermann, and Richie's home address, as well as searched Richie's Facebook page (five times daily), his Instagram account (three times), and Twitter account (three times daily). Bennie didn't cross-examine, because sometimes, a lawyer had to know when to shut up.

Judge Patterson faced the jury. "Ladies and gentlemen, this has been a lot of testimony to absorb in a short time. You are dismissed for a midmorning break."

CHAPTER FORTY-SEVEN

Bennie and Lou headed down the long hallway of white cinder-block, which led to the secured conference room for defendants and defense counsel. Bennie looked over at Lou, hoisting her purse to her shoulder. "How are we doing, Coach?"

"Not bad."

"That's what I thought," Bennie said, tense, as they walked along. "Do you think I needed to recross Stokowski?"

"No, you made the right call." Lou flashed her an encouraging smile. "I like the way it's going in, but we got hurt on motive statements from the uniform. The jury didn't like it."

"I know."

"And the computer stalking. The jury didn't like that, either. It hurts us."

"I had to leave it alone. It is what it is."

"Agree. On the plus side, the mugshot really worked. Before that, they were shooting Jason the hairy eyeball. But once that picture came up, I think they felt sorry for him."

"Good."

"I'm watching two guys in the back row, a black one and a white one. They're about my age, the accountant and a steamfit-ter, and they look at each other every time you talk. I can't tell if they don't like what you're saying or they can't hear you. Talk slower."

"I hate talking slow."

"They're both from Delaware County, one from Norwood and one from Aston. Throw in some Delaware County references. Show 'em you know the terrain."

"But I don't."

"Say Pica's, it's a pizza place. Everybody knows Pica's. Even that brunette from *30 Rock*, she's talking about Pica's all the time. She's from Upper Darby, you know?"

"Really? Tina Fey?"

"Yes, everybody knows that. You need to get out." Lou chuckled, then it faded. "I'll tell you another thing, the press is trying to figure out why you're on this case. I told them no comment, but all they have to do is Google your name and Jason's to connect the dots."

"Actually, it's not that easy. Jason's records were sealed because he was a juvenile and they were eventually expunged. Anyway I don't have a problem with that. Let them do their homework." They reached a locked gray door, where a uniformed sheriff standing guard broke into a dentured smile when he saw Lou.

"Lou Jacobs, as I live and breathe!"

"Dan, that you?" Lou clapped him on the arm. "I thought you were retired."

"I'm tired, not retired." The sheriff unlocked the door. "How the hell have you been?"

"Can't complain," Lou answered, standing aside to let Bennie into the conference room, a small windowless box with scuffed white walls and four black chairs, one of which held Jason, his hands cuffed.

"Hey, Jason," Bennie said, sitting down with her purse and pad on her lap, while Lou closed the door behind them and sat down.

Jason looked up, nervous. "Bennie, I'm confused. You told the jury it was self-defense, but like I said, I was framed. Somebody put the knife in my hand."

"Jason, you keep saying that, but as I keep telling you, we tried everything to investigate who might have framed you and we couldn't come up with anything." Bennie stayed patient, even

298 | Lisa Scottoline

though she had explained this many times before. "Nobody on Richie's side would talk to us, and now it's time for trial. I can't just say 'he was framed' because I have nothing to support that theory, so I came up with a theory I can support. Self-defense. You knew I was going to do that, remember?"

"Yes."

"And you said it was okay, which it is. It's my job."

"Yes.

"I don't understand one other thing." Jason bit the cuticle on his thumb, despite his handcuffs. "You said to the jury that it's never the defendant's burden to prove anything. So why do we need a theory and support and all that?"

"Good question." Bennie could see how she had confused him. "Support and proof aren't the same thing. We don't have to *prove* anything, that's harder, but we have to come up with something to say, *anything*. That's not proving a theory, it's supporting one. I'm trying to do that without you because I can't put you up and I have nothing else, no other choice."

"But you can say it was self-defense, like you told the jury. Why isn't that good enough?"

"Because I'm not a witness. I'm not sworn in and I have no personal knowledge. What a lawyer like me says in court is not evidence. It's argument. That's why in an opening, lawyers always have to say 'the evidence will show that,' or 'the testimony will be that.'" Bennie tried to explain. "I'm doing exactly what you called me for. I'm giving you a perfect defense, with nothing to go on. You need to get on board with this. I won't put you on the stand, but you have to let me do my job. Do you know what the penalty is for first-degree murder? It's life without parole."

"I know that, I know that."

"You didn't want to enter a plea because you don't want more time in prison. If we lose, that's exactly what's going to happen."

"I know that, too." Jason bit his nail again, and Bennie could see that his fingers were trembling.

"Do you want to change your mind and make a deal? I think I could get it back. Martinez doesn't know that you don't want to get on the stand. He thinks you're going to get up and say that you killed Richie in self-defense."

"But if you make a deal, I have to go to prison, for like, ten years."

"Yes, at least, that's right." Bennie recalled that they had discussed it at the prison, too.

"Can you get less?"

"No. Remember what I told you, it's all about the economics, the money. When we turned down the Commonwealth's offer, we made them spend money. They have to prepare a case, and that takes lawyers, investigators, secretaries, and staff. It's expensive, and if you make the Commonwealth pay, then they hold it against you."

"But the guys in lockup, they've been telling me what a ball-buster Martinez is. It's not like I never told a lie, but if you put me up there and he starts working me over, I'll screw it *all* up."

Bennie knew it was true. "I said, I won't put you up there and ask you to lie. That's suborning perjury. I've never done that before and I'm not going to do it now."

"Then what are you going to do?"

Lou looked over, frowning, and Bennie knew he had the same question.

"I will keep developing reasonable doubt and I'll try to offer support for our theory the way I have been, by inference. You never know. Maybe a witness will give me an opening, or maybe I can make the cross-examination seem like more than it is. That's up to me."

Bennie looked at Jason. "Is there anything else you want to ask me? Any questions I missed or anything you think I should cover?"

"No." Jason bit his lip, showing his jagged incisor. "I'm sorry, I feel like I'm really messing this up."

"You don't have to drive this bus. I do." Bennie turned to Lou. "How about you, Coach? Anything I should be doing that I'm not?"

"The Delco reference. Pica's."

"I'm above that sort of chicanery."

"The hell you are." Lou smiled. "By the way, how did you know it was hunting season?"

"I didn't." Bennie turned to Jason. "Was I right?"

"Yes."

"The hits just keep on coming," Bennie said, managing a smile.

CHAPTER FORTY-EIGHT

Emily Ratigan, the waitress from Eddie's, looked miserable as she was sworn in and sat in the witness box, casting a regretful eye at Jason. Her red hair was longer, falling to her chin and framing her soft baby face. She'd covered her freckled cheeks with foundation, but she had only light makeup on her greenish eyes, and she'd dressed up for court in a cropped navy jacket, with a white camisole and jeans.

Martinez addressed her at a distance from the witness box. "Ms. Ratigan, you did not want to appear today to testify in court, did you?"

"No."

"And you're appearing today only because you were subpoenaed to appear, isn't that correct?"

"Yes."

"Ms. Ratigan, why is it that you had to be subpoenaed to appear to testify?"

"Because I like Jason and consider him a friend."

Martinez faced Judge Patterson. "Your Honor, I would like to qualify Ms. Ratigan as a hostile witness."

"No objection," Bennie said, having no grounds. Martinez's calling Emily as a hostile witness enabled him to question her as if he were cross-examining her.

Judge Patterson nodded. "Proceed, Mr. Martinez."

Martinez faced the witness. "Ms. Ratigan, please tell the jury how you came to be friends with the defendant."

"I wait tables at Eddie's, and he comes in there to eat dinner."

"Ms. Ratigan, isn't it true that he comes in to eat dinner almost every night, that he sits at the same table?"

"Yes, he's a regular."

"Isn't it also true that his table is out of the way and is not easily visible from other areas of the bar?"

"Yes."

"Ms. Ratigan, isn't it true that the restaurant is divided from the bar by a wooden divider that also conceals the defendant's table from view of the bar area?"

Emily pursed her lips. "I wouldn't say it *conceals* it, but it makes it hard to see the table."

"Fine, I stand corrected." Martinez paused. "Isn't it true that defendant, when he sits at his table, always sits at the seat on the right, which gives him an unobstructed view of the bar?"

"Yes."

"And isn't it also true that the defendant has been in the dining area a number of times when the victim in this case has been sitting at the bar, alone or with friends?"

"Yes, that's true."

"Ms. Ratigan, you said you consider yourself friends with the defendant, yet he did not tell you that he knew the victim in this case, did he?"

"No," Emily answered, after a moment. "But I don't think that means anything. There's a lot about his life he didn't tell me. He didn't tell me that he was in Kids-for-Cash—"

"Move to strike as unresponsive." Martinez whirled around to face the judge.

Bennie rose. "Objection, Your Honor. There's no reason to strike that from the record. It was completely responsive, and Mr. Martinez just didn't like the answer he got."

Judge Patterson arched an eyebrow. "Ms. Rosato, spare us the editorializing. Still, there's no reason to strike the witness's answer. Please proceed, Mr. Martinez."

"Ms. Ratigan, moving on to the night this murder occurred. You were there that evening in the bar, were you not?"

"Yes."

"Ms. Ratigan, how did the fight in the bar start?"

"Objection, Your Honor." Bennie stood up. "This has been asked and answered. We provided for this by stipulation, and I would stipulate to Ms. Ratigan's testimony as well."

Martinez looked over. "Then I have no further questions, Your Honor."

Judge Patterson turned to Bennie. "Ms. Rosato?"

"Yes, Your Honor, I have a few questions." Bennie approached Emily with a smile. "Thank you for coming today. We're interested in hearing the truth, so you don't have to feel bad about being here."

"Thank you."

"Ms. Ratigan, please tell the jury, since you're a friend of Jason's, what kind of person is he?"

Martinez rose, frowning. "Objection, Your Honor. Is defense counsel turning the witness into a character witness, as we speak?"

Bennie addressed the judge. "Your Honor, as a matter of fact, I am. Evidence Rule 404(2)(c) is an exception to the general rule and provides that in a homicide case, the prosecutor may offer evidence of the victim's so-called 'trait of peacefulness' to rebut evidence that the victim was the first aggressor. That applies as well to the defendant."

"Correct, counsel. Overruled, Mr. Martinez. Proceed, Ms. Rosato."

"Ms. Ratigan, please tell the jury what you think of Jason's nature, in this regard."

Emily tilted her face toward the jury. "Jason is a definitely peaceful, very nice man. We always talked when he came in for dinner and he was always very kind. He never raised his voice or made any fuss at all. Everybody on the staff likes him, and he always tips us really well, even though he doesn't make a lot of money. He left me a—"

"Thank you, Ms. Ratigan." Bennie preempted the testimony about the hundred-dollar tip. "I have no further questions."

CHAPTER FORTY-NINE

Detective Mike Gallagher looked every inch the big-city homicide detective on the stand, dressed up in a light gray suit and shirt with a gray tie. His demeanor was more professional than the night Bennie had met him, and his affable grin was in check. He sat comfortably in the witness box and knew to adjust the black stem microphone upward, and Bennie predicted he would be a formidable witness for the Commonwealth.

After Detective Gallagher was sworn in, Martinez took him through the preliminaries, eliciting his twenty years of service on the force and ten as a homicide detective, the many cases he had investigated and cleared, then bringing him to the night of the murder, when he interviewed Jason in the Roundhouse.

Martinez stood before the witness box. "Now, Detective Gallagher, you were the primary detective assigned to this case, isn't that correct?"

"Yes."

"Detective Gallagher, you interviewed the defendant on the night in question, did you not?"

"After I gave him his Miranda warnings, yes, I did interview him."

"Detective Gallagher, at that point, had he asked for a lawyer?"

"No."

"And what did the defendant say to you at that time, with regard to the victim?"

Bennie listened without objection, since it wasn't hearsay because it wasn't coming in for the truth of the matter asserted. However, something else had drawn her attention. Karen Engstrom, the veteran reporter who had been sitting behind her on the defense side of the courtroom, had moved to the Commonwealth side of the courtroom next to Doreen.

Detective Gallagher was testifying, "He told me that he and Richie had had bad blood since they were children, and that he was glad that Richie was dead."

Martinez paused to let it sink in. Even though the jury had already heard it from the arresting officer, the detective's corroboration reinforced the cold-heartedness of the statement, and Marathon Mom made a note in her blue booklet. Bennie found herself distracted again by Karen, who leaned over to Doreen and whispered something.

"Detective Gallagher, in your capacity as the detective on the case, did you have occasion to find trace evidence, such as hair, fiber, blood, and DNA that will be relevant to this matter?"

"Yes, I did."

"Detective Gallagher, let's begin with the results of your investigation, mainly with respect to blood evidence." Martinez returned to counsel table, collecting the flurry of exhibits that Bennie expected, so she raised no objection as he showed them to Judge Patterson, entered them into evidence, had them marked as Commonwealth exhibits, then began his line of questioning. Detective Gallagher testified knowledgeably, explaining to the jury that his investigation had found Richie's blood on Jason's hands and clothes and vice versa, samples of Richie's hair on Jason and vice versa, and fibers from Richie's black down parka on Jason's dark green winter coat, and vice versa.

Bennie listened during the testimony, though she knew all of it already because the Commonwealth had turned it over to the defense, constituting the so-called Brady materials required by law. She knew the testimony would be damning, and she kept an eye not only on the jury, but on Karen and Doreen. The two women's heads were bent close together, and they seemed to be passing notes, Karen writing on her skinny pad, then handing the pen back to Doreen.

Bennie felt her gut tense, losing momentary concentration. No good could come of Doreen's talking to reporters, especially Karen. The media always needed an angle and would always pick the low-hanging fruit. If Doreen was talking to Karen and Bennie wasn't, the story would be that Richie was the tragic victim of a brutal murder.

Martinez finished with the line of questioning about hard evidence and made a great show of retrieving a set of surveillance videotapes from a box, and Bennie didn't object as he moved them into evidence, because she knew what they were, as well. She kept an eye on Karen and Doreen, who had begun whispering to each other in a way that ratcheted up her concern. Bennie tried not to look over for fear of catching Declan's eye, but even he inclined his head toward Doreen and Karen.

Martinez cued up the videotape on a TV cart that he had rolled over. "Detective Gallagher, can you please explain what Commonwealth's Exhibit 15 is?"

"Yes, it is one of the surveillance videos taken the night of the murder, for the relevant time period."

"Why do you say one of the surveillance videos?"

"There were approximately seven surveillance videos, all of which showed the same thing at the same time. This one had the best resolution, and also the time counter and correct date, which not all of them had. The quality of surveillance videos tends to be variable, depending on the source. Convenience stores have the best resolution, but there wasn't one of those in the vicinity."

"Detective Gallagher, where did this surveillance video come from?"

"From the traffic camera at the intersection of Pimlico and Dunbar."

"And that would be here, this corner at the head of Dunbar Street, which leads to the alley where the murder took place?"

Martinez stepped to Commonwealth exhibit showing the orientation of Eddie's Bar.

"Yes." Detective Gallagher nodded.

"Thank you." Martinez turned on the TV, and the monitor showed gray static, then he picked up the remote control and froze the image on the screen. The film was black-and-white, and the resolution good enough to show a man with a light jacket standing at the corner of Pimlico and Dunbar Streets. "Now Detective Gallagher, would you explain what this video shows, while I put it on play?"

"Yes, of course."

"Thank you." Martinez pressed PLAY, and the image sprang to life, with a man walking toward the alley.

Detective Gallagher testified, "Our investigation identified the man on the screen as the victim, Richie Grusini, and as you can see, he's walking toward the alley, which is on Dunbar Avenue."

Bennie glanced over to check on Karen, who still had her head bent with Doreen. Declan was looking at the video monitor, and Bennie turned away quickly, to not catch his eye.

Detective Gallagher continued, "You can see the victim enter the alley, where his pickup truck was parked, at approximately 11:10. Then, you don't see anything else for about the next five minutes."

The courtroom fell silent, with the jurors riveted to the TV monitor, and the reporter and Doreen had stopped talking, too. Jason watched in utter stillness, and Bennie felt the same way that she did whenever she saw surveillance video on the TV news. It was horrifying to see someone walking down the street, talking blithely on the phone, not knowing it was his last moments alive. The video had an impact all its own, and Martinez didn't overplay his hand, so Bennie had nothing to object to and was powerless to dispel the mood.

Detective Gallagher continued, narrating the video, "Now you can see the defendant appear in the frame, walk down Dunbar Street, and enter the alley."

Jason lowered his head and didn't watch his image on the

screen. Bennie could hear him emit a quiet sigh that she prayed was sadness, even if he would never admit as much.

Detective Gallagher testified, "Now, the surveillance video continues, but neither the victim nor the defendant come out of the alley. Nothing happens at the alley until approximately 11:45 P.M., after 911 has been called and police arrive at the scene and arrest the defendant."

"Detective Gallagher, who called 911?"

"A couple who was walking past. You will see them cross in front of the alley and stop at approximately 11:37."

Martinez asked, "So if I fast-forward, that's what we will see?"

"Yes."

Martinez fast-forwarded the video, then set it on PLAY again. The video showed the police arrive on the scene, their lights flashing, though there was no audio to hear their sirens. Bennie didn't object because she couldn't, so she remained impassive during the video, which was as damning as the hard evidence of blood, hair, and fiber had been. The video didn't even show the wound on Jason's forehead, because it was taken from too far away, so he looked every bit the guilty party, handcuffed and pressed by the head into the back of a waiting cruiser. She told herself this was the worst it was going to get for the defense and prayed that she was correct.

Detective Gallagher continue testifying, "There you can see the defendant, as he is being taken into custody."

"Thank you, Detective. I have no further questions." Martinez snapped off the television, for emphasis.

Judge Patterson looked at Bennie, her expression newly grave. "Ms. Rosato, I assume you have cross-examination?"

"Yes, briefly." Bennie rose and approached the witness. "Detective Gallagher, good to see you again."

"You, too, Ms. Rosato," Gallagher said, though he probably knew what Bennie was up to. One of her tricks was to befriend the expert when possible, because it established her as an authority, but Gallagher was experienced enough to play her game. In any event, her goals with his cross-examination were modest.

"Detective Gallagher, let me take you back a moment to the trace evidence that is Commonwealth Exhibits 15 through 27."

"Fine."

"Your testimony was that you found evidence of Mr. Grusini's blood, hair, and fibers on my client, isn't that correct?"

"Yes."

"Detective Gallagher, isn't it true that the same trace evidence would have been found if Jason had killed Mr. Grusini in self-defense?"

"Objection." Martinez rose. "Calls for speculation."

Bennie faced Judge Patterson. "No it doesn't, Your Honor. It's a reasonable question about this evidence and its probative value, that is, what it proves."

Judge Patterson motioned them forward. "Counsel, approach the bench."

Both lawyers walked quickly to the dais, but Bennie didn't delay, whispering. "Your Honor, we're asserting claim of self-defense in this case. We're entitled to ask the one-and-only detective on the case to interpret the probative value of this evidence. It's undisputed that these men had at least one altercation, which took place in the bar, and that's when any of this trace evidence could have been transferred—"

"Not the blood," Martinez interjected, gripping the dais tightly. "There's no testimony that there was blood in the bar fight."

"Fine, not the blood." Bennie had to concede something, if she wanted Judge Patterson to go her way. "But the fact is, my question is completely within the realm of this expert witness's knowledge, and it's not speculative at all."

Martinez whispered, louder than before, "Of course it's speculative. She's asking what-if. What-if is inherently speculative."

"Your Honor, it isn't what-if a spaceship landed." Bennie whispered loudly, just like Martinez had, because they were both really arguing to the jury. "It's what-if my client killed to defend himself, how would that change the evidence, and that question goes to the heart of my defense."

"I'll allow it," Judge Patterson ruled, pursing her lips.

"Thank you, Your Honor," Bennie and Martinez said, but only one of them meant it. Martinez went back to his seat, and Bennie returned to the witness stand. She didn't love that Detective Gallagher had had time to consider his answer, and he was looking at her with his bald head cocked slightly.

"Could you repeat the question, Ms. Rosato?"

"Yes." Bennie willed herself to stay calm. She was betting he was professional enough to tell the truth. "Detective Gallagher, isn't it true that you would've found the same trace evidence if Jason had acted in self-defense?"

"I wasn't aware the defendant was claiming self-defense." Detective Gallagher lifted an eyebrow, and Bennie acted unfazed, though she wasn't.

"My question remains, Detective Gallagher. Wouldn't you have found the same trace evidence if the defendant had acted in self-defense?"

"Yes."

"I have no further questions." Bennie turned, worried because Martinez was already on his feet, heading back to the witness box.

"I have redirect, Your Honor."

Judge Patterson nodded. "Go right ahead, Mr. Martinez."

Martinez turned to the witness. "Detective Gallagher, you testified that you questioned the defendant about the murder in question, did you not?"

"Yes."

"Detective Gallagher, you testified that, after you warned the defendant of his Miranda Rights, he agreed to speak with you about the murder in question. Is that correct?"

"Yes."

"And Detective Gallagher, after you warned the defendant of his right to have an attorney he agreed to waive that right and chose to speak with you freely. Is that correct?"

"Yes."

"Did he have any hesitancy whatsoever in speaking with you?"

"No."

"And he had the opportunity to tell you what happened in the alley that night. Isn't that correct?"

"Yes."

"And at no time did the defendant ever mention the word self-defense. Is that correct?"

"He did not."

Martinez shrugged. "I have no further questions."

Bennie stayed standing, but didn't go over to the witness box. "I have recross, Your Honor."

"Go ahead, counsel."

"Detective Gallagher, how long did you interview my client for before he asked for a lawyer?"

"Not long."

"Is 'not long' more than ten minutes or less than ten minutes?"

"About ten minutes." Detective Gallagher nodded, tight-lipped, and Bennie felt as if she was crossing swords with a pro, which actually got her juices flowing. A trial lawyer liked nothing better than a worthy opponent.

"Detective Gallagher, you testified earlier that you had investigated many, many murder cases, isn't that correct?"

"Yes."

"So that means you have interviewed many, many accused people, isn't that correct?"

"Yes," Detective Gallagher answered slowly, and Bennie could tell that he didn't know where she was going, but then again, neither did she.

"Detective Gallagher, when you're interviewing an accused person, how long does it usually take you to get the facts about a murder?"

"It varies."

"How often does it take only ten minutes?"

Detective Gallagher hesitated.

"I withdraw the question," Bennie said impulsively, then realized it was a pretty good move. "Detective Gallagher, during your interview of Jason, did you find out that he and Mr. Grusini had fought before, as far back as middle school?"

Martinez looked like he was about to object, but Bennie's stipulation covered these facts. She hadn't planned it that way, but it
was a lucky break.

"No," Detective Gallagher answered.

"Detective Gallagher, during your interview, did you find out
that Jason and Mr. Grusini had been enemies since they were
twelve years old?"

"No."

"During your interview, did you find out that Jason and
Mr. Grusini were both victims of the Kids-for-Cash scandal in
Luzerne County?"

"I found that out later, but not during the interview."

"So your answer is no, isn't it?"

"Correct. My answer is no."

"Detective Gallagher, did you learn why the date in question
was a special day to my client, Jason?"

"No."

Bennie checked the jury, and their arched eyebrows told her
she'd made her point. "Obviously, Detective Gallagher, there's
many facts you didn't learn during your ten-minute interview, isn't
that right?"

"Not facts that are relevant."

Bennie snapped, "The fact that my client Jason and Mr. Grusini
were lifelong enemies wasn't relevant?"

"Okay, that is."

"I have no further questions of this witness."

Judge Patterson turned to Martinez. "Mr. Prosecutor?"

"No further questions," Martinez answered.

Bennie went to her seat, catching Lou's eye.

He winked.

CHAPTER FIFTY

The next Commonwealth witness took the stand, and the men in the jury came to attention. It was Renée Zimmer, and Bennie knew her name from one of the license plates that Lou had investigated after their carb-laden stakeout. Zimmer was undeniably foxy, with long blonde hair, large green eyes, an upturned nose, a glossy pink mouth, and a curvy body shown to excellent advantage in a tight black cotton dress with a light black sweater. Bennie wondered what the possible relevance of Zimmer's testimony could be, since she wasn't at the bar the night of the murder.

Martinez flashed the witness a toothy smile. "Good morning, Ms. Zimmer," he began, his tone perceptibly warmer.

"Good morning," Renée answered, with a distinctive South Philly accent, so that it came out like, *Guh Morning.*

"Ms. Zimmer, thank you for coming today to court. I know this must be very difficult for you."

"I would do anything for Richie, and it's important for me to be here, to see that he gets justice."

Bennie noticed Computer Programmer Guy nodding and she bet that Cupid's arrow had already struck his coded heart.

"Ms. Zimmer, what was your relationship to the victim in this case, Richie Grusini?"

"Richie was my boyfriend."

"Ms. Zimmer, how long were you dating for?"

"Almost a year."

"And Ms. Zimmer, had you discussed marriage?"

Bennie thought about objecting because Martinez was going for the sympathy vote, but decided to let it go or the jury would think she was heartless. Nevertheless she shifted noisily in her seat, letting Martinez know that she was ready to object, like a base runner about to steal.

"Yes, we had." Zimmer blinked a few times, and Bennie was worried the witness was going to cry, so she half-rose.

"Your Honor, objection as to relevance, as Ms. Zimmer wasn't in the bar on the night in question."

Martinez turned to Judge Patterson. "Your Honor, as with Ms. Rosato, if I ask a question or two, I think the relevance will become clear."

"Fair enough, proceed," Judge Patterson ruled, and Martinez turned back to the witness.

"Ms. Zimmer, as you have heard, it is true that you were not with the victim on the night in question, were you?"

"No."

"Where were you?"

"I was at home in my apartment in Bella Vista."

"Ms. Zimmer, were you expecting to see the victim on the night he was murdered?"

"Yes, I was." Zimmer swallowed hard, and Brooklyn Girl pushed up her heavy black glasses, her lower lip puckering.

"Ms. Zimmer, how did those plans come to pass?"

"Well, if Richie was free, he would usually come over. That was the way it usually worked."

"Had you made plans earlier that day?"

"No."

"Ms. Zimmer, when did you make the plans for the evening in question?"

"That night, he called me around seven o'clock and said he wanted to come over, so I said great. I know the time because *Seinfeld* was coming on."

Bennie still didn't see the relevance, but she held her tongue.

"Ms. Zimmer, did you speak with him again that night, on the phone?"

"Yes."

"Ms. Zimmer, when was the next time you spoke with him?"

"A little after eleven o'clock, he said he was leaving the bar. It musta been jus' before, you know, he was killed." Zimmer's eyes filmed, and she kept her face tilted pointedly away from Jason.

"And how long did the call last?"

"A few minutes."

Bennie realized where Martinez was going, at the same time she realized that she had nothing to counteract the testimony.

"Ms. Zimmer, without telling me the substance of your conversation"—Martinez glanced over at Bennie, tacitly referring to her prior hearsay objection—"how would you characterize Richie's state of mind?"

"Happy and upbeat."

"Happy and upbeat?" Martinez repeated, needlessly.

"Yes. In a good mood."

"Ms. Zimmer, would you characterize his state of mind as angry, in any way, shape, or form?"

"No, not at all."

"Did Mr. Grusini tell you he'd been in a fight in the bar?"

"No."

"I've no further questions. Thank you so much, Ms. Zimmer." Martinez stepped away, and Judge Patterson nodded at Bennie.

"Ms. Rosato?"

Bennie felt the jurors swing their heads toward her, and she rose, unsure what to do. If she let Zimmer's testimony stand, it would damage the self-defense claim; obviously, the implication was that Richie wasn't in a state of mind to attack Jason. Martinez had been shrewd to put Zimmer up now, reinforcing Detective Gallagher's suggestion that the self-defense claim was aftermarket, which it was.

"I have a question or two, Your Honor." Bennie crossed to the witness stand, getting an idea. "Ms. Zimmer, it sounds like you and Richie were very happy together."

"We were."

"And if you intended to marry him, then you obviously considered him what I like to call 'husband material.'"

Zimmer smiled, her eyes still glistening. "Oh yes, totally."

"Ms. Zimmer, what were you looking for in a husband?"

Martinez opened his mouth as if he were going to object, but didn't.

"Somebody who was a good guy. And a fun guy. Richie was the life of the party, you know, but he would also be a good father and could take care of me and his family."

Bennie noticed the grandmotherly juror in the front row soften, but she pressed ahead. "So Ms. Zimmer, you considered that Richie would be the kind of guy who would take care of you, is that right?"

"Yes, totally." Zimmer nodded happily, and Bennie felt almost bad leading her, but not bad enough to stop.

"Would you also consider Richie the kind of guy who could protect you?"

"Yes, totally."

Martinez rose, frowning. "Objection, relevance, Your Honor."

Bennie faced Judge Patterson. "Your Honor, the prosecutor explored the relationship, so he opened the door."

"Fine, proceed, but make it fast."

Bennie returned her attention to the witness. "Ms. Zimmer, you were saying, Mr. Grusini was the kind of guy who would protect you."

"Yes, he was."

"Ms. Zimmer, would Mr. Grusini protect you by not telling you something that might upset you?"

"Totally, he didn't like to see me upset."

Bennie thought she had mitigated the damage. She would love to ask Zimmer if Richie carried a knife, but she didn't know what answer she'd get and that was outside the scope of direct examination, which Martinez had intentionally kept narrow. "Thank you. Your Honor, I have no further questions."

Judge Patterson swiveled around, facing Martinez. "Mr. Martinez, redirect, if you have any."

"I do, Your Honor," Martinez answered.

Bennie sat down, relieved.

Until she spotted Karen passing Kleenex to a teary Doreen.

CHAPTER FIFTY-ONE

Bennie got her bearings while Martinez called Dr. Jessica Chien, one of the city's assistant medical examiners. She was a slim Asian woman in her forties with a short, severe haircut and steel-rimmed glasses, which together with her grim grayish suit gave her a clinical demeanor. She sat so upright in the witness stand that she could have been balancing on her tailbone and she linked her fingers in front of her, in the most formal way. She wore no wedding band or any jewelry except for seed pearls in her earlobes.

Martinez made quick work of having the witness sworn in, taking her through her resume, qualifying her as an expert, identifying her as the person who performed Richie's autopsy, and moving into evidence a copy of her autopsy report, which Bennie had seen. Martinez took her through the preliminary questions about Ritchie's autopsy and elicited that she had found nothing remarkable during the internal examination. Then he fetched a photograph from counsel table, went to Judge Patterson with a copy, and brought a copy to Bennie.

Bennie glanced at the photograph, but didn't let her horror show in her expression. Richie's body lay on its back, crumpled in the dark alley, in a pool of bright light cast by the coroner's massive klieglights. His fixed stare faced heavenward, and his legs lay crumpled under him, bent at the knees, askew, a position that would've been completely unnatural in anyone living. His torso was raised slightly, which caused his head to fall back and opened the gruesome wound on the left side of his neck, a deep gaping hole. Blood glistened from the awful wound, soaked his jacket and the front of his shirt, and pooled around him on the filthy floor of the alley.

Martinez stood in front of the dais. "Your Honor, I'd like to move into evidence as Commonwealth Exhibit 28, a photograph taken at the crime scene."

"Objection." Bennie rose, knowing she'd lose. "Your Honor, this photograph should not be admitted because its probative value does not outweigh how prejudicial it is. The defense is willing to stipulate to the cause and manner of death in this matter, and the only purpose of these photographs is to inflame the jury's sympathy."

Martinez stiffened. "Your Honor, this photograph has obvious relevance, and the Commonwealth has done everything in its power to minimize any prejudice. There were other photos I could've shown that were considerably more inflammatory, and I have chosen only this one photo, so there is no repetition of evidence."

"Ms. Rosato, your objection is overruled." Judge Patterson set her copy of the photograph aside, her expression grave. "The photograph is admissible."

"Thank you, Your Honor." Martinez retrieved a mounted copy of the photograph from his desk, brought it over to the jury, and handed it to Computer Guy, who sat at the leftmost chair in the jury, nearest to the gallery.

Suddenly Doreen emitted a heartbreaking sob, and Bennie looked over to see her burying herself in Declan's embrace, next to Karen. Declan comforted her and tried to get her back in control. Every head in the jury box turned to them, and Judge Patterson was about to speak when Doreen quieted.

Martinez stood at the jury box. "Ladies and gentlemen of the jury, I know this is difficult, but I'm asking each of you to take a look at that photograph and pass it to the juror sitting beside you.

Please take as long as you like, and we will wait until all of you have seen the exhibit before I resume questioning."

Bennie watched as Computer Guy's unibrow flew upward and he passed the exhibit quickly to Brooklyn Girl, whose hand went to her mouth. Each juror had some variation of a horrified reaction, and the slow and deliberate passing of the photograph took on the ceremonial air of a funeral, which Bennie was powerless to dissipate. The grandmotherly juror stared worriedly at Doreen.

The exhibit reached the last juror, then Martinez took it to counsel table, turned it facedown, then returned to the witness box. "Dr. Chien, you have before you Commonwealth Exhibit 28, which is a photograph of the victim taken at the crime scene. Does this accurately reflect the wound that you found when you examined the victim's body?"

"Yes, it does."

"Excuse me, I should have asked you this earlier. Were you actually on the scene that night, Dr. Chien?"

"Yes, I was."

"And did you pronounce the victim dead in this case?"

"Yes, I did."

"Dr. Chien, what was the cause of the victim's death?"

"The victim died as a result of a knife wound to the neck, on the left side as you see here."

"Could you show us on the photograph?"

Bennie rose. "Objection, Your Honor, the photograph is the most prejudicial way to conduct this direct examination. If the prosecutor wants to take the witness through cause and manner of death, he could do that in a much less inflammatory manner by using the standard diagram contained in the autopsy report."

Martinez faced the judge. "Your Honor, the photograph is properly in evidence and the Commonwealth is entitled to examine the witness any way it sees fit."

Bennie shook her head. "I beg to differ, Your Honor. The analysis under the evidence rules requires an ongoing weighing of the probative value and the prejudicial nature of the exhibit. It's one thing to admit it, but it's another thing to make us look at it in detail for the next twenty minutes."

Judge Patterson paused, pursing her lips. "Mr. Martinez, I'm going to have to agree with Ms. Rosato. The jury may have the photograph and take it with them into the jury room, but questions of a technical nature would be much more appropriate using the autopsy report."

"Thank you, Your Honor." Bennie sat down, relieved. Even she didn't want to look at the photograph any longer, and she noticed that Jason hadn't let his eyes stray toward it, at all.

Martinez went back to counsel table, shuffled through his papers, and produced an enlarged copy of the diagram that was part of every autopsy report; a black-and-white outline of a male body. It was entered into evidence, then Martinez placed the diagram on the overhead projector, and after some doing, it showed on a white screen. Jurors shifted forward in their seats, eyeing the diagram.

Martinez turned to the witness. "Dr. Chien, could you explain to the jury in layman's terms what this is?"

"It's a diagram of the victim's body, on which I have made notations of matters that I observed during autopsy."

"Dr. Chien, is that standard procedure in the medical examiner's office?"

"Yes. This is, for want of a better word, I would say a *form* that we use in the medical examiner's office, for each autopsy performed." Dr. Chien pointed to a pen mark made on the left side of the diagram's neck. "I made this mark, per our procedure, which shows the location of the wound that caused the victim's death."

"Dr. Chien, what was the cause of the victim's death in this case?"

"The victim died as a result of a knife wound to the neck, which caused exsanguination."

"Did you find more than one stab wound during the autopsy?"

"No, this was the only stab wound."

"Dr. Chien, is it unusual for a single stab wound to be lethal?"

"It depends on where the stab wound occurs. Generally, stab wounds to the neck area tend to be lethal because the neck is so dense." Dr. Chien raised a delicate hand, touching her own Adam's apple. "Interestingly, a wound to the front of the neck is survivable because this is simply cartilaginous trachea."

"Dr. Chien, could you explain what you mean, in layman's terms?"

"The point I'm making is one can survive a knife wound to the front of the neck." Dr. Chien turned to the jury again. "You can try this yourself. If you rub your finger up and down on your throat, like this on your windpipe, you can actually feel the rings of your trachea. There are thyroid vessels there in front, and when they perform a tracheotomy, they go for the midline and avoid vessels."

Martinez blinked as the jury started running its fingers up and down its neck, and Bennie sensed that this wasn't the turn he'd hoped his direct examination would take.

Martinez cleared his throat. "Dr. Chien, you were saying that stab wounds in the neck area tend to be lethal. Why is that?"

"Lethal injuries to the neck are produced on either side of the so-called Adam's apple, on the left or the right. They're lethal on the sides because that is the location of the branches of the common carotid artery, which is a major arterial vessel." Dr. Chien moved her finger across her throat, which was slim and lovely, so the effect was inadvertently chilling, and Bennie felt Jason shift beside her in his chair.

"Dr. Chien, would you remind us what is the difference between an artery and a vein?"

Bennie didn't see the relevance, but didn't object. The more medical the examination got, the less dramatic would be its impact, and Dr. Chien had a professorial bent, happy to slide into jargon.

"As you may recall, arteries carry oxygenated blood, which is bright red, and veins carry deoxygenated blood, which is blue. Take a look at your hand and rub the top, where you see those bluish veins." Dr. Chien rubbed the back of her hand, and

324 | Lisa Scottoline

the jurors followed her example. "If you look on your own hand, you can see your veins and they look bluish, because they carry deoxygenated blood. Many people think their veins look bluish because they're older, but that is simply not the case. Interestingly, veins also are different from arteries in that veins have very thin walls. An artery, in contrast, has a very thick wall. In the case of the carotid artery, for example, there are three layers to the arterial wall. The inside layer is the intima, the middle layer is the muscularis, which contains muscle fibers, and the outermost layer of the artery is the endothelium. In layman's terms, I would say that arteries are very important vessels, and when one is severed, blood will spurt from it in a rhythmic fashion, gushing. In the case of a severing of the common carotid artery, there would be gushing that would reflect the beating of the heart and the pressure of the blood flowing from the heart to the brain."

Martinez blinked. "Dr. Chien, turning to this case, could you please describe the stab wound to the victim?"

"Certainly." Dr. Chien pointed to the neck on the diagram. "The knife made an upward-stabbing motion on the left side of the victim's neck, from underneath the jawline to the trachea. The initial motion would have incised the internal carotid artery and the common carotid artery—"

"Excuse me, are those two different things?"

"To be precise, yes, they are two different structures. The common carotid artery carries approximately ninety percent of the oxygenated blood from the heart to the brain, and it branches into the internal and external carotid. That common carotid incision alone could have been lethal, but the knife did much more damage in this case." Dr. Chien continued moving her elegant finger across the diagram's neck. "It also sliced through the exterior jugular vein, which as you recall, carries deoxygenated blood, not oxygenated blood like an artery. It also severed the vagus nerve, which controls the heartbeat."

"Dr. Chien, how deep was the wound?"

"About four inches, which is more than deep enough to be lethal."

"Dr. Chien, what, if anything, did you observe about the angle that the knife went into the victim's neck?"

"I observed that the angle of entry was approximately forty-five degrees."

"And did you draw any conclusion from that angle of entry?"

"The angle of entry tells me that whoever stabbed the victim was shorter than he was."

"Dr. Chien, did you measure the height of the victim in this case?"

"Yes, I did. The victim was exactly six feet tall."

"Dr. Chien, did you have an opinion to a reasonable degree of certainty about the height of the perpetrator of this crime, that is, the person who stabbed the victim to death?"

"It's hard to say with specificity, but I would say somewhere between four and six inches shorter."

Bennie tried to keep her face forward as some of the jurors looked at Jason, evidently double-checking his height.

"Thank you." Martinez reached behind him on counsel table and held up the bagged knife. "Dr. Chien, I'm showing you the murder weapon and asking you if your findings during the autopsy are consistent with the wound made from a weapon like this?"

"Yes, they are."

"In other words, this knife would've made that wound?"

"Yes."

"Dr. Chien, in your opinion, would that stab wound have taken much force?"

"No, not in such a vulnerable area." Dr. Chien shook her head. "A stab wound to the *front* of the throat would've taken force, but not to the side."

"Dr. Chien, was it the initial wound that caused the victim's death?"

"Only partly. The initial puncture and slicing would have done lethal damage in time, but the ripping motion produced by the withdrawal of the knife, as well as the withdrawal itself, created more bleeding."

326 | Lisa Scottoline

"Dr. Chien, is that because there was more tearing of these delicate internal arteries?"

"Please, use the term 'structures.' Only the carotid is an artery."

Martinez blinked. "Okay, structures."

"That's part of the reason, but not all of it. When a knife, or any foreign object, is removed, it creates more bleeding. It's counterintuitive, but very true. If the knife had been left in, it could've acted as a tamponide on the wound, which is a form of compression that can control or slow bleeding. But the fact that it was withdrawn negated that possibility and death was a certainty."

Martinez paused. "Dr. Chien, you testified that the victim died because he exsanguinated, which means bled to death, is that correct?"

"Yes." Dr. Chien nodded, warming to her topic. "However, when someone exsanguinates, death does not occur because there isn't enough blood to pump through the heart, as is sometimes thought. What happens as a physiological matter is something completely different. Think of blood as a freight train carrying fuel to a destination, and the fuel is oxygen. Red blood cells live about one hundred twenty days, then they get consumed by the spleen and reused. The tissues have to have oxygen, and why is that? Because oxygen is the final hydrogen acceptor."

Martinez looked like he was about to interrupt, but didn't. The jury looked interested, but no longer emotional, which satisfied Bennie.

Dr. Chien continued, "Any metabolism needs fuel to live, but when the fuel is spent, you have something like spent fuel rods. Unfortunately, these are toxic and the body has to get rid of them. The spent fuel rods are an acid and when they're used up, they leave you with a product which is a hydrogen ion, and that is what lactic acidosis is. If the blood level drops too quickly, like it did in this case, then the body has no way to get rid of lactic acid, and death results. The cells are essentially poisoned. We are merely biological engines and we're not very well designed, in many particulars."

"Dr. Chien, how quickly would death have resulted, in this case?"

"Death would've resulted in a matter of minutes."

"Thank you, I have no further questions." Martinez turned away, and Bennie rose slowly, not to appear disrespectful.

Judge Patterson motioned her forward. "Ms. Rosato, I assume you have cross-examination."

"Yes, Your Honor." Bennie walked toward the witness box, but stopped in front of the diagram on the easel. "Dr. Chien, I wanted to direct your attention to your diagram. The diagram shows the pen mark at Mr. Grusini's neck, and that represents the only stab wound on him, isn't that correct?"

"Yes."

"However, I noticed that the only other pen marks you made on the diagram occur on Mr. Grusini's right hand, here." Bennie pointed to pen marks on the knuckles of the right hand. "Did you make these pen marks on Mr. Grusini's knuckles?"

"Yes, I did."

"Dr. Chien, what did you find during his autopsy that caused you to make these pen marks?"

"There were contusions on the knuckles of Mr. Grusini's right hand."

"Dr. Chien, 'contusions' means bruises, does it not?"

"Yes, bruises."

"Dr. Chien, what conclusion did you draw about the cause of those bruises, if any?"

"I concluded that the victim had bruised his hand by impact injury, i.e., impact with a hard object."

"Dr. Chien, wouldn't the forehead of another person qualify as a hard object?"

"Yes."

"Dr. Chien, do you have a conclusion about how close in time that impact injury occurred in relation to Mr. Grusini's death?"

"I concluded that the injury to his hand was close in time to the mortal wound."

"Dr. Chien, isn't that the kind of hand injury that you typically see from someone who had punched someone?"

"Objection," Martinez said, half-rising. "There is no basis for that conclusion."

Bennie looked at Martinez like he was crazy. "You qualified this witness as an expert. She can give an opinion to that effect."

Judge Patterson shook her head. "Overruled. You may answer, Dr. Chien."

Dr. Chien nodded. "Yes, that is typically the kind of injury we see when there has been a punch thrown."

Bennie switched gears. "Dr. Chien, did you run tests on Mr. Grusini's blood?"

"Yes, I did, typical panels."

"Which panels are typical?"

"We always run an initial test for general screening purposes and blood alcohol content. Beyond that, for prescription drugs or other controlled substances, you have to request a test. No such request was made in this case."

"Dr. Chien, what was the blood alcohol content of Mr. Grusini's blood?"

"It was .16."

"And isn't that above the legal limit?"

"It's twice the legal limit. The legal limit in Pennsylvania is .08."

"Thank you, Dr. Chien. I have no further questions."

Judge Patterson looked over at Martinez. "Mr. Martinez, if you have redirect, please get on with it. I think we can break for lunch after this witness."

"I'll make it brief, Your Honor," Martinez said, succumbing to judicial pressure. No trial lawyer wanted to be the one who kept the jury from their free lunch.

Bennie returned to counsel table, sneaking a glance at Karen, who was leaving the courtroom with a distraught Doreen and Declan. She shot Lou a look, and he knew exactly what to do, rising.

The lunch break couldn't come soon enough.

CHAPTER FIFTY-TWO

Bennie met with Jason in the secure meeting room, huddled at the tiny table and wolfing down her cheese sandwich. She had to eat quickly because she had other plans for the rest of the lunch break. Lou was still outside, presumably spying on Karen and Doreen. He would be back any minute, if only for his roast beef special with extra Russian dressing.

"Jason, how you doing?" Bennie asked, between mouthfuls.

"How do you think I'm doing?" Jason had barely touched his sandwich, sipping Coke from a warm can.

"You should eat something. It's going to be a tough afternoon."

"Who are they putting on the stand?"

"I don't know."

"Then how do you know it'll be tough?"

"That's what's tough, that we don't know. So, eat." Bennie felt like his mother all over again, between answering his questions, encouraging him to eat, and dealing with his moodiness in general.

"I'm not hungry."

"Okay, so tell me what's going on with you."

"I don't know."

"Jason, you know." Bennie wanted to stay patient, but it wasn't easy. "Tell me what's happening. Was there something in the testimony you have a question about? Or do you have a reaction to anything?"

"I don't want to get on the stand."

"We're going to table that discussion for now. What else?" Bennie sensed his new mood was about the gory crime-scene photograph. "How did you feel when you saw that photograph of Richie in the alley?"

"What are you, my shrink?"

"No, your lawyer, trying to save your ass." Bennie met his gaze hard, and Jason looked away.

"I felt funny, okay? Is that what you want to hear?"

"Don't tell me what I want to hear. Tell me the truth. How do you feel?"

"Like I said, funny," Jason shot back, setting his soda can on the table.

"What else? Pick more words."

"Weird, strange."

"How about sad?" Bennie wasn't coaching him, she wanted to know.

"I don't know."

"Let's try another approach." Bennie popped the tab of Diet Coke. "When you went to the police station after Richie was killed, you said you were glad he was dead. When you looked at the photograph today, did you still feel that way?"

"No." Jason swallowed hard, finally meeting her eye, and the first word that came to Bennie's mind was, haunted.

"Okay, that's a start. You didn't feel glad. So you're not happy he's dead?"

"No."

"Okay, how do you feel if you're not happy and you're not glad?" Bennie sensed that Jason was inching toward something important, but she didn't want to put words in his mouth.

"I feel bad." Jason's thin lips turned down at the corner, twitching slightly. "I feel bad that it happened. I wish it were different. I wish . . ."

"Go ahead, Jason. Finish the sentence."

"I don't know, I just wish it were all different. I wish it never happened. I felt bad when I heard his mom cry. I know she's wacky and all, but I felt bad when I heard her crying." Jason's eyes filmed suddenly, and Bennie fought the impulse to comfort him because she didn't want the emotion to vanish.

"Good, I understand that feeling. I felt the same way you did."

"It's sad that she'll never get him back. It's sad for his mom." Jason's pale skin flushed, and he blinked his eyes clear.

"You know the way you feel now, sad for them all? Even for Richie? I want you to remember this feeling, because if I put you up on the witness stand and I think I'm going to have to, I want you to be able to say that."

"No, Bennie—"

"Yes, if you get up there, I'm going to ask you to say it to her and I'm going to ask you to mean it, from the heart. And you do, I know you do. I knew you did in that courtroom, and I know it now." Bennie spoke softly, but with conviction, feeling better about him again. "Hold on to that sadness. No matter what kind of a jerk Richie was, he was a human being and he didn't deserve to die in an alley like that. And if you're a human being, you *should* feel sad about that."

Suddenly there was a knock on the door and they both turned as the sheriff opened it and let Lou inside. He closed the door only partway, agitated. "Bennie, you need to get out there."

"What's going on?" Bennie grabbed her napkin, wiped her mouth, and stood up.

"Doreen got upset, and Karen took her into the ladies' room."

"Oh boy." Bennie gestured at Jason. "Please eat if you can, ask Lou any questions you have, and I'll see you back in the courtroom."

"Where are you going?"

Lou sat down, reaching for his wrapped sandwich. "She has to powder her nose."

"Nobody says that anymore, Lou." Bennie slipped out of the

door, hurried down the tile hallway, where she knocked until the sheriff let her into the courtroom. It was partly empty, with the staff eating lunch at their desks, and Bennie left the courtroom and let herself out into the wide corridor, which was emptying for lunch.

She passed through the elevator bank, entered the vast lobby, and made a beeline for the ladies' room. She opened the door to find Karen next to the sink with Doreen, who had stopped crying, but was holding a paper towel underneath her mascaraed eyelashes. Both women looked up, surprised at Bennie's appearance, and Doreen's mouth dropped open in outrage as she took the towel from her eyes.

"Get out of here!" Doreen spat out, her eyes burning in a way that took Bennie back over a decade.

"I'm here to speak to Karen." Bennie turned to the reporter. "Karen, I have half an hour right now, if you want to meet."

"Fine, great. Doreen, we'll continue this later." Karen gave Doreen's shoulder a final squeeze, then followed Bennie out of the ladies' room.

"Karen, I'm so glad we could grab a minute to talk," Bennie said, heading back toward the courtroom.

"Good, I'm glad, too." Karen fell into step beside her, toting a massively oversized messenger bag, standard issue for every reporter.

"Let's go to the attorneys' conference room, this way. It'll be more private."

"Great." Karen looked up at Bennie, hurrying along. "I've been trying to get ahold of you, but I know how you are with the press."

"That was then, this is now." Bennie walked her back toward the courtroom and entered the attorneys' conference room, another white windowless box with orange-padded chairs and a small Formica table. "Please, sit down."

"You don't mind if I record this, do you?" Karen dug in her bag, pulled out a small bronze-toned tape recorder, switched it on, and set it on the table.

"Not at all." Bennie sat down, easing into her mission. She

wanted to plant their side of the story and block Karen from spending more alone time with Doreen.

"Okay, so." Karen tucked a strand of dark, straight hair into a practical ponytail at the nape of her neck. "Why are you being so forthcoming? God knows, it's not like you."

"I'm not going to bullshit you, Karen. I've been watching you all morning, sitting with Doreen Grusini. I don't like that you're getting only one side of the story."

"Wow, okay." Karen's dark brown eyes lit up, and she flashed a smile that wasn't especially warm. She had on a plain brownish cotton sweater, jeans, and flats, a practical girl after Bennie's own heart.

"So ask me anything. I'm yours. Here, I can give you the background and information that I could never get into evidence in there."

"Are you gonna put Lefkavick on the stand?"

"Ask me anything except that." Bennie smiled. "You know I can't discuss the particulars of this case with you, not while it's ongoing."

"If you're not going to put him on the stand, who are your witnesses?"

"I'll get you a copy of my witness list, if you haven't seen it already."

"I got a copy of the witness list, but all you do is list their witnesses."

"It's an old habit of mine. I used to do it all the time in civil cases, and most civil lawyers do. You never know who you're going to need to call from their side and you don't want to be caught without a name on the list." Bennie shifted gears. "Now, let's get to what I wanted to talk to you about, because this case is not just a simple murder case, though it looks that way."

"You're trying to spin this?" Karen's eyes narrowed.

"No, I'm trying to make sure you understand that the story has a much larger dimension than you think, because you don't have all the facts. Do you want to write a big story or small story?" Bennie didn't *Pulitzer*, because she didn't have to. It was the first thing on any reporter's mind, especially with all the changes in the newspaper business. Winning a big prize was the only way to keep your job these days.

"Obviously, I'd rather write a big story."

"Then you need to talk to me, because I was there when this all began, over a decade ago in Luzerne County. It was right after 9/11 and the very beginning of the war in Afghanistan. I represented Jason Lefkavick in his juvenile action."

"You did?"

"Yes."

"Is that why you're representing him now? I admit, I was surprised to see you in a run-of-the-mill murder case."

"Yes, and now you know." Bennie prepared herself to eat crow, if it helped Jason's case. "The truth is, I have history with this defendant, and that's why this case is about a lot more than a run-of-the-mill murder case."

"What do you mean?" Karen reached into her bag, extracted her skinny reporter's notebook, and flipped it open. She'd stored a ballpoint pen in its spiral coil, and slid it out neatly.

"Well, you heard me talk in there about Kids-for-Cash, and how both my client and Mr. Grusini were victims of that scandal. I can give you details, right now, and I'd be happy to, exclusively."

"Great."

"To me, the real story here is about justice, and whether it can be attained in the wake of a judicial corruption scandal like that. It's a scandal that sent two judges to jail for decades, but when you see what's happening in that courtroom, you really have to wonder what justice means." Bennie warmed to her topic, which she believed in, even though she felt like a fisherman baiting a hook. "I can give you the transcripts and even the pleadings of the juvenile case. I have my client's waiver of his attorney-client privilege with respect to that action. You couldn't ordinarily get those papers because they're sealed and now the records have even been expunged, since the scandal came to light."

"I would really appreciate that." Karen smiled, scribbling away.

"You might also be interested to know that my client, and presumably Mr. Grusini, received compensation for their wrongful incarceration, to the tune of about $5000. But you really have to ask yourself how you can compensate somebody for a childhood. You really have to wonder how you can do justice, even now. Or ever."

Karen kept taking notes, and Bennie didn't need encouragement to continue. It was what she wished she could say in court but was restrained not to, and it never hurt to have public opinion on Jason's side. If she won an acquittal, it could even make Martinez think twice before filing an appeal.

Bennie continued, "You really need to ask in this story, isn't it true that when there is no justice, there is no peace? Is there a better illustration than in this case? Because in my opinion, I do not think we would be in this courtroom today, if it were not for the judicial corruption scandal that took place in Luzerne County."

"Really." Karen looked up from her notes, tucking a strand of dark hair behind her ear. "Are you prepared to say that on the record?"

"I just did."

"Okay, I have a few specific questions about that."

"Take your time," Bennie said, with another smile.

CHAPTER FIFTY-THREE

The trial resumed after the lunch break, and both Judge Patterson and the jury seemed fresher to Bennie, as well as more comfortable, having settled into the courtroom. She was also happy to see that the Commonwealth's next witness, an expert named Dr. Liam Pettis, was one she had faced before and even liked. Dr. Pettis came off like everybody's favorite uncle: bright blue eyes behind tiny gold glasses, an egg-shaped bald head with bright white tufts of hair above each furry ear, and jowls that had grown even softer with age. He had on a seersucker suit that she would have sworn he wore the last time she saw him, and it fit tightly on his small, pudgy frame.

Martinez took Dr. Pettis through his expert qualifications, which only made the witness flush with a modesty that Bennie knew was completely genuine, and she marveled again that such a sweet old man could be an expert in one of the most gruesome areas of forensic science, blood spatter analysis.

Martinez faced the witness box. "Dr. Pettis, we have established that you are a licensed physician, as well as a lecturer at police academies across the country on blood spatter analysis. Would you please explain to the jury, in layman's term, what is blood spatter analysis?"

"As I always say, blood spatter analysis is simply an analysis of the pattern of bloodstains." Dr. Pettis spoke directly to the jury, his voice creaky and soft, so they listened harder. "All it means is that when blood is acted upon by physical forces, it will deposit itself on items at a crime scene or the clothing of a perpetrator in a distinct pattern. We re-create and study these patterns in a lab, using the blood of pigs and other animals. By understanding these patterns, we can surmise much about the way in which the crime occurred."

"And Dr. Pettis, is this true whether the murder was committed with a gun, knife, or even a fist?"

"Yes, that's true."

"There has been testimony in this case that this knife, recovered from the scene, was in fact the murder weapon." Martinez picked up the bagged knife from counsel table and held it high again. "Dr. Pettis, have you had a chance to examine this exhibit?"

"Yes, I have."

"The medical examiner, Dr. Chien, testified that the wound on the victim's neck was consistent with this knife and—"

"I read the autopsy report, so I am familiar with that conclusion."

"I'm also going to show Commonwealth Exhibits 20 and 21, the parka and T-shirt worn by the defendant on the night of the murder." Martinez set the knife down, and picked up the bagged T-shirt, which he made a great ceremony of sliding from the evidence bag, unfolding, and holding up. He did the same to the bag that held Jason's parka, and the clothing had gone stiff with bloodstains that covered the front of the shirt.

The jury recoiled, even though they had seen both the T-shirt and parka during the testimony of Detective Gallagher, and Bennie noticed that the opening of the bloody clothes had released a stale odor of dried blood.

"Dr. Pettis, have you had the chance to examine this T-shirt and this parka?"

"Yes, I have."

"There has been testimony in this case that this is the T-shirt and parka that was worn by the defendant on the night of the murder. You can see the bloodstains on the shirt, and there has been testimony that the stains match the defendant's blood in particular. Is that consistent with your findings, Dr. Pettis?"

"Yes, I am aware there is some evidentiary overlap in this regard. But for the record, it is part of my function to perform a number of tests on the blood, conventional bloodwork for typing and so forth, as well as DNA testing."

"Dr. Pettis, did you test the blood on the sweatshirt and T-shirt and compare it for identification purposes with this sample of the victim's blood supplied by the Commonwealth?"

"Yes, I did."

"Dr. Pettis, in your considered expert opinion, to a reasonable degree of medical certainty, can you say that the blood on the T-shirt and parka is that of the victim?"

"Yes, and that's what I told Detective Gallagher and Dr. Chien. I wasn't in the courtroom when they testified, but they may have testified to that already."

"Dr. Pettis, my question to you is, is the spatter pattern on the defendant's clothes consistent with someone who stabbed the victim's throat?"

"Yes, it is."

"Dr. Pettis, can you explain to the jury why this is so, and how you arrived at your conclusion?"

"Spatter analysis is a fascinating subject, and the shape of the droplets, the pattern, the appearance, and the many other details of blood spatter can give an expert much information." Dr. Pettis gestured to the center of the T-shirt, making a circular motion. "Briefly put, this spatter pattern is consistent because it shows the generalized drenching that would've occurred from such a grievous and mortal injury. Anytime the carotid artery is severed, as it was in this case, a horrific volume of blood is produced, pulsing out in a rhythm in time with the heartbeat of the victim."

Bennie felt Jason shifting uncomfortably, but the jury was rapt by the expert.

"In addition, because the victim was stabbed in a standing position and the blood was being pumped upward from the heart to the brain, it is under a significant amount of pressure. As soon as the knife was removed from the victim's throat, as I understand it was here, blood would have gushed from the arterial and other slicing wounds, producing the drenching that you see on the T-shirt and the parka."

"I see." Martinez set the items down slowly, undoubtedly letting the information sink in to the jury. "I have no further questions, Dr. Pettis."

Bennie was on her feet. "Your Honor, I have a few questions, if I may."

Judge Patterson nodded. "Please proceed, counsel."

"Dr. Pettis, good to see you again."

"You as well, Ms. Rosato. You haven't aged a bit. I wish I could say the same for myself."

"Thank you." Bennie managed a tight smile, appropriate in the circumstances, but she was pleased that the expert had remembered her because it increased her credibility with the jury. "Dr. Pettis, isn't it true you cannot tell from the blood spatter on the defendant's T-shirt and parka whether or not the lethal stab wound was administered in self-defense?"

"Yes. That is true."

"Dr. Pettis, did you happen to know the blood alcohol level of Mr. Grusini's blood on the night in question?"

"Yes, I did."

"And isn't it true that his BAC was .16, twice the legal limit?"

"Yes, that's true."

"Dr. Pettis, didn't you also analyze my client Jason's blood alcohol content?"

"Yes, I did."

"And what was his blood alcohol content that night?"

"It was .10."

"So it was lower than Mr. Grusini's?"

"Yes, I reviewed the file and the defendant was a smaller man. I think he weighs 165 pounds to the victim's 205."

"Thank you." Bennie had gotten more than she hoped for, but Martinez didn't move to strike. "I have no further questions, Your Honor."

CHAPTER FIFTY-FOUR

Martinez squared up with the dais. "The Commonwealth calls Doreen Grusini to the stand."

Bennie kept her expression impassive, but Jason squirmed beside her, and everyone straightened in their chairs. Judge Patterson nodded gravely, and the jurors' faces fell into uniformly sympathetic lines, their collective gaze shifting toward Doreen, who stood up and left the pew. Even the court stenographer stopped her ceaseless tapping of the keys, and the courtroom fell completely silent as Doreen walked to the witness box, took the stand, and was sworn in. Bennie and Martinez had agreed, in light of the fact that Doreen was Richie's mother, to permit her to sit in the courtroom during the trial and not be sequestered in the hallway, as were the other witnesses. Her simple grayish-black wool dress, which she had on with a nubby black wool sweater, black tights, and black flats, made a somber and classy figure in the jury box. Bennie didn't know how, or if, she would cross-examine Doreen without appearing heartless to the jury.

Martinez linked his fingers together in front of him. "Mrs. Grusini, thank you very much for your testimony today. I know this must be very difficult for you."

"Thank you." Doreen's voice sounded predictably shaky.

"If you speak into the microphone, Mrs. Grusini, this might be easier on you."

"Thank you," Doreen said again, then glanced at the jury. "I'm sorry. I'm getting over a cold."

"That's okay," the grandmotherly juror said softly, then covered her mouth, realizing she'd spoken out of turn.

Bennie knew it wasn't a good sign, so she didn't react and neither did anybody else. The jurors had yet to choose a foreperson, which wasn't done until deliberations began, and it was a critical decision in any trial because a foreperson tended to sway the group, if not lead them. Usually, jurors would choose a man, deferring to a male authority figure out of habit or sexism, but they also tended to choose the most senior woman. If they picked the grandmother, Bennie could be in trouble.

Martinez cleared his throat. "Mrs. Grusini, you are the mother of the murder victim in this case, Richard Grusini, isn't that right?"

"Yes, he was my oldest son."

"How many other children do you have?"

"Two twin boys, both in college." Doreen gestured at the pew, and Bennie looked over to see only Declan sitting there. "They were in court today with their uncle, my brother, but I sent them out in the hall. I didn't think they should be here when I testified. You know how it is, when kids see their mom upset . . ." Doreen didn't finish the sentence.

Bennie saw with dismay that the grandmother nodded.

"Now Mrs. Grusini, I think it would be helpful if you told the jury something about Richie's reputation for peacefulness, as you have heard that the defense elicited that sort of testimony with regard to the defendant."

"Yes, okay." Doreen turned to the jury, resting her manicured fingertips on the black stem of the microphone. "Richie wasn't the person that is being portrayed by the defense, not at all. Growing up, he was a strong, happy kid, an excellent athlete, but he had a really soft heart. He was a big guy, and even if he was big, he could be hurt easily, very easily."

"Mrs. Grusini, can you please explain to the jury what you mean by that?"

Bennie wished she could object, but she'd have to keep her

objections to a minimum and not cross at all, depending on how the testimony went in. Better to get Doreen off the stand as soon as possible, since she was probably the last witness of the day.

Doreen turned to the jury again, with a pained frown. "Richie had a hard childhood because his father left us when he was little. The twins had just been born, and it just put his dad over the top and he was never responsible enough in the first place, he just, walked *out*"—Doreen's voice faltered, and her eyes began to film, but she held back her tears—"anyway, the point is that when Richie's father left, Richie was very hurt. They used to do a lot of things together, and Richie never got over it. It really wounded him, like, for the rest of his life. If he lashed out, it was only because he was hurting inside. He was a good person, with a good heart and it was a heart that was easily wounded. They say that anger really hides pain, and that was really true with Richie."

Bennie saw that Doreen had changed from the out-of-control, angry mother she'd been so long ago. She was coherent, but emotional, and the combined effect was working magic on the jury, who looked rapt.

"Mrs. Grusini, take us back to the origin of the history of conflict between your son and the defendant, if you would."

"You mean from middle school?" Doreen asked, sounding remarkably uncoached, and Bennie wondered if Martinez was improvising.

"Yes, briefly."

Bennie raised a finger, staying seated. "Relevance, Your Honor," she said, keeping her tone quiet.

"Overruled." Judge Patterson didn't even wait for Martinez to respond. "I'll allow it, briefly."

Doreen nodded, shifting forward. "Yes, I think that is an important thing to bring up, because the defense is making it sound like Richie was the instigator of the bad blood, but that's not the truth. The *opposite* is the truth, and I just can't sit and hear that my boy was anything but a peaceful, loving person." Tears sprang to Doreen's dark eyes, and a vein in her neck bulged. "It's just not the truth about Richie, about his character, and I want the jury to know, everyone to know, that it wasn't Richie who started the fight so long ago. It was Jason, not Richie."

"You're talking about the fight in the cafeteria, that sent both boys to juvenile detention, wrongly?"

"Yes, yes, truly." Doreen answered, her tone agonized. She looked every inch a mother defending her son, leaning closer to the microphone and holding on to it for dear life. "Even back then," she said, her voice breaking, "the boys were in the same seventh-grade class, but it was Jason who pushed Richie in the cafeteria. That's why Jason got a longer sentence than Richie did. Jason was sentenced to juvenile detention for ninety days, but Richie only got sixty."

Bennie doubted that she would cross Doreen about the real reason the cafeteria fight started. Doreen had known the real reason the fight had started, but she'd never admit it, not now. Besides, Bennie wanted to keep the jury's focus on the present, not the past. She was trying to do the same thing, herself. She didn't even think of looking at Declan while Doreen testified.

Doreen continued, speaking directly to the jury. "You all heard what they said, it was the same thing that happened in the bar. It was Jason who went up to Richie, not the other way around. You saw it on the videos, too, it's a pattern. It was *Jason* who went into that alley after Richie, it was never my son who started it. It was Jason, *always Jason*, and my son ended up dead in an alley, his throat sliced open—"

Bennie raised a finger again. "Your Honor, move to strike. This is argument, not testimony."

Martinez faced the judge. "Your Honor, defense counsel doesn't want the witness to finish her sentence."

Doreen's eyes began to glisten, and she turned to the judge in appeal. "Your Honor, I just want them to know the truth. They have to know the truth about Richie. They're getting the wrong idea about my son."

Judge Patterson nodded. "Mrs. Grusini, I understand that this is difficult for you, but please compose yourself. Please wait for me to rule before you answer any further questions, do you understand?"

"Okay, sorry." Doreen pulled a Kleenex from the sleeve of her sweater and dabbed her eyes. "I was answering the question, I was *trying* to answer the question. Richie's not here to speak for himself. He needs me to speak for him."

"Mrs. Grusini, take a moment to calm down. It doesn't help the jury understand anything if the evidence comes in in a disordered fashion." Judge Patterson sighed. "It's been a long day, and we can all understand how difficult this must be. But you must allow me to make my ruling, and we will proceed."

"Okay, sorry." Doreen seemed suddenly exhausted, easing back into the witness chair, and the court clerk rose quickly from her desk, poured a plastic cup of water, and brought it to the witness stand, where she set it down.

Judge Patterson turned to Martinez. "Mr. Martinez, I'm going to have to agree with Ms. Rosato. I've given you some latitude, but let's not get too far afield."

"Yes, Your Honor. I'll resume, I just have one or two questions after the witness takes a sip of water." Martinez backed off, making much of waiting while Doreen picked up the cup with a shaking hand and sipped some water, with every eye in the jury trained on her. After she had set the water down, Martinez began. "Mrs. Grusini, please tell the jury what your relationship with Richie was like, so they understand the factual basis for your opinion as to his peacefulness."

"I tried very hard, as hard as I could, to comfort him after his father left. He acted out a little, but he was always so special to me, especially after his father left." Doreen paused, wiping her eyes, leaving mascara smudges that only made her appear more forlorn. "We had a very special relationship, the two of us. His uncle, my brother"—Doreen gestured at Declan again, but Bennie didn't dare turn her head—"he used to worry that I showed favoritism to Richie and I suppose I did. He was the oldest, and when the twins came along, he understood that he had to take care of things that help me, like, be the man around the house."

Bennie glanced discreetly at the jury, and the grandmother had tears in her eyes and so did Brooklyn Girl.

"And Mrs. Grusini, is it true that your relationship with your son was very close?"

"Yes, absolutely," Doreen answered, more softly. She sniffled, wiping her eyes again. "We loved each other very much."

Bennie bit her tongue, wondering if Martinez even knew that Doreen's relationship with Richie was terrible, that she had lost custody of the children, that she even tried to kill herself. If Doreen was going to paint herself as mother of the year, Bennie would have plenty of ammunition to answer that, the equivalent of a nuclear option. But like any nuclear weapon, if she used it, nobody won.

"Mrs. Grusini, when was the last time you spoke with Richie?"

"Just three days before he was murdered. I sent him a sweater, and he called me to tell me he liked it."

"How often did you speak with him on the phone?"

"Every week, we spoke."

"Mrs. Grusini, so is it fair to say that Richie was a good and cooperative son?"

"Yes, absolutely, as best he could be."

Bennie heard Jason mumble something under his breath, then he picked up the ballpoint pen and commandeered her legal pad.

Jason wrote LIES! RICHIE HATED HIS MOM. HE TALKED SHIT ABOUT HER ALL THE TIME. I HEARD HE TRIED TO HIRE SOMEBODY TO KILL HER.

Bennie shot Jason a discreet warning glance. She didn't want the jury to see him scribbling away during Doreen's testimony.

"Mrs. Grusini, let's address the present circumstances, though that is difficult for you." Martinez turned to counsel table, picked up the bagged hunting knife, and showed it to Doreen, who recoiled at the sight. Her dark eyes filmed with tears again, and she swallowed visibly, a reaction that looked so genuinely heartbroken that Bennie felt moved. Martinez continued, "Mrs. Grusini, I didn't mean to upset you all over again, but I did need to ask you, do you recognize that knife as belonging to Richie?"

"No, it's not his knife, not at all."

"But Richie was a hunter, was he not?"

"Yes, and he had a hunting knife, but that's not his." Doreen wiped a tear away, nodding. "I know what his looked like because his father gave it to him. They used to bow-hunt together. That's absolutely not his knife. It's Jason's."

"Objection, Your Honor." Bennie half-rose, to make a point for the jury's benefit. "Mrs. Grusini is competent to testify that she doesn't recognize the knife as her son's, but there's no basis for her conclusion that it belonged to Jason. For all she knows, Richie bought the knife at another time—"

Martinez caught on. "Your Honor, defense counsel is testifying herself. If she wants to cross-examine the witness, she can. If she wants to make that argument to the jury, she can—"

Judge Patterson waved him into silence. "Mr. Martinez, I'll overrule Ms. Rosato's objection. The jury can decide on the probative weight of the witness's opinion as to the ownership of the knife, now that both you and defense counsel have made your arguments. But Mr. Martinez, I can't imagine what further questions you have of this witness. You are testing my patience."

Martinez swallowed hard. "Thank you, I have no further questions."

Judge Patterson turned her disapproval on Bennie. "Ms. Rosato, any cross-examination?"

Bennie made a decision. "I have no cross-examination, Your Honor."

Martinez nodded, still standing. "Your Honor, the Commonwealth rests."

"Excellent." Judge Patterson turned to Bennie. "Ms. Rosato, you're up, first thing tomorrow morning."

"Thank you, Your Honor," Bennie said, swallowing hard. She had no idea what she would do for a defense, and she still didn't know if she would put Jason on the stand. He would go to jail forever if she couldn't come up with something. She would have done him wrong, twice.

It was going to be a long night.

CHAPTER FIFTY-FIVE

Bennie and Lou hit the office, stepping off the elevator into the reception area just as Mary, Judy, Anne, and John were waiting for an elevator to go down. It wasn't that late, but the office had segued into summer hours. Marshall had already gone home, and Mary and the associates were apparently leaving for the day, their arms full of purses and shopping bags.

"Bennie, hey, how'd it go?" Mary asked, and the others clambered onto the elevator cab behind her, their expressions somewhere between Interested and We-Are-Missing-Happy-Hour.

"Okay," Bennie answered, distracted. Her trial bag weighed heavily in her hands.

"Great!" Mary hit a button to prevent the elevator doors from closing. "When do you go to the jury?"

"Tomorrow, after we put on a case."

Lou snorted. "After we think of a case to put on."

Mary smiled, in her uncertain way. "Are you kidding or do you really need help? We're going out for a drink, but I can stay and give you a hand."

"No, thanks," Bennie answered, touched. She had yet to get used to the fact that DiNunzio was her partner, but in any event, she'd have to deal with the case herself and she had Lou for backup.

"Looks like you're about to get some major press attention.

348 | Lisa Scottoline

They've been calling all day. Marshall left your messages on your desk, and John spoke with Karen Engstrom."

"Karen called here? When?" Bennie turned to Foxman.

"The reporter called in the morning, around nine thirty."

"Why'd you take a call from the press? We never talk to the press."

"Why not? We always did at my old firm. We thought it was good for business. Profile-raising. At Eastman, we—"

"At Rosato, we don't," Bennie interrupted, annoyed. She'd probably said twenty words to the kid since he started on the job, and she was already sick of his "at Eastman, we . . ." So was Lou. It was the reason they'd nicknamed him Eastmanwe.

"I answered the phone only because Marshall was in the bathroom."

"You can answer the phone, but not the reporters. What did Karen ask you?"

"She wanted to know why you're trying Lefkavick, since it's a small murder case—"

"No murder is small, Foxman."

"It was her term."

"So what'd you tell her?"

"That you were court-appointed."

"What?" Bennie's mouth went dry. "Why did you say that?"

"It's true. You told us."

"When?"

"When I started. You stopped in the conference room and told us why you'd taken the case. I remembered."

"You remembered that from *six months ago*?"

"Yes." John was pleased with himself, but Mary frowned, knowing it was a faux pas.

Judy nodded. "I remember that, too."

Anne asked, "Isn't that why you took the case, Bennie?"

Bennie fell momentarily speechless, her mind racing. So Karen had spoken with John in the morning, and Bennie had spoken with Karen after that, telling her that she'd taken the case because she'd handled Jason's juvenile case. That meant that Karen would have figured out that Bennie had lied to her associates. Karen had sandbagged her at lunch, and Bennie had fallen into her trap.

Mary met Bennie's eye, concerned. "Is it a problem?"

"I hope not." Bennie prayed it didn't matter. The elevator started beeping in protest at being held open so long.

Lou touched Bennie's arm. "Let's get to work."

"Sure, right. Bye, folks." Bennie turned away, heading toward the conference room.

"Take care, kids!" Lou called to them, as Mary released the button and the elevator stopped beeping.

"Bennie, call me if you need me!" Mary called back, just as the elevator doors closed.

Lou fell into step beside Bennie, through the reception area. "You think it's a problem that Eastmanwe talked to Karen?"

"I hope not, but I have bigger worries tonight, like what the hell we're going to do for a defense." Bennie charged ahead, on nervous energy.

"You can turn it around. You always do."

"It's never been this bad."

"No, it hasn't."

"Or this down-to-the-wire."

"That, too."

"I have faith in you." Lou led the way toward the conference room. The offices were still and quiet, with the late-day sun streaming into the hallway. "If you're so worried, why didn't you take Mary up on her offer?"

"It's our case, and it would take too long to bring her up to speed."

"She's such a doll. She always offers to help. She has your back, you know that? You were right to make her partner."

"She earned it," Bennie said, even though she'd thought almost the same thing. Something about the thought stuck with her, competing for attention with her new worries over Karen and her fears about pulling a trial strategy out of her butt. She and Lou trundled into the conference room, shedding trial bags, messenger bags, and her handbag.

"My prostate calls, be right back," Lou said, leaving Bennie alone with her jumbled thoughts.

She always offers to help. She has your back.

The conference room had been turned into a war room for Jason's case, and her gaze flitted over the legal debris without alighting anywhere: the rows of accordion files stuffed with documents, her pads of notes, photocopied exhibits, police investigation files, and other documents that Martinez had turned over. Empty Styrofoam cups dotted the table, and orangey sunlight shone in glowing squares from the panel of windows. The room had an eastern exposure, but the mirrored surfaces of the glitzy skyscrapers trapped the sun, reflecting it back. It was great in winter, but hot as hell in summer.

Bennie took off her khaki blazer and dumped it on the table, but it hit the mouse pad on her other laptop, which woke up the computer. The screen came to life with the last thing she'd looked at, the surveillance video that Martinez had showed the jury. The frozen frame showed Jason as he was about to enter the alley, and Bennie recalled it as her lowest point at trial. She flashed on the jurors, and if she had to pinpoint a moment that things went south, it was then, when Doreen had given her teary speech about Jason's pattern of starting the fights. It had all rung true, and Jason had morphed from being the defendant to being a murderer.

That's who he is. He always has my back.

Funny, Bennie remembered Jason's roommate Gail saying that, when they interviewed her. She pulled out the rolling chair in front of the laptop, sat down, and hit the mouse pad, her mind churning. The video started up again, and on the screen, Jason disappeared into the alley. She let the video play, but her thoughts strayed. She thought about how Mary always had her back, and then to Jason's roommate, who said that Jason always had her back.

Her thoughts corkscrewed farther back in time, and she remembered when she'd first met Jason, in the visiting room at River Street. He'd been a chubby boy with a toy in his hand, a beloved Lego figurine. She remembered she had found that figurine in his bedroom later, when she'd interviewed Gail. On impulse, Bennie got up and started digging in the boxes, finally finding at the bottom of one the little plastic toy, the blue knight who worked for King Lear.

Not King Lear. King Leo.

The name came out of nowhere to her consciousness, her memory jarred by the sight of the little toy in the palm of her hand. It all came back to her, what Jason had said about his Lego toy.

The coolest is Richard the Strong. He protects the Queen and the Princess. He helps.

Bennie brought the toy back to the seat and sat down, her mind churning. The video was still running, and Jason hadn't come back out of the alley yet, but she remembered when he had told her, about what had happened to provoke him during the cafeteria fight.

I'm used to Richie saying bad things about me, but I didn't like it when he said it about my mom.

Bennie thought a moment, trying to parse the memory. It was as if a conclusion lay just beyond her grasp, and just then Lou returned to the conference room. He'd taken his jacket and tie off and unbuttoned the top button of his shirt, and in his arms was an aromatic bag of Chinese food.

"Perfect timing, right? They just called from downstairs." Lou put the bag on the table and reached inside, unpacking the white containers. "Why are you looking at me funny? I'll share, you know I will."

"It's not that." Bennie was still trying to articulate a theory in her head. "Let me run this past you. You just said something about Mary, that she always offers to help."

"Yes, she does."

"You knew she would help because that's a pattern of behavior, a characteristic of hers. People behave in ways that are patterns. That's who they are."

"Sure, right. It's her way."

"Exactly. Like Richie's mother said today, on the stand. She said the pattern was the same." Bennie thought back to Doreen's testimony. "She said that Jason always provokes the fights. He provoked the fight in the cafeteria, back in middle school. He provoked the fight in the bar. And he provoked the fight in the alley, when he went inside."

"Right, I remember." Lou stopped unpacking the take-out bag, paying attention. "Where are you going with this?"

"But that's *not* Jason's pattern. That's not who he is. I know his pattern is different. Jason's pattern, or his characteristic, is that he *helps*. He *protects*. Like Mary. Like Richard the Strong."

"Richard the what?"

"This little guy." Bennie held up the Lego toy. "Think about it a minute, Lou. Jason's roommate told us that he protected her from the next-door neighbor, who gave her a hard time for being gay. And he started that cafeteria fight because he was protecting his mother's reputation. That's why this toy meant so much to him when he was little. It's a protector, a knight who protects a family."

"Okay, what's your point?" Lou pulled out the chair next to her, listening intently.

"So what do we know from this?" Bennie reasoned aloud, not knowing where it would take her. "We know that Jason can be violent, but only when he's protecting someone. You follow?"

"Yes."

"So that night in the alley, what if he was protecting someone? What if there was someone else in the alley that night?" Bennie felt her heart leap at the notion, whether it was hope or folly. "Remember my first instinct was that somebody could've been in the alley and gotten out the other side? Out the back? Remember we looked at it, and we saw that you could scale that wall?"

"Yes." Lou lifted a gray eyebrow.

"What if Jason killed Richie to protect somebody? What if there was a third person in the alley that night?"

"Why wouldn't he tell us that?"

"Because he's protecting them." Bennie turned to the laptop and started searching through the video files that Martinez had turned over to them.

"But who? Why?" Lou rolled his chair over, peering at the laptop.

"I don't know." Bennie scanned the directory for the video files, locating the one from Yearling Street, around the block from Dunbar. There had only been one, and she and Lou had watched it together, just to see if there was anything relevant, but there hadn't been.

She clicked the file, and a dark and grainy videotape popped onto the screen, showing a deserted city street around the corner from the alley. There was only sparse traffic on Yearling, which was one-way, and all she could see were blurry headlights in the darkness and the outlines of the cars, with only poor resolution. It was hard to see the sidewalk because there was only one street-light providing any illumination, and Bennie assumed the other streetlights were broken.

"I remember this, we watched this."

"Yes, we wanted to see if there were any witnesses, or anybody doing anything suspicious, like running down the street, as if they were running from the alley. We were trying to substantiate Jason's story that he was framed, too."

"Right."

"But we couldn't." Bennie watched the numbers of the time clock running at the bottom of the frame, before the murder. A shadowy figure appeared on the screen and started walking down the street, away from the camera, but the picture was so grainy, it was hard to tell what they looked like.

"So there's somebody, but that's before the murder."

"Right." Bennie remembered having gone over this and why they rejected it before. "And we dismissed that person as a witness, because Jason said there was no shouting during the fight. There was nothing to hear, so there was nothing to follow up on."

"Right."

"Now, watch. I think I remember there was somebody." Bennie and Lou watched the screen and stopped the video when 11:15 passed. "So this is roughly when the murder occurred. We can double-check it later and run the videos side by side, but I can't run two videos at the same time on the same screen and I want to keep going."

"You don't need to, I follow you. Jason enters the alley at eleven fifteen and he's in there right now."

"Correct." Bennie watched the screen, and another shadowy figure appeared. "There we go. Who is that person? What's that about?"

"It doesn't look like somebody running away from a murder or any kind of fight in an alley. That's why we didn't think it mattered. Someone walking calmly down a street." Lou leaned away from the screen to see it better. "I wish you could enlarge that."

"Let me try." Bennie enlarged the video as much as she could, but they still couldn't tell what the figure looked like, except that it appeared to be carrying something.

"Doesn't look like they were in the alley, Bennie. Not with a package."

"We don't know that. It's at least possible. Something could be in the package, something relevant, for all we know."

"So ask Jason. Confront him with it."

"He'll lie. He's a knucklehead, like you said. I'm just trying to save him from himself."

Lou paused, thinking it over. "So how exactly do you think it went down in the alley?"

"I don't know, but we need to find some better videotape." Bennie turned to him. "You have buddies on the force you can call, don't you?"

"You know I do."

"So maybe you could get us some new videotapes. Go call a few of them. We got videos from Dunbar, but ask them which traffic cams there are on Yearling, around the block from Dunbar. Or ask them which of the stores on Yearling have good surveillance video cameras. See if you can rustle up any more videos that show Yearling at the relevant time."

"I suppose I could ask around." Lou rose, hitching up his pants.

"Also stop by the Mayfair Bar & Grill and ask some questions.

See if you can find out if Richie made any enemies there, like maybe that guy he pulled the paring knife on."

"You really believe in this kid, don't you?"

"Yes. He's Richard the Strong."

"Well, okay." Lou reached for the bag of takeout. "I'm Lou the Hungry, and I'm taking my lo mein."

CHAPTER FIFTY-SIX

Darkness fell outside the conference room, but Bennie forked garlicky sautéed vegetables into her mouth and watched the video of the figure walking down Yearling, for the umpteenth time. The more she watched the video, the more she thought she was onto something. Maybe there really had been a third person in the alley, but she had no idea who. She kicked herself for missing it before, but she hadn't come up with her revelation about Jason's pattern of behavior until she'd heard Doreen's testimony. She fought the impulse to go see Jason and ask him, but she wanted more information before she confronted him. If she went prematurely, he'd just deny it, and she'd have shown her hand.

She slurped down a peapod dripping in sauce, eyeing the video files that filled up her laptop screen. The Commonwealth had turned over seven videos from Dunbar Street, and Lou had managed to get ten more via blue magic. Bennie thought again that if people knew how often they were filmed in public, they would never leave the house. She wondered if any of the other videos showed the unidentified figure entering the alley, but there was only one way to find out. She dropped her fork inside the take-out container, set it aside, and got to work.

Bennie began with the videos that the Commonwealth had

turned over and clicked through video after video, freeze-framing when she was unsure of what she was seeing. All of the videos were the same. None of them even started videotaping before nine o'clock, which made sense. The detectives would have focused their investigation on the time of the murder and worked backwards, and they would have stopped as soon as they had seen video of Jason entering the alley.

Bennie reached for her cell phone, scrolled to FAVORITES, and pressed Lou, who picked up after one ring. "Hi, did you find out anything?"

"Not yet, I'm working on it," Lou answered, over traffic noise in the background.

"Okay, but I forgot something."

"Milk, eggs, butter?"

"Find me some video from before Jason goes into the alley. Go back as far as you can."

"You mean earlier in the day?"

"Yes. Whoever went out of the alley had to go into it." Bennie flashed on something that Stokowski had said on the witness stand. "Remember, Stokowski testified that Richie always parks in the alley? If somebody knew he was going to park in the alley, then they could've gone in there to meet him, or even to ambush him."

"Okay, will do."

Bennie heard a beep on her phone, signaling that another call was coming through, and she checked the screen. "Lou, hold on, I'm getting another call, it's DiNunzio."

"Take it. I gotta go. I'll catch you later."

"Thanks. Bye." Bennie swiped END CALL & ACCEPT with her thumb. "DiNunzio, what's up?"

"Bennie, have you been online recently? I'm just giving you the heads-up." Mary sounded nervous. "I have us on Google Alert, and that reporter Karen just posted a story about your murder case."

"Great." Bennie simmered. "If she reported anything that hurts my client, I'll sue. The jury isn't sequestered, and the last thing we need is a mistrial."

"The story isn't about your client. It's about you, personally."

"About *me*?" Bennie felt her gut tense as she navigated out of the video. "I thought she liked me. I gave her the interview."

"I'm really sorry John talked to the reporter. He's sorry, too. He's going to apologize to you."

Bennie's heart started to thump. She went online, pulled up the front page of the paper, and spotted the Court News column. The headline read, HELL HATH NO FURY LIKE A LAWYER SCORNED. The lede began:

> Superlawyer Bennie Rosato is defending her first murder case in years, and it may just be a coincidence, but the murder victim, Richie Grusini, happens to be the nephew of an old flame of hers, who ditched her over a decade ago, fellow barrister Declan Mitchell. Reliable sources reveal that the famously single Rosato had a romantic relationship with Mitchell, which he ended when things got dicey, since she was then representing his nephew's bully, Jason Lefkavick, in a previous juvenile action.

"Oh my God." Bennie felt mortified. She'd had the press take shots at her before in print, but never about anything private. Now Mary would know about Declan and so would all the associates. Her friends would know. She'd never felt so embarrassed.

"Bennie, don't worry about it. It doesn't matter. I know you took that case for the right reasons, and nobody's going to believe a word of this, least of all me."

"I did take it for the right reasons!" Bennie shot back, stricken, as she read on:

> Lefkavick and Grusini have gone public as being caught up in the notorious Kids-for-Cash scandal that arose in Luzerne County. Lefkavick is currently standing trial for first-degree murder in the stabbing death of Grusini. When questioned by this reporter, Rosato admitted to having represented Lefkavick in the juvenile action, but neglected to

reveal that she had been romantically involved with his uncle and ultimately rejected by him.

"Bennie, if there's anything I can do to help you, I'll do it. If you're still at the office, I can come over."

"No, I'm fine." Bennie felt her face aflame. She realized what must have happened. Karen must have started digging, then Doreen had spilled the beans, or the other way around. Either way, Bennie's love life, or lack thereof, was online. She thought of Declan, then unaccountably, of their baby. That must be why the story rattled her. Thank God nobody knew about that. She hadn't told a soul.

"Bennie, this is just gossip, nothing more. You know that, right? I mean, really."

"But if the jury reads it, it could affect the merits of the case."

"No it can't. How?"

"Because it compromises my credibility." Bennie felt heartsick. "I have to stand up in front of them and tell them that my client killed Grusini in self-defense."

"Bennie, you've talked to tons of juries in your time. You have credibility for miles, and the jury doesn't decide a murder case based on what they think of the lawyers anyway." Mary's voice turned uncharacteristically authoritative. "We both know they decide on the facts and the witnesses. You've told me that yourself."

Bennie knew it was true. She'd given all the associates that lecture. Still, she fell silent as she read:

Rosato has gone to great lengths to conceal her motivation for taking the murder case. She told her partner and associates at her law firm that she was court-appointed on the case. Yet a subsequent search of court records reveals that Rosato was not appointed to the case, raising major questions. Why is Rosato lying to her own employees? Is Rosato using the court system for revenge at her ex-boyfriend? If so, isn't that a violation of the Code of Professional Responsibility, which lawyers are required to abide by?

"Bennie, I can tell you're reading it. You shouldn't even bother."

"But the jury will know, and so will the judge, the prosecutor, and everyone—"

"What will they know? So what?"

Bennie swallowed hard. The initial shock of the exposure was subsiding, and she regained her footing. "You're right. This isn't about the case. I don't think it will affect the case. It's just juicy gossip."

"Exactly. It doesn't affect the merits, even if the jury reads it."

"True, right." Bennie couldn't tell if she felt better or worse. She felt better because DiNunzio had made her feel better, but at the same time, she couldn't believe she had gotten herself into a position in which she was being comforted by DiNunzio, whom she'd raised from a baby lawyer. "DiNunzio, listen, I didn't keep it from you or the associates for any nefarious reason. I took the case to do right by the client, because I hadn't before."

"You don't have to explain it to me or anybody else. You want me to come back to the office? Everybody needs a girlfriend now and then."

Bennie didn't know how to respond. She'd had friends and business acquaintances, but she'd never had a true girlfriend. She'd always been on her own. Even back in college, rowing crew, she always rowed a single scull. She just wasn't a team player, and it had never bothered her before. She'd always believed that life was an individual sport, until now. "No, thanks, I'm fine."

"You don't sound fine."

"I am, or I'm going to be." Bennie's attention was drawn to the next sentence in the article:

Phil McGeer, President of the Criminal Section of the Philadelphia Bar Association, stated, "Certainly, it would be a violation of our Canon of Ethics for a criminal defense lawyer to undertake a defense for a personal reason of his or her own, or for any other reason other than advocating the best interest of his or her client . . .

Bennie cringed. She'd known Phil for thirty years. They'd served in the Young Lawyers' Section together. Now he knew about Declan and was being bothered for dumb quotes to give credibility to snark. She closed the webpage in disgust and navigated back to the videos. "Okay, my pity party's over. I have to get back to work. There's too much at stake in this case to worry about dumb stuff."

"Are you sure you don't need me? I can do research, draft briefs, prepare witnesses, whatever you need."

"DiNunzio, you did help me. Thanks for talking me through it. I really do feel better. I want to move on."

"That's the spirit!"

"Thanks. Now, let me go." Bennie clicked on the first video.

"Good luck and call me if you need me, any time of day or night."

"Good-bye, partner." Bennie heard the words coming out of her mouth with new warmth. She ended the call and set the cell phone down and clicked on the first video, starting over.

Bennie found herself engrossed in the video, though she had seen it so many times before. It was the first film that the Commonwealth had turned over, and the lighting and resolution were good enough to see a fair amount of detail, though there was no audio. She watched as Richie and Stokowski left the bar, walked to Stokowski's car, then Stokowski got in the car and drove away. Richie took a right turn and walked down the street, raising his cell phone to his ear. He must have been talking to Zimmer, his girlfriend, whom he was going to meet later. Bennie remembered that Zimmer had testified that Richie sounded happy and upbeat on the phone.

Bennie froze the video, remembering something strange. The video that Martinez had shown today had begun when Richie was on Dunbar Street. He hadn't been talking on the phone then. So Martinez had chosen a video from when Richie wasn't on the phone, though he put Zimmer up to testify about a phone call that Richie had made to her. Bennie thought it didn't square. She pressed PLAY and watched the video of Richie walking to the end of Pimlico, then turning the corner onto Dunbar. Bennie noticed something she hadn't before; Richie swiped the screen with his thumb, without breaking stride. She recognized what he was doing only because she had just done it herself with Lou, when Mary's call had come in.

Bennie rewound the video, then hit PLAY, and watched carefully. Richie's action was unmistakable. He'd swiped the screen of his glowing phone with his thumb. He had been on the phone, but another call had come in, and he had taken the call. She got up, hurried around to the other side of the table, and rummaged through the evidence boxes until she found a copy of Richie's phone records, which Martinez had turned over to her. She'd read them over when she first got them, but now they took on a new significance.

Bennie scanned the phone records, which were a corporate iteration of a common phone bill, issued pursuant to a Commonwealth subpoena, with a list on the right of the times of the incoming or outgoing calls, their duration, and the phone numbers of the caller. She scanned the list until she got to the bar fight, which occurred at 11:00, then Richie was thrown out, and Bennie could see that there was an outgoing phone call at 11:04. She scanned across for the phone number—267-555-1715. That was the first call that Richie made coming out of the bar, and the record showed it lasted five minutes. There was a second phone call at 11:09, but it was incoming, lasting three minutes. The phone number of the second call was 215-555-2873. The Philadelphia area code was 215, and 267 was given to more recent cell phone numbers.

Bennie blinked, mulling it over. So there had been two calls, not one, before Richie was killed. One of those calls had been to Renée Zimmer, who testified on the stand about it, but Bennie didn't know who the other caller was. It could have been anyone, even his killer. Maybe Jason really had been framed. She hustled the phone records back to her laptop, watched the video, and matched the time of the first call to the phone records, by using the time clock on the video. Richie pressed his phone at the very moment the 215 call came in, ending the first call to the 267 area code. Bennie had been correct.

She didn't know whether the 215 or the 267 number was Renée's and thought about calling them to see who answered, but then she'd be busted. Then she remembered that Renée had testified that Richie had called her earlier, at seven o'clock, so Bennie scanned the earlier calls and spotted an outgoing call to the same number, 215-555-2873, at 7:02 P.M. That meant the 215 number was Renée's, and the 267 call was the unknown caller.

Bennie got online and found a webpage for a reverse cell phone lookup. It wasn't a free service, so she went digging in her purse for her credit card, plugged it into the website, and searched the 267 number. The answer popped onto the screen. Declan P. Mitchell, Esq.

Bennie blinked, surprised. It wasn't what she'd been thinking, but it made sense. Declan was probably the only other person who knew the true significance of Richie getting into a bar fight with Jason, so Richie would probably call Declan right after the bar fight. Doreen would have known as well, but Richie wasn't close to her, no matter what she'd testified to in court.

Bennie processed the information. Martinez had put Renée on the stand to testify that Richie was upbeat after the bar fight, thus refuting that he was in a murderous state of mind. But Renée wasn't the only person Richie had spoken with, and she wasn't even the first person, facts that Martinez deliberately omitted. On the contrary, Martinez had implied the opposite to the jury. Bennie would almost have admired the sharp practice, if it hadn't been against her client.

Bennie reasoned that if Martinez hadn't called Declan to the stand, then Declan must have had a different conversation with Richie. But there was only one way to find that out, and it was risky. Besides, she didn't know if she had the heart for it, especially after the online revelations about them. The office phone started ringing on the credenza, interrupting her thoughts. It had to be the press calling, undoubtedly in response to the news story about her and Declan. She ignored the call, returned her attention to the laptop screen, and got back to work.

She worked through the night, reading and rereading the file, reviewing every exhibit, grisly crime-scene photographs, and expert and police reports, trying to see if there was anything she had missed. The office phone rang and rang, and her email bin filled with reactions to the article about her and Declan, but she ignored the issue. She drank a fresh pot of coffee and she got a second wind until Lou reappeared, coming into the conference room.

"Well, well, well, is this a sex goddess of the Philadelphia Bar Association?" Lou said wearily. "You saw that you and Sergeant Right are all over the local Internet news. You gotta love the media, don't you?"

"I know, right?" Bennie checked the laptop clock: 4:45 A.M. "Any luck?"

"No. I'm sorry, Bennie, I tried." Lou eased heavily into the chair beside her, sighing. He wiped his face, which looked slightly greasy, and his shirt was limp. "I talked to a couple of my buddies and looked at video from the other surveillance cams. None of them showed anything better than the ones we already saw or the one we have on Yearling Street. I brought them for you anyway." Lou leaned over, fished in his pocket, and pulled out a plastic zip drive. "The problem is that Yearling isn't as commercial as Dunbar. There's a lot fewer video cams, and the lighting is too crappy to see a damn thing."

"Thanks." Bennie picked up the zip drive. "What about earlier videos from Dunbar Street? Were you able to get any of those, so we could see somebody entering the alley, much earlier?"

"I got two, and they're both on the zip drive, but there were people walking up and down the street all afternoon. Remember, the L stop is at the end of the street? You can't tell who goes into the alley and who doesn't." Lou gestured at the zip drive. "Fire it up. Check it out yourself."

"I will, just in case." Bennie inserted the zip drive into her laptop.

"But I'm telling you, bottom line, I got *bupkis*."

Bennie waited for the zip drive to open, making a decision. "If that's true, then I have a Plan B."

CHAPTER FIFTY-SEVEN

Morning came too soon, and they headed to the Criminal Justice Center in heavy foot traffic. Bennie felt tense after a night of no sleep, an office shower, and a spare khaki suit she kept at work. Her topknot was slightly wet, but she girded herself for the day ahead. White TV news vans clogged the street, their microwave towers spiraling into a clear blue sky, and reporters thronged in front of the courthouse.

"Here goes nothing." Bennie glanced at Lou.

"Don't let them get to you, kiddo."

The reporters, photographers, TV people, and stringers came running toward them. "Bennie, Bennie!" they hollered on the run. "Look up, look up! Over here!" "Just one picture!"

Bennie ignored them, plowing forward, and Lou took her arm. They couldn't move fast carrying the trial bags, though she had a roller bag of files, which she considered using as a battering ram. She didn't know where all these reporters had come from, then she realized that gossip had replaced real news and she was looking at the usurpers. Cameras snapped all around her and video cameras were shoved at her face, their rubbery black lenses like so many eyes.

"What's going on with you and Declan Mitchell?" "Any comment on the story?" "Is this revenge or a legitimate case?" "Look up for a picture! On the right, on your right!"

"No comment," Bennie answered, shaken. She'd been bothered by the press before, but not like today. She felt newly vulnerable, with an irrational fear that if they knew one of her secrets about Declan, they could know the secret that really mattered. The secret that even Declan didn't know.

Lou tugged her along, parting the crowd. "People, stand aside. We're coming through, coming through!"

The crowd of reporters ran backwards, calling out questions. "What's the story, Bennie?" "Were you and Mitchell engaged?"

Bennie powered through the crowd, though she could feel her face aflame. It was so strange to hear Declan's name coming out of the mouth of complete strangers. She assumed that he would run the same gauntlet when he came to court.

"Come on, you've given us a comment before!" "If the story isn't true, just say so!" "Why did you lie?" "Why did you really take the Lefkavick case?" "Don't you want to tell your side of the story?"

Bennie and Lou pushed their way into the Criminal Justice Center, joined the attorneys' line, and hustled through to the metal detector. Bennie felt heads turning to look at her, but that could've been her paranoia. They grabbed a crowded elevator, and when they reached the ninth floor, ignored the reporters waiting outside the courtroom door, hoping for comment.

Bennie and Lou entered the courtroom, and the court staff looked up when she headed for counsel table, their gaze lingering. She assumed they had read the article, if only because of the hubbub. The court stenographer lifted an eyebrow, but the court clerk only smiled slyly. The gallery was filling with reporters, yammering to each other, glancing at her, and taking out their skinny notebooks and smartphones. A courtroom artist set up in the front row, opening up his long sketchpad, with its characteristic darkened paper.

Lou leaned over to unbuckle the roller bag. "Looks like we got an audience," he said under his breath.

Bennie felt too tense to reply, unpacking her laptop and plugging it into the court's AV system. Suddenly there was a commotion in the gallery as reporters turned to see Martinez entering the courtroom with Declan, Doreen, the twin boys, Renée Zimmer, Stokowski, and his wife. Bennie kept her head turned away, busying herself with unpacking their files.

Lou unpacked beside her. "Plus, did you see we got a sketch artist? We're coming up in the world. 'I must be in the front rooooow.' Do you know who said, 'I must be in the front roooow'?"

"What?" Bennie asked, preoccupied, but when she saw the crinkly warmth in Lou's gaze, she realized he was trying to help. "No, who?"

"Bob Uecker. Mr. Baseball."

"Who's that?" Bennie unpacked the rest of her stuff, side by side with Lou. She ignored Declan telling the reporters "no comment" as they squeezed into the gallery. Martinez sat down at counsel table, the staff went to their desks, preparing for court to begin.

"Bob Uecker made a great beer commercial in the seventies. He gets thrown out of his seat in the ballpark, but they put him back in the nosebleed section, not in the front row."

"Really." Bennie grabbed her legal pad and pen, then sat down in her chair, beginning to get her act together. She reminded herself that she was at home in a courtroom and she had the trial experience to pull a defense out of a hat. Or her butt.

Lou placed a hand on her shoulder. "You can do this, honey. Good luck."

"Thanks." Bennie ignored the lump in her throat, and just then Jason was brought into the courtroom. He looked pale and tired, and she rose and went to his side, touching his arm. "Hi, Jason."

"Hi." Jason's panicky blue eyes took in the packed gallery. "Yo, what's going on? This is a full house."

"Good luck, buddy." Lou returned to his seat in the front row of the gallery, as Jason offered up his wrists and the sheriff unlocked the jingling metal handcuffs.

"I'll fill you in later." Bennie realized that Jason was the only person in the room who didn't know that the story about her and

Declan had gone public. She guided him to the chair beside her, and they sat down.

"So what's going on, with me?" Jason whispered, leaning over. "You know I'm not testifying, right? I can't deal with Martinez."

"Relax, I have a new plan." Bennie projected a confidence she didn't feel, but the last thing she wanted today was for him to appear nervous in front of the jury. "Don't worry. Just remain calm, don't make any faces, and follow my lead."

"Okay." Jason faced front, and the courtroom deputy opened the pocket door that led to the judge's chambers.

"All rise for the Honorable Judge Martina Patterson, this Court is now in session!" he bellowed, and the judge swept into the room, with fresh lipstick on and a new lacy collar at the top of her judicial robes.

"Good morning, everyone," Judge Patterson said, ascending the dais.

"Good morning, Your Honor." Bennie didn't know if Judge Patterson had seen the article, but put it out of her mind.

"Good morning, Your Honor." Martinez shot Bennie a knowing look as they both sat down, and she worried that he'd try to make something out of the story about her and Declan. She'd have to stay on her toes.

"Tania, would you fetch the jury, please?" Judge Patterson gestured to the courtroom deputy, already heading to the jury room. Tania went inside and reappeared a moment later, leading the jurors.

"Good morning, ladies and gentlemen," Judge Patterson said, as the jurors entered the courtroom, and they responded with a cheery chorus of "good mornings" and "thank yous" and "good to see yous."

Bennie watched as Brooklyn Girl, Computer Guy, Marathon Mom, the grandmother, and the others took their seats, picking up their blue booklets. A few of the jurors looked at her, and she smiled back pleasantly. The jury had been instructed not to read anything about the case, but there was no way of enforcing the rule. Bennie chose to trust them, since she believed in the goodness of people, especially those without law degrees.

"Ms. Rosato?" Judge Patterson turned to Bennie. "Ready to begin?"

"Yes, Your Honor." Bennie rose, suppressing her fear. She couldn't think about the fact that if she lost, Jason would spend most of his life in prison. "The defense would like to call Detective Gallagher to the stand."

CHAPTER FIFTY-EIGHT

Bennie sized up Detective Gallagher while he was being sworn in. He still looked completely relaxed, though he couldn't have been happy she'd called him back. He had on a different suit and tie from yesterday, a lightweight wool in charcoal color with a solid blue tie. His bald head shone slightly because the air-conditioning wouldn't cool the courtroom properly until noon.

"Good morning, Detective Gallagher." Bennie didn't want to come on strongly adversarial or she'd never get what she needed out of him. If she laid the foundation with him, the fireworks would come with other witnesses.

"Good morning." Detective Gallagher leaned back in the chair.

"Detective, I'd like to take you back to your testimony of yesterday, with regard to the alley off Dunbar Street, where the murder in question took place. Okay with you?"

"Sure."

"Excuse me a moment." Bennie crossed to the exhibits leaning against the easel, picked the one she wanted, and placed it on the easel. "Detective Gallagher, I'm showing you Defense Exhibit 10, an enlarged photograph of the alley in the daytime, on which is superimposed the dimensions of the alley."

"Okay."

"Detective Gallagher, in the back of the alley, there is a wall, is there not?" Bennie pointed with her index finger, and the jurors watched, interested.

"Yes."

"The wall is five feet tall and it is made of cinderblocks, isn't that right?"

"Yes."

"On the other side of the wall is Yearling Street, correct?"

"Yes."

"And the width of the wall is the width of a standard cinderblock, which is about six inches, isn't that correct?"

"Yes."

"Detective Gallagher, you can see here, in front of the cinderblock wall, there is a blue recycling bin on wheels, approximately four feet tall, and next to that a galvanized steel trash can, resting on its side, isn't that correct?"

"Yes, I mean, I take your word for it."

"Detective Gallagher, you visited the alley on the night of the murder, didn't you?"

"Yes."

"You did so as part of your investigation, isn't that right?"

"Yes."

"And you saw the alley in the daytime, isn't that true as well?"

"Yes, I did return in the daylight."

"Detective Gallagher, does this exhibit represent what the alley looked like when you saw it in the daylight?"

"Yes."

"Now the left wall of the alley is where Mr. Grusini's truck was parked, and it does not contain doors at all, such as would be the back entrance to any businesses, is that correct?"

"Yes."

"In other words, it's an unbroken brick wall on the left."

"I would call it the west wall, but yes, it's unbroken."

"Good point. The west wall. I'm directionally challenged." Bennie smiled, accepting the correction. She knew she'd made a friend when she noticed Brooklyn Girl nodded. "Now the oppo-

site wall would be the east wall, and it contains the back en-
trances of two businesses, isn't that correct, Detective Gallagher?"

"Yes, I believe so."

"And that would be the butcher shop and the medical supply
store, isn't that right?"

"Yes."

"Did you happen to notice the position of the recycling bin and
the trash can, at that time?"

"Yes."

"Detective Gallagher, did you determine to whom either the
recycling bin or the trash can belonged?"

"Yes, they both belonged to the butcher shop."

"You knew that how?"

"We asked."

"The butcher shop would be the closer to the wall of the two
doors, is that correct?"

"Yes, but again, I would call that the northernmost door."

"Right again, Detective." Bennie smiled briefly. "Do you happen to know if that's where they commonly keep their recycling
bin and trash can?"

"Yes." Detective Gallagher hesitated. "But they don't use either
bin. They don't recycle, and their meat scraps are picked up by a
private hauler."

"Thank you, that was my next question." Bennie pointed to the
trash can and recycling bin on the exhibit. "Detective Gallagher,
during your investigation of the alley, did you happen to consider the possibility that someone had used the recycling bin or
the trash can to climb up and over the wall?"

Martinez jumped up. "Objection, relevance Your Honor."

Bennie faced Judge Patterson. "Your Honor, I believe I'm
entitled to understand the detective's investigation of the crime
scene."

Martinez looked over at Bennie, frowning. "If your theory is
that it's self-defense, then what difference does it make if somebody could climb over the wall?"

Bennie kept her face front, addressing the judge. "Your Honor, this is a general exploration and it won't take much longer."

Judge Patterson paused, sucking in her cheeks slightly. "I'll overrule the objection, Ms. Rosato. I'm inclined to give you some latitude under the circumstances."

"Thank you, Your Honor." Bennie hid her relief and faced the witness box. "Detective Gallagher, did you consider that as a possibility when you went to the scene?"

"As a matter of fact, I did."

"And did you consider that because it didn't appear to be that difficult, is that correct?"

Detective Gallagher pursed his lips. "I considered it because it wasn't outside the realm of possibility, which I believe was your question."

"Again, I stand corrected." Bennie wanted to appear as reasonable as possible in front of the jury. "And I assume that wasn't outside the realm of possibility because it's easy to see that somebody could climb up on the trash can to the recycling bin, and since the wall is fairly thick, go over the other side, isn't that correct?"

"Basically, yes."

"Thank you." Bennie breathed a relieved sigh. "Your Honor, I'd like to move into evidence a surveillance video that the prosecutor turned over to the defense, and I would like to mark it as Defense Exhibit 23."

Judge Patterson turned to Martinez. "Mr. Prosecutor, any objection?"

"No." Martinez shrugged.

"Thank you."

"Detective Gallagher, I've already cued up the video, so let me play it while you watch along." Bennie hit PLAY, then picked up the remote control, and walked toward the witness stand. Detective Gallagher and the jury watched the video, which showed the darkened scene of Yearling Street, the light traffic coming toward the camera, and the deserted sidewalk. Bennie pointed to the bottom of the video. "You'll see that the time clock is running here and we're approaching the time at which we believe the murder of Mr. Grusini occurred, approximately eleven fifteen."

"Okay." Detective Gallagher kept watching, and so did the jury, and Bennie knew that they were all experiencing the same foreboding as yesterday, the realization that a murder was about to be committed.

"Now this is about the time that we believe the murder occurred, and you will see that within the next few minutes, there appears a figure on the other side of the wall, where the alley would be, and that figure is walking down Yearling Street."

Detective Gallagher remained silent, but Bennie could see out of the corner of her eye that the jurors edged forward in their chairs.

"I'll freeze it right there." Bennie hit STOP the moment the shadowy figure appeared on the street, then she turned to the witness stand. "Detective Gallagher, you have seen this surveillance video before, haven't you?"

"Yes."

"Didn't you in fact obtain it as part of your investigation?"

"Yes."

"Didn't you consider it in the realm of possibility that this person, whoever they are, might have information that would help you in your investigation?"

"Objection, Your Honor." Martinez was on his feet, not bothering to hide his annoyance. "What's the relevance, again? It has nothing to do with anything."

Bennie kept her face front and her tone reasonable. "Your Honor, I'm briefly exploring the general investigation that the Commonwealth conducted in this murder case."

Martinez shot back, "But what does it have to do with a self-defense claim?"

Bennie ignored him. "Your Honor, I'm certainly entitled to explore more generally than a theory of the defense. The prosecutor turned over the video, and the witness agreed that what I've asked him isn't outside the realm of possibility, so I think that's prima facie evidence of relevance."

Judge Patterson nodded. "I'll allow it. Proceed."

Bennie faced the witness again, though his lips were pursed, more guarded than before. "Detective Gallagher, didn't you think this person, who was passing by the alley, almost immediately after a murder was committed on the other side of the wall, might have some information about this matter?"

"Yes, I did think that."

"Detective Gallagher, didn't it occur to you that that person might've heard something, such as an argument or even a cry for help?"

"Yes, it did."

"Didn't it also occur to you that the person might've seen something?"

"Yes."

"Didn't it also occur to you that that person might in fact have committed the murder and then escaped over the wall?"

Detective Gallagher shook his head. "I did not consider that as a possibility after I furthered my investigation."

Bennie took it on the chin. "But just so we're clear, at one point, that was in the realm of possibility, was it not?"

"Yes, it was. Previously."

"Detective Gallagher, whether this figure committed the murder or not, you certainly thought that he might have information, might have heard something, or might have seen something, so my question to you is, did you make any attempt to identify or locate this person?"

"Yes, I did."

"What did you do in order to identify or locate this person?"

"My partner and I canvassed the neighborhood, which means that we asked around, and we tried to determine if anyone had seen this person in the vicinity on the night in question."

"Detective Gallagher, what did you determine?"

"That no one knew who he was."

Bennie was almost home free. "And that remains true today, does it not? That is, you have not identified who this person is."

"Correct."

"Thank you, Detective Gallagher." Bennie nodded. "I have no further questions, Your Honor."

"Proceed, Mr. Martinez." Judge Patterson nodded to Martinez, who was already on his feet and approaching the witness.

"Detective Gallagher, you have been professional enough to indulge defense counsel's general exploration of your investigation, and thank you for that."

"You're welcome." Detective Gallagher smiled, and Bennie suppressed an eyeroll.

"And you described to her theories and thoughts that you explored early in your investigation of this crime, isn't that right?"

"Yes."

"But there came a time when you rejected your early theories and thoughts, isn't that true?"

"Yes."

"And the results of your investigation were that the defendant murdered Mr. Grusini, isn't that correct?"

"Yes."

"Detective Gallagher, do you presently have any doubts about the correctness of your conclusion?"

"None at all."

"And finally, in your opinion, does it matter who this person seen walking in this video is?" Martinez pointed at the freeze-frame on the television.

"Not at all."

"I have no further questions, Your Honor." Martinez strode quickly back to counsel table.

Bennie caught Judge Patterson's eye. "I have no redirect either, Your Honor."

"You may step down, sir," Judge Patterson said to the detective.

Bennie tensed as she got ready for her next witness.

CHAPTER FIFTY-NINE

Bennie felt Jason shift beside her as soon as she called Gail Malloy. He tried to catch Bennie's eye, but she ignored him, watching Gail walk to the witness stand, trim in a chambray shirtdress and denim espadrilles. She wore only light makeup, so she came off as wholesome and reliable, with a feathery cap of short brown hair and small gold hoops in her ears. She didn't even appear nervous as she was sworn in, and Bennie recalled that she had been eager to testify on Jason's behalf.

Jason wrote on Bennie's pad, WHY DO WE NEED GAIL?

Bennie ignored him, keeping him in the dark for reasons of her own. She prayed her gambit paid off, but she wouldn't know for sure until the jury returned with its verdict.

Bennie went to the stand. "Good morning, Ms. Malloy. Thank you for coming today. Would you tell the jury how you know my client Jason?"

"I'd be happy to." Gail faced the jury with a sweet smile, as if she'd been coached to do it, which she hadn't. "Jason is my roommate. We share a house in Port Richmond. I hired him to work for me at Juarez, a restaurant in Fishtown. I'm the manager, and he's a waiter. So I guess you could say that he's my roommate, but he's also my employee and my friend."

"Thank you." Bennie caught Brooklyn Girl and two other jurors smiling, and they were off to a good start.

"Ms. Malloy, how would you characterize Jason as a person?"

"Jason is a total sweetheart." Gail paused. "He has a good heart, and my partner and I, we always say that he's the kind of guy who catches spiders and puts them outside, rather than killing them. He actually does that."

Bennie smiled, and Brooklyn Girl nodded in agreement.

"In fact, once I caught him putting a *cockroach* outside, and I said, 'no way, that's the limit.'" Gail chuckled, and so did Brooklyn Girl.

Bennie glanced back at Jason, and a pained smile crossed his face, which made him look softer and more vulnerable. He liked Gail and it showed, which was what Bennie had been hoping for.

"Ms. Malloy, how would you characterize Jason at work?"

"He's the best I have. He cares about our customers and they all like him. Everybody on the staff likes him, even the chef. If you ever worked in a restaurant, you know chefs are big prima donnas and they never like *anybody*." Gail snorted, and Computer Guy nodded. "Jason is never late and he's the first one to ask for extra hours when I have them." Gail beamed, glancing over at Jason. "I couldn't think more highly of him than I do."

"Ms. Malloy, has he ever gotten into any fights or fussing at work?"

"No, never."

"Ms. Malloy, has there ever been an occasion that you know of when Jason has been less than peaceful, let's say, outside of work?"

"Yes, but only one time," Gail answered, after a moment, and Bennie understood her hesitation, because she hadn't prompted Gail about what she was going to ask on the stand, wanting unrehearsed testimony.

"Ms. Malloy, would you please tell the jury about the one time at which Jason was, shall we say, less than peaceful?"

"Well, there was one time Jason did get angry and shout at my neighbor, but to be honest, I appreciated it." Gail stopped.

"Ms. Malloy, please tell the jury what happened."

"Well, my neighbor next door is really a jerk and he always

gives me and my girlfriend a hard time when we're together, because we're gay. We're open, and sometimes we hold hands, but he hates that." Gail's face darkened, her short forehead buckling. "So one night my neighbor was calling us rude names, like *really* rude. I don't want to repeat them."

"You don't have to," Bennie interjected gently, because she could see that Brooklyn Girl and Marathon Mom were already feeling for Gail, their expressions almost identically empathetic.

"Anyway, it was really ugly, and one night it got to me, and I just started to cry. It's really hard when you have a happy moment that gets ruined by someone hating on you. It's just hard." Gail's eyes filmed at the memory. "Anyway, Jason was there, and he went up to our neighbor, who was sitting on the stoop, and he yelled at him, 'It doesn't matter who she is, it matters who *you* are. So be a gentleman, at all times.'" Gail wiped her eyes, with a triumphant smile. "I thought that was so nice, and that was really true, and that was very much the way Jason has always been to me and to everyone. He's just a good guy, with a good heart, and he always has my back. At home, and at work."

Bennie couldn't have said it better herself. "Ms. Malloy, when Jason stood up for you to your neighbor, did Jason physically harm him in any way?"

"No."

Bennie faced Judge Patterson. "Your Honor, I have no further questions."

"Thank you, Ms. Rosato." Judge Patterson turned to Martinez. "Mr. Martinez, do you have cross-examination?"

"I certainly do, Your Honor," Martinez answered, his tone stiff.

Bennie walked back to counsel table, sat down next to Jason, and put her arm around the back of his chair, implicitly vouching for him. She used to do that to send a signal to the jury, but this time it came from the heart. She knew that the Jason whom Gail had described was in there somewhere, underneath that hard shell he'd grown in prison.

"Ms. Malloy, how long have you known the defendant?"

"Six months."

"Not very long." Martinez sniffed.

"But we live together," Gail added quickly, turning to the jury. "You really get to know somebody well when you live with them. I know Jason very well."

Bennie almost cheered. She loved nothing better than a witness who stood up for herself, but Martinez wasn't about to let it go.

"Ms. Malloy, did you know that the defendant and Richie Grusini, the victim in this case, were both involved in a fight that led to their incarceration?"

"Yes, I did. I knew that they were both involved in the Kids-for-Cash scandal."

"So then did you know that the defendant had a grudge against my client for these many years?"

"Objection, Your Honor. That's not a fair characterization of the testimony." Bennie didn't want to come on strong, in contrast to Martinez, who was beginning to bristle.

"Fine, I'll rephrase, Your Honor." Martinez pivoted to the witness stand. "Ms. Malloy, did you know that the defendant had animosity toward my client?"

"Same objection, Your Honor," Bennie said, again without rising.

Judge Patterson paused, in thought. "I'm going to sustain the objection. Mr. Martinez, be more specific."

"Yes, Your Honor." Martinez linked his hands in front of his body. "Ms. Malloy, did you know that the defendant and Mr. Grusini had a history of conflict, which dated back to middle school, in fact?"

"Yes, I did."

"Did you know that because the defendant told you?"

"Yes."

"Did the defendant complain to you about Mr. Grusini?"

"Jason didn't complain to me. He told me he didn't like him."

"Ms. Malloy, did he seem angry to you when he discussed Mr. Grusini?"

"Yes," Gail answered, her tone noncommittal.

"Ms. Malloy, did you also know that the defendant stalked Mr. Grusini while he ate at Eddie's bar?"

"Objection," Bennie said, modulating her tone. "Again, not a fair characterization of the testimony."

"Sustained." Judge Patterson frowned slightly at Martinez.

Suddenly Gail raised her hand, like the smartest girl in school. "I can answer that, I knew that Jason ate dinner every night at Eddie's bar. So if Richie Grusini went there only sometimes, who's stalking *who*?"

"Move to strike the answer as argumentative." Martinez faced the judge.

"Granted. Ladies and gentlemen, you are to ignore the response provided by Ms. Molloy and are instructed not to consider it under any circumstances when the time comes for you to deliberate." Judge Patterson couldn't hide a slight smile.

Martinez straightened up, trying to recover. "I have no further questions of this witness," he said, his tone disgusted, and Bennie knew it wouldn't play well. The jury had liked Gail, and the defense had scored a tiny little point.

Judge Patterson turned to Bennie. "Ms. Rosato, any redirect?"

"No, thank you," Bennie answered, bracing herself. "Your Honor, the defense calls Declan Mitchell to the stand."

CHAPTER SIXTY

Bennie kept her expression impassive, even though the reporters shifted position in the gallery, whispering, wheeling their heads around and craning their necks to see better. The sketch artist drew madly, looking back and forth between her and his pad. This was the show they'd been hoping for, and it was about to happen before their eyes. Marathon Mom and Brooklyn Girl inched forward in their chairs, newly interested as Declan rose, whispered something to Doreen, then strode to the witness stand, his head up. Bennie reminded herself that nobody in the courtroom knew that they had made, and lost, a child together.

She tried to accustom herself to the sight of him, which seemed silly, but required effort. He was more handsome than ever, his dark eyes clear and his thick hair wavy, shot through with silver at the temples. He cut a tall, well-built figure in a dark blue suit, with a traditional striped tie. His shoulders looked strong underneath his jacket, pulling the lightweight cloth across his back, and it wasn't padding because Bennie knew what his arms and back looked like underneath. She flashed on him sleeping beside her, but she pushed those memories away. She'd never cross-examined somebody she'd loved. Still, she wanted Jason acquitted, and this was the only way.

Judge Patterson nodded. "Ms. Rosato, you may proceed."

"Thank you, Your Honor." Bennie stopped in the middle of

the courtroom, as close as she wanted to get to the witness stand. She looked at Declan, her expression a professional mask, and he met her eye, his expression equally oblique.

"Mr. Mitchell, you are the uncle of Mr. Grusini, are you not?"

"Yes."

"And you would have characterized your relationship to Mr. Grusini as close, would you not?"

"Yes." Declan pursed his lips just the slightest, and Bennie knew she'd have to elicit the information she needed without trashing Doreen, or the whole testimony would go south.

"Mr. Mitchell, isn't it true that you two became close because you spent a lot of time with Mr. Grusini when he was growing up?"

"Yes." Declan set his lips firmly together, as if they were sealed, but Bennie had gotten what she needed for the moment.

"And it's true that you served as something of a father figure for Mr. Grusini, is that correct?"

"Yes."

Bennie didn't ask another question about Richie's father, because she didn't want to elicit any further sympathy for him. "Mr. Mitchell, during the time that Mr. Grusini was growing up, you served as a state trooper with a mounted unit, is that true?"

"Yes."

"But since then, you have become a lawyer and now practice in the Mountain Top area, isn't that true?"

"Yes."

Bennie had Declan establish his background because she wanted the jury to understand that he was a credible and upstanding citizen, incapable of lying on the witness stand. She was betting that he wouldn't lie on the stand, and in her heart, she knew that he wouldn't lie to *her*.

"Mr. Mitchell, you were aware that Mr. Grusini, your nephew, resided in Philadelphia, weren't you?"

"Yes."

"Mr. Mitchell, do you know when Mr. Grusini moved to the city?"

"Yes."

Bennie suppressed a twinge of admiration. Declan was testifying like a true cop, answering the question asked, but only the question asked. "Mr. Mitchell, please tell the jury when Mr. Grusini moved to the city."

"About five years ago."

"Mr. Mitchell, during that time, did you and Mr. Grusini stay in regular touch?"

"Yes."

"Did you stay in touch by phone or by visits?"

"By telephone." Declan blinked, and Bennie wondered if that was related to her, at all.

"Mr. Mitchell, generally, did Mr. Grusini call you, or did you call him?"

Martinez raised a hand. "Objection, Your Honor. Of what relevance is this testimony?"

Bennie knew what Martinez was afraid of. "Your Honor, the relevance of this testimony will be clear in just a few more questions. It's certainly well within the parameters."

Judge Patterson nodded. "The objection is overruled."

"Generally, Richie called me," Declan answered, without being prompted.

"Mr. Mitchell, how often did you speak with Mr. Grusini, would you say?"

"Once a week."

"Your Honor, I would like to move into evidence as Defense Exhibit 24 Mr. Grusini's phone records from the date of the murder, which the Commonwealth turned over to the defense." Bennie picked up the copies of the phone records from counsel table, walked one to Martinez, then headed for the judge, with hers. "May I approach the bench, Your Honor?"

"Certainly." Judge Patterson accepted the records, then raised her eyes to Martinez. "Any objection, Mr. Martinez?"

"No," Martinez answered flatly, and Bennie knew that he'd guessed where she was going.

"May I approach the witness, Your Honor?"

386 | Lisa Scottoline

"Yes."

"Thank you." Bennie walked to the witness stand, placed the phone records on the ledge, and moved away. "Mr. Mitchell, I'm showing you Mr. Grusini's phone records for the night in question. Could you please read the highlighted line of those records to the jury?"

"It says '11:04 P.M., outgoing call, phone number 267-555-1715.' "

"Mr. Mitchell, isn't that your cell phone number?"

"Yes." Declan set down the paper, stony-faced.

"Mr. Mitchell, did Mr. Grusini place a call to you at 11:04 P.M., on the night in question?"

"Yes."

"Did he reach you?"

"Yes."

"In fact, it appears from these records, and is consistent with your testimony, that Mr. Grusini called you immediately upon leaving the bar after the fight, isn't that correct?"

"Yes."

"Mr. Mitchell, let me direct your attention to the second highlighted call *after* the call that Mr. Grusini made to you. Would you please read that entry to the jury?"

"It says 11:09 P.M., incoming call, 215-555-2873."

"Mr. Mitchell, those are the only two calls after eleven o'clock, correct?"

"Yes."

"Mr. Mitchell, you were present in the courtroom when Ms. Zimmer testified about her conversation with Mr. Grusini, were you not?"

"Yes, I was."

"Mr. Mitchell, isn't it clear from this phone record that you spoke to Mr. Grusini *before* Ms. Zimmer did?"

"Yes."

"Yet the prosecutor did not summon you to the stand to testify to the fact, did he?"

"No." Declan frowned, and so did the jury, collectively. Bennie knew she had made her point, and it had scored. She guessed from Declan's expression that he hadn't wanted to hide the call, but Martinez must have. The cover-up was always worse than the crime, but if prosecutors ever got that message, there would be no such thing as prosecutorial misconduct.

"Mr. Mitchell, you heard Ms. Zimmer testify that Mr. Grusini's state of mind after the bar fight was 'happy and upbeat,' did you not?"

"Yes."

"Mr. Mitchell, you also heard her testify that Mr. Grusini was not angry or unhappy in any way, did you not?"

"Yes."

"When Mr. Grusini called you that night, where were you when he reached you?"

"I was driving home from my office."

"The conversation took five minutes, is that correct?"

"Yes."

"Mr. Mitchell, when you spoke with Mr. Grusini that night, he wasn't happy and upbeat, was he?"

Declan met Bennie's eye, momentarily letting his guard down, and Bennie saw pain flicker behind his eyes. He was hurt that she would put him on the stand, and ultimately that she would use him in a way that benefited Jason's defense. But there was nothing to be done about it now, and she pushed the past back into the past.

"Mr. Mitchell?"

"No."

"Mr. Mitchell, so we're clear, it is your testimony that Mr. Grusini was not happy and upbeat when you spoke with him, directly after the bar fight?"

"Yes, that's my testimony."

"Mr. Mitchell, what did Mr. Grusini say to you when he called you after the bar fight?"

"Objection, hearsay, Your Honor." Martinez jumped to his feet, which Bennie anticipated because it was rank hearsay, but that didn't stop her.

"Your Honor, the prosecutor will go to any lengths for the jury

388 | Lisa Scottoline

not to hear this information, which he intentionally omitted from his case—"

"Ms. Rosato." Judge Patterson waved Bennie into silence.

"Your Honor, I'll rephrase the question." Bennie turned to Declan. "Mr. Mitchell, without telling us what Mr. Grusini said to you, what did you say to him during that phone call?"

"I told him that he should calm down."

Bennie glanced at the jury and saw the reaction she wanted. Two of the jurors in the back row looked at each other, and eyes rounded in the front row. The grandmother wheeled her head around to look at Martinez, her disapproval plain. Bennie addressed Declan, softening her expression. She'd known he wouldn't lie to her, and he hadn't, and, somehow, it broke her heart.

"Mr. Mitchell, isn't it true that you said that to Mr. Grusini because he was upset and angry after the bar fight?"

"Yes."

"Thank you." Bennie approached the witness box and took the phone logs from the ledge. "Mr. Mitchell, without telling us what Mr. Grusini said, did he speak to you with a raised voice?"

"Yes."

"Without telling us what he said, did he use profanity?"

"Yes." Declan swallowed, his Adam's apple tight against his cutaway collar.

"Mr. Mitchell, did you do anything or take any action as a result of your phone conversation with Mr. Grusini?"

"I called Richie's mother, my sister, Doreen, and I told her that I was concerned about Richie. Later that night, I tried to reach Richie, but it was too late."

Ouch. Bennie hadn't seen that coming, but she let it go. She had already made her point and she could see the impact it had on the jury, from their collective frown. Still, as good as it was, it wasn't a homerun. She would have to go forward with her next witness. She looked up at Judge Patterson. "I have no further questions, Your Honor."

Judge Patterson turned to Martinez. "Mr. Martinez, cross-examination?"

"No, Your Honor," Martinez said, half-rising.

Judge Patterson turned to the witness box. "Mr. Mitchell, you may step down."

"Thank you, Your Honor." Declan rose stiffly, left the box, and on the way back to his seat, shot Bennie one last look. She caught the expression on his face and wished she hadn't.

Bennie took a deep breath. "The defense calls Jason Lefkavick to the stand."

CHAPTER SIXTY-ONE

Bennie crossed back to counsel table, where Jason remained seated as if glued to the chair. His eyes had gone wide with disbelief, and his palms lay flat on counsel table.

"What, me?" Jason asked, his voice a whisper. His head wheeled from Bennie to the judge and back again.

"Jason, please take the stand." Bennie walked over to him, then touched his arm, trying to guide him from the seat.

"I don't want to, I don't want to take the stand." Jason shook his head. "You didn't tell me I had to go. You didn't say you were going to put me up there."

"Jason, please take the stand." Bennie lifted him bodily out of the seat. She would have warned him that she was going to call him, but she wanted him unawares. Only if he was off-balance did she have a fighting chance of getting the truth out of him.

Meanwhile, Martinez eased back in his chair, a finger to his lips, his expression nonplussed, and the jurors looked equally astonished, with Brooklyn Girl lifting an eyebrow. The reporters in the gallery whispered to each other, and the courtroom artist grabbed his entire box of chalk.

"But I don't want to." Jason snapped his head around to Judge Patterson. "Judge, do I have to go up there?"

"Oh, my," Judge Patterson faltered. "Mr. Lefkavick, your attorney could subpoena you if need be, but that will only result in delay of these proceedings. You are protected by the Fifth Amendment right against self-incrimination, so you have the right to refuse to answer whatever questions are asked of you, but you are nevertheless compelled to take the stand."

"Bennie, no." Jason turned to her, his eyes pleading, but Bennie took him by the arm and led him to the witness stand.

"Jason, please go sit down. Don't be nervous, just answer any questions I ask you honestly and directly, okay?"

"But—"

"Go, now." Bennie pointed, and Jason climbed into the witness box and held up his right hand, his eyes darting anxiously around as he was sworn in, then he sat down and perched on the edge of his seat. The jury watched his every move and gesture, their lips parted and eyes wide open. They were smart enough to understand they were seeing something out of the ordinary, if not downright crazy, and Bennie tried not to think what a massive risk she was taking, with Jason's life.

"Jason," she began, intentionally using his first name, "you've just been sworn in, and so, as you heard, you have to tell the truth, the whole truth, and nothing but."

"I did already, I told you the truth."

"Then you have nothing to worry about, do you?" Bennie needed to get him settled because she didn't want the jury to misconstrue his nerves as evasion. "Jason, take a look at the jury. They're just regular people like you and me, and they want to hear what you have to say."

Jason turned to the jury, his eyes wide as he scanned the first and second row. The grandmother smiled at him in a reassuring way, which encouraged Bennie. Jason wasn't acting like a hardened criminal, but a scared kid, which was the truth, and so far, it was working.

Martinez rose, shaking his head. "Your Honor, objection. Is this a civics lesson or murder trial?"

Bennie faced the judge. "Your Honor, nobody in this courtroom is more aware than Jason Lefkavick that this is a murder trial. If Mr. Martinez would stop objecting, which is only making

Jason more nervous, then perhaps we can get the truth about what happened in the alley that night. Unless, of course, Mr. Martinez is going to hide the truth, like he did with Mr. Mitchell's phone call and—"

"Ms. Rosato, you can stop testifying." Judge Patterson held up a manicured hand. "You must admit this is rather unorthodox. As for Mr. Martinez's objection, it's overruled."

"Thank you, Your Honor." Bennie nodded, and faced Jason. "Jason, let's begin simply. You grew up in Mountain Top, isn't that right?"

"Yes."

"Do you have any brothers or sisters?"

"No."

"How old were you when your mom passed away?"

"Eleven."

"Would you mind telling us how she died?"

"She had a heart attack." Jason flushed under his thin skin, but Bennie was relieved to see that he was more sad than angry.

"How did you get along with your mom?"

"Good, really good." Jason nodded in a jittery way, his fingers knitting in his lap.

"That must've been very hard for you, when she passed."

"It was. My dad, too."

"After she passed, how did you get along with your dad?"

"Yes, good, it was just him and me, and the dog." Jason glanced at the jury. "I mean, sorry. But we really, I mean, she was a great dog. I guess me and my dad, we both, kind of, put the wagons in a circle."

Bennie waited until Jason finished talking, noticing that his nervousness was making him talkative, which was fine with her. Soon Martinez would object to relevance again, so she switched up the order of her questions, on the fly. "Now Jason, let's fast-forward to the night of Mr. Grusini's murder. Was there any significance to that date, in your mind?"

Jason hesitated. "It was the anniversary of my dad's death. He died, his heart got him."

"And how did it impact your state of mind that night, when you went up to Mr. Grusini in the bar?"

Jason blinked. "I was just feeling sad, really sad that night, and I know my dad always blamed Richie, like going way back, for what happened to us, going to jail and getting stuck in Kids-for-Cash."

Bennie could see Martinez roll his eyes, but there was no basis for an objection, so she continued. "Jason, why did your dad blame Mr. Grusini for you both getting incarcerated? If you know."

"It was because we got into that fight in the cafeteria, when Richie said my mom got a heart attack because she was fat—"

"Objection," Martinez said, on his feet. "Move to strike the answer as hearsay."

"Your Honor." Bennie faced the judge. "It's only hearsay if it comes in to prove the truth of the matter asserted. We're hardly discussing whether Jason's mother was overweight or why her heart attack—"

"I see your point, Ms. Rosato, but I still think it's hearsay and I'll strike it." Judge Patterson turned to the jury. "Ladies and gentlemen, as I reminded you earlier, during the testimony of Ms. Molloy, you are once again instructed not to consider the previous answer provided by Mr. Lefkavick and you are instructed not to consider it under any circumstances when the time comes for you to begin deliberations."

"Thank you, Your Honor." Bennie knew it was impossible to unring the bell anyway. "Jason, without going into what Richie said in the cafeteria that day, what did you do?"

"I pushed him, and that's when the principal told the cops, and the cops came and arrested us both and we went to River Street."

"Please explain to the jury what River Street was."

"It was juvie hall. Really, jail." Jason's face fell, and he averted his eyes. "I did push him, but it just got me mad, thinking about my mom, and I wanted to stand up for her."

"Okay." Bennie seized the moment. She slipped her hand into her pocket, pulled out the plastic figurine of Richard the Strong, and set it on the ledge. "Your Honor, I would like to move into evidence as Defense Exhibit 25, one of Jason's childhood toys."

"What's that?" Judge Patterson leaned over the dais, squinting.

"Objection, relevance!" Martinez leapt to his feet. "Your Honor, this is a blatant attempt to gain sympathy for the defendant by introducing his *childhood toys*! Should I begin to introduce Mr. Grusini's toys? He had toys, too!"

Judge Patterson shot Martinez a warning look. "Mr. Martinez, I won't have you grandstand in my courtroom." Then the judge turned to Bennie. "Counsel, what possible relevance does this have?"

"Your Honor, it is completely relevant, and I was just about to connect it to the murder at issue. Perhaps if I could first authenticate it, then move it into evidence, I could make its relevance plain." Bennie noticed that the jury leaned forward, peering at the toy, and Computer Guy's face lit up with animation, evidently a fellow Lego fan.

"Please do." Judge Patterson leaned back in her chair.

"Jason, would you please identify this toy for the jury?"

"That's Richard the Strong." Jason picked up the toy, turning it this way and that in his hands.

"Why was Richard the Strong important to you as a child?"

Jason hesitated, blinking. "I don't know, I just liked him."

"He was a protector, wasn't he? Isn't that why you identified with him?"

"Objection!" Martinez shouted, his tone newly snarky. "She's leading the witness, and are we really going to discuss the significance of a childhood toy, in a murder trial?"

"Your Honor." Bennie faced Judge Patterson. "I'm entitled to explore Jason's state of mind on the night of the murder. I think this toy is key to his state of mind at that time. If Mr. Martinez would let me ask one more question, I think I can explain the relevance of this exhibit."

"One more question, Ms. Rosato." Judge Patterson kept her eyes narrow, but Bennie changed tacks, improvising out of necessity.

"Jason, please tell the jury what happened on the night in question, from the moment you went into the alley."

"I went in the alley because I admit, I was mad at Richie and I wanted to talk to him. That's why I went to him in the bar, too. I wanted to tell him it was the anniversary of my dad's death and he didn't even care, he didn't care about anybody but himself."

"So what was Mr. Grusini doing when you entered the alley?"

"He was, well, he was just done urinating against the wall."

"Then what happened, Jason?"

"I went up to him to tell him what I thought of him and all of a sudden, he hauled off and hit me, he punched me in the face, and I fell backwards, and when I woke up, he was lying there in the alley, and Richie's throat was all cut and bleeding." Jason grimaced, his horror clearly authentic. "There was a knife in my hand and blood all over me, on my forehead, and my eye was killing me where he hit me, and I don't know what happened."

"Jason, you didn't kill Mr. Grusini in self-defense, did you?"

"No, I didn't kill him, at all," Jason answered, as the jurors blinked or shook their heads in confusion, and the packed gallery burst into loud chatter.

"Order, please!" Judge Patterson banged her gavel on the desk, trying to settle everyone down.

"Objection, Your Honor!" Martinez's voice rang out, angry. "*What* is going on here? Did defense counsel just change her theory of the case?"

Bennie moved quickly, taking advantage of the chaos. She crossed to her laptop, hit a button, then grabbed the TV remote on the fly, coming back to the dais. "Your Honor, there's no basis for objection. I'm merely eliciting from my client the facts—"

"Hold on, Ms. Rosato." Judge Patterson fixed her glare on Bennie. "I agree with you, there is no basis for objection. But I also agree with Mr. Martinez, that you appear to be changing your theory of the case."

"Your Honor, I was wrong about my initial theory, and I am now attempting to elicit what really happened."

"I knew it!" Martinez threw up his hands, making the most of the moment for the benefit of the jury. "I *knew* that was a lawyer's theory! Your Honor, she misrepresented her case to the jury and Your Honor should—"

"Your Honor!" Bennie broke in. "I learned the truth only late last night, and if the prosecutor would allow me to ask a question—"

"Counsel, quiet, both of you!" Judge Patterson grabbed the gavel and banged it again. "Ms. Rosato, we will proceed with your case, but only in an orderly manner. First, are you seeking to move the admission of the Lego toy into evidence? Mr. Martinez is objecting to its admission, on relevance grounds."

"No, Your Honor, I'll withdraw my request to admit it into evidence." Bennie didn't really need it admitted, only shown to Jason, to bring those emotions back to him.

"Second, are you changing your theory of the case and abandoning your self-defense claim?"

"Yes, and what really happened in the alley will be proven right now." Bennie was determined to get at the truth, and the only way to do it was through cross-examination, even if it was of her own client, in open court.

"Thank you." Judge Patterson faced Martinez. "Mr. Prosecutor, please take your seat."

"Thank you, Your Honor." Martinez sank into his chair.

"Ms. Rosato, please proceed."

"Thank you, Your Honor." Bennie clicked the remote on the television, bringing the videotape of Yearling Street back onto the screen, with the shadowy figure. "Jason, I would like to refer to Defense Exhibit 23, the videotape that was the subject of Detective Gallagher's testimony today. Did you hear Detective Gallagher's testimony regarding the identity of this person?"

"Yes."

"Jason, you heard Detective Gallagher agree that this person appeared on Yearling Street right after Mr. Grusini was murdered, did you not?"

"Yes."

"And you also heard Detective Gallagher testify that he initially thought the person had committed the murder, did you not?"

"Yes."

"Objection, Your Honor," Martinez said, tentatively. "The question has been asked and answered."

Bennie faced the judge. "Your Honor, I'm entitled to press my client."

"Overruled." Judge Patterson nodded, and Bennie didn't miss a beat before she turned back to Jason.

"Jason, did you hear Detective Gallagher testify that the police tried to find out who this person was, but they were unable to?"

"Yes."

"Jason, you know who this person is, don't you?"

"No."

Bennie's gut wrenched. "Jason, I remind you that you're under oath. You have to tell the truth. Please, who is this person?"

"I don't know who that is." Jason's jittery gaze fled from the TV.

Martinez rose. "Objection, Your Honor, she's harassing the witness."

"It's my witness and my client." Bennie had started down the path and there was no turning back. The reporters wanted a courtroom drama, and they were going to get one. "Your Honor, I'm entitled to question my client any way I see fit, when it's in his best interests to do so. The prosecutor has no standing to assert my client's interests, as against me."

Judge Patterson arched an eyebrow. "Ms. Rosato, this is certainly unconventional, but you are correct. Overruled, Mr. Martinez."

Bennie faced the stand, trying to control her growing frustration. "Jason, would you please tell the jury who that person is?"

"I don't know who it is."

"Jason, you were in the alley with that person, weren't you?"

"No."

"Jason, tell the truth!" Bennie shouted, desperate.

"I *am* telling the truth!" Jason shouted back.

Martinez jumped to his feet. "Your Honor, objection! This isn't direct examination, this is cross-examination! She's cross-examining her own client!"

Bennie whirled around to face Judge Patterson. "Your Honor,

I'm now exercising my right to call Jason as a hostile witness, so I may cross-examine him."

Judge Patterson blinked. "Your *own* client?"

"Yes." Bennie doubled-down. Jason had been worried about Martinez cross-examining him, but he had never worried about his own lawyer. "It may be unusual, but it's entirely within the rules. This young man is on trial for murder, and I'm going to get the truth out of him, one way or the other."

"Fair enough, the objection is overruled." Judge Patterson shook her head, and Bennie couldn't tell if her reaction was admiring or nonplussed, but didn't care.

"Jason." Bennie advanced on the witness stand. "I represented you a long time ago, in the juvenile action regarding the fight in the cafeteria, did I not?"

"Yes, you did." Jason looked shaky.

"And you know that it's very important to tell the truth in any court proceeding, do you understand that?"

"Yes." Jason seemed to grow pale, his face draining.

"Jason, you know there was someone else in that alley with you, don't you?"

"No, there wasn't." Jason began to waver, but Bennie felt her own anger growing, not only at him, but at herself.

"Jason, you need to tell this jury who else was in that alley!" Bennie shouted, feeling herself lose control.

"There was no one else! There was nobody in that alley but Richie and me!"

"You're lying! You weren't framed, you're protecting somebody! You're protecting that person on the video! Who is this person? I *know* you know who this is!" Bennie pointed to the screen. She could see the jury react, looking back and forth. She could hear the gallery shift and murmur.

"I don't know, I don't know who it is!"

"Yes you *do!*" Bennie hollered back, desperate. Her strategy was blowing up. Her cross-examination was backfiring. She had violated her own rules. Jason knew the truth but he wasn't going to give it to her. Her defense was going to hell in a handbasket.

She exploded, throwing up her hands. "You're protecting some-one, aren't you? Just like you protected your mother! Just like you protected Gail! You're Richard the Strong, Jason! You're a pro-tector, not a killer, isn't that right? You know who it is!"

"I don't, I don't know who she is!"

"*She?* How do you know it's a *she?*" Bennie exploded. "Jason, who is *she?*"

"Objection!" Martinez shouted, and chaos broke out again. The reporters chattered, the jurors' mouths dropped open, and Judge Patterson reached for her gavel.

Bennie ignored everyone. "Jason, you spent the best part of your life in jail, do you want to spend the rest there, too? You didn't belong there then and you don't belong there now! *Who* is she?"

"Counsel!" Judge Patterson's eyes flared. "I will *not* be defied in my own courtroom!"

"Your Honor, I can't stop now!" Bennie cried out, but suddenly she became aware that the gallery behind her was in an uproar. She turned around to see what was going on, just as someone shouted:

"It's me! I'm the one on the TV! He's protecting *me.*"

CHAPTER SIXTY-TWO

Bennie whirled around, astonished to see a tall woman in a flowered shift standing up in the second pew. She looked to be in her thirties, with determined blue eyes, chin-length brown hair, and a small mouth. She'd been sitting with Paul Stokowski, whose mouth had dropped open in astonishment. Paul tried to pull her back into her seat, but she wrenched her arm away and began moving out of the packed pew.

"Judge, my name is Linda Stokowski! I need to tell what happened! I was in the alley—"

"Miss, refrain from saying anything further until I dismiss the jury!" Judge Patterson gestured to her courtroom deputy, who was already hurrying toward the jury box. "Jurors, please return to the jury room forthwith. I apologize for the inconvenience."

The excited jurors jumped up from their seats, and the courtroom deputy hurried them from the courtroom and slammed the heavy door behind them. A horrified Paul Stokowski was on his feet, reporters scribbled away, and the sketch artist turned around, rapidly drawing Stokowski's wife Linda, in motion.

Meanwhile Bennie had hustled to the second pew and extended her hand. "Linda, this way, please."

"Wait one minute, Bennie!" Martinez jogged to Bennie, but she had already grabbed Linda by her slender arm and was leading her through the bar of court.

"Members of the public and the press, leave forthwith." Judge Patterson frowned as the grumbling reporters took their belongings, shuffled out of the pews, and left the courtroom. "Members of the victim's family, you may remain, but you are cautioned not to disrupt this proceeding."

"Thank you, Your Honor," Declan called back, but Bennie couldn't be distracted, ushering Linda through the bar of court.

"Your Honor, I call Linda Stokowski to the stand," Bennie called out, on fire.

Martinez faced the judge. "Your Honor, Ms. Stokowski isn't on the defendant's witness list! She can't be called to the stand!"

Bennie pressed Linda toward the stand. "Your Honor, obviously, the defense had no notice of this woman's existence, so she couldn't have been on our list."

Martinez blocked Bennie's path. "Your Honor, there's already a witness on the stand!"

"Counsel, stop right there!" Judge Patterson banged her gavel. "Allow me to run my own courtroom. I won't have a mistrial at this point, nor will I have my record spoiled in the event of an appeal. Do you understand, both of you?"

"Yes, Your Honor," Bennie answered, in unfortunate unison with Martinez, who had grabbed Linda's other arm, like a legal tug-of-war.

Judge Patterson eyed Bennie in disapproval. "Ms. Rosato, does Ms. Stokowski appear on your witness list?"

"No, Your Honor, but I had no knowledge of her existence. Neither did the Commonwealth. I have no further cross-examination of my client, and in the interests of justice, Ms. Stokowski should be permitted to take the stand."

Judge Patterson faced Martinez. "Mr. Martinez, what is the position of the Commonwealth?"

"Your Honor, I find myself placed in a very untenable position. I have an indicted defendant on trial in a murder case, but of course, the Commonwealth is as interested in justice as the defense. So for that reason, we will waive our procedural objection to Ms. Stokowski's giving testimony. I gather that Your Honor intends for me to question Ms. Stokowski on the stand, in essence, taking a statement from her?"

"Yes." Judge Patterson nodded. "Mr. Martinez, did you intend to cross-examine the defendant?"

Martinez frowned. "Yes, Your Honor, but any cross-examination I have could be informed by whatever Ms. Stokowski has to say."

Judge Patterson nodded. "Then we'll take Ms. Stokowski out of turn. You may postpone your cross-examination until after you have heard Ms. Stokowski's testimony. Ms. Rosato, if you have further recross, or redirect, whatever you choose to call it, then you may also do so at that time." Judge Patterson turned to Jason. "Mr. Lefkavick, you may step down."

"Okay, Your Honor." Jason rose and left the witness box, but as he approached Linda, he stopped in front of her. "Listen, you don't have to do this. You really don't."

"Yes, I do," Linda replied, shaken.

"Yes, she does," Bennie said firmly.

"No she doesn't," Martinez snapped.

"Silence, order!" Judge Patterson commanded from the dais, then she frowned at Bennie. "Ms. Rosato, the only open question is whether you and your client are entitled to be present during this questioning."

"Your Honor, Ms. Stokowski is an overwhelmingly important defense witness, and justice would be served if both the defendant and I were present, so that we could hear what she has to say firsthand and would be able to meet it better, if the case goes forward."

"And you'll behave?" Judge Patterson lifted an eyebrow.

Maybe. "Absolutely."

"Please take your seat."

"Thank you, Your Honor." Bennie crossed back to counsel table and sat down next to Jason, whose eyes were riveted on Linda Stokowski.

Judge Patterson peered down at the witness. "Ms. Stokowski, do you have information relevant to this case?"

"Yes, I do, Your Honor. I was in the alley that night. I can tell you everything that—"

"Silence." Judge Patterson held up a restraining hand. "It is my duty to warn you that any information you may give today could result in criminal liability. Do you have an attorney present to represent you?"

"No, I don't need a lawyer."

"Ms. Stokowski, you may well need a lawyer, and if you cannot afford one, I can call a public defender or have a lawyer appointed for you. They can be here before the close of court."

"No, I really don't want a lawyer." Linda shook her head. "I know that I could be incurring criminal responsibility. I thought about this for a long time. I know what I want to do. I just want to tell the truth and make things right."

Judge Patterson frowned. "Nevertheless, I heartily recommend that you allow me to appoint you a lawyer, and after consulting with him or her, you will be in a better position to waive your right to counsel, in a knowing and informed manner."

"No, I don't want to wait. I don't need a lawyer. I'm waiving my right to counsel. I want to tell what happened. I can't take it anymore."

"Fine." Judge Patterson paused, sucking in her cheeks slightly. "Ms. Stokowski, if it any point during the questioning you change your mind, say the word and we will get you a lawyer."

"I know I'm not going to change my mind. I've been thinking about this forever."

Judge Patterson's gaze shifted to Martinez. "Mr. Prosecutor, I think it falls to you to Mirandize the witness, then she'll take the stand, and I'll rely upon you to question her."

"Thank you, Your Honor." Martinez turned to Linda, Mirandized her, then guided her to the stand, where the courtroom deputy swore her in. She sat down, tucking a strand of hair behind her ear.

Martinez pointed at the video screen. "Ms. Stokowski, is this you in this video?"

"Yes."

"Have you been in this courtroom during this trial?"

"Yes."

"Ms. Stokowski, why were you in the courtroom?"

"I'm here with my husband, Paul." Linda bit her lip.

"Ms. Stokowski, were you in the alley on the night in question, with the defendant Jason Lefkavick and the victim Richie Grusini?"

"Yes, I was."

"Ms. Stokowski, please tell us what happened, to the best of your knowledge."

"Well, um, this is hard." Linda kept her face turned toward Martinez and away from her husband, Declan, and Doreen. "I went to the alley around nine that night to wait for him. I knew from Paul that he and Richie would be at Eddie's, and I knew that Richie always parked in that alley, so I went to see him."

"Where did you wait for him?"

"By his car."

"Ms. Stokowski, why were you waiting for Mr. Grusini?"

Linda hesitated. "I wanted to talk to him. I only wanted to talk to him."

"Ms. Stokowski, what did you want to talk to Mr. Grusini about?"

"We had been having a . . . relationship, for about a year. It was a dark time for me, and I lost my way, that's why it happened. I decided I wanted to end it because, well, I was pregnant. I prayed on it and I realized I wanted to get things right with my marriage and start over, but the right way. I wanted to be honest with Paul and tell him about me and Richie."

Bennie felt a stillness in the courtroom that she knew was the impact of the revelation being absorbed. Paul would hear it, agonized, and she couldn't imagine what Declan was thinking. Jason stayed perfectly still, riveted to the stand.

"Ms. Stokowski, what happened in the alley?"

"Richie came in the alley, and he saw me. I told him that we had to end the relationship and tell Paul everything. He got angry, very angry. He said, 'you don't ditch me, I ditch you.' He said he didn't want Paul to find out. He shoved me. I fell, which was really scary, because of the baby."

"Ms. Stokowski, how many months pregnant were you?"

"I was six months pregnant. When I hit the ground, it worried me. I worried for the baby."

Bennie remembered that the figure in the video appeared to be carrying something. The figure was Linda, and the bulge must have been her pregnancy. Then Bennie flashed on the pacifier that she'd seen in the alley, wondering if it belonged to Linda.

Martinez cleared his throat. "Then what happened, Ms. Stokowski?"

"I got really nervous, like, I was scared out of my mind that he was going to hurt me. Richie had a terrible temper. He got, like abusive, calling me a whore and whatnot, so I pulled out my knife, it's a hunting knife. I bought it a long time ago and I kept it around the house for protection."

"Ms. Stokowski, where did you pull a knife from?"

"It was in my coat pocket." Linda shook her head. "I brought it that night for protection. Just in case. I wasn't going to use it. I swear to you, I didn't want to kill Richie, or anybody. I just needed it in case Richie tried to hurt me. I wouldn't have done it otherwise. I'm so bad with it that I dropped it when I hit the ground. Richie picked it up."

"Ms. Stokowski, did there come a time when the defendant appeared in the alley?"

"Yes. All of a sudden, Jason, the defendant, he came in the alley." Linda gestured at Jason. "He saw me on the ground and he said to Richie, 'Hey, stop, stop this.' Richie told him to 'get the eff out' of there, but he wouldn't go. Jason told Richie to leave me alone, but Richie picked up the knife. I'll never forget what he said—'Bitch, I'm going to cut that effin' baby out of your belly.' "

Bennie recoiled, imagining how terrified Linda must have been.

"And then it happened so fast. Jason rushed at Richie, but

Richie punched him really hard in the forehead, and the knife went flying." Linda's eyes widened, the memory horrifying her. "Jason went down, he wasn't unconscious, and right then I, like, dove for the knife and got it. I stood up, I held it out toward Richie. I didn't want him to come near me or the baby. I tried to back up but Richie came after me. He tripped and fell forward. The knife got him in the neck."

"And he fell down, the knife in his neck?"

"Yes, he fell down, like to his knees. I didn't know what to do, so I took the knife out." Linda grimaced, agonized. "Blood went all over. There was so much blood it got on Jason and me. Then Jason got up and came up behind me and he said, 'give me the knife and go.'"

"Ms. Stokowski, what did you do or say when the defendant said that?"

"I said, 'no, I'm not going to go.' I said to him, 'why do you want me to give you the knife, you didn't do anything, you saved my life, my baby's life.'" Linda faced Jason, her eyes glistening. "He said, 'you're a mom and you can't go to jail and leave your baby. I know what it's like to grow up without a mother, and I don't want to do that to your baby, so give me the knife. You go over that wall over there, I'll help you.'"

Bennie heard Jason emit a low sigh.

"Ms. Stokowski, why did he want you to go over the wall, if you know? Why not run out the front of the alley onto Dunbar Street?"

"Richie's body was right behind us, and there wasn't room, it was just horrible. So I went to the wall, and he helped me climb up on the trash bin, just like Jason's lawyer said." Linda exhaled, her eyes spilling with tears that she wiped with the back of her hand. "I didn't need the help anyway, and I got over easy, and so I walked slowly away, down the street. I got away with it, all this time."

"Ms. Stokowski, why did you come forward today?"

"Because of what his lawyer said, when she was asking him questions." Linda gestured at Bennie. "She said that Jason was in jail his whole life and now he is going to be in jail the whole rest of his life. She was right. He didn't deserve to go to jail for what I did, and I knew it was wrong to stay quiet, to let him take the blame. I did it for my kids, I knew they needed me. But I can't sleep at night, I can't live with myself any longer. I feel like a hypocrite, when I pray."

Bennie glanced over to see a distraught Paul Stokowski next to Doreen, who was being held by Declan.

On the stand, Linda wiped her eyes. "I'm so sorry, honey. I'm sorry for what I did. I didn't mean to kill Richie, I really didn't. I didn't mean for the affair to happen, either. I'm sorry, Doreen, Declan, the boys. I don't know what will happen to me now, but all I know is, I have to do the right thing. Before God. Now. Finally."

Bennie's mouth went dry. She should have felt relieved, but she wasn't finished yet. Jason didn't move or make another sound.

Martinez turned to Judge Patterson. "Your Honor, in view of this confession, the Commonwealth is charging Ms. Stokowski with general murder and taking her into custody."

"Sheriff?" Judge Patterson turned to the sheriff, who approached the witness stand with several uniformed police officers. Linda stepped out of the witness box, teary and upset, but came forward to meet them. She offered her wrists to the cop, and he clamped the handcuffs around them, then informed her she was being charged with murder and recited her Miranda rights again.

"Linda!" Paul Stokowski rushed to the bar of the court but a uniformed officer kept him from coming through. "I love you, honey!"

"I love you, too!" Linda called back, without looking over her shoulder.

Bennie and Martinez watched motionless as the uniformed officers escorted Linda through the pocket door into the secured part of the courthouse. Hoarse sobs came from the gallery, but Bennie didn't dare look in that direction. Jason slumped, ashen-faced, at counsel table, and behind him, Lou looked stunned.

408 | Lisa Scottoline

Bennie turned to Judge Patterson, her heart pounding. "Your Honor, I request that the Commonwealth dismiss the charges against my client. Jason Lefkavick did not commit this murder and he should not be prosecuted for it any further."

Judge Patterson turned to Martinez. "Mr. Martinez, what is the Commonwealth's position?"

Bennie held her breath, her heart pounding.

CHAPTER SIXTY-THREE

Martinez pursed his lips. "Your Honor, the Commonwealth will agree to dismiss the murder charges against the defendant. But—"

"But *what*?" Bennie snapped.

"The defendant will be charged with perjury, obstruction of justice, providing false information to police, and hindering the arrest of another."

"Your Honor, that's *outrageous*!" Bennie exploded, turning to the judge. "It's undisputed that my client lied only to save the life of a woman and of her unborn child. How can the Commonwealth even *think* of prosecuting him for perjury? And when they try him, who will they put on the stand to prove it? Ms. Stokowski herself?"

"Ms. Rosato, please." Judge Patterson raised a calming hand. "The matter of any remaining charges against your client need not involve this Court. They should be hammered out between you and—"

Bennie turned to Martinez, on fire. "Come on, do you really think that Ms. Stokowski's going to make a great witness in a perjury trial against my client?"

"Ms. Rosato?" Judge Patterson called from the dais, but Bennie wasn't about to stop now, realizing an emotion deep within was powering her.

"Martinez, you'd better not *think* about bringing an obstruction-of-justice charge. You charged him with a crime he didn't commit and you had him in jail for over six months after he had already spent an *entire childhood* in jail, thanks to Kids-for-Cash!" Bennie felt herself lose control for the first time in court, or maybe anywhere on the planet. "Is that *justice*? The Commonwealth is the one who should be charged with obstruction of justice, not Jason Lefkavick. The *entire system* should be charged with obstruction of justice, not my client, who is its *victim*. Shame on you!"

"Order!" Judge Patterson banged the gavel. "Ms. Rosato! Ms. Rosato!"

"Martinez, let my client go home today or there will be *hell* to pay. I will scream bloody murder in front of this courthouse. I will talk to every reporter I can. I will bring charges against your office for malicious prosecution and civil rights violations."

"Order! *Order!*" Judge Patterson kept banging the gavel. "Ms. Rosato, I'll hold you in contempt! How dare you ignore me!"

Bennie bore down on Martinez. "Think about it. Be smart. If you dismiss all charges against him, we can walk out together, talk to the media, and present a united front. I can make you look good or I can make you look bad. There's already egg on your face. You want to make it worse or you want to make it better? Your choice, Martinez. Decide."

"Order! *Order!*" Judge Patterson slammed the gavel even harder, and Bennie stopped short of telling her it was giving her a headache.

Martinez sighed heavily. "I see your point, but I have to call my boss."

"And you'll recommend that the Commonwealth dismiss any and all charges against Jason Lefkavick?"

Martinez nodded. "I'll recommend that and I feel confident that he'll agree, in view of this surprising turn of events."

"And my client will be released immediately?"

"That I can't promise you. It could take a day or two, procedures and all." Martinez shook his head. "Let me make the call first, would you? Sheesh!"

"Counsel! *Counsel!*" Judge Patterson shouted, throwing the gavel at them, which brought Bennie out of her reverie. She had pissed off judges before, but never to the point of assault with a deadly weapon.

"Your Honor, I'm sorry." Bennie tried to soften her tone. "I got carried away, please accept my apologies."

Martinez faced the dais, chastened. "I apologize as well, Your Honor."

"Good Lord, counsel!" Judge Patterson shouted. "You're lucky I'm not tossing you two in jail, *together!* Do you mind if I run my own courtroom?"

"No, Your Honor," Bennie answered, though it might have been rhetorical.

"Apologies, Your Honor," Martinez added.

"Now." Judge Patterson sat upright, composing herself. "Ms. Stokowski's voluntary confession having been heard, and both counsel having agreed, it is clear to my satisfaction on the record that the murder charge against defendant Jason Lefkavick shall be dismissed. And somebody get my gavel back!'"

"Thank you, Your Honor." Bennie looked at Jason, who still looked dazed.

"Mr. Lefkavick?" Judge Patterson peered down from the dais. "The murder charges against you are hereby dismissed. You will remain in the custody of the Commonwealth until such time as you are released. Please remain seated while the jury returns to the courtroom and I dismiss them."

"Thank you, Your Honor," Jason said, quietly.

"Counsel, please return to your seats," Judge Patterson ordered, and Martinez was already in motion.

Bennie returned to her chair and sat down. She felt lost in her own thoughts, distanced from everything around her, even as the jury returned to the courtroom and settled excitedly into their chairs, only to find out that they were leaving. Judge Patterson

412 | Lisa Scottoline

told the jury that, rather than spending an inordinate amount of time explaining the details of what happened while they were out of the courtroom, she advised them they would almost certainly get all of the information they needed when the account of what had taken place in their absence would be reported by the media the following day. Judge Patterson gave them general instructions on talking to the media, picking up their *per diem* checks, and getting their parking validated, but Bennie barely listened, sensing a deep sadness settle into her bones.

She was relieved that Jason wouldn't go to prison, but it was still so awful that Linda would, and it struck her that all of the despair and death was so needless, the horrific result of an incarceration that began in a middle-school cafeteria, of all places. If not for being sent to River Street, Jason would have been a different man and Richie would still be alive, having grown up a different man, too, especially with Declan in the picture. Bennie didn't think that anybody had gotten justice, even today. Justice wasn't what people really wanted, anyway. What people wanted was everything back the way it was. Justice was only a consolation prize.

"Court is adjourned." Judge Patterson banged the gavel, which someone must have retrieved for her. "Thank you, ladies and gentlemen."

Bennie looked over at Jason, who looked back at her, his haunted eyes brimming with tears. Neither of them could say anything, and neither of them knew what to say. There was too much and too little, both at once. Bennie reached for him and gathered him in her arms, holding him like she used to, when he was just a little boy. It struck a chord in her, and she thought of her own baby, gone so long ago.

She found herself glancing back at the gallery, looking for Declan.

But the pew was empty, and he was gone.

CHAPTER SIXTY-FOUR

Bennie and Lou stepped off the elevator, dragging their heavy trial bags, and entered the reception area, where they ran into Mary, Judy, Anne, and John, who were just going out, a happy gaggle heading for lunch.

"Hey, everybody." Bennie managed a smile as she set down the bags.

Mary's face fell. "You lost? Aw, I'm sorry."

Judy looked over, her lower lip puckering. "Bennie, nobody wins 'em all. It was such a hard case. The evidence was overwhelming."

Anne nodded. "Right. Bennie, you did your best and that's what counts. No lawyer can guarantee a result, especially in a jury trial."

John stepped forward. "Again, Bennie, I'm so sorry I spoke to the press. I'll never do that again, I swear. I feel terrible about it."

Bennie reddened at the reminder that all of them knew about Declan. She was facing them for the first time and suddenly she couldn't meet their eye, not any of them. She felt embarrassed and flustered, even as Lou, standing beside her, started chuckling.

"Cheer up, kiddos," Lou said, smiling. "We didn't lose, we won."

"You *won*?" Mary's eyes flew open, incredulous. "Congratulations, Bennie!"

414 | Lisa Scottoline

"You won! Yay!" Judy cheered. Anne and John joined in, Marshall hustled from the reception desk, and they all enveloped Bennie and Lou in a group hug, which was evidently becoming an office tradition, to her dismay.

"Thank you, everyone," Bennie said, flushed, when they'd released her.

Mary grinned, but looked puzzled. "Bennie, if you won, why are you so bummed out?"

"I'm just tired, is all." Bennie picked up the bags, turning toward the conference room. She didn't want to explain anything. Only she knew why she felt like she'd lost, even though she'd won.

"It's because of me, isn't it?" John called after her.

"What?" Bennie paused, setting down the bags again.

"You're upset because of the article, aren't you? It's my fault." John frowned deeply, with uncharacteristic animation. "I'm sorry, but to be honest, you shouldn't be embarrassed. *He* should. Whoever this guy was, he was crazy to let you go, and I can say that, as a guy."

Lou threw up his hands. "I told her the same thing!"

Mary came over, her eyebrows sloping in sympathy. "Bennie, all of us have been broken up with. You're not the first, and you won't be the last."

Judy nodded. "Bennie, that's true. Frank and I just broke up, after years together. It happens to everyone. There's no reason to be embarrassed."

Anne flared her lovely eyes. "Even *I've* gotten broken up with! I mean, hello, what's up with that?"

Everyone laughed except Bennie, whose throat tightened with emotion. "Well, thanks," she said, touched. "It's just new to me, everybody knowing my personal business."

Mary shrugged, smiling. "So what? You're a human being, just like the rest of us. It didn't change anything, except that we all feel closer to each other."

"We do?" Bennie asked, only half-joking.

"Yes, we do!" Mary grabbed her arm and tugged her back toward the elevator. "We're taking you to lunch to celebrate!"

"No, no," Bennie protested reflexively, but Lou took her other arm, while Judy, Anne, and Marshall came around her back, and they all carried her forward as if they were a team and she were a winning coach.

Which, she realized, was actually true.

Even if it didn't feel that way.

CHAPTER SIXTY-FIVE

That night, Bennie almost fell asleep in the back of the cab, going home. It was dark, and the air felt warm, lulling her into a fugue state. She'd enjoyed the celebratory lunch with the gang, but when she'd gotten back to her desk, her moodiness had returned. She knew it was about Declan, but she'd pressed him from her mind. She'd closed the door to her office, busying herself with answering emails and catching up with clients, but she was distracted. She'd checked her email, but he hadn't written. She'd checked her phone, but he hadn't called or texted. He was gone.

The cab lurched around the corner and turned onto her block, and she opened her eyes, rousing herself. She briefly entertained the fantasy that Declan would be sitting on her doorstep, like he was before. She edged up on her seat, checking her front stoop, but there was no one there. Her house was bare and dark, her neighbor didn't even have the light on. Declan was gone, for good. Maybe it was for the best.

Bennie stifled an inner sigh as the cab came to a stop, and she paid the driver and thanked him, getting out of the cab, closing the door behind her, and walking between the parked cars, fumbling in her bag for her keys on the way to the door. There wasn't enough light to see her house key on the key ring, but she found it by feel because it was the only one with the rubber top, a must-have accessory for workaholics, who always came home after dark.

She climbed her front steps, trying not to think about Declan. Maybe it was time to get a new dog. She still missed Bear, but she wanted something to come home to that was alive and huggable. She inserted the house key in the lock, wishing she could call a dog rescue and have them deliver a dog in twenty minutes, like takeout. The dog would be rescuing her, of course. She couldn't deny the feeling that she needed something to get her through the night.

"Hey," said a soft voice, behind her.

Bennie stood still at her door for a moment, without turning around. She couldn't tell if it was her imagination. If it was, she'd lost her damn mind. She turned around and blinked. It really was Declan, standing there. His face was in shadow, but she would know his silhouette anywhere. Suddenly, she felt flustered. She had gotten her wish and didn't know what to do.

"May I come in?" he asked quietly.

"Sure, right, yes." Bennie finished opening the door, swung it wide, and went inside the house, dumping her purse in the entrance hall and turning on the light, wanting to see his face, to gauge how he was feeling.

"Thanks." Declan closed the door behind him, averting his eyes, and Bennie scrutinized his handsome features, but couldn't get her answer. His expression was tired, even defeated. He had a five o'clock shadow, and his thick, wavy hair was layered, as if he'd been raking his fingers through it. He had on the same suit as he'd worn in court, but it was wrinkled and his tie was loosened, the top button of the shirt unbuttoned.

"So, can I get you something to drink?" Bennie flicked on the lights, illuminating the living room. She didn't know what he wanted or why he was here, and she didn't know what she would say.

"No, I'm fine. Can we talk?"

"Sure. Yes. Please, sit down." Bennie gestured awkwardly at the sofa on the left, and she sat down at the one on the right, facing him. Between them was a coffee table and God knows what else—love, hate, passion, joy, anger, resentment, and a baby, long gone.

"Thanks." Declan sat down on the couch, perching on the end of the cushion and raking his hands through his hair.

"So." Bennie braced herself.

"So." Declan looked up. "I don't know where to begin."

"Good, because I don't know where to end." Bennie was only half-kidding.

"First." Declan drew himself up, with a sad smile. "I'm sorry. I'm sorry that I gave you such a hard time for representing Jason. I'm sorry for all the bad things I've been thinking about you for doing that. I'm sorry that I came here and gave you that ultimatum." Declan paused, working his jaw. "I'm sorry for everything that happened to Jason that Richie caused. I'm sorry that Richie is dead." Declan's eyes filmed, but he blinked them clear. "I heard the truth today. I'm not stupid. I know that Richie didn't grow up to be a good man. But he started out a good boy. And it wasn't his fault, that he went wrong."

"I agree." Bennie could see that Declan was still in deep grief, which only set her nerves more on edge. He was feeling the loss of someone he considered his son, but Bennie could tell from the warmth in his voice that it seemed as if he wanted her back. If he did, she'd have to tell him about the baby he lost as well. She thought unaccountably of Linda Stokowski, telling the truth today to relieve a guilty conscience, no matter what the personal cost. Bennie wondered if she had the same courage. And if she did, would it cost her Declan, all over again.

"Second, I wanted to say congratulations." Declan straightened up, smiling more easily, though his eyes still showed the pain. "Just as I predicted, you won. Because of you, Jason goes free tomorrow, and Linda Stokowski goes to jail."

"She might get off on self-defense," Bennie said, then realized that was the wrong thing to say.

"She might." Declan nodded, swallowing hard. "And I hate to admit it, but I think she should be acquitted. Doreen might never accept it, but I'm not Doreen. I hate to think what Richie was going to do in that alley. She was well within her rights to protect herself." Declan sighed, then eyed Bennie with emotion, his crow's-feet wrinkling. "You were great today, and . . . I love you."

Bennie swallowed hard, but couldn't say anything. She loved him, too.

"So I'm wondering if we could rewind. You still have feelings for me, and I still have all the feelings I always had for you, and then some." Declan chuckled, uncomfortably. "I mean, this is weird, the two of us are sitting down like lawyers."

"That's what we are now." Bennie had to decide what to do. Whether to tell him, and how.

"But it does take some negotiating. It always would have. We knew that. I still like where I live. You still like where you live. We both have our own law firms, but they're in different places. Long-distance is never fun. You know I'm not being cavalier. You know I understand this, right?"

"Right," Bennie answered, because he was waiting for a reply.

"I'm also aware that this trial has been a trial for both of us. In every way imaginable. But I think we can put it behind us. I think we can get back to each other again. If you'll have me back." Declan met Bennie's eye directly, with the richness of the love and passion that had been there, before. He rose, opening his arms in an embrace. "What do you say, babe? Can we give it another chance?"

Bennie looked up at him, wanting to jump into his arms. It would be so easy. It would feel great. They would get back together and they could run upstairs. He never had to know. She could keep it to herself, handle it on her own, the way she did everything.

"What?" Declan blinked, his face falling. He lowered his arms and they hung down.

"It's hard to say." Bennie stayed still. Frozen, sitting on the couch, her hands in her lap.

"Just say it."

"Okay." Bennie found herself standing up, because she always felt better on her feet, a natural-born trial lawyer, facing the biggest trial of her life, right now. "Declan, there's something you don't know. Something that happened after Jim Thorpe."

"What?" Declan frowned, puzzled.

Bennie steeled herself, then told him. Declan rushed over to her, wrapping his arms around her, telling her he was sorry, comforting her, and she surrendered to his embrace, burying her face against the smooth silk of his tie and the rough cotton of his shirt, as if she were burrowing to his very heart.

"I'm so sorry," Bennie heard herself saying, not knowing until this moment how much she'd been blaming herself for losing the baby, thinking back to the sleepless nights when she'd gone over everything she'd done that could've caused what had happened. Somehow she felt better and worse, both at once, knowing the depth of the emptiness, but feeling the void fill up faster than it could empty.

And, finally, she understood that in sharing a burden, there was the true love.

ACKNOWLEDGMENTS

This is where I thank the many experts who helped me with the factual background for this novel, and there are more than usual. Spoiler alert: You might not want to read the following until you have finished *Corrupted*.

My inspiration for this novel was a true-life judicial scandal that took place in Luzerne County, Pennsylvania. I have always written about the intersection of justice and law, and my novels often examine how law is often disconnected from justice or even thwarts justice. There are few better examples than the Kids-for-Cash scandal, wherein two Pennsylvania judges wrongly adjudicated thousands of juveniles as delinquent for personal monetary gain.

As a lifelong Pennsylvanian, I followed the scandal as it happened, but I knew I didn't want to write about it per se. I'm a novelist, not a reporter, and though it took me a few years to process the corruption scheme, I finally hit upon a way to do it: by looking at the children who had been incarcerated and trying to explore the lifelong effects of such rank injustice.

I hope I was able to make a moving and even instructive novel herein, and my first thanks go to the cofounders of the Juvenile Law Center in Philadelphia, Robert Schwartz, Esq., and Marsha Levick, Esq. This amazing team of lawyers investigated the scandal, made vital constitutional law, and saved young lives when they brought the scandal to light. Both Robert and Marsha were both extraordinarily helpful to me in my research for this novel, but that's only one of the reasons they have my deepest thanks. Robert and Marsha are heroes, and they exemplify the best in the legal profession. They prove that law can ultimately lead to justice, at least of sorts. And that may be all that we can ask for.

Special thanks to Terrie Morgan Besecker, a great reporter who took the time to answer my questions about Kids for Cash. She is another hero in this nonfiction background because her reporting was the first to shed light on the fact that there were grave improprieties with respect to juvenile law in Luzerne County. If you wish to learn more about the actual scandal, read the book *Kids for Cash* by William Ecenbarger, and you can also rent a wonderful documentary, *Kids for Cash* by Robert May.

Thank you to the staff at Crestwood Middle School, who were so helpful to me when I dropped in to interrupt their day. Thank you to the journalists at the *Mountaintop Eagle,* who were equally welcoming and told us lots of on-the-ground information about what took place during the scandal. Thanks to the current staff at PA Childcare, who answered my questions as well as they could, with proper respect for the confidentiality of children incarcerated there. I would have it no other way.

Thank you to the Luzerne County District Attorney's Office, Public Defenders' Office, and everyone at the courthouse who helped me. Thanks to the Luzerne County Bar Association, which made me an honorary member so many years ago. You are doing what's right to promote the best of Luzerne County and your gorgeous courthouse, and you have my admiration.

Thank you to Lisa Goldstein, M.D., a psychiatrist specializing in children and adolescents, who spent time with me explaining the tragic results of childhood incarceration. Dr. Goldstein is warm, brilliant, and impossibly kind. I'm not surprised that such a gentle soul does such vital work.

Now onto my other experts. First thanks go to Detective Tommy Gaul of the Homicide Division of the Philadelphia Police Department. Detective Gaul deserves a medal, not only for what he does, but for taking the time to meet with me, answer all of my questions, and show me around the squad room and Arraignment Court. Special thanks to the Homicide Division for their brilliance, devotion, and hard work around the clock, trying to bring justice to my hometown.

Thank you to Lieutenant Funk of the Pennsylvania State Police for helping me in every way possible, and also for all that he and the PSP do for all of us in the Commonwealth, every day. Special thanks to Trooper Jason Fritz, Corporal Brad Zook, Corporal Carrie Neidigh, and Betty Houser of the Pennsylvania State Police Academy for all of their help. Thanks to Jennifer Traxler, Esq., of the Prothonotary's Office of the Superior Court of Pennsylvania and to my dear friend and former co-clerk at the Superior Court, Charles Thrall, Esq., who knows more than anyone in the Commonwealth about Pennsylvania legal procedure.

Thanks to my great friend Nicholas Casenta, Esq., Chief of the Appeals Division of the Chester County District Attorney's office. Thanks to Jerry Dugan, Esq., for his criminal defense advice and expertise, and special thanks to Nino Tinari, Esq., who taught me all the inside information that criminal defense lawyers only share with family. Thank you to the staff at the Criminal Justice Center, who answered all of my questions. Thank you also to David Zilkha.

Now onto my publishing family!

Thank you to my amazing editor, Jennifer Enderlin, who improved this manuscript so much, even though she now is publisher of St. Martin's Press! Jennifer is a one-in-million person, publisher, and mom, and I am lucky and blessed to know her. Big love and thanks to John Sargent, Sally Richardson, Jeff Dodes, Lisa Senz, Brant Janeway, Brian Heller, Jeff Capshew, Nancy Trypuc, Kim Ludlam, John Murphy, John Karle, Caitlin Dareff, Stephanie Davis, Angela Craft, and all the wonderful sales reps. Big thanks to Michael Storrings, for astounding cover design for the new Rosato & DiNunzio series. Also thanks to Mary Beth Roche, Laura Wilson, Esther Bochner, and the great people in audiobooks. I love and appreciate all of you.

Thanks and love to Molly Friedrich, and to the amazing Lucy Carson. Thanks to my wonderful agent, Robert Gottlieb, and the ace staff at Trident Media Group, including Claire Roberts, Molly Schulman, Nicole Robson, Nicole McArdle, Brianna Weber, Emily Ross, and Alicia Granstein.

Thanks and another big hug to my dedicated assistant and best friend, Laura Leonard. She's invaluable in every way, and has been for over twenty years. Thanks, too, to the great Nan Daley and to George Davidson!

Thank you very much to my friends like Franca, Paula, and Sandy, who suffered along while I wrote this book, and especially to my amazing daughter, Francesca, for all of her support and love.

Reading
Group
Gold

CORRUPTED

by Lisa Scottoline

Behind the Novel

- "What Inspired Me to Write *Corrupted*":
  A Note—and Photo Essay—from the Author

Keep on Reading

- Ideas for Book Groups

- Reading Group Questions

Special Extra!

- An excerpt from the next Rosato & DiNunzio
  novel, *Damaged*

For more reading group suggestions,
visit www.readinggroupgold.com.

St. Martin's Griffin

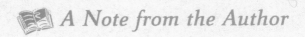

Dear Reader,

It started with the character: Bennie Rosato, such a strong, confident woman. But I wanted her to explore self-doubt and regret. Why? Because I feel that she's really become real to me—and, as I've gotten older, I think about my own life with regret. I can't pretend I don't have one or two, and I became tempted by the idea of a second chance. We always think we want a second chance and we would do something differently, and Bennie has lived her whole life with that illusion, which is the flip side of regret.

Bennie has a legal case that she regrets deeply, not only because she didn't get justice for her client but since it also compelled her to leave behind a man she loved. And she hasn't been in love with anyone, for real, since then. When confronted with the second chance, what would she do with it? When Jason is confronted with the second chance, what does he do with it? And the same is true of Declan, the love of her life: What does he do with it? All of these decisions illustrate character, because I always think that action is the best way to show character—as in life.

Here is a series of photographs that served as inspiration for *Corrupted*:

The adorable and quaint town of Jim Thorpe, where Bennie and Declan spend time together.

The Luzerne County Courthouse in Wilkes–Barre,
Pennsylvania, which dates back to 1899, where Bennie tried
to investigate how Jason ended up incarcerated.

The gorgeous and gleaming hallway of the basement floor of
the Luzerne County Courthouse.

Every detail, from floor to ceiling, is visually stunning at the
Luzerne County Courthouse.

*Behind the
Novel*

A grand view of the inside of the courthouse, where Judge Ciavarella presided.

The courtroom at Luzerne County Courthouse, where Judge Ciavarella incarcerated juveniles unjustly.

The now abandoned juvenile prison in Wilkes-Barre, Pennsylvania, which was central to the Kids for Cash scandal.

A view from the back of the old juvenile prison, which sits on a hill and overlooks a men's adult prison.

Behind the Novel

The conditions at the old juvenile prison were poor, and the building was overcrowded, facts that were used to push for the new PA Child Care facility.

The castle-designed men's prison, which sits at the bottom of the hill, just below the original, and now abandoned, juvenile prison.

The view from the original juvenile prison, which sits on a hill right above a men's prison and is surrounded by houses and businesses.

The new PA Child Care facility in Pittston Township, Pennsylvania, which was at the heart of the Kids for Cash scandal that rocked Luzerne County. This brand-new building opened in 2003, to much controversy.

This gleaming new facility came at a very steep price to so many juveniles in Luzerne County, Pennsylvania.

Ideas for Book Groups

I am a huge fan of book clubs because it means people are reading and discussing books. Mix that with wine and carbs, and you can't keep me away. I'm deeply grateful to all who read me, and especially honored when my book is chosen by a book club. I wanted an opportunity to say thank you to those who read me, which gave me the idea of a contest. Every year I hold a book club contest and the winning book club gets a visit from me and a night of fabulous food and good wine. To enter is easy: All you have to do is take a picture of your entire book club with each member holding a copy of my newest hardcover and send it to me by mail or e-mail. No book club is too small or too big. Don't belong to a book club? Start one. Just grab a loved one, a neighbor, or friend, and send in your picture of you each holding my newest book. I look forward to coming to your town and wining and dining your group. For more details, just go to www.scottoline .com.

Tour time is my favorite time of year because I get to break out my fancy clothes and meet with interesting and fun readers around the country. The rest of the year I am a homebody, writing every day, but thrilled to be able to connect with readers through e-mail. I read all my e-mail, and answer as much as I can. So, drop me a line about books, families, pets, love, or whatever is on your mind at lisa@scottoline.com. For my latest book and tour information, special promotions, and updates, you can sign up at www .scottoline.com for my newsletter.

Lisa Scottoline

The Bunnies Book Club of Scottsdale, Arizona, submit their photo for Lisa's book-club contest.

Reading Group Questions

1. In *Corrupted,* we are reminded that the justice system isn't always just, which is a travesty, but even more devastating when juveniles are involved. What did you learn about the juvenile justice system that was surprising to you? What kind of changes need to be made to protect children?

2. In writing this novel, Lisa wanted to look at the long-lasting effects incarceration has on juveniles. Unjustly imprisoned or not, what are your thoughts on the way we deal with juvenile offenders? What can we do differently as a society to work toward helping them at a younger age, and potentially rehabilitating them? Should innocently incarcerated victims be less accountable for their actions later in life? To what degree is the justice system responsible for creating future criminals?

3. Adding to the hardship of Jason's incarceration is the fact that his father was billed to cover some of the costs for keeping him. Do you agree or disagree with this idea? Should parents have to foot part of the bill when their child is convicted of a crime? Why or why not? Should adults incur the same costs for their imprisonment? Why do you think juveniles are treated different than adults, even though they are supposed to have the same rights in the eyes of the law?

4. You can't help who you fall in love with. Certainly, Bennie's love in *Corrupted* is not without complications. Ethically, Bennie was fully within her right to date Declan. What obligation, if any, did Bennie have to share information about her personal life with her client? What did you think about Jason's father's reaction to finding out? What could Bennie have done differently?

5. Like many women, Bennie always puts others' needs before her own, and she tends to lead with her head, not her heart. In *Corrupted* we see her finally do something strictly for her personal happiness and it backfires. When in your life has this happened to you? Knowing the outcome, would you do it again the same way, given the chance? Why or why not? What have you done outside your comfort zone that has turned out great?

6. Although he was the aggressor, Richie became a victim of the system, too. As you learn more about Richie and his life, how does your opinion of him change? Had Richie not been caught in the scandal, do you think Richie's life would have turned out differently? In what ways?

7. In the Commonwealth of Pennsylvania, judges are elected, not appointed. Do you agree or disagree with this practice? Why or why not? What are the benefits to having elected judges, and what are the risks? Judges hold immense power in our legal system. Do you think that the system adequately monitors them?

8. The Kids for Cash scandal happened after Columbine and around the time of 9/11. "Zero Tolerance" became an important concept at the time. What do you think about a zero-tolerance policy when it comes to kids? In what ways is it necessary, and in what ways have we taken it too far? Are we, as a society, smothering our children's creativity and individuality with our intense scrutiny of every move they make, or is it necessary, given the times in which we live?

9. Lou plays an important role in Bennie's life, although he likely doesn't realize how much she needs him, not only professionally but also personally. Other than your parents, who are some of the most influential people in your life? Whose advice do you value the most? Are there people in

your life for whom you are the unsuspecting role model?

10. Bennie is a bit of a lone wolf. Although surrounded by people all the time, she tends to stay on the outskirts, especially at the law firm. Why do you think she does this? Is it her personality, or just a necessary part of being the boss? Do you think that bosses can be truly friends with their colleagues? What are the benefits and what are the challenges?

Reading
Group
Gold

*Keep on
Reading*

Turn the page for a sneak peek at
Lisa Scottoline's next novel

DAMAGED

Available August 2016

CHAPTER ONE

Mary DiNunzio hurried down the pavement, late to work because she'd had to stop by their new caterer and try crabmeat dumplings with Asian pears. Her stomach grumbled, unaccustomed to shellfish for breakfast, much less pears of any ethnicity. Her wedding was only two weeks away, and their first caterer had gone bankrupt, keeping their deposit and requiring her to pick a new menu. She had approved the mediocre crabmeat dumplings, proof that her standards for her wedding had started at Everything Must Be Perfect, declined to Good Enough, and ended at Whatever, I Do.

It was early October in Philly, unjustifiably humid, and everyone sweated as they hustled to work. Businesspeople flowed around her, plugged into earbuds and reading their phone screens, but Mary didn't need an electronic device to be distracted, she had her regrets. She'd made some stupid decisions in her life, but by far the stupidest was not using a wedding planner. She earned enough money to hire one, but she'd thought she could do it herself. She'd figured it wasn't rocket science and she had a law degree, which should count for more than the ability to sue the first caterer for free.

Mary didn't know what she'd been thinking. She was a partner at Rosato & DiNunzio, so she was already working too hard to take a honeymoon, plus it was a second job to manage her wacky family in full-blown premarital frenzy. Her fiancé, Anthony, was away, leaving her to deal with her soon-to-be mother-in-law, Elvira, or El Virus. Meanwhile, tonight was the final fitting for her dress and tomorrow night was her hair-and-makeup trial. She was beginning to think of her entire wedding as a trial, a notion she hated despite the fact that she was a trial lawyer. Maybe she needed a new job, too.

Mary kicked herself as she walked along, a skill not easily performed by anyone but a Guilt Professional. She had no idea why she always thought she should do everything herself. She only ended up stressed-out, every time. She was forever trying to prove something, but she didn't know what or to whom. She felt like she'd been in a constant state of performance since the day she was born, and she didn't know when the show would be over. Maybe when she was married. Or dead.

She reached her office building, went through the revolving door, and crossed the air-conditioned lobby, smiling for the security guard. The elevator was standing open and empty, so she climbed inside, pushed the UP button, and put on her game face. She was running fifteen minutes late for her first client, which only added to her burden of guilt, since she hated to be late for anything or anyone. Mary's friends knew that if she was fifteen minutes late, she must have been abducted.

She checked her appearance in the stainless steel doors, like a corporate mirror. Her reflection was blurry, but she could see the worry lines in her forehead, and her dark-blonde hair was swept back into a low ponytail because she didn't have time to blow it dry. Her contacts were glued to her eyes since she'd spent the night emailing wedding guests who hadn't RSVP'd, which was almost everyone. She had on a fitted navy dress and she was even wearing pantyhose, which qualified as dressed up at Rosato & DiNunzio.

Mary watched impatiently as the floor numbers changed. Her legal practice was general, which meant she handled a variety of cases, mostly state-court matters for low damages, and her client base came from the middle-class families and small businesses of South Philly, where she'd grown up. She wasn't one of those lawyers who got their self-esteem from handling big, federal-court cases for Fortune 500 clients. Not that she got her self-esteem from within. Mary was the Neighborhood Girl Who Made Good, so she got her self-esteem from being universally beloved, which was why she was never, ever late. Until now.

"Hi, Marshall!" Mary called out to the receptionist, as soon as the elevator doors opened. She glanced around the waiting room, which was empty, and hurried to the reception desk. Marshall Trow was more the firm's Earth Goddess than its receptionist, dressing the part in her flowing boho dress, long brown braid, and pretty, wholesome features, devoid of makeup. Marshall's demeanor was straight-up Namaste, which was probably a job requirement for working for lawyers.

"Good morning." Marshall smiled as Mary approached.

"Where's O'Brien? Is he here already? Did you get my text?"

"Yes, and don't worry. I put him in conference room C with fresh coffee and muffins."

"Thank you so much." Mary breathed a relieved sigh.

"I chatted with him briefly. He found you from our website, you know. He's an older man, maybe in his seventies. He seems very nice. Quiet."

"Good. I don't even know what the case is about. He didn't want to talk about it over the phone."

Marshall lifted an eyebrow. "Then you don't know who your opposing counsel is?"

"No, who?" Mary was just about to leave the desk, but stopped.

"Nick Machiavelli."

"Machiavelli! The Dark Prince of South Philly." Mary felt her competitive juices flowing. "I always wanted a case against him."

"Machiavelli can't be his real name, can it? That has to be fake."

"Yes, it's his real name, I know him from high school. His family claims to be direct descendants of the real Machiavelli. That's the part that's fake. His father owns a body shop." Mary thought back. "I went to Goretti, a girl's school, and he went to Neumann, our brother school. We didn't have classes with the boys, but I remember him from the dances. He was so slick, a BS artist, even then."

"Is he a good lawyer?" Marshall handed Mary a few phone messages and a stack of morning mail.

"Honestly, yes." Mary had watched Machiavelli build a booming practice the same way she had, drawing from South Philly. The stories about his legal prowess were legendary, though they were exaggerated by his public relations firm. In high school, he had been voted Class President, Prom King, and Most Likely to Succeed because he was cunning, handsome, and basically, Machiavellian.

"Good luck."

"Thanks." Mary took off down the hallway, with one stop to make before her office. Her gut churned, but it could have been the dumplings. The real Niccolò Machiavelli had thought it was better to be feared than loved, and his alleged descendant followed suit. Nick Machiavelli was feared, not loved, and on the other hand, Mary was loved, but not feared. She always knew that one day they would meet in a battle, and that when they did, it would be a fight between good and evil, with billable hours.

Mary reached her best friend Judy's office, where she ducked inside and set down a foam container of leftover dumplings amid the happy clutter on the desk. Judy Carrier was one of those people who could eat constantly and never gain weight, like a mythical beast or maybe a girl unicorn.

"Good morning!" Judy looked up from her laptop with a broad grin. She had a space between her two front teeth that she made look adorable. Her cheery face was as round as the sun, with punky blonde hair framing her pretty face, with large blue eyes and a turned-up nose. Judy was the firm's legal genius, though she dressed artsy; like today she had on a boxy hot pink T-shirt with yellow shorts and orange Crocs covered by stuck-on multicolored daisies.

"Please tell me that you're not going to court dressed like that."

"I'm not, but I think I look cute." Judy reached for the container. "What did you bring me? Spring rolls? Spanakopita?"

"Guess what, I have a new case—against Nick Machiavelli."

"Ha! That name cracks me up every time I hear it. What a fraud." Judy's blue eyes lit up as she opened the lid of the container. "Yummy."

"I'm finally going up against him."

"You'll kick his ass." Judy opened the drawer that contained her secret stash of plastic forks.

"Don't underestimate him."

"I'm not, but you're better." Judy got a fork and shut the drawer. "What kind of case is it?"

"I don't know yet. The client's in the conference room."

"Meanwhile, I thought you were going vegetarian." Judy frowned at the dumplings. "This smells like crabmeat. Crabmeat isn't vegetarian."

"It's vegetarian enough," Mary said on her way out. "I gotta go."

"There's no such thing as vegetarian enough!"

Mary hurried to her office; dumped her purse, mail, and messenger bag inside; grabbed her laptop; and hustled to conference room C.

CHAPTER TWO

"Good morning, I'm Mary DiNunzio." Mary closed the door as O'Brien tucked his napkin in the pocket of his worn khakis, which he had on with a boxy navy sports jacket that hung on his long, bony frame. His blue-striped tie lay against his chest, and Mary noticed as she approached him that his oxford shirt had a fraying collar. Edward's hooded eyes were an aged hazel green behind wire-rimmed glasses, with visible bifocal windows. His face was long and lined, and his crow's-feet deep. Folds bracketed his mouth, and age spots dotted his temples and forehead. His complexion was ruddy, though Mary could smell the minty tang of a fresh shave.

"Edward O'Brien," O'Brien said, walking over, his bald head tilting partway down. He was probably six-foot-two, but he hunched over in a way that made him seem like a much older man than he was, which was probably in his seventies.

"Please accept my apologies for being late." Mary shook his slim hand.

"Not at all. And call me Edward."

"Great. Please, sit down." Mary sat down with her laptop and gestured him into the seat, catty corner to her left.

"Thanks." Edward sank into the fabric swivel seat, bending his long legs slowly at the knee.

"So how can I help you, Edward?"

"This is a free consultation, correct? That's what it said on the website." Edward frowned, his forehead lined deeply.

"Yes, completely free." Mary opened her laptop and hit the RECORD button discreetly, so he wouldn't be self-conscious. "I hope you don't mind if I record the session."

"It's fine. I'm here because of my grandson, Patrick. I'll begin at the beginning."

"Please do." Mary liked his reserved, gentlemanly manner. His teeth were even but tea-stained, which she found oddly charming.

"Patrick is ten, and he's in the fifth grade at Grayson Elementary School in the city. We live in Juniata." Edward pursed his lips, which turned down at the corners. "He's got special needs. He's dyslexic, and I think I need a lawyer to help with his school. I should have dealt with it before."

"Okay, understood." Mary got her bearings, now that she knew this was a special education case. Under the Individuals with Disabilities Education Act, a federal law, students with learning disabilities were entitled to an education that met their needs at no cost. She'd been developing an expertise in special ed cases and had represented many children with dyslexia, a language-based learning disability. There were differences in symptoms and degrees of dyslexia along the spectrum, but most dyslexic children couldn't decode, or put a sound to the symbol on the page, and therefore couldn't phonetically figure out the word because the symbols on the page had no meaning.

"He can't read at all. He thinks I don't know, but I do."

"Not at all, even at ten?" Mary didn't hide the dismay in her tone. Sadly, it wasn't unheard of in Philly's public schools.

"No, and his spelling and letters are terrible."

Mary nodded, knowing that most dyslexic children had spelling problems as well as handwriting problems, or dysgraphia, since handwriting skills came from the same area of the brain as language acquisition.

"I read to him sometimes, and he likes that, and I guess I kind of gave up trying to teach him to read. I thought he'd pick it up at school."

"Have they identified his learning disability at school?"

"Yes. In second grade."

"Does he have an IEP?" Mary asked, because under the law, public schools were required to evaluate a child and formulate an individualized education program, or an IEP, to set forth the services and support he was supposed to receive and to help him achieve in his areas of need.

"Yes, but it isn't helping. I have it with me." Edward patted a battered mailing envelope in front of him, but Mary needed some background.

"Before we get too far, where are Patrick's parents?"

"They passed. Patrick is my daughter Suzanne's only child, and she passed away four years ago in December. On the twelfth, right before Christmas." Edward's face darkened. "I have no other children and my wife, Patty, passed away a decade ago."

"I'm sorry."

"Thank you. My daughter Suzanne was killed by a drunk driver." Edward puckered his lower lip, wrinkling deeply around his mouth. "I retired when that happened. I'm raising Patrick. I was an accountant, self-employed."

"Again, I'm so sorry, and Patrick is lucky to have you." Mary admired him. "How old was Patrick when his mother passed?"

"Six, starting first grade at Grayson Elementary. He took it very hard."

"I'm sure." Mary felt for him and Patrick. Special education cases could be emotional because they involved an entire family, and nothing was more important to a family than its children. Mary felt that special ed practice was the intersection of love and law, so it was tailor-made for her. This work had made her both the happiest, and the saddest, she'd ever been as a lawyer.

"Finally, he's doing great at home. It's school that's the problem. The kids know he can't read and they tease him. It's been that way for a long time, but this year, it's getting worse."

Mary had seen it before, though dyslexia could be treated with intensive interventions, the earlier the better. "How's his self-esteem?"

"Not good, he thinks he's stupid." Edward frowned. "I tell him he's not, but he doesn't believe me."

"That's not uncommon with dyslexic children. The first thing anyone learns at school is reading, so when a child can't do something that seems so easy for the other kids, they feel dumb, inferior, broken. It goes right to the core. I've had an expert tell me that reading isn't just about reading, it's the single most important thing that creates or destroys a child's psyche." Mary made a mental note to go back to the subject. "Are you Patrick's legal guardian?"

"It's not like I went to court to get a judge to say so, but we're blood. That makes him mine, in my book."

"That's not the case legally, but we can deal with that another time. What about Patrick's father? How did he die?"

"He broke up with Suzanne when she got pregnant. She met him up at Penn State. She was in the honors program, but when she got pregnant, she dropped out. Suzanne could have been an accountant, too." Edward shook his head. "Anyway, we heard he died in a motorcycle accident, two years later."

"And when Suzanne dropped out, did she come home?'

"Yes, and I was happy to have her. Patrick was born, and Suzanne devoted herself to him. Since she passed, I'm all Patrick has now. I'm his only family."

"I see." Mary's heart went out to them both, but she had to get back on track. "When did you notice his reading problems?"

"Suzanne did, in kindergarten." Edward ran his fingers over his bald head. "Then after she passed, I would try to get him to read with me, and we'd get books from the library. He didn't know the words, not even the little ones like 'the.' He couldn't remember them either. But he's smart."

"I'm sure he is." Mary knew dyslexic children had high IQs, but their reading disability thwarted their progress in school. They often had retrieval issues, too, so they forgot names and the like.

"He does better when there's pictures, that's why he likes comic books. He draws a lot, too. He's very good at art."

"So back to the IEP. May I see it?"

"Sure." Edward opened the manila envelope and extracted a wrinkled packet, then slid it across the table.

"Bear with me." Mary skimmed the first section of the IEP, and the first thing she looked at was Present Levels, which told her where a student was in reading, writing, math, and behaviors. Patrick was on only a first-grade level in both reading and math, even though he was in fifth grade. The IEP showed that Patrick had been evaluated in second grade, but not since then. Mary looked up. "Is this all you have? There should have been another evaluation. They're required to reevaluate him every three years."

"I didn't know that. I guess they didn't."

Mary turned the page, noting that Patrick had scored higher than average on his IQ tests, but because he couldn't read, he had scored poorly on his achievement testing, which a district psychologist had administered, and the IRA, the curriculum-based assessment test that the teachers administered. She looked up again. "Is he in a special ed classroom or a regular classroom?"

"Regular."

"Are they pulling him out for help with his reading?"

"No, not that I know of."

"How about any small-group instruction? Does he get that?"

"No, I don't think so."

"So what *are* they doing for him?"

"Nothing that I know of."

"So they identified him as eligible for services, but they're not programming for him or giving him any services." Mary wished she could say she was surprised, but she wasn't. "They're supposed to be giving him interventions, and he can learn to read if they do, I've seen it. I've seen wonderful progress with dyslexic children."

Edward brightened. "What kind of interventions?"

"A dyslexic child needs to be drilled every day for his brain to connect sound and symbol, then language. There are many great research-based programs, and they work."

"He hates school, more and more."

Mary had seen this before, with dyslexic children. Early on, they might use pictures to make it look like they were reading, but by fourth grade, when pictures were gone and the words took over, the fact that they couldn't read became more evident. They couldn't read aloud and avoided group projects. The axiom was that children learn to read, then read to learn, but that was a heartbreak for dyslexics.

"Patrick gets nervous, and when he gets really nervous, lately, he throws up. He did it in school a couple times, already this year. They sent a note home, then they called me. The teachers don't want to deal with it anymore. But it's not his fault, it's his nerves." Edward pressed his glasses up higher on his long nose. "The kids make fun of him, call him names. Up-Chucky. Vomit Boy. Duke of Puke. They make throw-up noises when he comes into the classroom."

Mary felt for the boy. "First, have you taken him to a pediatrician?"

"Yes, but she said there's nothing medically wrong."

"It could be from anxiety. Have they evaluated him to determine if anything else is going on?"

"Not that I know of." Edward blinked, uncertainly.

"They should have done a social-emotional assessment, like the BASC test, which will pick up how he's feeling. It's a questionnaire that asks the child a series of questions, and it tells the psychologist if he's anxious, depressed, or shutting down. The evaluation determines what his programing should be. If they don't do the evaluation, they don't know what services or counseling he needs."

"The teasing only makes him more nervous, and his teacher sends him to the guidance counselor. They say they send him there to calm down, but I think it's because they don't want him to throw up in the classroom. They said it's normal, they call it something."

"It's called a 'cooling-off room.' " Mary said, supplying him with the term of art.

"But he sits there for hours, like a punishment."

"The school can't punish him for behaviors associated with his disability. For example, a child with ADHD will have a problem completing assignments on time. The teacher can't say to the child, 'You have to stay in for recess or you can't go on a class trip.' They can't punish him for the manifestation of a disorder that he can't help. It's illegal and it's just plain—" Mary searched for the word, then found it "—cruel."

"But wait, Mary." Edward leaned over with a new urgency. "The worst of it is Patrick got hit in the face by a teacher's aide, Mr. Robertson."

"My God, what happened?" Mary asked, appalled. She had heard horror stories, but this was the worst. Teacher's aide was a misnomer; aides weren't teachers, they could be a bus matron or a cafeteria worker. They couldn't teach, nor were they trained to work with children with behaviors.

"Patrick threw up and Robertson made him clean it up. Patrick got some on the desk, so Robertson punched him in the face and told him to 'cut the crap.' "

"That's an assault!" Mary said, angry. "Robertson should have been arrested on the spot."

"Patrick didn't tell anybody what happened, and Robertson told Patrick that if he told, he'd beat him up." Edward frowned, deeper. "Patrick was so scared, he didn't say anything. When he came home that day, I asked him about the bruise on his cheek, it was swollen. He told me that he fell against the desk. I gave him Advil, I put ice on it. I believed him because he does fall, he can be clumsy."

"Were there any witnesses to the assault?"

"No."

"Any surveillance cameras that you know of?"

"No, only in the halls." Edward shook his head. "The next day Patrick was really afraid to go to school. He begged me not to make him, so I didn't. By Friday, I started to think something was really wrong, and over the weekend, he finally admitted it to me."

"Poor kid." Mary felt a pang. "Did you call the police?"

"No, I called the school and I told them what Patrick said, and they said they would look into it. So then the school called back and said that Robertson had quit. They denied knowing anything about Patrick getting punched. They said they were going to investigate the matter." Edward dug into the manila envelope again and pulled out a packet of papers. He grew more upset, his lined skin mottled with pink. "Then the next thing I know, yesterday, I'm being served with a lawsuit."

"Who would be suing you?" Mary asked, incredulous.

"Robertson hired a lawyer named Machiavelli, if you can believe that, and they're suing me and the school district, claiming that Patrick attacked Robertson with a scissors."

"*What?*" Mary felt her blood begin to boil.

"It's a complete fabrication." Edward handed Mary the suit papers. "Here, take a look. But I know my grandson, and he did not attack anybody with a scissors. He's not aggressive. He doesn't have it in him. It's not possible."

"Bear with me while I read this." Mary skimmed the cover letter on Machiavelli's letterhead, then she turned to the Facts and read aloud: "... the **Defendant Patrick seized a scissors from the teacher's desk and lunged at Plaintiff with the weapon, attempting to do him grievous bodily harm.**"

Edward scoffed in disgust. "That's false."

"Has Patrick ever been disciplined in school, for fighting or violence?"

"No, not once."

"What about when the other kids tease him?"

"No, never. He just cries or gets sick. He won't hit back, he's little."

"Does he tell the teacher?"

"No, he hides it, like with Robertson. He doesn't want trouble."

"Poor kid." Mary flipped the pages to the causes of action, where it set forth claims against the O'Briens for Battery, Assault, and Intentional Infliction of Emotional Distress. Again, she read aloud, "... **Plaintiff was so frightened by the assault and battery by Defendant Patrick that Plaintiff has been unable** to return to his position and was compelled to terminate his employment and seek psychiatric counseling. . . ."

Edward groaned. "Can he win on that?"

"Doubtful. He has proof problems with the assault and battery claims, and to qualify as intentional infliction, an action has to be extreme and outrageous. I doubt a court would find it met by a little boy lunging at an adult male, even with a school scissors."

"God, I hope not." Edward frowned. "Why are they doing this, then? Is it a money grab?"

"Yes, but you're not the deep pocket here, the school district is. Wait'll they find out it's not so easy to sue the district, they have immunity." Mary returned her attention to the Complaint and flipped to the causes of action against the school district, which were for Negligence and Breach of Contract. She read aloud: **"Defendant School District has a duty to keep the Plaintiff safe from harm while performing his jobs on school grounds and also has a duty to train Plaintiff on how to deal safely with violent and emotionally disturbed 'special education' students at the school. Defendant School District breached each such duty to Plaintiff and Defendant School District was grossly negligent in compelling the Plaintiff to deal with a violent, emotionally disturbed 'special education' student on his own, untrained and unsupervised."**

Edward shook his head. "Robertson punches my grandson, then turns around and sues us and the school?"

"It's hard to believe." Mary wondered if Machiavelli knew that Robertson was lying, but she wouldn't put it past him. To Machiavelli, the end justified the meanness.

"Robertson's asking for half a million dollars in damages, claiming he can't return to work, and he'll have psychiatric and medical expenses."

Mary fumed. "But wait, if Patrick really attacked Robertson, why didn't Robertson report it to the police? Or the school?"

"I don't know."

"I bet I do. Robertson didn't think of it right away. It's some story he thought up later, to drum up a lawsuit. Robertson will have to think of some reason to explain it, but it argues in our favor."

"Good point." Edward nodded. "The school called me this morning saying they got the Complaint and they said Patrick broke a school rule, using a weapon like a scissors, and he had to stay home on an at-home suspension pending their investigation. They said if he did it, he's getting sent to disciplinary school."

"Oh no." Mary knew that if a child was found with a weapon in a Philadelphia public school, he could get transferred to a disciplinary school, after a hearing. The problem was that disciplinary schools contained kids with more serious anger issues.

"Mary, so what do I do now?"

Mary collected her thoughts. "There are two different legal matters here, and we have to run them on parallel tracks. One is the civil-tort case, which is the Complaint just filed against you, and the other the special education case. Both have to be dealt with. First, we have to respond to the Complaint. I would like to call Machiavelli right now and tell him we won't be offering him anything in settlement."

"I agree." Edward nodded. "I'll be damned if I'll pay a penny, it's extortion."

"Second is Patrick's special education case. He needs to be in a school where they can program for his dyslexia and his anxiety, where he feels safe and nurtured, and gets remediation. The district is threatening to expel him, but I'm not sure I'd want him back at Grayson anyway. I know an excellent private school, Fairmount Prep in the Art Museum area."

"*Private* school?" Edward grimaced. "I have some savings and a trust set up for Patrick's expenses, but I had expected it to last his lifetime. We live frugally."

"Don't worry. You don't have to pay for private school, the school district does."

"Really?" Edward's sparse gray eyebrows flew upwards, the first bright note in their meeting.

"Yes." Mary felt happy to give him some good news. "Legally, if the school did not program appropriately for a child, they owe

454 | Lisa Scottoline

that child compensatory education, that is, funding for tutoring, educational services, and materials. But if the school district *cannot* educate him where he is, then they have to place him in a private school where he *can* be educated. In other words, they reimburse you for the private schooling. We don't have to wait to enroll him, it's already October. If you have the money for this semester's tuition, we can notify Grayson that we're placing him in private school, then we place him, sue the district, and go to a hearing for reimbursement. If we win, you don't have to pay my fees, either. The school district does."

"Great!" Edward smiled, and the deep lines in his forehead smoothed briefly. "Do you work on a retainer basis?"

"No, but my fee is $300 an hour." Mary hated the size of her fee, but as a partner, she was making herself get over it, especially since Edward could get reimbursed if she won.

"Okay, you're hired." Edward smiled again.

"Terrific. I'll send you a representation agreement." Mary patted his hand. "Don't worry. We can do this. We'll help him." She rose. "Let's get started. I'll go call the lawyer and be right back. I'd like you to call the doctor and see if you can take Patrick today, to get a look at that bruise on his face. See if the doc can determine how it happened and when. Tell him the situation."

"Okay. I'll go get Patrick in school now, because they are keeping him in the office until I can get back." Edward reached in his jacket pocket for his cellphone, and Mary picked up the Complaint. She left the conference room and headed for her office, mentally rearranging her calendar. She had other cases to work, but none of them involved a little boy being used as a punching bag, so this got top priority.

It wasn't about Machiavelli anymore, it was about Patrick.